Always, Always Choose Again

Chatuge Dam
Recreation
Area

Chatuge Shores
Golf Course

Lake Chatug

Georgia
Mountain
Fairgrounds

Beach
Park

Valley

Hiawassee

Falls

mapbox

Always, Always Choose Again

a novel

by Deb Whalen

April 2021

Published by the Georgia Mountain Journal
www.GeorgiaMountainJournal.com

First hardcover edition 2021

Manufactured in the United States of America
29 28 27 26 25 24 23 22 21   1 2 3 4 5

ISBN 978-1-7371821-0-8 (hardcover)
ISBN 978-1-7371821-1-5 (paperback)
ISBN 978-1-7371821-2-2 (e-book)

Design
The original watercolor on the cover
is by Carol Gay, of Blairsville, Georgia

Cover design by Spiro Books
Interior formatting by Spiro Books
Final Edit by Diane Wortman

Map sourcing through
© Mapbox, © OpenStreetMap

Contents

Chapter 1

When It Seemed Your Stars Aligned

"This is not about a secret; it is simply a private matter. It was a long-ago decision, far in the past. Leave it there, David."

Barefoot and headed for the paddle boards stored under the deck above her, Eli stopped still, more to avoid an embarrassing intrusion than to listen as she heard the conversation overhead continue.

"She is not a reporter. She's your biographer," the attorney advised, sliding back his chair, "and this is your story to tell as you wish."

Their voices faded as they entered the house. Eli quietly lifted a paddle off the hook and replaced it with her backpack, replaying every word until it was a retrievable loop in her memory. Not the most seasoned writer at the agency, Eli had to consider that she may have been chosen for her gullibility.

Rattled, Eli needed time to process, and her first solo glide on the river would work for that. Maybe quiet her mind as well as her heart rate. She hoisted a board from the rack, then looked across the pool to the river beyond. There was not a boat in sight as she laid the board on the two-wheel cart for the trek to the wharf.

Before leaving, Eli listened to be sure no one had returned to the deck above. Her reaction to hearing about this secret was a sort of betrayal. As tempted as she was to pack and leave, that would be clumsy. Would she end up a stooge? Become the writer whose glossy account of a celebrity's life was eclipsed by someone else's tell-all book?

No doubt she was enchanted by this client, the iconic actor-director-producer adored around the world as the quintessential American hero. Extensive research and countless interviews led to this week's stay in Beaufort near David and Ida Harrison's historic South Carolina home. The work had concluded with a tempting invitation to remain an extra day, for Thanksgiving with the Harrison family.

David and Ida would be welcoming oldest son and aspiring producer Marc; daughter Kylie, her husband Brad and family; younger son James Cary, the sculpted clone of his handsome dad with an equally stellar career path; property manager Molly James and her dazzling daughter Kit; and attorney-agent Victor Hernandez and his glamorous wife Liz. It would have been an opportunity to see the family dynamic, and to look for clues to this "private matter," but Eli already had plans back in Atlanta.

She continued walking beneath the deck, then past the pool before turning onto the sandy, palmetto-lined path to the wharf. Lost in thought, she barely noticed the change to hot lumber underfoot. Ahead, the door to the boathouse was tucked beneath a sundeck accessible by a birdcage elevator. Above, she could see a space for entertaining on the water, outfitted with a retractable roof.

Eli secured the cart to the rail, then leaned over to set the board and paddle against pilings on the swim platform below. After waving at security cameras all week, it seemed they should know the face by now, but she compulsively wiggled her fingers at a lens tucked under the boathouse eaves. A glance upriver revealed boat traffic was still light.

With the flush of anxiety waning, Eli struggled to imagine what her mentor Vivian Wright would advise her to do with this unsettling information. Until this afternoon, Eli had eased her grief by picturing Viv beaming over her protégé's handling of this project.

David Harrison's story was a prize production years in development, and Viv didn't live to see the first day of collaboration. The Wright Agency had lost its heart and Eli, her oracle. Eli had experienced surprises with clients before—and no one shares everything in their soul-baring narratives—but the Harrisons had been so generous and open, all access to every resource.

On this late November afternoon, the sun offered a soothing warmth, sprinkling the water with fragmented light. Eli reviewed the paddle board lesson from Kit James the day before, then pushed away, sitting back on her heels. Carving the paddle deep in the water drove the board toward the channel. Not entirely five feet three inches tall, Eli's slightly muscular build was a plus, lowering her center of gravity, powering her strokes.

A hundred yards beyond the wharf, farther than she meant to go, the board glided over a shadow crossing her route. Eli altered her course to follow, and just as the diamondback turtle neared the surface, it disappeared along the dense spartina grass at the river's edge. She held the paddle across her thighs and drifted, fading wakes from boats out in the channel rocking her gently.

This time yesterday she had been standing on the board, paddling behind the long silhouette of her companion until the sun came to rest atop Beaufort's waterfront. Tomorrow, she would be driving back toward the skyline of Atlanta for Thanksgiving dinner with Pete, the only family she had left.

Eli floated closer to the mud flats, watching fiddler crabs just below the surface skittering side to side, plucking at plant stems and waving an oversize claw in either warning or greeting. As a peace offering, she reached into her pocket and pinched a bit from her energy bar. It sank over a tiny crab that dodged the incoming missile, then quickly returned to check it out.

Another wake washed over her toes, cooler than the sun-warmed board beneath her. Eli's reflection in the water surface warped and stilled again, interfering with her view of the crab considering his crumb, shifting her focus. Gone was the invisible copywriter, all Birkenstocks, naked face, and loose braid. This visage was artistically conceived—contoured, shaped, and smoked from brows to jaw—intended to redefine her less than hollow cheeks and prominent chin.

This intense brushwork was crowned with a bedhead crop of bronze low lights among subtle highlights, all shot through her natural copper roots. Not a low maintenance look, and at thirty-six, she was beginning to miss being mistaken for a teen.

After so many weeks immersed in the life of David Harrison, she was reevaluating her idea of success. This man could not care less about the world's opinion of him. His family and broad circle of loved ones energized his life.

Eli had devoted this last year to divesting herself of her longest relationship, while becoming, as her late mentor had said, "someone worth knowing." Leaning closer to the watery caricature of Vivian Wright's last transformation, she wondered, *And what are you now?*

"Hey, Eli!" A well-aimed arc of cool river water splashed across her shoulder as Kit's board slid alongside—the surprise launching Eli into the soft mud flat in the marsh cord grasses.

"That's some startle reflex," Kit teased, pushing Eli's board within reach as she struggled in the gooey muck. "Tide moves out quick this time of day. Thought you might want to walk into town for lunch. With all that Thanksgiving prepping, I'm making myself scarce."

"I could eat. Maybe clean up first?" Eli drawled, slinging gooey residue in Kit's direction. "Euugh, what is this stinking stuff?"

"There's no stink to pluff mud. That's the organic aroma of decomp. Locals consider it the welcoming fragrance of home on return from our travels. Let's go."

Eli pushed the paddle in the mud as she jumped to her feet, hurrying to catch Kit already skimming the edge of the marsh towards the Harrison wharf.

They returned the boards after Eli's quick shower at the waterfront cottage Kit's mother Molly had meticulously restored alongside the Harrison estate. Eli put on her rinsed, wrung-out linen skort and open-weave tunic, figuring all would dry during the walk to town.

Kit dropped a shimmering lichen and cream caftan over her head, leaned to the mirror for a sweep of heavy liner to each lid, added a coral swash across her lips, then pushed her shining orb of tiny curls behind a gold braided band. Within that sixty seconds, she morphed into an Insta vision of Cleopatra awaiting her barge.

For Eli's new look, makeup required a quarter hour of sponge blending and tedious pencil work. Nothing but electronics, pens and paper in her Chanel backpack, a well-worn gift from Viv. Clean but bare faced and seriously wild haired, Eli created a mental meme of her waif self, carrying the hem of Kit's caftan as they walked along the crushed shell driveway.

"How far?" Eli belatedly asked, feeling her flats already.

"Less than a mile. One highway to cross. We can ride-share if you want."

As they ambled along the sand-glazed road, Kit began a descriptive tour of the grounds surrounding the Harrison's fabled Sunrise Shore estate. She named the year-round progression of blooms as they passed the gardens teeming with complementing layers of annuals that survive as perennials in the coastal climate. Plantings of azaleas, camellias, and everything that buds in between those seasons were loosely scattered below the three levels of porches scaling the façade of the old mansion.

Eli slowed to touch the silky maidenhair ferns banked against the gardens' brick and tabby walls, inset with iron gates at walkways. Overhead, a sprawling evergreen canopy of venerable live oaks breached the walls, waving long mossy strands above the roads.

"The last few years, David and Ida have spent more time here," Kit noted. "I think they consider this to be home over the houses in Malibu, Jackson Hole, or any of the others. When they sell it, Molly's house will be worthless behind their shoreline. She doesn't think about those things, though. Thinks they'd never screw her over."

"In the Georgia mountains where I was in high school," Eli said, ignoring the Harrison diss, "property varied like that. Huge mansions next to older cabins on Lake Chatuge. Didn't matter like it does in Atlanta, where nearby homes and comps drive pricing."

Eli wondered why Kit called her mother Molly. Maybe she was being clear for the writer she was escorting, but why that dig at the Harrisons? *Nah, just hit a nerve*, Eli decided, wincing as she recalled her steady refusal to address her own mother by her first name.

"Nobody in this district is worried about pricing," Kit assured her as they crossed Carteret Street. "You've either been here all your life and don't intend to leave, or you're a second-homer with the money to spend."

The tour went on from their start at the Pointe, past magnificent old homes lining streets, through the Commons between Sunrise Shore and Beaufort proper. Then Eli wanted to change the subject.

"Hope they won't mind me paddle boarding. I'd been interviewing Mr. Harrison and his attorney out by the pool. This perfect weather and the view to the river proved irresistible. When they left to return calls, I used the break to get on the water."

Eli worked to keep pace with her companion's long strides, noticing Kit's gaze was already fixed on the pub beyond the marina.

"I'm making myself a little too at home here, hoping to avoid so many meals alone," Eli mentioned, acknowledging her hotel across the road. "I had been keeping a professional distance, but the Harrisons have a way of drawing everyone in, almost as family."

"Yeah, they're all that," Kit replied, suddenly back in the conversation as she yanked open the pub door. "Basic frauds."

Once inside, Kit greeted staff and patrons, making her way to the end of the bar and slapping a seat for Eli. She was holding court with the regulars while Eli ordered salads.

Kit was at ease, her head resting against the wall behind her barstool as her slender six-foot frame stretched across several stools. The gauzy caftan over a thong and band swimsuit didn't hide much.

"I'd like your perspective on them—the Harrisons," Eli said, maneuvering into objective observer mode as fresh drinks arrived with seafood Cobb salads. "What's something people would be surprised to know about them?"

"Now what were you looking at in the mudflats?" Kit asked, as she stirred her drink, ignoring Eli's effort.

"Yeah, tiny crabs, one calypso dancing with a big claw stretched up to me. I think a shrimp or two went by, but they looked ghostly compared to the plump pink ones in this salad."

"There is another world below the surface, trying to survive us," Kit responded. "Waterways like these are nurseries for our oysters, blue crab, and shrimp populations. Coming home is what keeps me inspired to finish my marine biology studies."

"How close are you?"

"Done next year. I'm considering opportunities at a couple of east coast research facilities now."

"Will you be part of a project rehabbing shorelines or maybe working in aquaculture?" Eli knew little about marine biology.

"Mariculture, for me. I want to get in on the *sustainables* market," she mini air-quoted, "for saltwater food products, both animals and plants. What we learn in mariculture will go a long way towards our farms, hatcheries, and nurseries improving their quality and output."

So, Kit is a genius *smoke show with a career path that could save the world and earn billions,* Eli thought.

"Kit. Is that—"

"Katherine. And yours?"

Eli laughed, but didn't answer right away. "Until I was fifteen, I had gotten away with telling kids my name was Eliza, which would justify Eli. In fact, it's Elinor, after a relative my mother hoped would remember us in her will. Just don't call me that."

After more insights on Beaufort marine life and a few shared Charleston experiences, she managed to bring Kit back to the Harrisons.

"They met Molly when she was organizing a local fundraiser as they were moving to Beaufort. She's quite the community advocate. Molly managed the property for them before I was born, so this is all I've ever known, life in the swirling eddies of the mighty River Harrison. They're always *on*, you know? Deigning to help with everything. Playing the lead onscreen and off."

"When you say *on* do you mean faking it?" Eli asked. "It's show, for publicity?"

"They've got it made, always have. *Please.* They have Molly fooled, devoting her life to them as they breeze in and out of here and pretend to care. Hard pass," she said, smacking her glass on the table and signaling for a refill. "Now tell me, how'd you get this gig, celeb ghostwriter?"

"Better than ghostwriter, credited. Right place right time, maybe. David Harrison is my biggest project so far, and I can't imagine much bigger. My mentor, publicist Viv Wright of the legendary Wright Agency in Atlanta, had noticed my work when I joined her Charlotte office. Assignments improved. Now, here I am in Beaufort."

"Boyfriend? Married? Kids?" Kit pressed, mid-slurp.

"Married Ted at eighteen, my freshman year. He was graduating, off to the family business, and we eloped soon after—to *everyone's* horror. A few months later, we took in my five-year-old cousin. His parents had died when he was a baby—in a wreck, traveling with my mom.

"Both orphaned, Pete and I went to live with our great-aunt Ta. Fast forward, I was divorced six months ago. Pete graduated Colorado University and landed a sweet job in Denver."

"You divorced as soon as Pete was gone? Long, bad marriage? What?"

"Circumstances, mostly. Ted is brilliant, talented, super focused. His interests didn't go beyond himself and his pursuits. Thanks to Viv Wright, I realized he was some sort of—*wait for it*—narcissist, that we would always be leading disconnected lives, so I gave up on a love story and struck out on my own.

"Viv died a few months ago, after a cancer battle. Didn't get to see her friend David Harrison's book finished. It has been intense but getting better. It's good."

"Have another drink, girl," Kit advised. "You may say it's all good, but you are wound up tight."

"If you don't mind, I'll go on to the hotel. I'm leaving early tomorrow. Holiday traffic," Eli said, pulling her backpack from under the stool. "Call me when you're in Atlanta. Stay with me for the launch party. They expect the big names."

"Safe travels, Eli. If *you* don't mind, I'll skip that bougie party. I've seen those characters before."

She sent Kit her info and funds for lunch, leaving unnoticed while her new friend moved to grace a table of guys fresh off a fishing expedition, admirers sponsoring her bar tab.

At the curb, Eli checked her messages. A text from Pete said that he and girlfriend Grace had arrived in Atlanta early for their Thanksgiving visit. They were expecting to stay in the guest apartment of the Buckhead penthouse Eli had shared with Ted— a few floors above her new condo in the residential levels of the fabled hotel. Plans changed when Grace decided they were going to Virginia to see her parents, returning to Atlanta for dinner with Eli Saturday.

More relieved than annoyed, Eli promised Pete a fresh-catch pot of gumbo for dinner Saturday, then shot a text to her building's celebrated eatery asking to cancel all the meals on order for Eli Sledge, including a Thanksgiving dinner, to which they responded with a quick "Certainly, Mrs. Waller."

The ex-Mrs. Waller would be giving thanks alone.

———————

Earlier in the day, Eli had passed through the enormous kitchen to the porch as Molly and Ida were making their heirloom recipes for the feast, assisted by the Harrison's busy cook. Eli had truly wanted to get in on that.

Like a hometown preacher, school principal Aunt Ta was always invited somewhere for holiday dinners, even after Eli and Pete moved in. Never in her life had Eli beheld an *unbrowned* whole turkey.

As Eli was packing a folder of loose notes in her luggage, Ida Harrison called, asking her to come by for breakfast—granting Eli's wish for one more invite. She quickly accepted, citing her canceled plans.

"Wonderful, dear. All our kids are arriving tonight, and we still have a room to spare. Eli, please leave that hotel and stay here. We'll have a splendid Thanksgiving."

"I'd be thrilled to come," Eli rushed to say before her brain braked on this solidly inappropriate plan. When she passed the desk clerk, he advised that her ride was waiting out front. From the door she saw David and Ida in his beach Jeep.

"Like it or not," David playfully confided as he loaded her bags, "you're becoming one of the family."

No matter his age, David Harrison's presence was powerful. A global brand, those mesmerizing, crystal blue eyes—sheltered by unstyled, salt and pepper brows—appeared lit from within. His devastatingly easy smile, beguilingly framed by deep dimples in a gently weathered face, was known the world over. But that remark—was it the disarmingly insincere charm Kit described, or words typical of genuinely loving people? If only for tomorrow, Eli decided, *I believe.*

As the Harrison's daughter, Kylie, arrived with her gregarious tribe, Eli could see that Ida had wrapped her in the same enthusiastic embrace as was bestowed on each of the arriving family. She studied their interactions, indulging in imagining that she belonged in this sea of radiant kindness.

Kylie was introduced as a dermatologist from Atlanta, along with her sports agent husband Brad, their two adult children and spouses, then three grandchildren, whose names Eli would have to collect. Next, eldest Marc, familiar to Eli as the entitled, money squandering celebrity son of tabloid fame. Soon, youngest Harrison sibling James Cary, JC to his family, made an entrance that eclipsed previous arrivals as his delightful exuberance enlivened the atmosphere.

After introductions were finished and everyone headed to their quarters to unpack, Eli turned wide-eyed to Molly asking, "Just how many bedrooms do you have here?"

"Um, ten, and one is a bunkroom, optimistically designed to sleep six grandchildren. I can guess where your mind is going next, Eli. We have a base staff here of two housekeepers, two cooks, and three weekly visits from our chef. Armed protection is ever-present, and our maintenance tech is full time, as is the gardener. Oh, can't forget my executive assistant, Mary Beth. I'm in and out, but responsible for the estate and its satellite offices as it all operates here in Beaufort."

"Satellite offices?"

"Scheduling, transportation, guard services, procurement, community resources, charitable endeavors," Molly gestured, hands pressed together towards David's study. "It's more extensive that you might think. And that's just in Beaufort."

As Molly guided her to the Rose Room on the third floor, Eli admired the varying eras of architectural detail. Each of the old place's families had influenced its evolution, Molly related, citing gas lights in the 1880s, some indoor plumbing by the 1890s, a family kitchen with primitive appliances around 1900, ceilings lowered and coffered in the 1920s, garages replacing carriage houses by the '30s, "…and swept yards that became gardens surrounding pools. That's when my tabby house was built as an office for a doctor who once owned this place. Such history.

"The Harrison's biggest project was converting that top floor to bedrooms surrounding the open staircase beneath the louvered cupola—an early ventilation system. I was here for that, and it was an undertaking."

A late round of light snacks had everyone gathered near the fireplace—both Ida and Molly with laps full of excitedly chattering little ones. A pool game at the end of the grand room engaged the young adults as they caught up on one another's busy lives. Eli and Kylie were finishing the dishes in the kitchen with the help of David, JC, and Brad, with most of the conversation fixed on the upcoming football games.

When Eli retired to her room, she marveled that a house could hold so many graceful bedrooms, and each with a spacious bath attached. Soon she was falling asleep in the deep down and silken linens of the elegantly dressed antique rosewood bed as she imagined the entire layout of this historic mansion.

———◦———

Bird songs competing outside her window woke Eli at first light. Her view to the massive, outstretched branches of the live oak trees ruffled with resurrection ferns, was framed by French doors to the porch. It was still dark enough to venture out in her sleepshirt, one of Ted's oxford button-downs. She cracked the door and sidled into the shadows of the new morning for a peek at the awakening gardens—backing into Marc sitting in a rocking chair outside her room, e-reader in hand.

"Well, I was hungry for breakfast, but baby, you'll do," the way past his prime, face still mashed from his pillow, storied womanizer purred, as he flicked his Kindle to lift her shirttail well above where her panties would have been. Mortified, Eli stumbled back into her room, and locked the door, barely muting his revolting laugh.

No sooner had breakfast plates been cleared than a cart rolled out of the walk-in cooler with two vats containing brined turkeys to be readied for the ovens. Eli watched from a distance, taking part by peeling heaped vegetables awaiting pots. Lively chatter and bustle were building as the holiday dinner manifested.

The kitchen hummed as little ones helped with table settings, elders advised from afar, and a special few were assigned a dish or platter to prepare for serving. Kit's fruit tray was a sensation, laid out in the shapes of sea creatures and water birds. Eli could not imagine a more classic Thanksgiving than this.

Conversations rippled from one end of the vast dining table to the other, speckled with giggles and hoots when seniors attempted to sound tech savvy to the younger diners. As desserts attracted guests to the buffet, Marc took the opportunity to boom the news of his latest venture across the table to his father, who had already underwritten countless flops initiated by his eldest.

"Let's discuss that later, Marc, after dinner," David deferred. "So much going on now, eh?"

"No better time than now," Marc scoffed. "Kylie will want to invest in this, and JC is a contender for a role that could finally make him in the industry. I'm ready to get this off the ground and share my success. Let them decide, *eh*?"

And with that, Eli also witnessed just how quickly a Thanksgiving dinner can devolve into exasperating disagreements with one boorish attendee. As dinner was cleared and the last cleanup of the day got underway, voices in the kitchen were subdued. Frustrated, angry words carried from David's office where he, Victor, and Marc were discussing the possibility of more funding.

In the family room, several cabinets were open as Ida and Molly looked through albums for photos Kylie wanted to copy. They were flagging pages with sticky notes when Eli stepped in, using her scanner app to transmit each of the twenty or more images Kylie selected.

Between scans, Eli watched an uncomfortable interaction by the fireplace where Liz had cornered Kit. Liz held her drink loosely in a royal wave as she spoke. Kit was in a tighter stance, her knuckles pressing against her lips, eyes downcast.

In time, almost everyone had retreated to the back porch, with children popping in and out of the heated pool as Kylie and Brad sat nearby in close conversation. Eli and Kit were debating the pros and cons of a pluff mud cosmetic line when a slamming door signaled the end of the meeting in David's office.

Soon after, Victor and Liz were gone. As Eli was thanking Ida for including her, she heard Marc stomping up the stairs. To avoid another encounter, she waited until Kylie was taking a little one up to bathe, allowing Eli to fall in with them and dart into the Rose Room to get her things for the drive home.

⟶•◀

JC was waiting at the stair landing when Eli emerged with her bags, no doubt sent by Ida to ferry her to the hotel lot. As Eli hugged her hosts, goodbyes were heartfelt, knit with promises to get together soon. Enjoying a slow drive in the fading sunlight through historic Beaufort with a legit Hollywood hottie had Eli choking back her fangirl.

"I never expected Beaufort to be so idyllic. This is the way to see it," Eli declared, with a sweeping gesture above the vintage convertible.

"The vibe keeps bringing me back to see Mom and Dad. That's why they're here, I think. Totally chill place to be."

She plied him with semi-journalistic questions about his childhood travels until their destination appeared—the lot behind her stately old hotel. As he parked, JC stretched his arm across the seat behind Eli's head, a move that brought him well into her space.

"Don't take this as a come-on," he said, laughing. "This is a sincere question from someone who gets plenty of personal comments—what color are your eyes? I see mostly blue, but are they green in the middle? What's with the little gold sparks? Seriously," he said, peering closer. "What color?"

"Well, blue-green," she blurted, both uncomfortable and wildly flattered with the scrutiny. "Some say they're the eyes of alien creatures," she babbled, regretfully recalling Pete's informative sci-fi fan years. "I really don't have a clue why they're so weird," she expanded. "My mom's eyes were hazel."

"Definitely got mine from my dad. I was told that very light blue irises are the result of a lack of melanin, and that I should always wear shades in bright light. Not so good for my career," he added, his eyes still fixed on Eli's.

"You seem to be a quiet kind of person," he observed, after an eternity of silence. "I mean, for all that you have to say as a writer. A lot of writers I know in LA like attention. They're life of the party types. You do a lot of observing, is what I'm trying to say."

Eli looked away, flustered by the attention. "My boss said that. After a series of meetings with one client or another, she noticed that for all the useful ideas or suggestions I put out there, my input wasn't ascribed," she confided, glancing quickly at him. "That often people wouldn't remember I had been present. 'An invisible but resourceful consultant,' she said, and told me that just proves I'm a muse."

"A muse? Like what, a water nymph or something?"

"More a mythological force. A personified source of creative inspiration."

"So, an *alien!* I'm going to enjoy getting to know you, Eli—Eli who? Is there a last name, or do mythological forces use them?"

They exchanged info, and JC began loading her car as they talked about the coastal experiences they each had yet to try in Beaufort. He wanted to climb the lighthouse, and she intended to take a coastal boat tour, maybe visit Helena Island. JC fell silent when he thought he noticed something scurrying away from her rear tire.

"That was, uh, a squirrel," he guessed, walking to the back of the car for a better look. After he closed the hatch on her loaded SUV, Eli thought she detected something special in his farewell hug. Toes to temples, everything was tingling. If this week previewed the kind of experiences she could expect in her new life, she was more than ready.

And as for that secret? *Just knowing there is one,* she wondered, *isn't that the key to cracking it?*

Chapter 2

Why You Can't Get There from Here

Eli pulled out of the hotel lot ahead of JC. He had waited to see whether her car would start after sitting ten days, then to see her safely headed home before he left. *How different from Ted*, she thought. Despite his celeb status, JC had such warmth. Never without a smile, he would share his easy laugh, casually touch, talk with connection, she marveled, then remembered his Academy Award nomination.

Ted was surely as good looking, and only becoming more so, as many men are thoughtlessly inclined to do. His gift and his curse, she supposed, that astonishingly glorious construct of a mind. *Could it have hijacked circuits from the emotion sectors of his brain?*

After a seafood market stop to pick up fresh shrimp and crab, the GPS squawked about rerouting. It was still set in waypoints to Atlanta along roads too lonely and dark for this trip. She clicked instead on the route Ted always used and would have directed her to use as well. Taking orders had never been easy for Eli, now a devotee of obstinance—especially where Ted Waller was concerned.

Their parting had been long in coming and over as quickly as possible. Both had been careful to end things civilly. A pair for over half their lives, yet, it seemed to Eli, he now preferred to believe that she had never existed.

Long drives always took Eli's mind time traveling, and it seemed this trip would dredge up their beginning. She met him her first summer as a permanent Hiawassee resident. Even now, Eli could almost feel the boat spray from the cold mountain lake as Ted passed close to her rocky perch.

She had watched the university-bound freshman blasting around Lake Chatuge on his ski boat with his local friend, Mac Miller. Before she met Ted, Eli had known which of the magnificent North Carolina shore homes was his parents' summer house. A structure worthy of an exclusive Hamptons compound, the house faced southeast across the lake. The Wallers came for a few weeks every summer, never socializing, ensuring no one knew much about them.

Eli's mother, former Woodbine debutante Julia Sutton Sledge, spent her summers on Lake Chatuge as a child. Juju, as the family called her, existed in a cloud of personal and financial calamities but took care never to embarrass Aunt Ta. Eli's misfortunes, she felt certain, were known to all in the tri-state area. She, too, had spent every summer she could remember with the older couple in Hiawassee. Ta was her great-aunt Catherine—and Ta's husband, newspaper editor Jim Clark.

Catherine Sutton Clark had been a recurring force of reckoning, impressing Eli early on as a woman whose lens functioned in only the tightest focus. Aunt Ta got to know Ted when he agreed to sub in her bridge game. At first, she was impressed that he played, and then more by his skill level. Afterwards, not so much.

"This boy is cocky, arrogant," she decreed, "not someone you should be seeing."

"Aunt Ta, he's really very shy, and super intelligent. He's complicated."

"Unpleasantly complicated, Elinor. You must remember that for every action, every decision," Aunt Ta would endlessly remind Eli, "there are inescapable consequences."

Was it invoked consequence, fourteen-year-old Eli had wondered through tearful, sleepless nights that summer, that had taken Eli's mother Julia, her aunt Edie, and Edie's husband, Charlie, that late May night? Sweet Edie hadn't wanted to leave nine-month-old Pete, but JuJu insisted the relaxing getaway would be worth the angst. In truth, finding an ex of JuJu's whose circumstances had improved greatly was her latest misguided agenda.

Julia Sutton Sledge had one year left to live, Eli calculated, when she was Eli's age. How very different their lives had been. Eli recognized that she was likely at the pinnacle of her career—writing for perhaps the best known, most loved figure in American movie culture.

"Maybe it's time to bring my life in line with some objectives I choose," she confided in the rearview mirror.

Eli decided to model her new outlook on a combination of David Harrison's disregard for the opinions of others and marvelous Kit's me-first style—all made trickier without decades of world renown or the cutting-edge profession of mariculture. Never mind the spectacular physical presence of her subjects.

"No more Ms. Fixer," she shouted to the interstate traffic ahead. "No more being that impact-absorbing guardrail in everyone else's life. I am not a villain because I left a marriage of fidelity, civility, and affluence. The relationship was slowly killing me.

"I'm not going to be run off the road by Pete's freewheeling girlfriend *living in the moment* as she drifts in and out of everyone else's lane," she continued shouting at increasing volume. "And," she concluded in a softer, more thoughtful tone, "I'm not going to be the sucker whose name appears on the published collection of all the press releases ever issued on David Harrison. I really don't want to be that."

As she was pondering this attitude remodel, the trip back to Atlanta slowed with disturbing problems in her Sport's engine. Dash lights were flashing, accompanied by muffled bumps and scratching sounds. Ted had driven sporty, exotic cars while Eli stayed with sturdy, practical vehicles. *Wasn't this car all that and a nice upgrade?* "Maybe," Eli wondered aloud, "it's just time for coffee."

Several miles below Macon, Eli pulled in for gas, thinking the engine might recover with a restart. She felt around the passenger seat behind her purse for those energy bars she'd bought on the way down but found only wrappers.

With the tank topped off and sipping something less than fresh coffee, Eli continued up the interstate, alarmed that the engine was running rougher. A little while later, as she neared McDonough, fine debris was dusting the footwell. Symptoms were worsening.

"Great. Thanksgiving night. Nothing will be open," she groaned, signaling for the next exit. A Waffle House sign came into view, and she crossed under the roadway, finding a spot in the busy parking lot.

As she opened the door, something dark and shiny shot from behind her feet, disappearing against the asphalt. Eli was shrieking like an unintentional snake handler, afraid to exit but terrified of another something hopping onto the seat. "*Not* a squirrel," she wailed with a shiver.

Hours passed as Eli got to know the restaurant's staff, who steadily supplied her with caffeine until the tow truck finally arrived. Eli had been napping face-to-table in a back booth and awoke, disoriented, to the tow driver tapping her shoulder with his tablet. "They said you're the lady with the breakdown," he softly announced, trying to avoid startling her.

Lady? Okay, he's younger than I am, but... "Yeah, that's me."

Eli groggily gathered her things and struggled to her feet, briefly describing the car problem as she handed him the key fob to load her vehicle. With the bill paid hours ago, she tucked extra cash under the cup and thanked everyone from the kitchen staff to the cashier for their hospitality.

Reggie, the tow driver, had the car hood up and was asking where she had left it parked in Beaufort. "A downtown lot," she answered, "a block from the river."

"At a dumpster," he added, more a statement than a question.

"There was a dumpster," she agreed, "across the fence from my car. Behind a restaurant."

"Ma'am, rodents chewed your wiring. Can't believe you got this far. I think your car was full o' rats."

What is happening? she thought. *Now I'm a ma'am?*

"Wait, what? *Rats?*"

Soon they were on the road, with an exceptionally fine view from the cab of the tow truck, where Eli was pondering the need to disclose a rat infestation when trading in a vehicle. *Definitely ready for something with a tow truck view.*

Reggie cranked the satellite radio, and they spent the last hour of the trip vocalizing with Guns N' Roses, Alanis Morissette, and Red Hot Chili Peppers, arriving just ahead of sunrise.

Ending on the last chorus of "Nothing Compares 2 U," Eli thanked Reggie for the rescue and bailed out of his truck. As she approached the residents' entrance with her luggage and the cooler of seafood in tow, Eli recognized Hannah Collins, Ted's company accountant, leaving the private elevator at the penthouse garage.

"What brings her here?" Eli muttered. "And Waller Analytics is closed on Black Friday, anyway."

Upstairs, Eli raised her phone closer to the lock on her condo door—as if that would trigger the familiar click—but when she touched the lever, it was open. Before calling security, Eli peeked through and saw her fantastically expensive, *I will love again* silk peignoir—the one she kept hanging on the bathroom wall as fine art—billowing off her balcony.

She threw open the door and realized the silken cloud of hand-painted peonies did nothing to screen the sight of Grace, perched on the balcony railing in the peignoir, legs wrapped around Pete's bare backside, and both oblivious to Eli or anyone else in the potential audience of countless Atlanta skyrise neighbors.

Molten, Eli turned away yelling, "Off the balcony now," then pulled the door nearly closed behind her.

"Way to barge in," Pete roared, stepping into his pants by a dining room chair.

"You're supposed to be at Grace's parents' or staying in the guest apartment," Eli growled from the corridor, pointing overhead. "Tomorrow."

"We just wanted time alone after an entire day with my parents," Grace whined, adding, "Ted got us in. Why are you standing out in the hall?"

"Right, I'll just put these bags away," Eli mumbled, as Grace shook off the robe, holding out the wadded ball of silk to Eli as she passed the child-size frame of her bare-naked guest.

"Grace, you know…" She stopped. "This was…. *Keep it.*"

As she reached her bedroom door, the former sanctum of serenity was unrecognizable. Food containers had drizzled who-knows-what on the slide down the custom duvet heaped at the foot of the bed. A thong-like item hung off one of the sconces above the headboard, a wine bottle was dripping from the nightstand into an open drawer, and a not quite empty adult shoppe bag on the floor warned she might have already seen enough.

"How long have y'all been here?" she gasped in disbelief.

"Wow, Eli, you look terrible. Okay, so, two days before we left for Virginia, Wednesday night, and then we came back last night," Grace rambled, adding with feigned dismay, "Someone was already in the guest apartment, a friend of Ted's."

Eli slowly walked past Grace, threw open her guest room door to the undisturbed, thoughtfully appointed accommodations, then turned, both palms in the air, to comfortably still-naked Grace.

"That is a nice bedroom, Eli, but the other one is so dreamy, who could resist?"

Smoldering and exhausted despite the Waffle House nap, Eli shouldered past Grace, snatching clothes off her trashed bedroom floor, tossing them over her head onto Grace until she cleared a path to her closet. She reached for her bags, rolling them to the door, but froze at the sight of a flower-stenciled storage box open on the closet floor.

Grace was stuffing the collected clothes in her travel bag—except the wrap dress she had tied on over nothing. As Eli emerged from her closet stone-faced to confront Grace, the vacant box in her hand, she saw the missing contents—all her old journals—sprawled across the side table next to her reading chair.

Eli picked up one under the lamp, the one with a pen sticking out of it. The page had notes in the margin, notes Eli had not written. She suspected a stroke might be shutting down her thought processes as she looked up in shock, face-to-face with Grace, but could not speak. Of course, Grace could.

"I was reading all night, Eli." Grace sighed, no hint of apology in this, the second audio grenade of Eli's roller coaster week.

"So, Ted is probably not a narcissist, not even a subtle narcissist, as your *employer*-friend convinced you. Talk about HR violations. Eli, Ted may be an Aspie," she delightedly declared, as though she had unmasked a good wizard in a Potter story. "We're a beautifully neurodiverse world," Grace continued, moving to Eli's vanity mirror and sweeping a brush through the length of her glossy black hair as she delivered the clinical explanation of her suggestion.

"Actually, Asperger's is an obsolete term applied to myriad points on the autism spectrum—from kids who are clearly struggling to top executives whose difficulties can be imperceptible. Each person affected has a different experience from the next, with personalities just as varied as the neuro-typical population," she concluded, while applying Eli's gloss, popping her lips, then smearing a kiss on Eli's cheek before tugging her bag away.

"E, we're getting together for dinner, 'k? Oh, and your mom was probably neurodivergent, too. Not a coincidence that you basically married your mother. If you encountered issues similar to what you had with her, again in your interactions with Ted, your subconscious gravitated to behaviors you were accustomed to handling. And girl, a good therapist would not be wasted on you. Bye, now!"

Pete appeared with his luggage to find Eli standing dumbfounded, holding the trash bag brimming with food cartons, wine bottles, and assorted garbage.

"Better that we stay elsewhere tonight. I booked a room downstairs," Pete said, snapping her back from the brink of a meltdown.

"I know this isn't how you roll, Pete. I believed you'd be a grounding influence on Grace. Now I'm hoping she isn't nurturing a wild child phase in a guy who is just beginning his career."

"Yeah, we're working through a few things." His smile would always melt her heart. Pete mussed her trendy hair. "Will never get used to that look."

"Dinner at Maison Marietta tonight? Meet you at seven," Grace called through the closing door. And then it was all so quiet.

Not the no-place-like-homecoming Eli had longed for since she left Beaufort, but nothing could ease her stress as quickly as seeing

Pete. Caring for him had generated the love and laughter that carried them both through so many tough transitions.

Shy and plain, Eli believed she had never been special to anyone—certainly not her mother Julia—until Julia's half-sister, Edie appeared in their lives. Edie radiated kindness and joy; whereas JuJu was always happy—to capitalize on her little sister's generosity, or anyone else's. Uncle Jim referred to her as "the heiress" because she seemed to prosper as relatives aged out, living from one inheritance to the next, profitably dangling baby Elinor as the proposed beneficiary.

Having Edie in Eli's life softened everything. It wasn't lost on the little girl that she was being shuttled from doorstep to doorstep as JuJu parked her with elderly aunts or family friends for a weekend that turned into weeks. As soon as Edie was living with roommates off campus at Emory, Eli often appeared there, too, including one stint that lasted six weeks until Edie's furious mother broke up the babysitting ring. It was painful to leave.

Little Eli had been new to snuggles, hugs, kisses, and the unforgettable moments—Edie looking at her with such love as she would braid or ponytail Eli's hair, often taking her shopping and delightedly dressing her in clothes that, for once, fit.

Was Grace right? Had she married her mother? Found a person with issues that resonated? Even teenage Pete saw problems, saying Eli would benefit from therapy as much as he did.

When Aunt Ta died in a matter of weeks, newlywed Eli had been with her through it all. Afterward, Pete came to live with Eli. Their rocky reunion soon smoothed thanks to counseling to help the boy forgive Eli eloping with Ted, as well as easing the child's adjustments to a new life. If only she and Ted had tried a session or ten together.

Toxic waves of exhaustion and melancholy sloshed in her brain. Time to get over Ted so readily having forgotten her. Staying in the same building just in case he needed assistance with things she always managed, hoping they could go forward on a friendly basis, were pointless. "Time to stop setting yourself on fire to keep someone else warm," Viv Wright, a collector of trendy phrases had said, when Eli moved out—but only a few floors below Ted.

C'mon, you can't let a filterless med student shake you, Eli bristled. Had Grace just torpedoed her rationale for leaving Ted? Autism? A brilliant, accomplished titan of chemical analytics guy like Ted? Yet he was so much like her mom, once she thought about it. So many similar attitudes.

"You're tired, Eli," she said aloud on behalf of the voice in her head. "It will all look better tomorrow." Unlike Zen seekers who strive to banish the chatty voice of the mind, Eli tolerated hers as an occasional source of good advice erupting among judgy observations. A babbling stream of diversions from introspection.

She continued filling the trash bag—donut box, chips sack, Starbucks cup—and there, in a puddle on the floor next to the shower, ripped from the ensemble Eli had revered for months as a symbol of her new life ahead, lay the soggy silk corpse of the peignoir hanger. Ah, Grace, a doctor who will never know borders.

Eli passed on the dinner suggestion, reminding Grace by text that they were expected back at Eli's for supper Saturday if still interested. By late evening she had completed a vinegar washdown of her bedroom from the ceiling fan to the crevices of the hardwood floors and everything in between. Eli was beginning to see her cleaning fixation as more of a space cleansing exercise. That's what she was going to call it, anyway.

Still, she decided to sleep in the guest room. Pulling back the duvet, Eli slid in, fighting unsettling thoughts about Pete, Ted, and her client's secrets. "Bring it, Universe. There's nothing this girl can't handle," Eli challenged, intending to reassure herself.

By mid-morning, the onions, celery, and green peppers were chopped; okra was thawing; and a butter, flour roux was underway. Watching Molly peel shrimp had made it look easy, but Eli was battling shells and wiggly legs at a rate that would push dinner back to a sophisticated midnight plating. She had been running laundry through the morning and chuting bags of trash as her place returned to normal. And so far, no blowback from the building's board about the spectacle on the terrace balcony.

The roux was demanding attention to keep the sacred essence from scorching as it browned. Eli managed to get all the veggie ingredients added, in the order Molly dictated, by mid-afternoon. With the gumbo on a low simmer until she was ready to add the seafood, there was time to finish restoring her bedroom.

Eli picked up the last of her plundered journals and opened it to the pencil wedged inside, then paged back to the first notes Grace had made. Young Dr. G presented a legit case for her Asperger's opinions about Ted and JuJu. Eli was ricocheting through surges of astonishment, dismay, regret, and grief. "If all this is accurate," she choked through tears, "I've made a terrible, cruel mistake. I've been so smug. So righteous. *So wrong.*"

Pete and Grace were at the door and Eli was still reading journals, but with Grace's perspective, however misguided. Having someone else recognize the degree of loneliness in her marriage—the total absence of attention, approval, appreciation, or genuine affection from Ted—left Eli weak with gratitude for that understanding.

"Door's open," she called to welcome them back with a more humble, glad-to-be-together attitude. *So much give and take in life*, Eli thought, as she watched Pete and Grace banter.

The gumbo was as close to Molly's bowl of perfection as Eli dared hope. Pete's contribution of key lime pie was the perfect foil for the main dish, and Grace, well, Grace had reset Eli's unhealed heart with her usual sledgehammer technique.

As Eli walked them to the elevator, Grace turned to Eli. "You will never guess who was using the guest apartment this week. Hannah, the accountant! She has seen Ted's numbers and likes what she sees."

Eli appeared stunned, but she was confused by the idea.

Pete hit the elevator button. "Hasn't Ted mentioned it? Her house is being remodeled, and she had no place else to go."

"Poor baby," Grace whined, one eyebrow cocked. "That's a lame one."

"Then, if you're in the guest apartment tonight," Eli stammered, "where did she go?"

"Maybe back home," Grace cheered.

"There was a car club rally Ted was attending this weekend," Pete informed them, "and, when Ted was rationalizing the remodeling thing, it sounded like she invited herself to go with him. Eli, when was the last time you talked to him?"

"When we met with the attorneys before the divorce was finalized in May."

Pete looked at Grace. "Why am I not surprised? He is who he is, Eli. Move out of here and have some fun for once in your life." Pete gave her a wraparound hug, an especially good hug, after Grace had finally whispered an apology of sorts as she said goodbye.

"Voice in my head," Eli said, watching the elevator light reach the 26th floor, "you really know your stuff. How about singing me to sleep tonight?"

Chapter 3

Who Not to Call
Before You Dig

On that rainy, snoozy Sunday morning, Eli rolled out of her own bed and hurriedly dressed to meet Pete and Grace before their early flight to Denver. She was surprised that Ted had stayed in touch with Pete, but it was a nice surprise. Their shared fascination with analytical chemistry, perhaps.

Monday morning, she was emptying her backpack onto the dining room table when Eli noticed how neatly everything had settled in the haggard bag. She stacked notebooks filled with resource material, image lists, interviews, and follow-up notes in piles she could subdivide by subject and chronology.

That done, she opened her laptop to input the material and build background on interview subjects, but her search terms morphed into

"Asperger's partners," "Asperger's" or "narcissism," within authoritative websites—on and on until morning became afternoon and then evening. So much sounded heartbreakingly familiar.

She knew Ted to be a man of unfailing integrity, but emotionally absent. To most people—while he seemed like any other reserved guy—the lack of eye contact, discomfort with touch, invisible empathy, or disinterest in affection would not be obvious.

In his case—as far as Eli could tell—he may have warm feelings, he may harbor kind thoughts, but none had escaped the recesses of his mind. She went to bed, but hardly slept.

The next day, Eli had advanced through the piles of research on the book when a call came in from Megan Wright, the daughter-in-law who had taken Viv Wright's role at the agency.

"Hello, Megan. I was going to call you this morning," Eli said, noticing her teeth were clenched.

"To say you invited yourself for Thanksgiving with the Harrisons?"

"*No.* To say that meeting more of the family gave solid insights to the Harrison dynasty and brought out leads that will be worth pursuing."

"Uh-huh. Wrap it up, Eli, we have other clients." Megan's preference for taking the agency in what she considered a more relevant direction wasn't happening fast enough.

"I expect drafts this week."

"Can't, but I will stay on this and give you updates often. Okay, thanks, Megan, I'll—"

"Hold on, Eli. I want to know where we are on this project, and you're going to send me drafts. By Wednesday."

"And why would you need to see first drafts of my work? Viv never intruded on this process. It's my assignment. I'm working on schedule. You might see drafts, after review by the client, his editors, and after he has authorized me to share those drafts with you."

"We can't sell a saccharine fairy tale with regurgitated cowboy stories. This is my firm now. Drafts Wednesday."

"David Harrison selected my name for his contract," she answered, the phone trembling in her tight grasp. "This project is no hagiography, and I do not need your approbation to continue with it. Read his contract, Megan."

Eli made sure her phone was off before letting loose with a stream of unflattering adjectives preceding names of unseen body parts, ending with Megan. "No question I'm past my doormat phase." Eli declared, then conceded, "Not exactly badass if you save the good stuff for after the call." Eli took several deep breaths, then shifted her focus to the elephant sitting amid her research materials.

"Obviously David Harrison is worried about something he hasn't revealed," she stated, in review. "And his attorney, Victor, is intent on concealing it. Is it something liable to come out and sink the book after publication? Is it something old and buried that keeps him up at night, or a bit of nothing that only a decent person would be troubled by?"

Bombshell or dud, Eli considered how she might approach David. He had been completely open, leaving his personal office as her full-access workspace for the week and a half she was in Beaufort. The family was uninhibited with their stories and photos; she had unrestricted access to all the staff. *How do I proceed,* she wondered, *knowing a secret in his story is being withheld? A private matter. A decision made long ago. His story to tell.*

Eli decided against approaching David Harrison. He would have already shared it if he were willing. *Find a glitch,* she thought. *Something conflicting in the resource material.* That might be her opening to ask about other potential surprises.

For three days, Eli pored over every shred of information she had collected. Duplications in file categories were innumerable, but necessary. Nothing jumped out. It was time to wade through the images— decades of studio, news, personal, and publicity shots—few of which had been digitized until now.

Another day of annotating, caption searching, and identifying left Eli with a splitting headache that she wanted to attribute to the stress but suspected could be relieved by a pair of readers.

There, in the last batch of images from the Harrisons, the album photos scanned front and back for Kylie. In Ida's admirably fine hand-writing, noted and dated just as all the others, was a photo of a fashionably belted Ida with her arm around a term-ishly pregnant look alike, with the inscription, "Oahu, Hawaii, Sis & I. Jan '68."

Family info didn't mention a sister-in-law for David, but that could be for privacy reasons. His mother and sister were included in a few stories. And if correct, that photo date was the month before Marc Harrison was born. In Hawaii.

"There is absolutely no one I could trust with this," Eli shouted, rocking back from the mountains of stacked paper. Viv would have known how to handle it; Eli didn't know where to begin. She recalled an interview reference to Ida's early movie career, and seeking parts with her sister, Alma. Continued searching failed to turn up any further mention.

A little after midnight, too wired to sleep, Eli wanted to take a walk, go for a drive, something calming to clear her mind. None of her relaxation hacks were helping. Eli opened the balcony doors for some air and looked out on to the wide-awake city skyline.

"Forest bathing," Eli sighed. That's what this body needs—to soak in some Georgia mountain woodlands."

Whether it was triggered by the afternoons on the Beaufort River or the ache for family connection after Thanksgiving with the Harrisons, Eli was longing to be at the lake in front of the fire in that rambling house her grandfather's grandfather built when the land was still a creek-side farm.

As for bathing, it would take too much time and water to fill the oversize tub. *Okay*, she decided, locking the balcony doors behind her, *let's hit the shower.*

"A kitchen sink sprayer puts out more water than this," she griped, turning front to back and back to front, catching the near mist emitted by the showerhead. Nothing chased the image of Ida and Alma from her mind.

After several failed starts, Eli managed to turn off the shower. A few minutes with the blow dryer and she was fluffed enough not to dampen her pillow, soon in bed and snoring.

Before her eyes opened to the morning light, the image of the sisters sprang to mind. Was it all a dream? She grabbed a robe on the way to the bathroom, leaning to look in at the stacks in the dining room. *Not a dream.*

Eli yawned through her morning ablutions, waiting for a flash of inspiration on how to bring up this photo with David, or maybe Ida. "Or Kylie," she shouted, drowning out the breakfast suggestions from the voice in her head. Surely the doctor noticed this pregnant anomaly—if she didn't know already.

Nope, David is the client. I finish gathering the information, let my thoughts settle, and then take it all to David.

Steeled for another round of follow-up calls, Eli stopped at the kitchen bar to get her phone off the charger. No phone. She went to the bedroom where she kept the always charging phone with the ported line from her aunt's house at Lake Chatuge. She called hers and found it ringing under a folder on the table. "Totally need to put a password or thumbprint or anything other than facial recognition on that phone," she muttered. "Then when I do lose it…"

Eli noticed the file in her hand that had been over her phone. *What was I doing with my contract file?*

She returned to the stacks, focusing her attention on Ida, looking for clues to her sister Alma. Creating her own timeline for this ghost from the early sixties wasn't easy. Couldn't be much younger than Ida. That interview mentioned the two Garcia sisters had stayed with cousins in Los Angeles in the mid-sixties, working to develop film careers. Not much to go on.

Eli clicked the file showing David Harrison's films chronological-ly, skimming down to the very earliest roles and cross-referencing the producers. All but one was the same man, Jack Grant. His obituary showed a son still at the same swanky address. Johnny Grant was also listed as a production assistant on several films. Maybe he would re-member Alma.

Eli left a routine voicemail on his business line, seeking an inter-view for David's book. Johnny Grant called back in the early after-noon, sounding pleased to be included. Not so pleased when most of the questions were about Alma, whom he couldn't recall.

⟫━◆━⟪

Days passed with no search results on Alma. No financial histories, hospital records in Hawaii, nor verifiable court cases. Not a single cred-it report. Certainly nothing from the digital age. Hunger was gnawing at Eli's concentration. She looked at her phone. *December sixth?* The only items in the fridge were decomposing gumbo and lumpy orange juice. Time for a grocery run.

Halfway between produce and the deli, Megan called. *Crap, can't dodge her after last week. Can't call her names in the middle of the grocery, so this could work.* "Hello? Megan, listen, I'm—"

"Spare me, Eli. David Harrison has received a blackmail threat. This project is on hold pending the outcome of what their law firm ex-pects will be a criminal investigation. You are suspended until further notice. I'll deposit the balance due you before close of business today." And with that, the call ended.

Eli tossed a box of donuts onto the romaine and assorted veggies in the cart, then headed to checkout. Her fingers gripped the handle as her heart continued to pound. She needed that walk.

She drove to the Atlanta Botanical Garden, land of luxe forest bathing. Eli regarded the acres of magnificent nature-scaping as her spiritual spa. Her Aunt Edie often brought her to this verdant refuge in its early days. On this cold, gray afternoon, the vast Garden Lights, Holiday Nights displays were guiding her in from the street.

At the entrance to Sage parking, she whipped out her pass and membership card, leaving the veggies to chill in the near vacant lot while she and the remaining donuts took a hike. "No lunch at Longleaf today," she pouted, zipping her coat as she passed the celebrated Garden restaurant.

Crossing mosaic pebble paths to the canopy walk high over the Storza Woods, Eli slowed to hear the water stairs splashing as she continued the half-mile loop. Thoroughly chilled, with donut glaze frosting her lips, Eli had thought through her involvements with the Harrisons, and could not pinpoint a catalyst for shelving the project, much less a criminal investigation.

From the edge of the fountain next to the restaurant, Eli was rinsing her sticky fingers in the pool when her phone rang again. The dealership had her car ready.

On her way home, Eli tried calling Jeff Wright, Viv's son and now the titular head of the Wright Agency while still managing his law firm. She didn't leave a voicemail. *Should have sent a text. Would look desperate now. Give it a day*, she thought, in a cloud of panic.

Jeff returned her call. He'd been talking with David's attorney, Victor Hernandez, who confirmed there had been a blackmail demand, and that Eli was involved as the leak—whether intentional or not should soon be determined. Jeff asked if she had legal representation.

"A lawyer? Well, for the divorce."

"Ask if he could recommend someone, Eli. A litigator. If this escalates, I represent the Wright Agency."

Wheeling in the residents' parking deck, Eli gave her key fob to the doorman, swearing, "I won't be ten minutes, Leon, I promise." Pushing a bellman's cart from the service room, Eli barged onto an elevator, parting a venerable couple—she, clutching her Bichon, and he, taking her hand through Eli's cart to steady them both.

In the condo, she scooped the few fridge items in a trash bag, emptied the bins in the bath and bedrooms, then jogged down the hall, slamming the bag in the garbage chute. She loaded the laundry basket with her laptop and desktop, wedging two wall mirrors against a duvet full of printed files, then filled the bare bedsheets with the contents of her closet and dresser drawers, knotting the ends and squashing the mound onto the cart.

She piled on her towels and finally the travel bags full of shoes, vanity supplies, chargers, and surge protectors; then threw the guest room linens over the bars above the cart, tucking hems under the heaps beneath. Eight minutes in, she shoved out the door and onto an elevator.

Eli came crashing out of the residents' doors, crammed the car to the headliner, and was pulling away for good, leaving Leon aghast with the empty cart, profound apologies, and a grateful hug as she slipped him the last two twenties in her wallet. Enough gas to get above Atlanta registered in the tank, then she could stop for fuel and look at the deposit that had pinged while she was loading up.

Geez, no. Eli cringed at the numbers on her screen as she was paying for gas. This wasn't as much as her unfiled November expenses. Unlike her insanely pathetic I-can-take-care-of-myself divorce settlement, Megan wasn't going to scapegoat *and* swindle her.

Despite her avowed political pacificism, she would battle Megan from the mountaintops, or at least from a mountain lake. "A low budget war," she amended, relieved to be easing off I-575 onto Highway 515 North, and not far from a glimpse of the mountains.

Traffic thinned north of Jasper, and Eli had been estimating financial resources in the stop and go of the early evening commuters, but with the rising vistas, she entertained more pleasant thoughts. Her last drive up was to bring Pete and Grace to join Eli's former brother-in-law, adorable Lewis Waller, and his teen son for a day on Lake Chatuge. It had been July Fourth.

Independence Day traffic that early morning had been light, allowing them the time to check on her aunt's lake house, but Pete hadn't been interested in stopping on the way to the cookout. They did stop for a sack of Carlotta's po'boys—lunch for a tour of the lake.

Eli felt uneasy returning to the grand Waller lake house. She was waiting alone on the dock with the picnic basket when a wide shadow passed over her. A bald eagle sailed past, banking low, reversing direction and cruising over her again. *A Carlotta's fan?*

Her fond memories of the day—decorating, then riding in the boat parade, Lew's fantastic spread at that evening's cookout under the fireworks—paled compared to the sight of that magnificent raptor.

That was months ago. Eli meant to spend a summer weekend cleaning the house she and Pete inherited. Cabin-minding services in the area checked outdoors twice monthly, maintained lawns, and would clean house as requested. Eli hadn't placed a cleaning request in a year—probably three. Time had flown since their uncle, Jim Clark, died.

Now Eli was barreling back to that lonely house, seeking solace where losses had been the theme for decades. The sense that her life was imploding overwhelmed her. "It's time to put yourself first," Viv told Eli many times, advising Eli to, "Push away negativity and accept nothing less than respect from those around you."

Still, Eli was swimming in a current of negativity. She couldn't think of anyone who respected her at this moment. "I've never mastered that power of choice thing," Eli declared, still taunting the universe.

Snow flurries were swirling across the windshield as she passed through Blue Ridge, but roads were warm enough to keep it a lovely distraction. "Isn't snow good luck?" she asked the night sky. "Nah, that's on a wedding day. Maybe in Japan," she added, dismantling the thought.

Two hours earlier, she had been an ATL high-rise dwelling celebrity biographer. Now, she'd come to hide in the place she blissfully slipped away from eighteen years ago.

From a ridge just west of Blairsville, the clouds thinned enough to reveal the moonlit undulation of the Appalachians across the horizon. Clearing the last rise before Towns County opened a view to the gentle sweep of the snowy Wolfpen Ridge, confirmation of a traveler's entrance to the Enchanted Valley nestled among the ancient balds of North Georgia.

Finally turning off the highway onto the familiar road, winding up and around, down but not quite to the end, Eli passed a few homes sporting Christmas lights. Driving beyond one more shadowy bend, she recognized the falling fences bordering the barely graveled drive.

The woods were overgrown from the road to the house. The old place loomed against a river of light trailed across the lake by a gibbous moon. Oh, the torrent of spectral memories that greeted her here. If this moment could spin back to the night before she'd eloped with Ted, how differently Eli could live the years that lay ahead.

Somewhere in the console were the house keys, and possibly the clunky old remote for the garage door. She scrounged for several minutes and decided to call a locksmith in the morning. Her loaded car held her pillows and blankets *somewhere*, Eli recalled, as she vacantly studied the clouds pacing across the moon.

A sudden deep breath roused her, and Eli burst into tears, crying harder than she had when she'd signed the divorce papers. More uncontrollably than when Viv died. But none of that occurred to her, so deep in her grief for the new life she was building. And for the one before that.

"Please, help me let go of all this," her entreaty began, as she back-tracked on her inclination to nose-thumb the universe, "to not be consumed by my stupid mistakes. I've ridden the pendulum from cowering and frightened to arrogant and so damned smug. Oh, Edie. Viv? Okay, you've never heard me before, God, but please, help me."

Barking dogs woke Eli. Startled, she could barely move in response, cocooned in a parka and quilted coat with her feet wrapped in a bathrobe and towels. She snaked one hand down to press the brake pedal, using the other to push the starter and warm the car.

She desperately needed to whiz, but not in the driveway. Eli struggled to push off enough layers to reach the glove compartment, where she had finally remembered moving several things the night the car was towed. "House keys!"

She hurriedly felt around in the footwell for her shoes, then paused in the headlights to select the key. She was beyond relieved to get inside and flip light switches as she rushed to the bathroom. Toilets and drains were freeze-treated, and the water was off, but first things first.

As she came through with another load from the car, the gritty floors and stale air distracted her. Despite adjusting the thermostat, nothing changed. She released the water cut-off and began dusting until the water heater kicked in.

Wasn't happening. A quick round of vacuuming would surely scatter any spiders or other things no one wants to think about in these situations. Then a little mopping. Maybe some online counseling for cleaning disorders.

———◆———

At first light, she tried to back the car in the garage, but the overhead door wouldn't budge. Eli released it and managed to hoist the stiff door. After unloading, she tried swinging from it to close the door.

Nothing. At least the trees blocked the sight from the road. There would be service calls to make.

As Eli stretched out on the sectional facing the kitchen's view to the lake, she saw the sun was already coming up. Just as her eyes closed, she glimpsed a small figure staring in at her through the sliding doors. An imperious, golden cat sitting with its head cocked and nose to the glass. She considered letting it in to scout for mice. Maybe after her nap.

Bumping noises in the garage slowly roused Eli until she was awake enough to think that it might be a bear foraging in her car. She eased to the bay window and remotely started the car. More bumping ensued until an enormous dog, obviously a Great Dane, went bounding south across the yard.

"Lots more pets here than I remember," Eli muttered, walking back to the kitchen and noticing the handsome cat lounging on the sunny patio.

Eli started her calls, first looking up garage door repair. Amazingly, there were now three services in the area. She picked the most distant, hoping to keep her arrival from being noticed. In the divorce, Eli had petitioned to revert to her maiden name, Sledge, since Pete had remained a Cooper and she didn't want any Waller ties.

Next, Eli shopped her phone for a replacement fridge—no sense trying to repair a dead thirty-year-old model. *Delivery from nearby Blairsville tomorrow?* Life in the mountains had definitely become easier.

Looking around the space in daylight was more despair-inducing than comforting. Aunt Ta had died eight months after Eli married, and the furniture that was showing its age then was layered now with a grimy patina of neglect. Eli grabbed her jacket. Time to walk.

Out across the patio, leaves were deep with a slick, decaying layer beneath. Another project for another day. Eli was devoting her every thought to creating a refuge from this crumbling place. It was no Sunrise Shore, but there was plenty of room—for improvement. After all, this might be her forever home. She could work it out with Pete.

Naming the lake house could be inspiring. The Waller estate was dubbed Pastoral Point. She searched the opposite shore, trying to recall other names. Nothing cutesy, certainly nothing pretentious. Her pre-dawn first sight of this place in years came to mind—Falling Fences.

As she walked through the trees towards the lake, Eli was yanking saplings, mostly poplars, from the soft, wet soil. Rustling leaves behind revealed that the cat had trailed her to the water. It scampered to the end of the dock, shot up a post, and raced back, proving at least the catworthiness of the structure.

Above the shoreline, stone benches surrounding the firepit were hidden in winter-withered weeds, never having been part of the lawn cutting program. "Good golly, I should be carrying a clipboard," Eli grumbled. Grounds would have to wait for the spring list.

Rumbling on the gravel drive had Eli sprinting for the house. Finally, the garage door was going to close. Instead, the side window sticker on an immaculate, not-yet-antique Mercedes SUV identified a real estate agent.

"Hello there," a woman called to Eli as she left her car. She was a generously curvy, 40ish woman with true twinkling eyes, dimples, and a bouncing auburn ponytail. Each squishy step risked the wedge mules that matched her slacks and the sea green check of her gingham top as she came marching through the brush to Eli. "I'm Beth Parker, tending to your neighbor's house. Are you moving in?"

Eli was not ready to be discovered. "Just here to get some repairs done," she answered, with a low wave she hoped would turn Ms. Parker around.

"Getting it ready to go on the market then," she called back as she neared, slipping her arms in a jacket.

"Oh no, not selling," Eli said, but Beth had arrived, hand out-stretched. "Eli Sledge," she conceded in defeat, as their hands clasped. "Part owner."

As Eli attempted to walk her back to the car, Beth proceeded to give an update on the neighborhood. The house she mentioned was one of the newer large homes built on the small lots around the point where the two lanes narrowed to one at the last turn in the road.

As Eli had always known, that was once the entrance to the old Sutton farm, her family homestead, perhaps two generations older than Eli's great-grandfather, a respected Atlanta commercial devel-oper. He was Aunt Ta's father and had made a gift of it to Ta and Jim Clark when they married. Since then, the Clarks had steadily sold off portions for extra income, leaving the house on its last three acres amid a lakeside neighborhood.

As Beth ran down the roster of homeowners, her effusive descrip-tions detailed previous places of residence, professions, and family members, citing these numbing facts house by house. Her tone hard-ened as she included an expansion within the family of the couple Eli remembered across the road, who since had added homes on the property for their child and most recently, grandchild.

"I'm sure you've noticed the son's appliance repair truck always parked at the road behind the mailbox. Two of those houses encroach on the setbacks." Beth reported, shuddering.

With that, she went on to describe Eli's next-door neighbor to the south as "a veterinarian who lives on the estate of her missing friend, Beau Johnston—"

"Beau?" Eli choked. "Beau Johnston went missing? He was a MacGyver-esque legend when I was in school here," she recalled, imagining a hunting or fishing accident.

"Beau was a contractor in the Middle East." Beth seemed pleased to finally have Eli's interest. "Very successful, from a prominent family.

I believe Mela had moved in to take care of his aging parents while he was gone, but he's never come back."

Eli's mind was blown. *Mela, the quiet, super-student, had been living with Beau, the adventurous, ingenious guy said to have skipped more classes than he attended? How could someone like Beau just disappear?* Ted's life-long lake buddy, Mac Miller, never mentioned any of this. Or if he did, Ted never passed it along to Eli.

"Now, on the other side of Mela is that sad, sad lady, Ann Arnold. Never seen her myself, but, well, so sad." As Beth gathered her thoughts on Ms. Arnold, Eli jumped in to say she had to prepare for a repairman who was on his way.

"Oh." Beth continued, disregarding Eli's escape plan. "Those ten marshy acres at the end of this road? Some secretive kazillionaire has built in there. Months of concrete trucks, trades, and subs racing in and out. And then—"

And then, the garage door truck appeared. Eli waved him around Beth's car and inside the parking court, trotting away behind the vehicle, gagging in the dust. "Note to clipboard: Price asphalt driveway and maybe a gate."

Dude, as Eli had christened the ever-present Great Dane, reviewed every truck that came while work continued. Ten days and several thousand dollars later, the house had a functioning HVAC system, operating garage door, a patched roof, cleaned fireplace, and new refrigerator.

Next came plumbing repairs—completed after Eli's first attempt at a soaking bath in the ancient clawfoot tub. The pipe had become so heavily corroded just below the drain that as the plug was pulled, it disintegrated. Water pooled onto the tile floor, flooding the hall, and could be heard collecting in the basement below. Fans and heat ran hard for days.

Aside from Beth dropping in, Eli had maintained her seclusion socially while the steady stream of craftsmen revived the old house.

Fluffy, the cat, had earned an indoor pass after sneaking in the kitchen and pouncing on a field mouse he'd been watching through the door. Fluffy became especially fond of assisting the HVAC techs during their visits.

The chief tech and now owner, Gary, had been to the house for system issues over the years, and during this call he showed Eli the attic opening above the larger guest room. When the first part of the house was built, a ladder connected that single room cabin to the upper sleeping area. The walls of that 18' x 18' guest room and the joists beneath the floors were made of hand-hewn timbers that had become impenetrable by normal drill bits. Those old stories Aunt Ta told were coming to life.

Eli felt safe and productive in the company of the talented tradesmen working to make the old place habitable, but the shock and misery she had locked out of her awareness began leaching into her dreams to an intolerable degree. For the exhausted fugitive, sleep was no longer an escape.

Chapter 4

Where You Once Knew

To avoid seeing people she might have known, Eli's runs to the grocery and building supply stores were early morning ventures. Not that any hurried Christmas shoppers would notice someone in jeans, a puffy jacket, and a hooded sweatshirt pulled over a knit cap.

Projects kept Eli too busy to dwell on the Harrison crisis. As work was slowing at the house, Eli was thinking more and more—not about her situation—about Mela. Catching up with Mela would mean ripping the lids off the hammered compartments of her messed up life, and as well as Eli believed she was functioning, she wasn't up for scrutiny.

Chunk by chunk, Eli had hauled away pieces of two old recliners, the sectional sofa, and made three dump drops with a mattress over her sunroof. Rather than trading her Sport in on a truck, her solution was to drag the long part of the sectional sideways through the sliders out to the firepit to burn it. She just couldn't get the thing to scooch around the glass slider. *Not happening*, the ol' inner voice advised. *Environmentally reprehensible, Elinor.*

"This won't go in or on my car," she shouted, in counterpoint. "As often as I go to Home Depot, how do I not have a freaking chainsaw?"

Attached pillows were holding the sofa upright in the open door. Eli elected to slice away the upper cushions to allow the bulky frame to move through. The box cutter released the top pillow, revealing its hidden zipper as three folders sealed in plastic bags slid to the ground.

At her feet, she saw a newspaper clipping under the plastic. The headline: "Three Dead in Mountainside Wreck." A chill crawled up her spine as one of her internal hammered compartments cracked open.

<hr />

The day after Aunt Ta's funeral, as Ted was leaving for his flight home to Dallas, kindergartener Pete was standing next to the rental car, watching. Eli had been away for weeks, with no return date determined.

Ted wasn't sure she would come back to Texas without Pete. When Uncle Jim asked about the possibility of the child going to living with the newlyweds in Texas, Ted's only response to the old man was, "That's a lot to consider."

Pete stepped away from the car door as Ted approached without speaking, and the child raised his arm for a farewell handshake. Ted obliged, then swung the door open. As he used his handkerchief to brush cookie dust off his fingers, he turned back to Pete. "I guess I'll see you in Texas?" Oblivious to the adoration radiating from the boy, Ted slid into the driver's seat and looked over at Eli, dropping his gaze as if to say, "You win," and was gone.

Every Sunday afternoon at four, Eli and Pete would call to check on Uncle Jim. Despite his proclivity for drinking more than he should, the first few years he was fairly clear-minded and full of stories—often the same stories—when she called, but always asking when they could come again.

Eli never realized how desperately important those visits were. She was busy, Ted was never happy about them, and Pete seemed upset by them, perhaps wary of being returned.

Ted was relocated within Waller Analytics twice more over the next four years. Life became even busier, little Pete more reluctant to visit, and Uncle Jim more frail in the years after he sold the newspaper. He often chastised Eli for not calling in months despite her near daily calls and became weepy when she reassured him.

Eli arranged a large celebration for his eighty-ninth birthday, and she came for the week. This time from Ted's latest posting in Charlotte, which was close enough for Ted to drive over the day of the party in his favorite roadster.

During that week, Eli was shocked by the evidence of her great-uncle's deterioration. Stacked boxes of check orders covered his desk above drawers of unpaid bills. Spoiled food ruined his refrigerator. Bathing, it appeared, was of no interest to him.

Eli took Uncle Jim to see his doctor twice that week and then, on the doctor's recommendation, to tour an assisted living center in town where he would receive his meds, meals, and have help with hygiene—a place where he would be welcome to retell stories to his heart's delight.

Eli was able to visit more often as a division writer with the Wright Agency branch in Charlotte, but it mattered less, as he would forget before she was out of the building. He died the week before Pete's high school graduation. Pete and Ted arrived the day of the funeral. Eli rushed home for Pete's big day and back to quickly settle accounts before catching up with her own life.

Clearly there had been more accounts to settle. In one of the sofa's hidden folders was a savings deposit record from late in the year of the wreck that took Juju, Edie, and Chuck—Julia Sutton Sledge, Edith Sutton Cooper, and Edie's husband, Charles Cooper. A letter from Eli's maternal grandmother citing ill health relinquished custody to the Clarks, along with executorship to Aunt Ta.

Clipped articles about the crash included pictures of the wrecked SUV off the side of a mountain near Bristol. Eli wouldn't read them. Her mind was on custody documents. *Where was that paperwork?* Three death certificates were behind the articles. Edie's mother and father were dead before the accident, and Eli remembered hearing Chuck had aged out of the foster system.

Ted had asked Eli many times about provisions for Pete. Had there been a will, an insurance policy, anything that should be invested for Pete, but she knew of nothing other than their college funds from their grandfather, George Sutton. Given his many marriages, he had established an education trust for future grandchildren. Pete still had funds remaining. Eli had gradually used most of hers on expenses for Pete that she didn't want to debate with Ted.

In the second bag, the folder held Eli's report cards, some essays, and university acceptance letters, piled atop a mound of photos that ranged from the old couple's earliest years to a lakeside picture of Pete, Jim, and Eli, the last of them together.

The third bag held four pouches—one crackled leather, the other three bright plastic. Eli zipped open the first and found it was stuffed with twenty-dollar bills. "Aunt Ta's sunroom," Eli gasped. The second, a newer pouch, was filled with one-hundred-dollar bills, as were the third and fourth.

She remembered the times when her great-aunt would open a drawer and withdraw cash from the leather pouch for a book, a dress, or other teen necessities, saying, "This is important. A porch can wait."

She never did get her sunporch. Neither Eli nor Pete ever had a need unmet in that home.

The last three pouches might represent the sale of the newspaper, which Eli had wondered about since she'd taken over his finances before Jim's death. Not a note, a clue of any kind in the bags. How easily it could have all turned to ash. *I need to call Pete,* Eli thought, then realized she was supposed to be hard at work in Atlanta.

That night, Eli made sure the curtains—floral sheets from the T.J. Maxx in Blue Ridge lined with white sheets from Walmart in Blairsville—were tightly closed as she hollowed out the loofa sponges from the basket by the tub. She filled them with fifty-four thousand, eight hundred and sixty dollars in rolls of cash, batches freshly laundered in her work glove bag—a lingerie bag in a former life.

Days later, Eli had stopped looking at her phone. There hadn't been a single call from Atlanta or Denver since she'd left over two weeks ago. She hadn't sought legal representation, and no one had come to apprehend her. "Nothing says *guilty* like leaving town in a dramatic hurry," she said, in summary. This was no way to spend Christmas Eve. Time to go for a drive.

Beth had invited Eli to stop by her shop, Fancy This, an upcycled selection of pre-owned home furnishings and local goods. Nonstop projects had left Eli pleased with what had been accomplished, unwilling to consider the damage to her finances, and profoundly weary.

Wanting to see a little Christmas in Hiawassee, Eli planned to explore on the way, first driving past Young Harris College. She was astonished by the huge new buildings across what had become a four-year institution. East of the campus, the Mayor's Park sparkled with lights illuminating all the trees and outlining the playground's rail fences. Small town magic at its finest.

On the way to Hiawassee, Eli noted an array of new facilities. A vast EMC complex had been built to look more like a great Adirondack lodge. An extravagant spa, sited opposite the entrance to the sprawling Brasstown Valley Resort, was tucked into the edge of the golf course.

Then she passed a county rec center the size of a big box store; marina expansions dwarfing a lakefront resort; and a wide, sandy beach that had appeared at a new park near the bridge coming into town. "Maybe everyone who winters in Florida was required to bring back a trunk full of sand," she suggested to the empty passenger seat.

Brasstown Bald was snowy, as it often is in winter. Eli always loved the sight of so many frosted mountains visible from Lake Chatuge and surrounding Towns County. From the Bald crowning the wide Wolfpen Ridge to the often hoar-frosted Chimney Top above the college, the snow depth always varied, usually dustings on the lowest elevations and elegant mantles among the peaks.

Coming to Hiawassee, the white crested Long Range beyond the south end of the lake enticed her to stop for a photo. *And was that Hightower Bald to the northeast, and maybe snowy Standing Indian up near Franklin, visible across the lake in North Carolina?* Eli was awed by the majestic backdrops in every direction. She had her Christmas card moment, if nothing else enthralled her in town.

There were no disappointments ahead. Lush Fraser firs forested the vegetable stand just off the lake, with garland and handmade wreaths in heaps by the wood stove. Eli couldn't resist buying a wreath and a swath of garland, if only for how delightfully the fragrance filled her car.

Lights twinkled and snowmen waved brooms and bows in greeting as she passed the half-dozen shops along the highway. One of the older buildings in the heart of town, Fancy This, was festooned with mixed lengths of fir, pine, and cedar around the door and windows, all radiant with vintage-look multicolor lights.

Beth was at the side of the building, overseeing loading of the delivery truck. One item was a chamfered-edge, kitchen island to which she had added shelves on three sides, then finished in dry-brushed layers from a midnight blue to dark teal and finally an Irish Sea blue green. A pair of deepest navy barstools were being wrapped to go, too. *If this is upcycling*, Eli thought, sliding her fingers over the deftly blended paint, *it's better than new.*

Inside the shop, Eli was amazed by the fine condition of every item, even upholstered pieces. She was test-lounging when Beth came in. "That is one yummy sofa," Beth said, plumping pillows in the opposite chair. "It's a light fabric. Will your doggie be around it much? Are you staging the house for sale? I can include staging if you're ready to list."

She went behind the counter and poured cups of hot cider, giving Eli a chance to consider. "I'm not sure what's happening," Eli responded. "Oh, and not my dog. Some neighbor's." Her answers trickled as she was admiring the many local views within the framed art on the walls, lots of clever antique furniture revisions, and beautifully curated accessories all around.

"Beth," Eli asked, still craning to see everything the shop had to offer, "how do you find time to do all this, sell real estate, and manage a family?"

She handed her guest a cup of cider and a blueberry scone, then settled in the chair across from Eli. "My side hustle is organizing," she began. "And that generates plenty of inventory when people are paring down. Then there's the steady buying and selling when owners upgrade their weekend houses. So, lots of sellers getting rid of things reasonably, and others looking to furnish without overdoing it. All of my gigs are intertwined."

"But these exquisite finishes. You don't *find* it like this. Do you have a workshop, a basement full of projects?"

"No, nothing in the basement here, no," Beth answered, smoothing the arm cover on her chair. "We did have a workshop at home, but we downsized to a townhouse. One in Gainesville. The twins are like, UGA sophomores now, so hubby helps, you know."

Behind those deep dimples, Eli saw something—not sadness, not overwork, but a detached look. *Huh, probably the marriage,* she decided. *Those things will kill you.*

There was no denying it. Eli was smitten with the sofa. And the chair Beth was in. And so much more. If this moment were an ad on television, Eli thought, the announcer would be addressing her unchecked manic disorder and its pharmaceutical solution.

After all the house repairs, Eli was aware she was racing through her settlement from the divorce faster than she anticipated, and with no paycheck, but this was reasonably priced and looked flawless. Eli collected several pillows, an ottoman, and looked away from the dry-brushed table that would be perfect for the kitchen nook.

For her furnished condo, she had bought only linens and the two mirrors to brighten the dark spaces. Eli had left behind everything in the penthouse with Ted, hoping to maintain all-important continuity for him. *All but his mother's antiques surely donated by now.*

With the back-up resource of the Bank of Loofa, Eli creatively rationalized buying the things Beth would be delivering the next week—a rationale constituting another box ticked on the involuntary commitment roster.

She stopped by the paint store for brushes and enough Alpine green and Sierra Skies blue to transform Aunt Ta's kitchen table and chairs. Projects were keeping her functioning, and Eli clung to that.

Painting supplies were parked on the table as Eli got the wreath and garland from her car. The former motorized-rat-habitat wafted the fragrance of Nova Scotia fir forests. Inside, Eli laid the garland across the mantel from the home's 1890s remodel and propped the wreath at the center. "Rustic," she decreed.

And then she was off to watch Christmas Eve shoppers at Walmart in Blairsville. It was late, but last-minute buyers still crowded the store. Eli was putting cans of cat food and some dog treats in her cart when she slowed for a man ahead of her with an oversized bag of dog food under one arm and an intense phone conversation underway.

"When did this happen?" she heard him ask. "Where have they taken him?" Eli recognized the voice. It was Mac Miller, who had been a few years ahead of her in school and was Ted's oldest friend. "I'm on my way, Buddy. I'll see you there." With that, he pivoted towards her, nearly falling in her grocery basket.

"Dammit, kid, watch where you're—Eli, where the hell did you come from?" Mac hopped a step on his right foot. She realized he must have torqued his prosthesis on her cart's wheel. Eli hadn't seen him since his separation from military service. Since he lost his lower left leg.

Mac balanced the dog food on the corner of her cart and searched her face, wondering what she'd heard. "Sure good to see you, gal," he said, deciding whether to share the news he'd just received.

"You, too, Mac. I think about you often. Hoping you're taking good care of yourself, especially when you're hanging out with the crazy Waller Racing crew."

"Listen, Eli," he said slowly. "There's some bad news. Someone you know."

Eli's heart was slamming. *It's Ted. Something happened.* "Was that Lew? Where is Ted? Mac, tell me!"

"Lew crashed testing a car at the Speedway tonight. Airlifted to Grady. Ted's driving his boy John up from the track, and I'm going to meet them. Want me to call you when I know something?"

Oh, Lewis Augustus Waller. She cringed at the thought of his reckless racing style, and at her own relief over this not involving Ted. "Would you let me come with? We could take my car, and I'll wait for your call in the parking deck? I know Ted wouldn't want me there, but I can't stay this far away. Lewis is a brother to me, not an ex-brother-in-law."

"I don't want to add to the load on Ted right now, Eli," he said quietly. He saw those words land hard.

Eli looked down, fumbling in her purse, trying to breathe. "I do understand that," she whispered, without raising her head.

He stepped around to her, lifting her chin to bring her gaze to his.

"I promise to let Lew know you want to see him. I promise to let *you* know something as soon as I can. I've got your number. Now I need to call Mela and ask her to get my dog. I may be gone a few days."

"Mac, please don't let Mela know I'm here. I haven't called her yet."

"Roger that, Eli. Now you get home safe. I will call."

She watched him moving through the crowd, on the phone with Mela, no doubt. Eli checked out with his forgotten dog food, too, and after a few minutes of tapping info onto her dash, turned south onto Highway 515, with Grady Hospital on the GPS.

She was backed in a spot opposite the parking deck guard station, a Christmas miracle, when Mac's call came through a little before 1 AM "Sorry if I woke you," he said. "Thought you might be waiting."

"Wide awake, Mac, thanks for calling," she answered, killing Bluetooth as she realized the call was resonating on speakers inside her car.

"Lew is still in surgery—was when I got here. He's got some head trauma, not much, thanks to the Hans. Got some serious spinal injuries, broken left arm, ribs. Left knee is damaged. He'll have a long road back once we get him through the next week or so."

"Has John seen his dad?"

"Waiting with us. Lew was buying the car for John to rebuild. Maybe now he won't be pushing the boy to race. John's mother is on the way up from PTC to take him home with her. He was spending Christmas with Lewis this year."

"How's Ted doing?"

"I think this has him pretty shook up, but it's hard to tell. It's Ted, remember."

"Will you call again, when you have the chance?"

"Count on it, Eli. Now turn over and get some sleep."

With all the cameras in a hospital, Eli couldn't go skulking around corners, peering inside surgical waiting areas while trying to avoid everyone gathered there. After a quick sneak to the restroom and by the vending machine, she tied her hoodie, pulled her hands inside her sleeves, and leaned back in the heated seat to wait for Mac's call.

"Open up, Eli," someone barked at her car window. Suddenly awake, she peeped through the shrunken aperture of her hoodie. Mac was waving a Denny's bag and looking none too happy to see her there in the first light of day.

"Open. *Now!*" Eli bolted upright, not wasting the time to raise her seat, and lowered the window—a little.

"What?" she responded, somewhat muffled, and not particularly happy to see him, either.

"I guess you've been here all night? Lew has been upgraded to serious from critical and we got this. Now you eat and then drive your little ass home, wherever that is for you today. I will call. Now git."

He dropped the bag in her lap through the narrow opening, grabbed the back of her head, pulled it to the window, and planted a kiss on her forehead. "Trust me on this."

Christmas Day was appropriately cold and bright. Eli remembered to unload the edibles from the car lest creatures invade. An emoji-filled text from non-observers Grace and Pete wished her a Happy Holiday. Perfect for her season of desolation.

Eli looked around at the empty, spotless house. Tomorrow she would buy a bed. Soon Beth would deliver the furniture. For now, she built a fire, layered her comforters on the floor as she had every night for weeks, and slept until Christmas was over.

Mac kept his word, calling or texting at least twice a day from Atlanta. Lew was conscious but heavily sedated. Mac mentioned that Ted was planning to attend his weekly staff meeting on Wednesday morning, as usual.

Eli took the cue and arrived as early traffic in Atlanta was settling down and Ted's meeting was underway. Lew was in the ICU and a nurse was at his bed, taking vitals. Eli went to the opposite side, holding her questions until the nurse was finished.

"And you are?" the nurse inquired, looking up at Eli.

"Family. Sister-in-law, actually," Eli lied, gently slipping her fingers under his hand. Lew's eyes fluttered.

"Mr. Waller?" the nurse called to him, then louder. "Mr. Waller, can you hear me?"

"Of course, yes," he whispered hoarsely. His eyes cut over to Eli, who was beaming, fighting the urge to embrace his bruised, bandage-strapped body.

"Indestructible Lew Waller," Eli said, trying to warm his chilly fingers.

"I'd say the destruction is near-complete," he groaned, eyes closed.

The door brushed open and a doctor strode in, introducing himself and his phalanx of residents. "Yes, doctor," Lew said, "I remember."

"Should I wait outside?" Eli asked.

"Don't you let go of me," Lew answered.

The specialist reviewed Lewis' situation post-surgery, his prognosis, and the additional procedures and therapies that would be necessary to determine whether he would walk again. "Will you be ready to do the work once you graduate to the Shepherd Spinal Center, Mr. Waller?"

Lew flipped his right thumb in the air. "Thanks, docs. Everything's going to be fine."

Eli felt days of tension draining away. Lew wasn't giving up—he was coming back.

⟫•◦•⟪

By midafternoon on New Year's Eve, two beds and mattress sets had been delivered. Eli wanted to be sure Pete and Grace had a room if they visited Georgia before she could pull her life out of this tailspin. The antique pieces Eli had saved—some cabinets, side tables, a hunt-board, and bookstands—were pushed to the front bedroom with a bay window matching the one in the living room. Eli intended to make that an office if she stayed on.

That afternoon Beth rolled in, trailed by a box truck and two young men who made quick work of bringing in the furniture. They earned extra tips after helping Beth demonstrate the different furniture arrangements that Eli might use according to the seasons.

"Sofa to the fireplace, with the game table behind for winter," Beth advised. "And in summer, the sofa turned to face the sliding doors onto the lake, with the chairs here," she gestured, indicating placement to the amiable movers.

Before the boys left, Beth had all of the wood pieces installed as bedside stands, side tables, and entryway displays. That big bedroom had become Eli's retreat—her own bath, a writing desk in the window nook, and that comfy chair from the living room with an ottoman for window gazing. With Beth's deft touch, it bore no resemblance to its previous condition.

Eli was impressed with Beth's imagination and talent. "There are two chairs in the shop that would be even better in your living room than these," Beth said, drained and leaning against the back of the chair in Eli's bedroom after scooting the matching chair in the guest room.

The rearranging had been fun. Eli hadn't laughed like that since she was in Beaufort. They were enjoying hot cocoa in front of the fire when Eli noticed the time. "Beth, it's almost midnight on New Year's Eve, and you have to get over the mountain to Gainesville. Does your husband know you're here? Want to give him a call and stay tonight?"

"Oh, yeah, yeah, I did lose track," Beth said, looking at the fire. "I have been texting him though, and I do this all the time, over the mountain late, so not a prob at all."

Eli thought she seemed reluctant to go. Obviously tired, Beth found her coat and purse, took a look around the room, and seemed pleased. She had overseen the grouping of Uncle Jim's paintings of local landmarks above the mantel, then the wide antique mirror set over the huntboard at the front door. "I can never thank you enough for what you've done here, Beth. It is truly a transformation."

Beth went to the kitchen with her cup, then noticed the paint store bag on the table. "I'm hoping to try something like the finishes you had in the shop," Eli confessed, flipping on the light as they walked onto the front porch. "I hope you don't mind."

"I'm flattered," she answered, her hand on her chest. Eli walked her to the car as Beth asked, "So you're settled in now? This should feel like home instead of a survivor challenge. I'll come back and help if you want."

"Sure this isn't a DeLorean? I think you've figured out how to time travel, the way you get so much done," Eli said, as Beth's vehicle backed onto the driveway. "Come anytime," she shouted.

She went inside to call Lew, who was in a regular room and could answer his phone, but placing calls was still out of his skill set.

Chapter 5

What You Can't Resolve

New Year's Day brought glorious sun and temps warming fast in the dry air. Eli finished sanding the kitchen table and chairs as the temperature reached a brisk forty degrees. Fluffy was sunning on the low wall surrounding the patio, and Dude was leaning against Eli's lower back as she sat on her heels, sanding a spot she'd missed on a chair rung.

"Wooof." The dog's booming bark so close behind her was a shock. She lurched away but felt her feet pinned under the relaxed dog as he tossed his head in the air for another loud, "Wooof."

"Oh, crazy dog," Eli groused. "Shut *up*."

Then she heard someone calling. The voice was moving closer, and Eli could make out, "Astro, c'mon, boy." As she struggled to free her feet, a lithe, thirty-something woman in blue scrubs appeared. She wore her thick hair pulled into a wispy bun, and held her phone out as though she were following it.

Upon seeing Eli wedged beneath the Great Dane, her fierce whistle brought the dog scrambling to her side. "Good Lord," she said, pulling Eli to her feet, "Are you okay? I was using the tracking app for my dog. Sorry for the trouble. He's very old, almost deaf, but—Eli? Eli Sledge, er, Waller, ohmygosh, Eli!"

She threw her arms around her old friend, rocking side to side. "How long have you been here? I live right over there, now," she said, pointing southeast along the lake shore.

"Mela, it is so good to see you. So good," Eli replied, regretting hiding from her, and hoping Mela wouldn't find out she had known they were neighbors for weeks.

"Looks like this is more than just a house check," Mela noted, settling in a spring chair and studying the furniture.

"I've been finishing a project," Eli hedged, "and thought I'd come here to get away from the distractions in Atlanta."

"Yeah? Last I heard you were in Charlotte, but I know Ted's work keeps you moving around. How's everybody?"

She doesn't know about Lew, Eli thought. *Well, she doesn't know Lew…*

Mela tried again. "And little Pete?"

Eli smiled at the thought, relieved by the easier topic. "*Little* Pete is working in Denver. That's where his love interest is finishing med school. He's in a good place." Eli drifted away, looking across the lake Pete adored as a kid.

The sleeping cat had awakened to the activity, pulled a long stretch, and wandered under Eli's chair, where he curled for another nap. The dog stuck his head under the chair, nosing the cat until he growled, eyes still closed. Mela snapped her fingers, pointing to the stone floor where the dog quickly sat beside her.

"By the way, this is Astro. I hope he hasn't been bothering you. He's a rescue and not big on making new friends. The cat's Pharaoh, and he just doesn't make friends. Comes by for the occasional meal."

Eli remained quiet. Mela was running her hand down the dog's back and looking out at the lake, too, not sure what to make of Eli. She looked exhausted, with raw, cracked hands, a gauntness to her face, and dark, swollen eyes. The girls in her office would say Eli was "ratchet." Mela knew a creature in crisis when she saw one.

She moved near her friend's chair, taking her hands as she crouched beside her. "Now what's going on with you, Eli? Would you let me help?"

Experiencing kindness, tenderness of any sort, never failed to dissolve Eli, revealing—she believed—the neediness within. Mela's compassion reduced her to a weeping mess, and it shamed her deeply. Lately, tears had become just another losing battle.

As she regained her composure, Eli dusted off and invited Mela in for something to eat. "If not for those superb Epic take-outs, I'd have starved my first week here. Did you know he's opening a restaurant in Hayesville?"

"Karl? Yes, it's going to be busy."

"I'll make sandwiches. Dude is waiting for his snack, and Fluffy will expect—"

"You've already met Dude? Mac's Dude?" Mela exclaimed. "Did he swim over? He is Super Dog."

"Sorry," Eli stammered, washing up at the sink. "I meant Astro. And, what's the cat? Farrah, with the golden mane?"

Mela's quick peal of laughter lightened the energy in the room. "P-H-A-R-A-O-H," like an Egyptian ruler. You know, regal, aloof, and expecting to be served."

"And Astro, I *get*."

"Yeah, that's Beau, all futuristic simplicity."

"You and Beau became a thing, then?" Eli was treading lightly. "I thought he wasn't into girls."

"No, he isn't. But he'll always be the dearest person in my life. This is going to sound, well, different things to different people—moronic, insulting, certainly fraudulent. Eli, Beau and I, *we married.*"

Now it was Eli's turn to look delusion square in the face. "Tell me about that," Eli said, carrying turkey sandwiches to the patio and giving scraps to the four-legged diners.

"You remember how protective he was of me in school when I came here."

"Wasn't Beau two years ahead of you?" Eli asked, calculating. "And you were ahead of me; but I saw him every summer, and stories of his exploits echoed."

"Yep, that's right. Seems like you were always here, though."

Lunch was hardly touched, with Mela reminding Eli that she was the last of the children adopted by the Orr family, recalling her long struggle to fit in, Beau championing her until she did. Then getting her B.S. from UGA and on to a stint at University of Tennessee Knoxville Veterinary School before coming home to replenish her funds.

"I was working in Dr. V's office when Beau came in, and I don't know which of us was happier to see the other." Mela's eyes brightened at the memory as she popped a potato chip in her mouth.

"We met for dinner, and he told me about his work in the Middle East as a restoration contractor. Lucrative, but extremely dangerous. He had come back to persuade his elderly parents to move to a senior living community. They wouldn't budge.

"We came up with a plan. That night, Beau told them I needed a place to stay. I moved in to look after them and work, which was a good situation for a while, but as they were weakening physically, Beau's work was intensifying. Sometimes we couldn't reach him for weeks.

"He came home that spring determined to move them to a full-time care facility so that I could get back to UT, but they were in their late eighties, adamant, unnerved, pleading with me to stop him. He only had a few days. It was chaos. We went to the lake for a private conversation.

"Beau was walking in circles around me, telling me he had researched the options for leaving his world in my hands, so to speak, and the most expedient, ironclad thing he could see was that he marry me.

"He looked up with this impish grin, like this was where I was supposed to walk away or shake hands. Of course, he loves me like a sister. I guess I love him like a superhero.

"I knew he was thinking about his parents, the high risk work he was doing. I hoped he knew then that I will joyously hand it all back and resign the position when he's finally home."

"Okay," Eli said, still processing the story. "Am I the first to know this?"

"There were a few people who knew. Listen, I need to feed my animals before I go by the clinic to check on patients this afternoon," Mela said, looking at her watch. "Want to walk over and meet the barn crew?"

"You have a crew for your barn?"

"Crew *in* the barn. Quite an assortment. C'mon."

———◆———

Walking down the dog path through the woods between the homes, Astro at their heels, Mela said that Beau had come home just four times after they married. When both his parents were gone, Mela had returned to UT, finishing her DVM.

"I know he was insanely busy and more than a little damaged by what he was dealing with. And he didn't hide that he had a place outside London and that a friend named Lenny lived there. He talked about him so fondly. Lenny was a university professor, and not a well man."

Mela had come back almost every weekend to check on Beau's house, pay bills, and meet frequently with attorneys over his parents' estate and probate issues. Privy to the family's accounts, she told Eli the wealth surprised her. "But that's nothing compared to the Wallers, huh?"

"I know Ted's family had tons, just no idea how many. We were fortunate in that our housing was always a corporate perk as we moved around, and they paid him well, but I had no interest in finding out what he was worth in the divorce. Just settled and left."

Mela stopped to absorb that news, leaving Eli walking alone until she reached the pasture and saw the exquisite simplicity of the modern post and beam style, built when Lake Como villa look-alikes were the houses everyone wanted on their waterfront lots.

"Wowser, Mela, this is subtly magnificent. It's—"

"Did you say divorce?" Mela hollered from the tree line. "You divorced the gorgeous, talented Mr. Waller?"

They both turned to the lake, looking for the source of a scraping noise. Mac was dragging his canoe onto the bank as Astro was rushing to greet a powerfully built dog standing by Mac. *Looks like a yellow lab on 'roids*, Eli thought.

Mela reached Eli as Mac approached. "Sounds like you two are all caught up. And," he added, with a sweeping gesture to the water, "so is everybody on their docks this beautiful afternoon."

"Water's pretty cold to be out there in a canoe," Mela chided, massaging the ears of Astro's friend. "With your *dog.*"

"Cold is good for everybody," Mac declared, adjusting the foot of his water prosthesis. "Especially dogs. Ain't that right, Dude?"

"Are y'all kidding me?" Eli asked. "His name is not Dude."

"Since he was a puppy," Mac answered. "It was lil' Dude, but for obvious reasons, Dude now."

"I don't remember ever seeing you with a dog, Mac," Eli said, internally wincing at the thought that this might be a post-injury support dog. Eli noticed athletic Mac Miller had become studly Mac. *He should be registering high on the hot meter*, she thought, *although I've known him since his dorkhood.*

"Not while I was in, no. He's still young, just nine months old, but he's sharp. Mela, show me that dead spot in your perimeter cameras?"

"I was going to introduce Eli to everyone in the barn," Mela protested sweetly. "I'll show you the glitch, then you can come down if we're not back at the house by then."

Eli watched the two of them walking away as she veered to the barn. There was leaning in, Mela touching his arm, laughter between them. Mac's heat wasn't lost on Mela, whether she knew it or not.

Mela was a few minutes behind Eli, coming to make the rounds from pigmy goats to burros and assorted horses snatching bits of hay scattered by chickens wandering in the loft. She named every resident, as a preset ration of grain or food pellets was delivered by chute to each stall from a central hopper overhead. Water troughs refilled automatically and gates to the round pen and pasture opened remotely.

"Amazing, right?" Mela said, watching Eli take it all in. "Wedding gift from Beau's parents. All my little pens in the landscape were kind of tacky, but this—it's anybody's dream. Beau's dad was an architect, and they planned this one afternoon on a scrap of paper. Still, this is all something of a farce; it's not like I expected to be here half as long as I have."

"Yeah," Eli said softly. "I do get that."

No sign of Mac as they approached the house. Eli stopped at the edge of the deck, mesmerized by the quiet elegance of the structure. The roofline soared out towards the lake, sheltering a wall of glass from the peak beam to the ipe flooring that flowed onto the deck.

From the lawn, Eli could see inside to the timber frame exposed against walls faintly tinted to a shade of fine parchment. Understated, solid stone pediments framed every entry point. The walls had to be eight inches thick. Tall glass doors moved with the touch of a finger. Inside, Mela darted down a corridor toward Mac's voice.

Eli was speechless. She gently perched on a sauvage leather recamier against the staircase. Winter light sparkled through clerestory windows along the south wall of the room. Below them, colossal groupings of ancient maps were hung with paintings of racing sailing ships, and softly rendered pastoral homes, all arranged among three pairs of French doors opening to the sunroom.

Eli glanced back to a kitchen sufficient to support a restaurant, but Mela had detoured out of sight. She looked beyond the deck to the terrace where Astro and Dude were on their feet, then bounding away. Eli noticed them running past the sunroom to the front of the house as Mela trotted from the kitchen and through the living room before the doorbell rang. *No surprises around here,* Eli thought.

A very southern voice carried from the foyer. "Hi, neighbor. Sorry to meet you this way after living next to you so long, but I just ran right over your mailbox. And I had help."

Mela waved her in—an elegant woman, in a collar-up, double-breasted navy coat with an intricately loomed scarf over one shoulder. Her glistening white hair was swept back over darker shades beneath; and her sparkling brown eyes shone with mischief.

"It was either take out the Fowler kid on that four-wheeler or your mailbox. Only time will tell about that decision."

Mela ushered the visitor in as Mac approached from behind Eli. "I'm Mela Orr. This is our neighbor to the north side of me, Eli Sledge Waller, and from around the lake, Mac Miller."

"Very nice to meet you all. I'm Annie Blanche Sutton," she said, with a thumb-point, "from next door. Unless you're writing me a ticket, signing my paycheck, or collecting my taxes, then it's Ann Arnold."

"Oh, Sutton." Eli struggled to remember. "You were my aunt's second cousin, or…"

"Catherine Sutton Clark, Yes," Annie agreed. "Somewhere back in the tree there's a common great-great. He settled in Tennessee, eventually, leaving a son this old farm. They used to move on when the soil was spent. My branch is still over on the west bank of the Ocoee, about halfway to Chattanooga."

"And *there's* the war hero I've read about," she said to Mac, with a familiar smile.

Mac reached in for the handshake Annie offered. "He's quite the alpha geek, too," Mela added, knowing Mac wouldn't enjoy either subject. "Have a seat, and I'll make coffee."

"I can't stay. On my way to work. Just had to stop and confess before you found the carcass on the road," Annie said, back at the door. "I pulled it up in the yard, but it's going to need a new post. I'll find someone tomorrow to replace it."

"Take it off your list," Mac said firmly. "I'd be honored to do it. I remember your kindness during the weeks my gran spent in hospice. Might not have made it back in time if you hadn't kept her holding on for me that last night. Count on me, ma'am."

"That's mighty generous, young man." Annie's lower lip quivered slightly as she continued. "I remember Nellie well. Just be sure to call me Annie Blanche from now on," she said, sharpening her gaze, "and I'll forget about calling you Sugar Punkin. 'K? Good to finally meet you all."

As the door closed on their goodbyes, Mela clapped her hands and turned to Mac. "Sugar Punkin? Something to do with the October birthday?"

"A little. I was sweet, back then," he said, by way of a challenge. "Wasn't easy keeping that handle under wraps. Especially when Gran's packages came to the base. With a first name like MacLellan, I had enough problems."

Eli was grinning at the energy of their exchange.

"Coffee?" the two women asked in unison, leaving Mac to raise his hand in agreement. Mela gave Eli a push as they rounded the kitchen island. "Like seeing Bigfoot, huh?"

"You mean Sugar Punkin back there? Eli asked, bemused, as she took a seat at the bar.

Mela stopped filling the coffeemaker and parked both hands on the edge of the counter. "Ann Arnold? She's lived there forty-something years, and that's the first time I've ever laid eyes on her other than her car zipping by."

"I don't remember her," Eli said.

"Momma told me about it when she came to live with me after Beau's parents were gone," Mela said, returning to the coffee. "She wanted to be friendly with her, but never got past the gate. Her disgrace, I guess you'd call it, occurred before I was part of the Orr family.

"Momma said she was a young, new nurse at the hospital, and a couple of nights a week she cared for the terminal wife of a doctor who was chief of the medical staff. The doctor and Annie got involved before the wife died. Annie was pregnant, he married her, the two kids despised her. Probably shunned by lots of the hospital staff, several churches worth of folks, and most of the people in three counties. The Arnold family was beloved around here."

"Geez, somebody with a worse backstory than mine," Eli said.

"Not the worst of it. Her husband, Dr. Arnold, was driving with their little boy to visit his daughter at UGA, somehow drove off Blood Mountain. Killed him, and I think the little boy lived a few days. Momma said it was like people blamed her for *everything*. She ended up with lots more problems for years after that."

"She stuck around to take care of the kids?"

"No, the oldest, a boy, was almost through at Georgia Tech, and the daughter had gone to live with her mother's sister. This lady was alone here as far as I know."

"That's really sad," Eli murmured. "Everyone ripped away like that."

"Hey, Eli," Mela said, extending her hand across the counter. "Are you having a hard time adjusting to being alone?"

Mac had been quietly sipping coffee through this gossipfest, but his sudden thumb-across-the-throat gesture to Mela caught Eli's attention, too. "Thanks, Mac, it's okay. The hardest thing has been adjusting to the damage, the things that will never heal. Realizing that I might have done the right thing for the wrong reasons."

"It's good you came up here," Mela assured her, patting Eli's hand. "You'll stay busy with your project. Just wish that house hadn't been such a nightmare."

"You could have called me when you got here, kid," Mac chided. "Would have saved you a couple of bucks."

"Truth is," Eli stammered, "my book project had been suspended the day I left Atlanta. They think I'm part of a blackmail scheme targeting my client, *the* David Harrison."

She watched for shocked reactions to her failings. What she saw was immediate concern in the faces of two people she hadn't bothered with in years. Neither one asked how she could let this happen or what she had done to jeopardize the project—their mutual response was indignation over the accusation.

"Time to fight back, Eli, to protect yourself," Mac suggested, resting his hand on her shoulder. "Do we have any details? What's the claim? Who received it? How were you implicated? Has your attorney received any specifics on how it was transmitted?"

"No details, no information at all, and no attorney," Eli admitted. "I know that looks bad, taking off, but I didn't do anything. I don't have a connection at the Wright offices anymore. The Harrisons think I betrayed them."

"And you don't have Ted to protect you," Mela added softly.

"Ted Waller, as far as *I know*, never stepped in to protect anyone in his life," Eli shot back. "Not his style. When it came to me, he always launched the very first stone." Eli looked at Mac, defensive, defiant, waiting for him to try and set her straight.

"I know a kick-ass attorney who can get you through this," Mac said. "When you're ready, I'll get you an appointment with Larry. Meanwhile, mind if I examine your devices? Complete a few scans?"

"I'd be most grateful, Mac," she said, as he walked back to the office for his phone. "And Mela, I'm sorry—"

"Un-huh, Eli, that was just me thinking about how Beau always looked out for me, even before I saw anything coming."

"Your camera blind spot is gone," Mac said, after finishing up in the office and zipping his phone in his jacket's dry-pocket. "I widened the angle, causing a small drop in resolution, but you've got plenty of pixels to spare in that system. You two stay out of trouble."

Standing at the door with Mela, watching Mac and Dude push off into the lake, Eli wished she could prolong this sensation of a huge weight being lifted. Mela, however, was already late to work. "Anything I can do at the clinic to make up for wiping out your morning?" Eli asked, not sure what answer she hoped to hear.

Holiday staffers have everything under control, or I'd have heard. I'd like to start our patients' new year right," she said, clinking her mug against Eli's.

"Mine looks better already," Eli added to the toast.

Chapter 6

Who's Your Ally?

On a Wednesday morning in mid-January, Eli left before dawn to beat Atlanta traffic. Lewis Waller would soon be transferred to the Shepherd Spinal Center for rehab. He was sleeping when Eli crept across his room but woke to her kiss on his cheek. "That's an intoxicating scent, angel. Is that the smell of success? Doing a Harrison screenplay, too?"

"I've taken up chemistry in my scant free time," she announced, fanning fragrance to him. "The gentle art of combining essential oils with fine organic lotions. I can't sew, do algebra, or cook over fire, but this works."

"Before you hit the retail market, I have a connection with *the* top analytical chemistry firm," Lew advised. "But I can't help if you're going to make medicinal claims. Don't want to tangle with the feds."

Eli wanted to play along but was determined to avoid any mention of Ted. "I'll give that careful consideration. Thank you, Lewis. Now tell me, any nurses you're especially fond of this week?"

"I wasn't going to bring up Ted, honey. You missed him by minutes, though. Waiting in the hall for him to leave?"

"No, I thought he'd be in his meeting. Mac says you're going to the Sportscar Vintage Racing Brickyard Invitational. That's fabulous—as a spectator."

"Maybe SVRA at Watkins Glen in September—as a driver. Talk to me about Eli," he said, struggling to shift his position.

"I'm great. Pete's coming to see you next weekend. Think John might be around?"

"Yeah." He laughed, shaking his head. "Johnny wouldn't miss Pete. You sleeping okay, Eli?" His voice was gentle with concern. "If that book is what's wearing you down, time for a little fun. If it's my brother, you have to let go. You were way too much horsepower for him. Ted had you throttled down to a crawl."

"Lew," she opened cautiously, "have you ever heard of something called Asperger's? Asperger's syndrome?"

"Yep, more than once. It has been a point for discussion on Ted's evals for the firm since he moved into management. It was suggested that his abrupt communication style contributed to a reputation as a total SOB in the branches.

"Ted resented the idea. Like it was a suggestion of flawed character. He never told you? Wait, part of that included a psychologist who came to talk to you and Pete."

"No, Lew. Not through the firm or anywhere else. Ted believed that simply taking Pete for therapy would destroy the kid's future employment opportunities."

"Dad required Ted to submit to that interview not long before his last heart attack. He thought this was the solution to making Ted an officer. Then Dad died, and the board wanted superstar Ted to replace him. No one else could touch his level of expertise. But he wasn't interested in improving his connectivity with clients or staff, so in the end, I had to take over. Then, as you know, a while later I left to go racing, and he wanted the job."

"Maybe there was a guy," she recalled. "Ted never invited anyone over, yet, he brought a man home one evening. Introduced him as someone he worked with who was visiting from headquarters.

"Wouldn't stay for dinner, not even a drink. The strangest part was that this guy was asking personal questions. Pete was there. I remember being careful not to say the wrong thing.

"He was asking about what we each liked to do most for entertainment, what things we did as a family, favorite vacations. It was like a *3rd Rock* episode because we did not have many *normal* answers. I've always wondered."

"In Dallas?"

"Yes."

"So, the boss's son set his own ground rules. I thought he had loosened up once he ascended to the big desk," Lew said, staring at the ceiling. "Then again, maybe I was just glad to be out of there. I saw what I wanted to see."

"Oh, he did get easier over those last three years, fewer meltdowns," Eli agreed. "Pete had gained lots of insight during his years of therapy. He was a freshman at Colorado when he overheard me ranting after a call with Ted. Pete thought it was massive anxiety that made Ted a life master of staging a strong offense as the best defense. It made me think.

"After that, I would carefully probe to find out how Ted saw our relationship. Couldn't tell it ever crossed his mind. While he did get nicer to the world in general, he has never thought much of me."

"What makes you say that?"

"As unbelievable as it sounds, he never spontaneously said one kind, supportive, appreciative, understanding word to me. Not one. I was listening closely for anything beyond the steady sniping commentary.

"After an argument, I begged him to tell me one thing he liked about me. It took a minute or two, but he seemed truly pleased with his answer: 'You do nice things for me.' I felt like a four-year-old's nanny pathetically fishing for affirmation."

"I'm sorry for spewing all the negativity, Lew," she said, lifting his head a little to adjust his pillow. "This was supposed to be a happy visit."

Eli was smoothing his bedding, lifting the light blanket from his feet to tuck in the sheet, as he responded. "We both love the guy, but we can't—"

Lew caught his breath sharply, startling Eli. "What?"

"I *felt* that. You touched my foot, my goddamn foot, Eli, and I felt it. Grab the bottom of my foot. Please!"

She lightly grasped each foot and applied gentle pressure. He raised his right hand across his face. She couldn't tell whether he was suppressing a laugh or cry. When he lowered his hand, she saw joyous relief.

"Look out, Watkins Glen," she said, pressing the nurse call and getting in a farewell hug ahead of the fresh medical assessment.

———◦———

A text pinged as Eli left the elevator. Mela wanted to make good on their intentions to start walking the neighborhood regularly, saying she would be home after her last patient, around noon. Eli texted her same ETA and headed north.

Mac was already at Mela's when Eli arrived, tamping in the mail-box on the new post. "Ms. Sutton really clocked this box," he swore, laughing as he tamped the dirt. "This one's set in concrete. She might get some damage if she swerves to miss that kid again."

"For sure," Eli answered, absorbed in her phone screen. Five weeks tomorrow since the call from Megan telling her the Harrison book project was suspended. Mac lifted her phone and closed it in his truck before asking if she was ready for him to review her devices. "Don't talk about this until we know something?"

"Yes, sir. Here you are," she said, slapping keys in his hand.

"And don't tell me you have the same password on everything."

"Only thing *with* a password is my laptop."

"The only thing worse than one password for all," he boomed. "Hit me with it."

"Yeah, that." Cringing, she called out, "8noDAD4me" citing caps and numerals.

"Any digital assistants? Camera system? Voice remote?"

"Geeez no. Laptop and CPU are on the desk in the east bay window. All yours. Mela and I are going for a stroll around the neighborhood."

"If you're going with Mela, you won't be strolling. She didn't tell you she's a marathoner?" he said, loading his tools in the back of his Jeep pickup.

"Is that a short joke, tall man? Because I'm, okay, I *was once* damned athletic."

"So is she, and—just an observation, not a short joke—her legs are about twice as long as those," he drawled, waving his screwdriver back at her while reaching behind his seat, peeking through the back window as he continued taunting her. "Being the athlete that you are, you might could overtake her where she turns around at the marina."

"Wait, the marina? Eli pictured the steep hills and busy highway on that route. "That's at least six miles one way."

"Almost three, but yeah, that's her usual. On a nice day like this," he added, looking up at the brilliant blue sky strewn with mare's tail clouds.

With that, he waved from the departing truck, disappearing in Eli's driveway just as Mela's SUV came in view. Without a phone Eli couldn't fake being called away.

Mela yelped when Eli asked to skip the marina run. "Oh, no. He's totally messing with you. I was thinking we might start with getting to the main road and back. No running, though. I don't *have* running shoes."

Their leisurely pace brought them to the intersection with the two-lane road where a girl in bike shorts and a sports bra began a pre-run stretch as they approached. "*Hiii*," she called out from a near headstand.

"Hard to believe it's the middle of January, right?" Eli responded, as they continued on.

"Yeah, did you see, down the road you came from?" She gestured in a tippy toe posture to indicate the topography. "Did you see the juicy bro down there?

Eli's face must have registered her confusion, appearing to blow goldfish kisses as she silently repeated the description.

"You know," the runner pressed, eager to elicit information from a more senior neighbor, "like *a hot guy* with a shovel back there?"

Mela shot Eli a look of disbelief, a whispered, "Naaaah."

"I saw him there when I got home a few minutes ago," she added, tugging at an overburdened bra strap.

"He was putting in a mailbox, but he's gone now," Eli informed her, with a reinforcing sad face.

"Aaaaw," she wailed. "He's in a black truck. If you see him—hey, 'k if I go with a ways?"

"Sure," Mela said, picking up the pace, "but any running you'll do solo."

"I'm Carly," she said with a giggle. They quickly introduced themselves.

"We all have bro names," she continued. "Mine's after my dad, Carlson. And Eli? That's a guy name. Oh, oh, Mela? Was your dad Mel? This is amazing. We are so connected!"

"Looks like it," Eli grumbled, pushing herself to keep up.

Conversation improved on the downhill sections as they learned Carly had rental houses, ran a cabin concierge business, and was taking college courses—all when she wasn't traveling for work from the Atlanta airport.

"How did you even notice the mailbox guy?" Eli had to know. "I'd be in a coma after working all night."

"Long hours make for shorter weeks, and that gives me lots of days off for business. Most of my classes I can get online."

"When do you sleep?" Mela droned, reminded of her nights on call.

"Blackout curtains in the downstairs bedroom, and I sleep whenever I can," she said brightly.

Her abundance of enthusiasm and energy had Mela curious about her age. "Does your family live on the cove?"

"It was me and my dog. Really, he was my ex's dog, and he came back for him," Carly noted, suddenly subdued.

"Last February, before the wedding, we bought this house," she said, looking up the cove. "He was going to work remotely from here while I finished school a couple of days a week in Dahlonega. After two months, he was ready to move back to his Miami high rise, but I wasn't interested. He missed the clubs and his friends. I'm trying to keep the house, but it's crazy expensive to do.

"Hey, here comes my neighbor," Carly shouted, as she flagged down the wary woman driving towards them. "Hi, neighbor, I'm Carly Lane. I've missed seeing you drive by lately," she said, arms folded on the window of the car. "These are neighbors from the little road down the hill—Mela and Eli."

"I've been away recently, and I'm only checking on your neighbor's, but, yes, I've seen you around..." Beth responded, as Carly turned away to introduce her companions. *"And heard your music and cleaned up after your dog,"* she whispered faintly, before speaking audibly again.

"I know Eli, and hello, Mela. Lovely to meet you. I'm Beth Parker," she said, projecting around the body in the window. "I was just at your neighbor's house, a pocket listing, but they live in Florida, so I'm—"

"Oh, where? I'm from Florida," Carly shouted, throwing both arms to the heavens.

"St. John's River," Beth answered. "In a senior community."

"This is a very senior community," Carly declared, palms waving again.

"Well, this is a resort area, not a big job market," Mela said defensively. "Mostly people looking for a beautiful, quiet place to live in the mountains. Can't imagine anywhere better."

"Maybe a few more shops," Carly suggested.

"Beth, I've meant to come by and tell you how much I've enjoyed the furnishings you brought," Eli said. "Feels like home, now."

"I appreciate that," Beth responded. "Y'all starting a track group, or what?"

"Mela and I are making good on a commitment to walk as often as we can," Eli answered. "And we just found Carly along the way today."

"Let's start with thirty minutes every morning at seven, 'k?" Carly directed. "By then if I'm working, I'm usually off and it's before business hours. Are we a thing?"

As Mela and Eli were exchanging why-not shrugs, Beth joined in. "Cool, I've made a resolution to walk. I can do my house checks early. Eli, bring Mela and Carly next time you come by. See y'all tomorrow."

"I believe we've just had our mornings co-opted," Mela said, taking a look at her phone where the signal might be strong. "I'm on call," she added, her voice trailing off.

"Confession," Eli said. "We do know the black truck guy. He's not exactly social, but I can introduce you."

"Involved with anyone? He's a snack, so sure he is. 'K, we'll talk in the morning," Carly sang, jogging down the hill to the cove.

"Hey, Eli, listen, um…" Mela reluctantly continued. "This is from Mac. He was working on your phone when a text popped on the screen. He says you should see it."

"Ask him to forward it."

Eli was swirling in dread, but hoping she was, as usual, over anticipating. Then Mela read the screenshot from Mac: "As of today, January 16, Eli Sledge is no longer employed by the Wright Agency in light of evidence she has engaged in behavior harmful to the company's reputation with our client, David Harrison. Call to arrange a settlement meeting with HR. Hard copy to follow."

It was as cold as Eli had imagined. She had been expecting this for weeks, wounded and waiting for the kill shot. "Megan must be dancing on her desk," Eli calmly deadpanned, as she created an appropriate meme tweet in her mind.

It was a short walk back to Eli's house, with Mela's consoling words not registering. "Who the hell have you pissed off?" was the scribbled greeting Mac held up as they came in. He pointed to the patio doors and they went through. Once outside, Mac delivered more news.

"First, Eli, I apologize for how you got that message. And from what you've said, Ms. Wright would have done things differently." Mac waited for her to look up, then turned his screen around, showing her a log of intrusions on her laptop.

"There's evidence that someone has compromised your communications devices. Whether that's related to the blackmail I can't say, but I've been discovering tracker apps, open microphone bugs, and file transfer traps on all your devices," he advised. "It may take some time to determine where this is going. The surveillance has been in place for several months.

"However, the non-linear junction detection has indicated a new device," Mac continued, busying himself adjusting cords on his scanners as he concluded. "I think it's in the nightstand next to your bed. Anyway, *you* look in there. If you don't find anything, then I'll find it."

"Oh, right, I have another phone. The one with the old landline number from this house." She darted to the bedroom and returned with the phone, which Mac promptly started scanning with the first of several tools.

"Who would want to spy on you, Eli?" Mela asked, as they sat on the stone wall watching Mac work.

"Not Ted. The divorce is long over, and he's moved on with someone. As the saying goes, I am dead to him."

"'K. Seemed like a lot of hostility in that text. What would your boss have to gain from ruining the book deal? Doesn't sound like she's a fan."

"Whoa, not my boss," Eli snapped, flinching at her own inaccuracy. "And losing this project, probably losing David Harrison as a client, well it might be a win for Megan's agency transformation, but Viv could never have let that happen. And Viv's son—he knows that.

"Megan dislikes me because Viv *did* like me. She thought I was getting preferential treatment from Viv, but truly, I was just the last of her rescues."

"Mac," Mela said, "am I out of line to wonder if Ted might be behind this?"

He worked on for a minute, then responded. "Let's just say he has a curious streak, one that I'm familiar with, and that there are some men who have an irrational fixation on knowing what, and whom, their exes are doing."

Why that would bring Eli close to tears she wasn't sure, but she wasn't going to crumble again in front of these two. Having them buffer the blow of that text was a wonder of timing. Having them here, beginning the investigation she had shrunk from, had a whiff of providence about it.

"Doesn't look like we're up against a pro. This phone's clean," he said, disconnecting the radio frequency spectrum analyzer and handing her the Hiawassee line back. "Don't put any apps on it, don't open a browser, just use it to make calls until I get the other devices back to you. Then we start eliminating suspects until we find our intruder. I hope to God it isn't Ted."

⫸∙◦∙⫷

That night, sleep was slow to come, but knocking at the front door woke Eli from a sound sleep. "Not even six? We said seven, dammit." Eli moaned, throwing back the covers and trudging to the door.

"Open up, Eli, it's Pete!"

She cracked the door, wishing it could be a clumsy bear, a process server, anyone but Pete.

He looked furious as he stormed in on a gust of arctic air. "I have a ten o'clock meeting in Atlanta, but I'm here because you weren't at your condo, didn't come home last night, and haven't answered any of my calls.

"Then, Mac Miller answers your phone at two in the morning and tells me you're here at the lake." As he raged, his gaze took in the furniture, repainted walls, and immaculate status of the house. "Eli," he said, sinking into the sofa, "what's going on?"

Pharaoh had snuck in with Pete to escape the cold, and as Eli turned toward the kitchen to gather her thoughts and make coffee, he hopped on her dragging robe.

"And now you have a cat," he observed, his concern deepening.

"Not my cat. Book contract was canceled, and I'm suspected of the blackmail attempt that shut the project down. Oh, and I'm the subject of a covert surveillance operation. Been a rough month or two."

"And you didn't call me?"

"Why would I visit my *stuff* on you, Pete? On the upside, I have some things to show you," she called, shuffling down the hall and returning from the bath. "I wasn't sure how to let you know when I found it a couple of weeks ago."

She laid the loofas on the kitchen table, then opened a drawer and handed him a discolored folder inside a plastic bag. He saw his name on the bank statement atop the clippings and pulled out the papers as Eli was shaking cash from the sponges. "Stuff that turned up when I was cleaning," she said.

"Uncle Jim made sure we had everything on the college funds, his checking and savings, the deed to the house, but these things, he never mentioned. Maybe things he forgot about? But this cash, almost fifty-five thousand dollars.

"I think this is a combination of Aunt Ta's sunporch savings, and possibly the cash from payments Jim received on the sale of his newspaper to Hank Norton and his partner. There were a lot of bank closings around that time and who knows what he was thinking. I can't find his tax records that far back."

"Stop treating me like a kid, Eli. You should have let me know."

"I'm all grown up, too. I promise I can take care of myself," she countered.

"Then why's Miller answering your phone?" he asked dryly, glancing down the hall.

"A girl I knew from high school, Mela Orr, lives next door now," she stated. "They're good friends, and he offered to help with the spyware. He took my phone home with him. Are you planning to see Lew? He wanted John there, too."

"Yeah, saw them yesterday. Ted and I went by, and Lew is coming along well at Shepherd. His progress is astonishing."

"You saw Ted?" Eli said, stricken. "You let Ted know you were coming, and you hadn't called me until yesterday afternoon?"

"Ted's the reason I'm here. He's made me a fantastic job offer. I want to accept it. He's even offered to help Grace get her psych residency here."

Eli went from surprised to wildly paranoid. This contact had been going on for a while, just like the bugs Mac found. Was Ted, Mr. Integrity, behind all of this? Was he trying to drive a wedge between her and Pete? Now that she was ruined, was he having his old friend Mac remove all the evidence from her devices? Pete was waiting for her response. She felt catatonic.

"What will you be doing?" she managed to ask.

"Well…" He hesitated, trying not to sound patronizing. "I'll be working with micro and nano-fabrication techniques for interfacing with biological systems, to start."

"That sounds amazing, really amazing. I'll be so happy to have you closer," she added, sounding like a calm, reasonable human in a normal conversation.

"Pete," she said carefully, "I have to ask you, to tell you, it is critically important not to mention anything I've said about my situation to anyone—not Ted, not even Grace—until some of the mystery is unraveled. Please, can you do that for me?"

"You mean the firing, the blackmail? This money? What exactly?"

"Everything, but mostly the surveillance," she said, her gaze intense. She was choosing to believe Mac's motivation was to help her.

"It's probably tied to the blackmailer, but the more people who know, the greater chance of a compromised investigation," she warned, hoping to suggest a formal, official inquiry was underway. "Forget I said anything about it, please."

"Yeah, sure," he said, sliding back his chair.

Distancing from the crazy lady? The voice in her head suggested. As Pete put an old folder inside his coat, Eli asked what they should do with the cash.

"You hang on to that. Looks like you've put plenty into making this place livable again. We'll figure it out later," he said, cuffing her shoulder. Pete pulled up his scarf against the collar of his coat as he walked to the door.

"Travel safe, Pete," she said from a few feet away, determined not to force any show of affection. He stared back at her, the silence setting her heart racing. Had he, too, come to hate her? Was she oblivious to her own toxicity?

In one step he reached out, wrapping her in his arms. "If anything ever happened to you... Please, Eli, be careful. I need to know what's going on." He wiped a tear from her cheek and left.

Oh God, he thought I was shutting him out? Is that what's happening? I'm shutting everyone out and blaming them? Pete's headlights caught a figure jogging along the road. *Who jogs in a predawn Siberian Express? Carly!* Eli raced to throw on her warmest sweats.

Trotting up the drive, she saw Carly was jogging in place, encased in a quilted parka zipped from her knees to the fluffy trim encircling her face. Her companion, a towering Darth Vaderesque heap of layers, was waving a flashlight and saying, "Y'all know sunrise is 7:40 this time of year?"

"Yes, but in a month, it will be an hour earlier," Carly pointed out cheerily.

"Probably colder," the heap replied, through chattering teeth.

"Then in March," Eli teed up their enthusiasm, "sunrise will move to five minutes before eight."

Beth's Mercedes parked and Mela jumped in the front seat, demanding the highest heat setting. Carly and Eli hovered over the engine. "Just to the highway and back?" Eli suggested, coaxing Mela from the car.

"This is insane," she responded, slamming the door and whipping out the flashlight again. "Let's go. I have to get to work."

"You'll never guess who you missed this morning, Mela," Eli teased, on the flat stretch along the Fowlers' fence.

"Oh, I saw a cute guy leaving in a pretty little car, but I wasn't going to say anything," Carly said coyly.

"Not Ted," Mela panted.

"It was Pete. That's my cousin," she said over her shoulder to Beth and Carly. "He flew in yesterday to see Lew at the Shepherd Center. Lew is my brother-in-law, recovering from a racing accident," she added to the list of clarifications.

"When can I meet your cousin?" Carly asked, dancing backward up the hill.

"Next time he shows up at six in the morning, I'll bring him along."

Eli thought she saw a worried glance from the bundle that was Mela, but it was still too dark to be sure.

"You wear the cutest hats," Carly squealed, admiring Beth's wool Stetson.

"I have a closet full," Beth answered, fading fast. "They belong to my great-aunt."

"Let's don't add any more people to our squad," Beth huffed, shining Mela's light ahead to see how much more incline was left. "We don't need an online group or anything, right? Social media creeps me. Sorry, didn't need to say that."

"I lost a good friend over that life-warping sideshow. She became obsessed, very political, determined that I should see things her way. I'll never understand what happened."

"I'm so sorry, Beth. That's awful. The only experience I've had with it is trying to get information about businesses, which you're not welcome to see without *joining*," Mela answered. "I have zero interest."

"Not my thing either," Eli echoed.

"I was on it for a while," Carly said, "but just so my exes can see how happy I am."

"Was that plural ex, more than one?" Eli stumbled as she asked.

"Yeah," she answered. "Married twice, both times less than six months."

Carly," Mela asked, "is the one with the dog actually your ex?"

"Canceled, hundo P."

"Is that a court sanctioned hundred percent," she pursued, "or just your relationship status?"

"I'm not paying for another divorce," she fumed. "Tyler can pay for something. And he hasn't helped at all with this house. The down payment was all my money."

"Carly," Beth advised, "home values are climbing, especially here, and you wouldn't want him at some point to force you to sell and get half after you've been paying, maybe years. A divorce now could be cheaper."

"Got it. That goes to the top of my list."

Beth slowed, sinking onto a boulder along a fence. "Speaking of lists, how about some topics for a no-fly list? Like politics, religion, kids, money, grandkids?"

"Why would you bring up no-fly lists?" Carly asked warily.

"I mean a list of things we don't discuss. Things that might cause friction."

"You're the only one with kids, or the threat of grandkids," Eli said.

"Yeah, yeah, I mean in general."

All responses were affirmative.

"Then we're in agreement."

"If we don't freeze before spring."

"Hey, y'all," Mela shouted. "We do not do this in the rain. Or if we do, it has to be warm rain."

"Don't you birth breeched calves in blizzards?" Beth challenged.

"I mean it, women!"

Soon Mela was off to work, Carly off to bed, Beth off to her shop, and Eli to pack away her Harrison files until she was cleared or needed them for court.

Chapter 7

Where the Road Takes You

S everal rainy mornings offered breaks from pre-dawn walks as January became February, including a rare Sunday when Eli slept especially late. Maybe it was the rain, or maybe the absence of drama for a few weeks.

Later that morning, Mela and Eli drove to River's End Café on the Nantahala for a waterside breakfast. Mac was meeting some of his 82nd Airborne buddies who were at Brasstown Valley Resort for a reunion. They would be kayaking in from a few miles upstream and taking out at the café, where Mela and Eli would be waiting.

As they arrived, the kayakers were a colorful spectacle, scattering all the mallards surfing the current just outside the dining room window. The boaters trickled through old slalom gates, then stowed their boats beyond the footbridge over the river.

Still in wetsuits and pumped from the exhilarating run on the rain-filled river, their banter reflected the familiarity that had unified them in a very different time and place. Throughout the meal, they carried on with several tables of diners on the open porch, all enjoying the unusually mild mid-February day.

After breakfast, Eli drove as they dropped Mac and one of the guys at the trucks that they had left upriver. On the way home, Mela suggested they take the missed morning walk. "I'm loath to admit it, but I feel better all day after walking."

As they started out from Mela's, Eli turned south on the road. "Let's find this estate we've been hearing about."

"I saw Dr. K's mobile veterinary van go in, but that's been a while," Mela said, as they passed the Johnston estate. When they reached Annie Blanche Sutton's property, the sound of a fast-approaching car echoed from her driveway. No sooner had a Mini Cooper come into view than it was careening around the gate and past the walkers, who had jumped the roadside ditch to escape.

"Whoa," Eli exclaimed, as the car screeched to a stop and reversed.

"I always attributed burning trash, nasty language, adverse possession, random gunfire, and squealing tires on this road to the Fowlers," Mela remarked. "Seems I may have misjudged the tires."

"Hey, girls," Annie called through the passenger window. "Heading to the grocery," she announced to her recent acquaintances, offering to shop for them, perhaps to settle any unneighborly dust her passing had kicked up.

"Thanks, but I'm going tomorrow after work," Mela answered.

"It will be wild there," she advised. "Snow coming in tomorrow night."

Eli was having doubts about this woman's stability on such an exceptionally pleasant afternoon. Mela took it as gospel. "Big snow?"

"Saying six or more inches, but a steep temperature drop, and you know how icy parts of our road to the highway stay," Annie replied.

"And I was planning to put some logs in the firepit this evening to roast hot dogs," Eli mentioned, reconsidering.

"I haven't done that in years," Mela said, abandoning all thoughts of snow. "I'll text Beth and Carly," Mela offered. "Annie? Marshmallows?"

"Y'all have a good time, just get that fire out before the winds come up. Supposed to be rain in the morning turning to flurries, but mark my words, we're getting a nice snow. Bye now."

As they walked, their conversation shifted to the snowstorm of '93, before Eli arrived in Hiawassee. Mela called it a frozen hurricane, recounting the difficulty in reaching residents in remote areas, saying three-and-a-half feet of fallen snow created drifts high enough to isolate some homes for days.

"It was impossible to walk or drive through it, and the few snowmobiles available for rescue were blocked by the fallen trees. Power was out for weeks in lots of places. No one talks about it much. People died."

Their trek had brought them to a wide asphalt drive—no gate—framed by two columns. "We won't go near the house," Eli reassured Mela. "Just to where we can see."

Not far past the posts, an electronic voice sent shockwaves through them, powerful enough to drop Eli to a squat. "How can I help you?" rumbled through the forest around them.

Mela ran back and, bracing her hands on her quads, answered into the speaker, "Hello, we're out for a walk. Thank you."

Eli was turning in circles, looking for concealed cameras in the trees as Mela waved her back to the road. "What is this, a secret military base on Chatuge?" Eli asked the post as she passed by.

That afternoon, Eli was dragging the first load from a garage packed with boxes of newspapers suitable for igniting kindling in the firep- it. As she stuffed newsprint balls under the piled tree limbs collected from the yard, Eli looked back at the old structure. She realized it was an old barn that evolved into a 1940s garage.

Massive, tightly fitted stones created benches around the fire pit—a later addition to the property than the barn, Eli speculated. A fieldstone floor encircled the wide pit. Short walls on each level were also stone, making a solid backrest around the seating area. The shape reminded Eli of Aunt Ta's koi pond off the patio—the one that was repeatedly emptied by a persistent blue heron.

An ice chest of soft drinks and wine coolers had Astro's attention, solely for the package of hotdogs atop the drinks. Eli was stripping white oak branches for roasting marshmallows when Mela led Beth and Carly down through the woods.

"We could see the smoke from the road," Carly called. "This is perf right here on the lake."

"Nice spot," Beth echoed, leaning wearily against the stone seating around the pit. "You know," she continued, a fingertip pat- ting her lips, "you two have enough space between your houses to carve out another very valuable home site. Have you thought of that?"

"Gosh, don't think so." Eli tried to sound as if she might have considered the idea.

"That isn't my house, it's Beau's," Mela answered.

"I've talked to an attorney, and he thinks I should sell my house, even though it is mine because I bought it before the wedding," Carly announced. "But I'm going to try finding a roommate first. Oh, sorry, Beth, didn't mean to talk about finances."

"Well, if you decide to sell, I can handle that," she quickly an- swered. "And I can screen some roommate candidates if you'd like."

"I would love," she said, clapping.

Hours later, as the sun dropped behind them, the fire was going strong. "Let's keep adding small limbs to heat up the fire and get it to ash quickly," Carly suggested, bringing a load.

"Great idea," Eli shouted, gathering more wood in the fading light. The sound of a whining engine drew her eyes to the hill above, where headlights were shining as they passed the house.

A camo dune buggy came zigzagging through the trees, whipping around to the lakeside and sliding to a stop. Annie Blanche hopped out, breathlessly saying, "Hey y'all, didn't think I'd make it but here I am."

She sprinted past them, grabbed the near empty cooler, and staggered to the back of her vehicle, slamming it on the narrow cargo shelf. "Should anyone ask, I've been here all afternoon, got it?" she said, sitting on a large stump next to the fire to catch her breath. "All afternoon."

"So, what's going on, Annie?" Eli asked, trying to sound casual.

Beth pretended to reach for something behind her as she whispered to Mela, "Could that be the mysterious Ann Arnold?"

"There may or may not have been an incident at the church up the road that I may or may not have been involved in," Annie answered, swigging an Aranciata from the cooler. "Criminal mischief. Nothing a person could do time for."

Before anyone else could speak, a sheriff's deputy came shuffling through the woods toward them. "Y'all let me do the talking now," Annie said softly, tossing a stick into the roaring fire.

"Evening, ladies," the deputy called from the path above them. A subdued volley of "hey" and "hello" greeted him as he arrived fireside. "I'm looking for someone who just vandalized church property. Fled the scene in a UTV, described like that one over there," he noted, shining his phone light on Annie's ride. "Whose is that?"

"It's mine, officer, been here all afternoon," she swore through her most charming smile.

"Infrared camera says otherwise, ma'am. That engine is plenty hot right now."

"Oh shoot, did I leave it running again," she said, wrapping her sweater in her best old lady imitation and easing over to take her key, faking a shutdown.

"Bless your sweet heart, officer. I hope you find your man. Be safe out there," she urged him, calling Astro over to make her look as small as possible.

"All afternoon, huh?" he asked.

"Honest to God, sir," Beth responded.

"Would you like a hotdog?" Eli asked.

"Been right here," Mela muttered, looking in his direction but avoiding his gaze.

"Can't leave flames unattended," Carly called out, stooping to stoke the fire.

"Okay, ladies," he said, returning to the path. "Good night."

A boat heading back to the marina passed close to the old dock as the deputy became a silhouette in the woods. Wake lapping on the shore and the cracking fire were the only sounds until his flashlight completely disappeared.

"Would you like a hotdog?" Annie mimicked. "That's your idea of shutting down an interrogation?"

"What did you do to the church?" Mela asked solemnly.

"That preacher needs antidepressants in the worst way," she answered, adding, "and now that you're all after-the-fact accomplices, would y'all please call me AB? Annie is my grand momma, and Annie Blanche is such a mouthful."

"Annie, A.B." Eli said, starting introductions. "This is Beth Parker. She owns Fancy This in Hiawassee in addition to doing real estate; and over there is Carly Lane, another busy neighbor from the cove."

"Hello, girls." Annie smiled as she waved. "Lovely to meet you. Pardon my entrance."

"Did you desecrate a grave?" Beth queried.

"You put trash in their dumpster, right?" Carly guessed. "I've thought of doing that."

She bristled with contempt as she answered. "I took a dust mop to that stupid sign out front. Every week that fool comes up with the most awful threats to people passing by. It's a disgrace to Christianity."

"AB, you know that pastor's wife died awhile back," Mela cautioned.

"No, I did not," she said softly, poking at the fire again. "I met someone nice who went to that church. I would see her walking among the tombstones a summer ago, just like I go and do some evenings. She thought he was *wonderful*—brave and kind and wise. I think he's a pompous jackass."

"What did he do to you?" Eli asked.

"Nothing to me," she acknowledged. "I never met the man, but those damned signs are driving me crazy. 'Stop, drop, and roll won't work in hell.' 'Weather never changes in hell.' He's all hellfire and damnation, and I'm damned tired of it every time I drive by."

"Oh," Beth started, eager to contribute. "There are some good ones out there. 'Don't let worries kill you, let the church help' and um, 'We love hurting people,' my favorite. Oh, and 'Have the donkey and elephant let you down? Turn to the lamb,' and—"

"Beth, that's politics," Carly cautioned.

"Yeah," AB said through a faint smile. "We got the drift."

"So, what's that hot rod you hid under the cooler," Eli wanted to know.

"That's my Kaw. I use it around the property and to ride up to the quick mart."

"Or the church?" Carly teased. "I've heard of a UTV mule, a gator, but cow?"

"Short for the brand name."

"Well, girls," Mela said, rising from the stone bench, "I've got surgeries in the morning, and AB has promised us a nice snow, so I'm turning in after we get this fire out."

"Let's do this again next week at my place," AB suggested.

"No cops," Beth barked.

"Weather permitting," Eli confirmed, with a thumb's up.

"I have to work Sunday evening," Carly said, "but I'll stop in."

"Just damn," AB hollered. "Here's my mop I threw in the lake when that officer was tailing me. It's just floating back to the shore, little plastic letters stuck in it. That's what I call a smoking gun."

Carly and Eli walked over to get the ice chest from the Kaw, both remarking on the air temperature noticeably dropping. Carly unloaded the last two wine coolers while Eli took a pic of AB seatbelting the incriminating mop to her ride. As AB throttled up the shoreline, they dumped the ice water onto the fading embers, creating a cloud of steam that left the pit dark.

Chapter 8

When You See It's Not a Train

Winds were howling early that night, forcing Eli out past the patio to look for flames resurrecting in the firepit. She stumbled over Pharaoh as she reversed direction, then reached down to give him an apologetic scratch. "Fella, your ears are freezing," she said, wondering how old he might be.

Pharaoh crept to the sliders and dashed through, going straight to the soapstone hearth at the fireplace. Eli curled up on the sofa, drowsily watching the furry shadow grooming in the firelight. "You should make sleep-inducing videos, old man," she muttered.

Eli woke up to a darkened fireplace and a golden cat fleece snoozing on her side, purring like one of Ted's racing engines. Eli found the contentment contagious.

When she roused to faint light in the bay windows, Pharaoh was at the front door, waiting to leave. It was not yet the sun, but moonlight reflecting on snow, with gusts lifting duck-feather flakes in loops and swirls. Despite the wind, her car had over six inches in rounded mounds on the hood and roof.

Eli bundled in a blanket to let her companion out and was surprised by a snowdrift standing flat where the door had been. In a split second, Pharaoh left an oval hole in the frosty wall. She expected him to burst back through, but saw him springing along, cartoon bunny style. As a rookie cat lady, she wasn't sure whether a rescue or discreet disregard was in order, but once he cleared the drift, he had no trouble bounding his way to Mela's.

Beth would never get across Blood Mountain. All agreed by text this snow qualified as an excuse not to walk, and the same dispensation applied to Tuesday as well. Eli skipped walks on Wednesdays for her trips to see Lew. It took special permission to sneak in an early morning visit at the Shepherd Center, but as always, Lew knew who to call.

On Wednesday afternoon, Eli found a note in the door from Mac. He had uncovered the spyware source and passed some pertinent information to the Harrison's investigative team through several channels, keeping his name and connection to Eli unreported. "Will come by Sunday after we're finished at the track to explain."

Still in her coat, she sat at the kitchen table re-reading Mac's note. There was some relief at being exonerated, but Eli was surprised at her who-cares reaction. No yearning to ninja-jump Megan, rubbing the report in her face until fake eyelashes, garish lipstick, contour shadow, and brow gel had rearranged into exquisitely abstract art.

She could never fully believe it had been Ted, although he was a persuasive candidate. She just didn't care who had used her to get to the Harrisons. She was collateral damage. Maybe now she could have the bugs removed from her devices. Maybe now she could move on. To what, she had no idea.

On Thursday, AB joined the walkers, celebrating the snow melting. "High of fifty-five today, ladies," Beth crowed. "Spring is just two weeks away."

"What?" Carly shot back. "You're three weeks off," she said, double-thumbing her phone.

"If you're looking up first day of spring, try meteorological spring." Beth smirked. "March first."

"Can't right now," Carly answered. "I'm turning in my homework. Class in an hour."

"Well, I'm ready for some spring, more time outside after work," AB declared, slowing for the others to catch up.

"I'm considering starting a blog," Eli said. "Maybe something about living in our part of the Georgia mountains. Think anyone would find that interesting?"

"Your posts could be about doing things people would like to try," Mela replied.

"Maybe things we could do together?" Eli wondered if that sounded too eager to her companions.

"Sign me up," Beth answered. "There are so many festivals and places I've wanted to see."

"Let's do hikes," Carly added, without looking up from her phone. "I can show y'all my AT section."

"Your what?

"You know, AB, a section of the Appalachian Trail that I volunteered to maintain."

"Oh yeah, sure." AB rolled her eyes. "Seriously, our morning spins are a big deal for me."

"What's something you'd like to do?" Eli asked her.

She answered quickly, "I'd like to take a class at John C. Campbell Folk School."

"Can we make it a weekend one?" Carly begged. "When I'm off?"

"Could you do a weekend, Beth?" Eli said, as they reached their turn-back point.

"Yes, let's accommodate the golden girl."

"We need to figure out a class," Mela suggested, hoping the group hadn't reached the comfy-enough-to-snark phase of the new relationships.

"I'll get a catalog, and we can decide at our bonfire," AB promised. "Carly, look up Sunday's weather?"

"A start in the low thirties, becoming sunny and a high of fifty. Woohooo!"

"My subscription forecast," Beth countered, "says a high of fifty-four."

"I defer," Carly said with a curtsy.

The walk back covered every class they could recall from origami to blacksmithing. AB was considering Contra Dancing—assuring Eli's blog would have entertaining stories.

⟫•◊•⟪

Eli and Mela met Sunday afternoon for the walk to AB's house. Mela had hotdogs and buns; Eli's bag had chips, marshmallows, and two squirt bottles—one Ghirardelli sea salt caramel, the other dark chocolate. "Trade me now, and you may never see me again," Mela offered.

As they reached the house, a real estate sign papered with an arrow and "campfire" hand lettered, directed them to the lake path. Centered on a beautiful fieldstone square, a wide cedar table was draped with a red and white checkered cloth, covered with dips, appetizers, and condiments.

The shoreline was serene, with hemlocks framing the clear lake water. A dock off the stone-paved area appeared as weathered and weary as Eli's, but with missing boards. An ancient boat lift stood bare—the roof long gone. Eli and Beth built the fire into an inferno and joined Mela and AB in perusing the JCC Folk School catalog.

On her way to AB's house, Carly had stopped at Eli's to drop off her AT club scrapbook. As she returned to her car, black SUVs pulled in behind. A woman was waving from a backseat window in the first car. "Hello, darling, could you tell me, is Eli at home?"

Carly noticed the cute driver, who stared straight ahead as she approached the woman. "Thank you, dear. I'm Ida. This is my husband, David. Dreadful to drop by this way, but we had so hoped to see her."

"I'll show you where she is. It's two houses down this road," Carly told the woman.

"Could we wait here?" Ida asked. "Might she be long?"

"You should come. We're five neighbors getting together for a weenie roast. Eli wouldn't want to miss your visit," she assured Ida, while observing the others in the vehicle and peering around at the SUV behind.

"We won't take long," she promised Carly, who was studying David as though she knew him from somewhere.

The black caravan backed out, allowing Carly to lead them to AB's house. The first SUV pulled in behind Carly, and two men opened the doors for their passengers. Ida walked to Carly, taking her hand as they strolled the path to the lake, leaving David waiting beside the house with his driver.

Stunned couldn't begin to describe Eli's reaction to seeing Carly and Ida walking toward her. She easily recognized the distant figure by the house. The pulse in her ears was deafening as she watched Ida stop a few yards away. "Excuse me," Eli said to AB, trembling as she hurried to Ida.

"Thank you, darling," Ida whispered, patting Carly's hand as she released her guide to join her friends.

Ida opened her arms as Eli approached. "Can you ever forgive us, Eli? We've behaved so shamefully, letting technicians and law firms accuse you while we stood silent. We've come to apologize. To tell you what happened and ask for your forgiveness, in time. Would you speak with David?"

"Yes, of course," Eli answered, grasping Ida's hands.

"Let's go tell him so."

As they climbed the hill, David met them in a few long strides, wrapping an arm around each of them as they admired AB's spread on the table ahead. Carly was describing her encounter, when a long gasp was heard from AB, alerting Beth and Mela, who were similarly struck by the sight of the man walking their way. Carly looked back and forth at the man and her friends, bewildered by their reactions.

"Ida, David," Eli began, wide-eyed. "These are my friends, Annie Blanche Sutton, Beth Parker, Mela Orr, and Carly Lane. Girls, meet Ida and David Harrison."

After a few minutes of fawning welcome—during which Beth spontaneously collected her friends' phones and piled them on the table, followed by a hands-up gesture to the security team—David asked to speak with Eli. They walked down to a log seat below the firepit where he straddled the bench to face Eli.

"This is the most cowardly episode of my entire life, and you bore the brunt of it. When the Wright Agency contacted Victor about a blackmail threat, he turned it over to our investigative firm. The usual steps were taken, but this time it involved a series of personal photos from an album in our Beaufort home. These were photos that you generously scanned for Kiley, and that's how you were dragged into this."

"No explanations necessary, Mr. Harrison," she said quickly. "These things happen. I'm relieved you know now it wasn't me."

"We never thought that for a moment. Victor defended you at every turn, but things had to happen in order to find the person responsible. We had help from places we still can't identify, but in the end, it was a hacker who apparently accessed our daughter's cloud storage and sent a blackmail demand along with the images. Because your phone transmitted the photos to Kylie's, you became involved."

"I completely understand. I do." Eli stopped him again, blinking back tears. "I wish you hadn't come all this way. I'm truly glad it's over," she said, standing to return to her friends.

"Please, wait," he said, taking her chilled hands in his. "You have as much of an investment in this book project as I do. And it is time you got a story you can work with. If you will work with me again?"

"Yes," she said, clearing the catch from her throat.

David signaled the driver, still posted at the back of the house, who sprinted down the hill with a leather binder. He handed it to David, who then nodded, sending him back. From the folder he extracted photos—some Eli hadn't seen before, a sheaf of papers and a digital recorder, which he placed between them on the weathered log. He started the recorder.

"In your interviews, what I said was the same thing I've been saying since my very first studio contract needed a press release: 'Itinerant Midwest farm family, hard scrabble, post-Depression era, getting by, until I was discovered as a horse wrangler on the set of a TV show.'

"What it didn't say was that at fifteen, I'd been hired out doing field work on farms for over ten years already. My age was likely obscured by regular beatings from my old man, at least until I was big enough to stop him. When he left us that time, he didn't come back.

"Being a ranch hand paid better than field work. With all the moving, I never got past tenth grade. But I was a smart kid—too much like my old man—and was looking for easier money to pay my rent and take care of my mom and sister back home.

"I was delivering horses to this location shoot, making good money for a kid my age, but I had plans. Stupid plans to take a truck, trailer, and four nice horses to New Mexico, sell them all for plenty of money to cover my mom while I found better opportunities, maybe in Arizona.

"That was the same afternoon that the man who would change my life's direction pulled me aside. He was easily the most popular actor in the show, but walked straight over to me, this nobody. He lit a cigarette, stared hard at the horse trailers and said, 'You're better than that, Davey. You've got a test this afternoon for a part as one of the trail hands, a regular part? This is your chance, kid.'

"He took another drag, looked steadily at me, and all I could think was, did he know what I was planning? Could he see my old man, that sleazy bastard, in me? Maybe he was simply giving me my career-break pep talk, but even now I'm not so sure he didn't yank me up and set me on solid ground.

"I got the job. It lasted a few years, and then several of us from that cast were off to Italy for a couple of shoots and back to LA. By then I was getting a few offers, and I tried to be like the guy who got me my break—his demeanor, his dedication, maybe his haircut and shirt maker, and for sure his grab-life-while-you-can attitude.

"I was becoming a little too much like him, or so he seemed to say. By then he had his own production company, and as we were walking back to our trailers on a crusty mud road, he looked at the woman—not his wife—going in his trailer and said, 'A wise man learns from the mistakes of others, Dave, and some of us, well, we have to learn every damned thing the hard way.'

"What mistake did he mean? There was no one special in my life, and every night was another party. I was sending money home, but my days revolved around working hard and playing harder. I was young and successful. Isn't that the objective?

"Around that time, I met Ida on the set of my first not-a-Western. There was something unforgettable about her, but I couldn't get her to notice me. That year we were both cast in the same production, and I realized I was changing my ways, hoping she would see a different guy. She made me want to be a man worthy of her time. Sappy, I know.

"And then the big breaks started coming. My first roles were bit-part bad guys in studio features; then guys who get what's coming to them, but in wider released movies; and soon I was winning leads, the misguided guy who finds his way, the reluctant man who rallies the team, the superhero who saves civilization.

"One night Ida approached me at a party, said she admired my changing performances. She described her favorite scenes—also mine—where the character seems to grow a little. *She gets me*, I thought. And that led to me finally getting the girl, who has been my world ever since.

"I only wish it had been as beneficial to her life as it was mine. Unfortunately, my old man reappeared about the time our wedding made the news, bothering my mother and sister for money. I will always regret that I lured him out to California with a job on the set.

"He was as worthless as ever—lying, stealing, cheating every which way. I had arranged for Ida's sister, Alma, to work as an extra, so they were both staying in our new home in LA. Soon, Alma was pregnant, and he was in the wind. Yes, Marc was born in Hawaii, just not to Ida—to her older sister, Alma Garcia.

"With help from Victor, we filled out all the papers as though he had been born to us. We made sure Alma was as much a part of Marc's life as we were. Then she up and left before he was three months old.

"Ida couldn't understand it because Alma had just started getting her life together. I think she was dating my producer's son. When I heard talk that Ray Harrison had been seen at the studio with Alma, there wasn't a doubt for me that my old man had come back and taken her to Mexico with him. I knew it. Not one word all these years.

"We were always going to tell Marc. Ida was sure her sister would be back, but months, then years went by, and we didn't know how to tell him—with no answers for the questions he would have. He was our blood, both of us, and he will always be our son.

"That's the picture of Alma standing next to Ida, just before Marc was born. That's her holding Marc with Ida. Those are the pictures the blackmailer had sent. Eli, we knew you did nothing wrong. We were barred from contacting you until now."

Eli finally looked up from the log's ridges she'd been tracing with her thumbnail. "I hope you both truly believe that, because I... There's no way I would ever betray you or your family. You've all been wonderful—"

David stood and reached down for Eli. "Ida says everything happens for a reason. I believe that," he told her, as she tucked into his embrace, his chin resting on the top of her head. He could feel the sobs she was muffling, as well as the deep affection she held for his family.

"We'll need to get ol' Marc through this revelation, to let the sleuths finish their paperwork, and the lawyers rewrite your contract and then, Eli, I think you'll have one helluva book to finish for us."

With AB's blessing, Ida had sent for more hotdogs, buns, chips, and drinks to have plenty for the three men accompanying the Harrisons. As they ate, and to Ida's delight, AB grilled David with questions about movie sets and co-stars. Mela was propped on her elbows, absorbing every word. Beth was pitching properties, and Carly was fascinated—mostly by the hunky security crew—but miserable when she had to leave for work. Doubly so when sworn to secrecy over the visit.

⟫―◦―⟪

After the Harrisons left for their flight out of Atlanta to LA, and after Eli had been fully debriefed, everyone headed home. Eli unlocked the front door and was startled to see Mac sitting at the table working on her laptop.

"How'd it go?" he asked, without looking up from his work.

"How'd you get in?" she responded, pulling a chair beside him.

"Hooh, you are a smokey blend of charred oak and burnt hickory," he complained, fanning her back from his work.

"You could have come down for a hotdog, Inspector Gadget." That brought him up from the laptop.

"There are a few things I couldn't tell you before you saw the Harrisons," he confessed.

"You knew they were coming?"

"I heard something about it. Not from anyone close to them. You're such a crappy liar, I couldn't risk telling you this before you met with them." He studied the slender tool in his hand. "The taps on your devices were traced to Waller Analytical systems. A foreign hacker with celebrity trolling inclinations was *not-exactly*-framed as having accessed the Harrison's daughter's cloud storage, the source of the images that you had scanned for her."

"You framed somebody?"

"I didn't frame anybody. The Waller insider did the framing. Well, baited him into framing himself." Mac looked directly at her as he slowly said, "Eli, Ted is looking good for this. Real good. He has access and motive."

"No, that's Machiavellian, beyond Ted Waller's scope of malice." So much like the day Grace had explained Asperger's, Eli could almost see puzzle pieces drifting into place.

"I did get this odd text from him in July saying 'loving life,' with a shot of him in his boat. I'd never known him to take a selfie. Thought it might have been a 'happy without you, don't wish you were here' thing. Mac, could that have carried spyware? A virus? I've made myself paranoid thinking about all this, but if he wanted to spy on me—to then steal my work and use it to destroy me? That isn't in him."

"Somebody did this, and yes, to you, not the Harrisons. They were a means to an end. There's no one else out there we've found so far. Certainly no one else who used Waller systems in the process."

"What about Megan Wright? She's had plenty of electronic access through emails and files," Eli suggested eagerly.

"Cleared. Previous clients, cleared. Also assorted former coworkers, neighbors, and friends."

"You really think I go around pissing everybody off?"

He raised an eyebrow but didn't answer, just bounced her phone in his hand. "I'm installing countermeasures on your phone and computers that must not be discovered. Do not misplace any of these. Nobody touches your phone or computers. Try not to let them out of your sight until I'm finished with the case."

"What kind of a case? Who else is in on this?"

"You think I have a half million plus in scanning equipment? This stuff isn't mine, Eli, it's, well, it's not mine," Mac said, reaching for his buzzing phone.

From Mac's side of the conversation, Eli could tell it was Lew, and that Pete was with him. After a brief discussion of Lew's progress, he handed his phone to Eli with a finger to his lips to remind her as he said, "Pete."

"E, I hope you're taking care of yourself. Lew looks good, and he's expecting more brownies from Melissa's Bakery when you come Wednesday. So, here's the thing. I'm planning on taking Ted's job offer. Are you okay with that? I need to know, because if—"

"No ifs about it." She stopped him, her heart in her throat. "Pete, go for it. I'm glad that it's working out for you. I promise. And I have some news for you, which has to be another just between us thing for now. The book contract is being revived. David Harrison told me today."

"Sweet," he answered, then hesitantly continued. "If you're going to be at Chatuge for a while longer, could I use the condo until Grace gets here in April?"

"Move right in. Promise you'll stay off the balcony?" Dead air. "'K, too soon for that. Did Ted forget to offer you the guest apartment? So much nicer. Bigger and better furnished."

"Yeah, that's occupied. Indefinitely. Still Hannah Collins."

The silence was long enough that it was Pete's turn to wonder whether the call had dropped. "Huh," Eli finally responded. "Guess the paint job turned into a remodel. Really I'm surprised she hasn't moved in with Ted already."

"Nah. Ted mentioned something about getting his place ready for Lew once he's released from here," Pete said. "And you know Ted—even two's a crowd."

"Interesting, but I'm especially glad to hear he's looking out for his big brother. Like I said, you're welcome to the condo. Per the divorce agreement, I have it to the end of March, and Ted would surely let you stay longer. I'll bring my key Wednesday. Love you, Pete Cooper."

——➤•◀——

Monday morning's walk buzzed with observations about the Harrisons, their fascinating protection team, David's most memorable scenes, and Carly's intention to binge-watch all his movies. "You'll need serious vacation time for that," AB advised.

Beth asked to ride to Atlanta with Eli on Wednesday for a camera upgrade on her drone. "I'd love the company if you don't mind a stop at the Towers to drop off my key," Eli answered.

Beth's curiosity about that prestigious buildings' privately owned residences above the hotel levels and some of its well-known inhabitants eventually led Eli to reveal her ex occupied a penthouse, which had previously been the home of his parents. Beth was desperate for a tour, but Eli quickly nixed that idea, assuring Beth she was not interested in running into anyone.

"But you go on Wednesdays because he's always in a meeting, so why shouldn't we snoop a little?" Carly asked, adding herself to the passenger list.

"Really, Carly? *We?*" Beth protested.

Eli and Beth met Carly near the Young Harris campus. They stopped for Lew's brownies in Blairsville as Carly made a wardrobe change in the back seat. "A flight attendant and you can't be ready on time?" Beth remarked, as Carly pulled a fresh sweater over her head.

"Flight attendant?" Carly responded, exasperated.

"Yeah, tough job, jetting here and there, meeting all sorts of people, getting hit on all the time," Beth riffed, to Carly's consternation.

"What I do is a lot harder than selling houses on a mountain lake," Carly answered, trying to contain her irritation and understand the problem.

"Whoa, Beth, what if Carly does fly free in a job? She runs two business and is working on her degree in her spare time. Did you know that?"

"No, I didn't," Beth said, turning to look directly at Carly. "I'm sorry, Carlz. Things have been weird for me lately and, well, I saw you as a privileged kid with everything going your way. I've been an ass. You and I are probably a lot alike."

"I appreciate that, Beth. I think you're amazing," Carly said, sounding subdued.

"Crap, that's the nicest thing anyone has ever said to me. So, we're good?"

"We've always been good."

The visit with Lew, and Beth's camera repair, finished in time to meet Pete for an early lunch in the hotel restaurant. Beth and Carly planned to shop Buckhead Village for an hour or so while Pete and Eli checked out the condo and advised management of his arrival. They would regroup in the parking deck.

As Eli was standing on the balcony waiting for Pete to measure a wall for the maximum TV screen size, a drone came wobbling down the face of the building, banked sharply, and disappeared. At first, she was incensed by the invasion. *Damned spies and hackers.*

Then she thought about the coincidence—a drone outside the building Beth wanted to see; Beth's drone with that new camera. She leaned over the rail to look at the parking deck. On an open level there was Beth, toggling the controls of the tiny aircraft as Carly watched the screen.

A quick hug for Pete, and she was dashing to the elevator. "Please don't let them be in the back of a police car," she pleaded, maybe to the guard monitoring the elevator camera. As she hurried out, Eli saw two security officers questioning her friends.

"I just told you, I'm getting video of the view that I forgot to get when I was upstairs getting the listing," Beth was claiming.

"For me," Carly added, implicating herself in the caper. "I'm buying her listing."

"Your ID is not the right real estate office," the senior-looking officer noted. "Every sale here goes through the same one, and it is not yours."

"Excuse me," Eli called across the parking deck. "Sorry," she panted, as she drew closer. "These are my friends, officers. I'm a tenant, and they were getting images for someone who will be moving in," she said, digging out her building ID card.

"No problem, Mrs. Waller," the lead officer responded, without looking at her ID—for Eli Sledge. "You folks have a nice day," he said, touching the bill of his cap then guiding his perplexed colleague away.

"Can I get one of whatever you showed him," Beth asked, pushing Carly in the front seat and easing in the back. "Cool that we had the same alibi, huh?"

"Those were not the same story," she shouted into the rear view mirror. "Why is everyone trying to get me evicted," Eli muttered, making for the exit.

"They weren't supposed to be home," Carly whined. Beth quickly regretted their seating.

Eli pulled to the curb in front of her building, not wanting to hear the worst while trying to merge on I-75. "Exactly what happened while you two were supposed to be shopping?"

"I wanted to be sure the camera was working properly before we left," Beth answered in a methodical recitation. "Why not do a test while we were waiting? I sent the drone to the top of the building and back down. They had confiscated it when you arrived. That's all."

"So where was home, and who was there that wasn't supposed to be there? Spill, Carly!"

"All those penthouse windows were big and bright. It was like we were in there," she exclaimed, followed by an "Oh, God" moan from the back seat.

"And we just kept looking around. That big staircase is amaz, like a castle or something. Eli, people were ice skating on the roof. Then at the bathroom window—"

"Please, no," Eli said, putting her face in her hands. "What bathroom window?"

"Well," Carly stammered, looking back into Beth's glare, "a huge bathroom under a travertine barrel ceiling, with vanities on either side, a steam shower with lots and lots of glass…"

"Ted's bathroom," Eli added flatly.

"So beautiful," Carly continued. "Then this lady came in, putting stuff under the counter, maybe a fridge. It was under the coffee station. I saw an espresso machine. We got it out of there before anyone saw us. Except the security guy."

"That entire building is wild with security," Eli growled. "They know everything you did. You're not leaving anything out? Wait, did you say a lady was in the bathroom, the one I said was Ted's? Was she cleaning?"

"No, dressed real nice. It was the only bathroom we looked in," Carly ruefully reported.

"What did she look like?" Eli pressed.

"That," Beth said, pointing at a woman entering the restaurant. It was Hannah Collins.

Beth was out of the car before Eli could react. She shot an okay sign from the door, hoping to redeem herself with a little reconnoitering. She reported by phone almost immediately.

"No worries," she whispered. "Got a menu in front of my phone in case anyone remembers me from lunch."

"Security gets complimentary meals there," Eli said dryly. "You, they will remember."

"She's placing her to-go order, for three of the same thing. Doesn't look like a big eater."

"She's going to put it in her dishes and make like she cooked dinner," Carly claimed. "I did that with my exes all the time. Three meals together look homemade."

"Come on, Beth. I'm ready to get out of town." Eli sounded weary.

Soon Carly was asleep, and Beth honored the silence until loud breathing commenced. "We good, Eli?" she asked, leaning to the gap between the front seats. "That was a bonehead move. I'm sorry, got carried away."

"We're good."

"You think she's moved in with Ted?"

"Yeah."

Beth stretched back in the seat, exhausted. "Yeah."

Chapter 9

What Things You Do for Love

F rigid temps banished thoughts of an early spring as "nope" texts circulated among the walkers. Beth cited appointments, and Carly had class catch-up. Mela and AB separately suggested breakfast at the Sawmill instead of risking frostbite. Over pancake stacks, crispy hash, and omelets, Eli filled them in on the Atlanta excursion before inaccurately innocent versions surfaced.

AB's reaction was stifled hysterics, while Mela was quietly horrified for Eli.

"Best we never speak of this again." Eli shuddered, laughing off the memory.

Eli did speak of it once more when she visited Lew in early March. Although Eli hadn't revealed her problems with the Harrisons nor mentioned the spyware, she did happily entertain him with Beth's determination to see the penthouse, resorting to drone access until busted by security.

When she said they saw Hannah alone in Ted's place, his laughter faded. "I knew she was moving in on him," Lew said, saddened by the news. "*Any* Waller will do. She knows how to work a guy's every angle, too," he added, clearly recalling something. A therapist came for Lew, and Eli was impressed with how easily he transferred to the wheelchair. Whether he would walk unaided was still uncertain. She watched him wheel away, sharing a prized brownie with his therapist.

⸺◈⸺

Morning walks were pushed back to the predawn light with the time change, sparking Beth's rant on the insane costs of semiannual upheavals for prime-time daylight. AB declared it a mess for shift operations, like the hospice she managed. Eli had learned to come prepared with alternative topics.

Another spectacular mid-March weekend arrived on the heels of several stormy days. Springlike temps helped Mac persuade Mela to bring Beau's sailboat out of storage on Saturday morning for some maintenance, and air it out sailing on Sunday.

When Mela suggested they meet after lunch at the dock, Carly quickly claimed sailing experience and a spot on the crew. Eli and Beth offered to bring a picnic for the cruise. AB begged off, citing a patient she planned to see.

Too early in the season for many boaters to be on the water, this classic spring day offered a steady but gentle breeze easing through the surrounding mountain ranges. Mounding white clouds grew higher than wide, allowing sunshine to spill to the forest floor, warming the last reluctant trilliums to rise.

Mac watched the wind dance across the glistening surface of the lake, recalling his last day sailing with Beau. They were mid-lake, constantly trimming the sails as Beau drilled him on minding the unpredictable winds on a mountain lake, and on heeding the main sail as it flaps along the luff. Beau made sure the Catalina 22 was too far from shore for his unhappily civilian friend to swim in any direction before he revealed his convoluted plan to marry Mela.

"It won't keep her on the shelf long," Beau advised his troubled friend. "If you love her as much as I suspect, get your head out of your ass. Come about for that course made good. I wouldn't want to see lovely Mela wasted on anyone else, Mac."

With five people on board, the Catalina sailed slowly from the marina to Sunnyside for the picnic, then back through the pass and along the North Carolina shore before tying up at Mela's for a bio-break. From the dock, Mela noticed someone on the terrace wagging a drink in her hand.

Crouched with her back to the house, Mela was securing a line at the dock as Eli stepped past her. "Anyone you know?" Eli finally asked.

She shot an aggravated look in the direction of the visitors. "Someone you know, too," Mela grumbled. "Leslie, and I think she's brought her daughter Sophie, although I can't be sure because I haven't seen either of them since Mom's funeral."

Eli and Mela took their time getting to the house. "Your car was out front, and it opened the garage door for us," claimed the woman in a midriff blouse and short shorts, windblown platinum strands shading her eyes. The young girl was getting a double headshot of herself and Astro, with kitty face filters.

"You aren't really my little niece?" Mela said to the girl, as she absently hugged her sister, who was sizing up Eli.

"I know you," Leslie accused, extending her pointy finger from her glass. "You're little Ellie, um, something." She circled, asking,

"Didn't you snag some big money? Yeah, you ran off with the nerdy Waller kid."

Eli raised the corners of her mouth to remove the hostility from her return stare. Leslie was just as snide and bitchy as ever. "Did I hear you're a granny?" Eli trolled.

"Where the hell did you hear that?" she roared, snapping her head back in disgust.

"I thought your married son had a little one," Eli replied dismissively.

"That's a step-kid, nothing of mine," Leslie clarified, stretching out on a chaise and studying Mac's approach.

"What brings you to Hiawassee?" Mela inquired, scrolling through the shots Sophie was showing on her phone and noting the earliest, in Mela's bedroom, was over three hours old.

"Sophie's on spring break and wanted to see her Auntie Melanie," Leslie purred.

"Think she could have picked me out of a crowd?" Mela responded, as the girl trailed Astro trotting out to meet Carly and Beth.

Eli held the door, creating an escape for those caught in the escalation outside. Mac hesitated as he reached Mela, gave Leslie a nod, and moved on to the kitchen. Leslie's gaze followed Mac until he was inside, then she whistled. "What a waste. Little ol' Mac, all grown up—hot, bothersome, and crippled."

"Why are you here, Leslie? Why now?" Mela demanded.

"Well, straight to the point," she said, belatedly. "There are four of us left, and I don't think you, as—I suppose—Mama's executor, have ever made any information available about the estate."

Mela stared dumbfounded at this fading caricature reposed on her chaise. "You know damned well that Dean and Margarite Orr were two hippies who took over an old campground, adopted all of us, and scraped by every winter on what they could earn the summer before.

When they sold the campground to developers, they were able to live decades on that.

"As Mama said when I brought her to live with me, I didn't have to climb over any of you to get to her. She was broke and alone. You know there has never been any estate, and therefore no need for an executor. So, I'm going to ask you again. Why are you here?"

"I had to leave. JT is having an affair, and he's cut me off," she whined, swinging her feet to the ground and crossing her arms. "Sophie doesn't know."

Mela thought about walking back inside. Not playing this game. Not offering shelter to this person she had no relationship with, nor any interest in building one. "Stay here a few days, get yourself together, then go deal with your life, Leslie. If you're headed for a divorce, go prepare for that. If you want to work things out, that can't happen from here."

"Okay," Leslie said, sliding her feet in strappy mules and tugging her shorts out of her crotch. "We won't be any trouble." She went straight to the sunroom, opened the bar, and mixed herself another drink. She detoured to the kitchen, where she wiggled as she snickered in Mac's ear and then leisurely returned to the empty terrace.

As she watched, Mela recognized the distinctive gold bracelet on Leslie's arm as the one Beau had brought from Italy. Mela realized the urgent need for setting some boundaries. She went to Leslie, pinned the braceleted forearm to the chaise cushion with her knee, and removed the wide woven wheat chain without a word—dropping it in her pocket and returning to the kitchen, repeating, "One week."

⟫◦⟪

Leslie showed no interest in the morning walks, in spring break activities for Sophie, or whether the girl had eaten recently. Wednesday afternoon, as Mela came in from the clinic and prepared to shower, she returned to the kitchen and saw Leslie thumbing through her wallet.

"Thought I'd get some groceries," Leslie said, without looking up.

"Do not touch my purse," Mela ordered, seizing it from her. "Do not go in my room or open my desk, and you definitely stay out of the bar," she added. "Got it? Tell me you understand what I'm saying."

She had noticed Sophie's head pop up next to Astro on the sunroom floor. "Why don't you take Sophie on a hike, or maybe horseback riding at the resort? Something fun for her?"

"Well, asshole, that takes money, doesn't it," she shouted, climbing the stairs. Mela went in the sunroom, playfully walking her fingers across Sophie's scalp on her way to check the bar. Every bottle was empty or gone, including some ancient grenadine mix.

She perched on the sofa above the eleven-year-old, not sure what to say. "If you're looking for your booze," Sophie advised, avoiding eye contact, "try my mother's room."

"Drinking problem, huh?" Mela replied, crediting the girl with a grasp of the issue she endured.

"I can't even," Sophie said, frustration rising in her voice. "Dad told her to get out and not come back until she was ready to get better. But I don't think she wants to. She's always wasted, she lies about everything, and Dad is going to cancel her. She says he doesn't want to talk to me, either."

Mela slid next to her, pulling Sophie closer, and taking her phone to show her things they could do together before she went home

"Mela," she said, looking directly at her, "my mother said we were never going home when she registered me at a school yesterday. She lied about my spring break, you know. It's next week."

There was no good in that news, but holding this heartbroken kid put the situation in perspective. "Your dad will have something to say about that, and I know he would never, ever *not* want to talk to his baby girl," she said, realizing she was rocking them both. Mela had always believed her "fur babies" were all the love she needed, but comforting a little human had a magic all its own.

⊰•◦•⊱

As Carly struggled on Thursday's walk, she veered to her driveway, passing on the last leg. "I have to sleep," she moaned. "Don't look for me in the morning."

Then Beth remembered Carly's birthday on Saturday, and AB suggested dinner together. "I'll get reservations at the Copper Door," she added. "I've never been there, but I met one of their managers, and that young man is adorable."

"It's in the top 100 restaurants in the country," Beth exclaimed.

"Then will we finally meet your hubby?" Mela asked, feigning astonishment.

"He's golfing this weekend. I'm free."

Mela called to boost the reservation by two when Leslie showed no inclination to leave.

"I'll have y'all know I put the last stitch in this outfit tonight," AB announced, executing an end-of-runway spin in a body-hugging teal suit outside the Copper Door.

"Are you saying you made that?" Beth asked, touching a shoulder seam.

"Used to make all my clothes," AB said thoughtfully, turning back a cuff for Beth's inspection. "That old machine still sews."

"This is wizardry," Beth exclaimed. "Can I come watch?"

"Anytime," AB said. "I'd forgotten how much I enjoy sewing. It's meditative."

Feeling underdressed in jeans with a blazer over her sweater, Eli complimented Beth's short jacket over a silk chemise.

"It was a Christmas gift for someone," she answered. "I've lost enough weight lately that I can wear it."

"Quite a lot," Eli agreed, concerned but reluctant to spoil Beth's evening.

Mela's group arrived, and everyone went in, awed by the handsome, wood paneled interiors and enormous stone fireplace hand-crafted by the owner and chef. Despite their early reservation, the restaurant was soon fully seated.

"I saw your car at Ruth's house this afternoon," AB said to Mela, as the Tusquittee salads were served. "Didn't her daughter take her little dog, Phoebe, when Ruth moved to hospice?"

Mela rested her fork on the plate, trying not to tense as she looked at Leslie. "What were you doing there?"

"It was on my way to the grocery. Ruth was Mother's best friend, and I wanted to see her. Forgot you said she was gone." AB looked across at Mela who appeared rigid with stress.

Carly was primed to enjoy the evening. Her lace tank over a pencil skirt and stilettos turned heads as she made a late entrance. Her effervescent style continued to claim attention as the table of seven carried on together.

When Sophie was able to get a word in, she wanted to ask their waiter for a straw. Her mother refused, saying it wasn't appropriate.

"Or environmentally responsible," Carly admonished, leading Beth to search her purse and pull out a slim case.

"Why are you waving a tampon holder over the table?" Eli asked in a strained whisper.

"*Straaaws,*" Beth responded, flipping the lid and fanning the folded flexible tops. "You can't get the real deal anymore," she said, offering the multicolor selection to Sophie. "Remember to give it back," she added, waving an empty zip bag. "Gotta recycle."

As they were served, plate envy escalated until samples were swapped. A sliver of filet exchanged for a spoonful of creole, a taste of lamb for a pinch of crispy duck breast. And Sophie allowing Mela to try her vegan bowl after her aunt relinquished the last of the popovers.

In attempting to thank her newfound friends for dinner together, Carly became tearful, and Mela rose to comfort her.

"If you're going for the check," Leslie said, smirking, "don't bother. I've taken care of everything." Mela's first instinct was to verify she had her wallet, but she resolved not to make a scene.

Beth signaled chill. "We'll settle up at the lake tomorrow."

"Excuse me a sec," AB said, scooting her chair. "Need to call the Center. Don't cut that birthday cake."

After a bit of nonchalant searching, AB found the young manager whose grandfather was in the hospice center. "Lee," she confided, "although we barely know one another, I hope you'll trust me on a delicate matter that may border on—okay, that doesn't matter yet. You see, I'm having dinner with some friends, and there may be a problem." He instantly looked to her table, relieved to see peaceful diners.

"I believe one of our party has mistakenly handed our waiter the wrong credit card, trying to pay our bill. If you could, well—this should cover our evening," she implored, slipping a thick fold of cash in his hand as she spoke.

"I'm sensing this isn't the usual check skirmish. As it happens, Ms. Sutton," he continued, reaching into his chest pocket, "your server gave me this to hold, not comfortable carrying it around. Shall I return it to her?"

"May I see it first?" she asked.

He put it in her open hand. "Lee, has this already been run?"

"Not yet," he said, becoming more curious.

"Could you call the credit card company," AB requested, letting the card slip from her fingers to the ground, where he quickly retrieved it. "Tell them y'all found it on the floor, so it can be restored to the family of Ruth Banks?"

He looked at her, processing, then nodded. "We have a protocol for that. It happens. Enjoy the rest of your evening, Ms. Sutton. We will get that cake right out," he promised, adding, "Heather and I will be by to see Pops tomorrow."

She rested her hand briefly on his forearm and returned to her seat next to Mela at the table. "Don't you worry, doll," she whispered. "Problem solved. Finish those scallops so we can bring out the cake and give Miss Carly something else to squeal about."

⸺⊶⊷⸺

On Sunday evening, Mela was the last to arrive. The bonfire was a sight to behold, with flames streaming up through the pyramidal log pile, sending fine golden embers drifting to the stone floor. She plunked a beer beside her. Unusual for such a cold, clear afternoon, but especially so for Mela.

"Leslie driving her little sister to drink?" AB asked directly.

"She still claims she's broke. I give her money to go to the grocery, and she comes back with this," Mela answered, taking another slug. "Maybe drink some before she does.

"I was letting Sophie call her dad from my land line, and we found out Leslie had blocked her own and Soph's number from their home, blocked her entire family's phones on my line, and, oh yeah, that she was cheating on JT, again, while siphoning their savings, again, to pay her insane credit card bills. Again.

"He says he'll arrange for one more round of real rehab, but he wants Sophie home immediately," Mela concluded, pulling a tube of antihistamine cream from her pocket and applying it under her shirt.

"Allergies?" Eli inquired.

"I can develop severe reactions when overexposed to OPD," she responded, watching Leslie approach the fire.

"Opioids," Beth said, glancing at Leslie, aghast.

"Other People's Drama," Carly stage-whispered.

"I used sublingual drops for my allergies," Beth said, pushing a hefty branch into the burning logs, "but I don't think OPD is part of the testing."

Leslie nearly tumbled down the steps but staggered backward to the stone bench. "Two hotdogs, all the way, to go," she shouted, laughing hysterically.

"Where is Sophie?" Mela asked. "You know JT will pick her up soon."

"Music was too fucking loud in her room to hear me say it was time to eat. Snooze you lose."

"Way to raise your daughter," Mela muttered.

"Like you would know anything about kids," Leslie shot back. "If we're going there, Melly, I'll tell you now you're just a manipulative lamer living off Beau's success and our parents' fortune. You're nothing but a conniving *taker*."

"That's a whole lotta projection with a side of delusion," Mela said, standing to leave. "And in that respect, remarkably insightful, coming from a freeloading, self-serving, opportunistic liar."

"Yeah, sanctimonious little Melly. Always there for everybody and every crawling thing," Leslie shouted, enraged. "Why haven't you helped *me*? You should have done something to help me!"

"You *first*, Leslie. Show me you are ready to change—to make good things happen for you and maybe even your daughter—and I'm there with you all the way. But no, you expect a single-dose pill, a magic wand, something that takes the responsibility off you."

Desperate for a change of topic, Carly brought up the house fire in Young Harris where the entire family and pets had been rescued by volunteer firefighters. "God had his hand on that family," she professed.

"Oh, Carly," Beth said, a rant on the wing. "God decided those people rated being spared, but others who die in fires aren't on holy radar? One guy survives a deadly interstate pileup, and a bystander says, 'God chose to spare him.'

"C'mon, we see it all the time on the news. Like, 'The good lord was with us,' some homeowner says, in front of their intact home in a row of tornado-stripped foundations. It's self-congratulatory ignorance. If there's a loving, caring god out there, it's viciously arbitrary and pretty well concealed."

"I get where you're going," AB cautiously interjected. "We'd be foolish to suggest we know how this ol' universe works. Yet our Higher Power hasn't imbued us with any more compassion, greater forgiveness, or deeper understanding than Heaven has for each of us. On our best days, we can muster the tiniest fragments. Maybe that's why we're marooned on this planet. To work on that."

"Well, clearly there is some merit in the adage about fools and drunkards. Good night," Mela said. They watched her walking the shoreline, soon invisible in the twilight.

"We should call these Sunday gatherings our ash-it-out-sessions," AB suggested, switching to a seat near Leslie. "How about moving on to addictions? I'm pretty well versed on that. What do you imagine would be your ideal road to recovery, Ms. Leslie?"

A lifelong aversion to wading into any fray had kept Eli silent, and she regretted not coming to Mela's defense. She took off, catching her just past the dock, and walked along with her, sharing stories of her mother's stunts while on binges.

As she finished the one about her mother and her soccer coach, she was trying to make out a silhouette ahead—*a woman maybe?* Eli looked to see whether Mela had noticed, too, and saw Mela was staring open-mouthed at the floor-length Palladian window in her brilliantly lit upstairs guest room, as a slender form twirled on a bedpost that would pass in this instance for a stripper pole. It was Sophie.

Apparently nude eleven-year-old Sophie, executing something of a backspin finale. Mela was frozen in place until an eruption of cheers and whistles sounded from the boat launch across the cove. When Eli looked back from the whooping throng of teens, there was no way she could catch Mela, already at the terrace. Whoever was walking along the shore ahead of them had vanished.

⸻◆⸻

Mela didn't come by as expected to walk on that bright, clear Monday, so Eli kayaked around and came to the deck, knowing the alarm system would announce her arrival. A disheveled Mela in shorts and a tee appeared at the cracked door.

"What? They're both gone. Sophie home, and her mother to the Holiday Inn. Okay? 'Bye."

A 'Not coming today?' text?" Eli asked. "I just wanted to be sure you're okay, that's all," Eli said, feeling intrusive.

"I'm fine," Mela grumbled, slamming the door.

Eli climbed on the deck rail to remain visible if Mela was still in the sunroom. She felt more connected to her friend than she ever had to anyone, and she wasn't going to leave until Mela let her in on whatever this was. After an hour on the rail, her aching backside sent her over to the window. She cupped her hands around her eyes, shouting, "Tell me you can hear me. You don't have to talk."

"Oh my God, I hear you, Eli."

"I get how private you are, I do. But when you're in crisis, and you must be, you have to let me in on the battle. You lifted me when I wasn't functioning on any level, and I love you for that and will not let you—you're not there, are you?"

"I went right behind you," she said from a deck chair.

"So, was I another discarded pet you found, or are we real friends? You're such a loving, giving—"

"Beau's attorney left a message about a meeting Tuesday morning."

"Oh. Then if things are changing for you, if you'll need a place to live or..."

"When I found Astro with you that day, Eli, I think I saw myself in your situation. You, too, love someone who cannot reciprocate in the way you expected. The more people you're around, the quieter you get. Me, too. And you did have a faint resemblance to something that had been subsisting on the roadside—hiding, underfed, and wary. So, one-part rescue, two-parts empathetic connection.

"As for the attorney, he was left instructions to take action when it had been seven years since anyone had seen or heard from Beau. I'm expected to have him declared dead, Eli. Death in Absentia.

"I have loved him since I walked terrified into that classroom with hair that didn't look like any of the other girls, skin that wasn't white or black. Despite the kindness, I could see only the withering side-eye, some sneering kids, a rattled staffer," she recalled, dabbing her eyes with her t-shirt. "Another novel addition to the crazy campground family.

"That day, Beau Johnston pulled a chair next to him in the lunch-room, included me, buffered me until I could open my own heart and become a part of things. His is a true and loving spirit. He is my soul-mate from another sexual orientation.

"I kept his home and his life here waiting, as his lawfully endowed best friend. Did he go on with a new life? Forgot I was here, keeping it all safe for him? Now they want to declare him no longer in existence, and I cannot do that. I will call you when I can, Eli," she said, going through the kitchen door.

That last week in March, Mela didn't show up to walk and hadn't answered calls. The clinic said she was out with the flu. Her autoreply to texts was "unavailable."

On a Thursday morning, Eli walked the shore to her fence line, feebly whistled for Astro, and then hitched a pass through the property security by crouching close to him, holding his transmitting collar as they approached the house. She wriggled through the pet door after him. *Some security.*

She trailed him to the master bath and saw Mela bent forward, holding a large handgun with the barrel to her face. Mela, who hated the sight of a gun. Astro jumped on the wide marble seat and laid his head across her arm—close enough to snatch that gun. She took several quiet steps back through the hall and softly called Mela's name.

"Get out," Mela roared. "Leave me alone." She heard the gun slide on the marble bench as Astro whined. Mela's head was in her hands and pill bottles were staggered along the bench beside her. Eli came in, fear overtaking her, as she realized the depth of Mela's despair.

"I can't do this, what my brother did," she cried softly. "What would happen to my creatures? What would Sophie think?"

Eli started toward her friend but was knocked to the floor as Mela pushed past, running out of the room. Eli saw the gun was gone. The bedroom door slammed behind Mela and next, the door into the garage. Then an engine was revving, backing out as Eli pushed open the slow cranking bedroom window and squeezed through, already in a full run when she saw the SUV was coming fast. Momentum sent Eli tumbling across the cobblestones as the Expedition skidded over her.

"Oh my God," Mela screamed, sliding from the seat to look beneath the truck—giving Eli a chance to get help for her distraught friend.

"My head, oooow, Mela…"

Eli heard bare feet slapping down the driveway as Mela raced to the house for her phone. She painfully scooched between the front and rear tires, pulling up on the running board. Eli felt for the gun, then slung it deep into the shrubs, silently giving thanks for the extra ground clearance a vet needs to navigate pastures.

Some toes felt mangled, her left eye was swelling shut, and that plastic guard beneath the front bumper had peeled away some flesh. *No emergency,* She moved back to injured victim position, but if someone didn't kill the engine soon, those exhaust pipes would create a problem.

Minutes after the paramedics arrived, AB had responded to the sirens. With savvy medical personnel attending to her wounds, Eli had to admit her eye was the only head injury, she hadn't lost consciousness, and both battered toes wiggled. A silly mishap that she hoped wouldn't make the newspaper's response report. As the EMS bus left, AB demanded answers.

"I was coming to see what was keeping Mela from walking this week," Eli responded, "and Mela was leaving in a hurry. Boom."

AB looked at Mela, expecting a better answer, and saw the more wounded party of these two, arms wrapped and rocking. "I have an appointment in Blue Ridge. Do I need to cart you two with me?" AB threatened.

"I'm done with everything," Mela admitted. "All I'm good for is taking care of people, animals, and I'm done. I'm empty. Tired and empty."

"You haven't slept since your muddled sister arrived," AB reminded her. "Go sleep. I'll be back this afternoon with something irresistible from Harvest on Main. You up to sitting on her, Eli? Propping that foot and sticking around until I get back? Can I get an amen?"

"I'm keeping my good eye on you," Eli warned, carrying one shoe.

"I'm so sorry, Eli. I'm losing my mind. I was looking through Beau's things and found the unlocked gun box. I'm so tired, it seemed he was giving me a way out. I thought I'd killed you," Mela apologized, trembling. Together they hobbled inside. When AB returned, Eli would get the gun to Mac for safekeeping.

Chapter 10

When Your *That'll Be the Day* Dawns

B y Sunday, Eli was able to walk with a boot AB had brought back from Blue Ridge—along with those box lunches from Harvest: their superb barbecue sandwich for Mela, and Eli's favorite Blue Ridge Hot-Brown with a side of mac and cheese.

AB waited at the driveway for Mela every morning that week, affording them a private chat before meeting up. AB confessed that she had checked on her sister at the motel and brought Leslie to her home, where AB could nudge her to contemplate the freedom of sobriety.

Eli offered to bring a stash of Kobe beef hotdogs from Bitter Creek Market with a slew of gourmet sides if they could use AB's place for another Sunday cookout. Seemed everyone was ready for an Ash-It-Out do-over.

The forecast called for evening thunderstorms, moving the cook-out to early afternoon. AB used her Kaw to ferry supplies and Eli to the lakeside terrace while Carly stoked the fire on this already cloudy, warm afternoon. Beth and Mela were at the dock, determining whether it was stable enough to moor Beau's sailboat. Beth spotted someone walking in their direction close to the trees along the shore.

"Here comes that lady who strolls by every evening." Mela reached for her jacket on the dock rail to get a quick look and wondered whether it was the person she had noticed minutes before the Sophie show that night. "You know, Beth, I think—"

A lightning blast burst from darker clouds over mountains to the west, striking directly across the lake.

"Look out," the beach walker shrieked, frantically running in their direction. She was beyond the trees when a second strike lit the air, shattering a tall pine as Beth and Mela waved the woman to join them on their run to the house.

With a tablecloth load of supplies in back, AB and Eli ignored the path and drove behind Carly as rain pounded. When they reached the deck, Leslie was watching it all unfold through the window, sipping what might have been coffee—or whiskey—in that teacup.

Inside the screened porch on the deck, AB was holding the door as Carly helped Eli in, trailed by Beth and a familiar face ahead of Mela at the rear. "Well, hello, Bern. Where did you come from?" AB asked, patting the newcomer with one of the dishtowels she was handing out. "Ladies," AB announced, "this is Bernie Carter, a friend and valued volunteer at the hospice."

Bernie peeked over the towel as she dried, twiddling fingers at the group when Beth added, "Better known as Bernadette Montgomery. Don't y'all recognize her? Everyone dreams of getting a reading with her. Montgomery Medium?" she coached.

"Accused of fraud, TV show canceled," Bernie recited, "and gone from the stadium circuit four years ago, so, *no*, nobody knows me now."

"Hey, *I* didn't say it," Leslie remarked.

"Sorry about the intrusion," Bernie said, blotting her wet clothes. "And," she added, looking apologetically at AB, "I'm very sorry I hid that I'm your neighbor, but not being recognized has its upsides."

"Well, without your wigs—"

Eli jabbed Beth in the back with a mustard bottle. "Ow, what?" Beth yelled. "I have wigs."

"I must confess," Bernie said apprehensively, "before I bought the property at the end of the road here, I was in an awfully paranoid place and, well, there were some backgrounds done. As wrong as that was, and I do so apologize—*with the exception of the Fowlers*—my neighbors are people I wanted to somehow get to know.

"Especially you, AB. Your energy is that of an extraordinary healer. And you, over there with the weaponized mustard, you have been lighting up my idled radar for two months now."

"Late arrival," Beth noted, thumbing Eli's way.

"Now, Mother Nature here," Bernie said, stroking Mela's arm, "there's a fella who has come to you in dreams. He's told you that he is in glorious peace, and you still have times you think you see him. He's had me strolling this lakefront, waiting for the opportunity to tell you how much he loves and appreciates you. He's smiling, knowing your life is finally about to begin.

"As for this bundle of shame and regret behind me," she said, turning to face Leslie as thunder rumbled, "the path you're on is short. Ms. Sutton here has pointed out a different path to you. One that you'd have to climb, not continue to slide down. Your body needs help. Heaven has renewal and joy in store for you.

"And while I'm on a roll, Miss Sunshine over there," Bernie continued, jutting her chin in Carly's direction. "Your light is so much brighter than you allow your friends to see," she observed, tilting her head from side to side. "You're too much for the average Joe, so keep right on growing that sweet soul. A man can wait.

"Ahhh, you," she said to Beth, pointing a spiraling finger her way. "You will soon have to rev—" White-gold light blinded them all, and then the room went dark as the thunderous blast subsided, reverberating across the lake basin.

"Storms are so weird in these mountains," Eli whispered in the dark. "Thunder sounds super deep, like an avalanche echoing through the ranges."

"Bernie Carter," AB called out, "you better not disappear before the lights come back on. Just don't."

"You do that?" Carly asked, shining her flashlight on the floor beneath them.

"Are you some kind of survivalist?" Beth demanded of Carly. "You're the only person I know who carries around more crap than me."

Lights flashed on again and stayed. "This stove is propane," AB stated, raising the flame on a burner. "So even if the power goes again, we can get these uber-weenies roasting."

"Do you think it says anything about us, that we're fond of roasting wieners?" Eli whispered to her host.

"Henceforth, I shall only refer to the main course of our Sunday roasts as frankfurters." AB laughed as she continued. "My personal impression is that we are a demonstrably weenie-friendly assembly, but not without significant individual issues in other matters. Roast in peace."

Bernie took a chair next to Leslie, and Beth moved beside her. "If you have information for me," Beth requested, "well, I'm a very private person, you know?"

"Oh, honey," Bernie assured her. "I *do* see that."

"AB, do you know how old this house is?" Eli asked. "If it was built by our common ancestor, it may be older than the cabin inside my place."

"Not sure. You want to take that?" AB asked Bernie, who waved her off.

"The newest part of my house is the spa pool that looks like a garage from the front. That was put in late in the last millennium, while Mela's place was under construction. Called the number on the truck, they put in my own little water park. Best thing I ever did for myself after getting sober."

"Nothing else in this place has changed since the 1950s," Leslie commented.

"My God, Leslie," Mela started.

"Uh-uh, girls," AB said, squelching the spat, then thumping her new coffee maker. "It hasn't been that long. But not much has changed in over forty years. It is due for some fixin' up. You girls have got me thinking about that."

"Filling a twenty-yard dumpster would be a good start," Leslie said, doubling down.

"Gimmie that cup," AB demanded, taking a sniff. "Huh, must be a touch of alcohol dementia. Maybe a dry-drunk thing," she said, glaring at Leslie.

"That's your professional opinion, addictions counselor, nurse practitioner, psychologist?"

"That's my version of the *ungrateful house guest, three-day-old fish* analogy. And keep your nose out of my office."

"Now, I'm hearing mention of interest in my passion," Beth said. "Interior *re*-design. Are you serious, AB?"

"As an alcohol addiction," she shot back, throwing a look at Leslie. "Where do we begin?"

"At Fancy This, her shop in Hiawassee," Eli suggested. "Beth transformed the house I'm in. Come see it, AB."

Long after the storm had passed, they were all, even Leslie, wandering from room to room suggesting use changes, fresh colors, and lighting ideas to AB.

"This energy I'm feeling," Bernie stopped the chatter to tell them, "is positively therapeutic. Y'all have something remarkable going on here that I would love to be a part of, if you're accepting new members."

"They have to," Leslie gloated, less menacingly. "It's part of *their* healing."

Bernie was waiting at the gate Monday morning, ready to walk, when she noticed AB collecting fallen limbs in the woods along her driveway. "What? Do you run on batteries or something?" she asked.

"Not yet. I prefer last shift hours, sometimes drop in on the weekends," AB responded. "I would say that it's because I can get more work done, but your busybody intuition has likely already told you I've lived a bat life to hide from the world."

"Ah, the lady knows more than she lets on," Bernie countered.

"Have to admit, I knew who you were when you volunteered. Didn't know you were my neighbor, though. Your show got me through some dark times. If you wanted to be just Bernie Carter, that worked."

"I am Bernie Carter. I'm from Montgomery, Alabama. Grandmama used to refer to me as Montgomery Bernie because we had so many Bernadette namesakes in the family, and that's where my branch settled.

"AB, when your neighbor's brother started bothering me about convincing her he's at peace, well, that was the first I'd heard from the other side since before things fell apart for me. The little screen in my mind," she said, swinging a finger across her eyes like a windshield wiper, "had been blank."

➤◆◀

April was well underway. The wild azaleas and Carolina Silverbells, local harbingers of spring in the mountains, were dropping their blooms for budding leaves. By this time, Eli's toes allowed her to rejoin sections of the morning walks.

Trees were greening around the lakes, and the walkers had already reduced their adventures list by a weekend class at JCC, a visit to the casino in Cherokee, and a Saturday shopping in Asheville's art district. On this Wednesday, Eli would be making the first trip to see Lewis since her foot injury. She was dreading the long halls at the Shepherd Center.

As she left the elevator, Eli could hear Lew's laughter, and from his side, it sounded like a very upbeat conversation with his son John. She waited outside his room until the call ended, smiling as Lew continued to chuckle to himself.

"Someone's having a good morning" she said, kissing his cheek and handing off his box of brownies.

"I have missed that face, and Melissa's momma's recipe," he told her, as she went to the chair already moved next to his bed.

"I'm not your first visitor today?" she inquired, hands on her hips.

"You just missed Ted," he said quickly. She glanced at the door but squared her shoulders and asked whether it had been a good visit, and why Wednesday.

"He's doing really well," Lew answered emphatically. "Ted came by on his way to catch a flight. Imagine, Ted skipping the Wednesday staff meeting, not taking the first flight of the morning. He sat right there, talking." Lew vigorously pointed at her chair. "He even made a joke. He has seemed more relaxed lately, but this is a very different guy."

"Being with Hannah is good for Ted," Eli observed solemnly. "Pete has mentioned Ted being lighter, too."

"On to other news," Lew said, reaching for her hand. "I've got my paperwork in for Watkins Glen. Hotel reservations made. If you miss your old racing team, you're welcome to join us."

"There's a book launch event then," she replied, immediately regretting the lie to avoid Ted.

"I wondered how that was going," he said, noticing her drift as she lost her concentration looking in his exquisitely kind eyes.

"Daydreaming about your Hollywood friends?" he probed.

"Just appreciating good people in my life," she confided.

"Enough socializing, young man," Lew's therapist announced, backing the wheelchair alongside his bed. "Time to work."

"Me, too. Love you, Lew," she whispered in a quick embrace once he was ready to roll.

They went right, in the direction of the ambulatory therapy rooms, as Eli turned left for the elevators. Then she backtracked to leave a note on his pillow. "On second thought," she wrote, "making my reservations for Watkins Glen."

Eli folded her notepad, tucking it into her purse as she stepped into the doorway. She smacked face first into a dress shirt with a scent that incapacitated her mind as the shirt's arms caught her body.

"Pardon me," Eli stammered, still mashed to this chest, and trying to sidestep the person without looking at certainly the chief of rehab or a visiting Waller Analytics exec.

"Hey, what is your problem?" she heard Ted react.

Ha! Same old Ted, the senior voice in her head heralded. He had a solid grip on her upper arms, as that intoxicating familiarity morphed into a cloud of unpleasant memories.

"It's you," he said, releasing her. "What the hell happened to your hair?"

No flash of fleeting fondness on his part, she alliterated, swirling away down the hall in her mind.

"I came to visit Lew," she said.

"He has therapy."

"I know, he just left. Okay, say hi to Pete for me," she murmured, attempting long, hobbling strides in her escape.

She heard his footsteps behind her and turned to face him, triggering yet another Eli-at-fault collision as he arched and spun to avoid flattening her. He then tugged his jacket back in place and walked ahead, punching the elevator button as the doors opened.

"Are you coming?" he said, sodden with condescension.

"Thanks, no. I'm all about stairs these days," she replied, darting out the fire door to the landing. She scrounged through her jacket pockets for a tissue, confused by the hot tears bubbling down her cheeks.

The closing door flew open as the guttural "Eli!" that had always signaled his extreme frustration with her blasted into the stairwell.

He can't do this to me anymore, she remembered, collecting herself to fend off the barrage of insults he was preparing.

"What did I do now?" he asked in an exasperated but softer tone. "What are you sad about?"

"Nothing," she whispered, disarmed by his gentle interest. "I've had a few rough weeks and a lot going on, but you have no part in it. I am not sad, just unnerved." She studied him, and saw nothing to suggest vindictiveness, satisfaction with her difficulties, or any sort of curiosity about her that would warrant surveillance.

"All right," he said. Still, he remained in his wide stance, hands in pockets, as though he were giving a troublesome race car engine the once over.

"Do you need help?"

This Ted was *new*. She was getting a peek at the happy-with-Hannah version.

"No, thanks. Don't you have a flight to catch?"

"Eli, if you're embarrassed about those texts, forget it."

"What texts?"

"Oh, c'mon."

"I do not know what you're talking about, Ted. You have received *nothing* from me since we met with the attorneys before the divorce. And I don't need any more photos of you on your boat 'loving life.' Maybe," she instantly regretted saying, "it was one of your girlfriends."

"I haven't sent you any pictures, and I would never say that," he answered crisply. "Remember, you left me."

"There's a reason we divorced. We never fit. You found me deficient in every way. Let's continue to avoid run-ins like this. You're doing well, and you're with someone. I've made new friends, my work is fulfilling, and I plan to be settled and successful soon."

Ted was looking away, his jaw tight, when she spoke those last words. Then he drawled, "Yeah, that'll be the da—"

A ferocious smack and her stinging hand confirmed she had slapped him, hard. Their eyes locked, both expressions registering that something unthinkable had happened.

Eli skittered down the stairs, hopping with the injured foot, fleeing to the mountains. If he disliked her before, he surely hated the new and improved Eli. Neither of them had ever resorted to violence, until this.

Ted hadn't moved from the spot, perhaps considering why, of all the remarks he could have made, he'd chosen to repeat the very words that ignited their breakup.

———◆———

That evening, another snow fell. This one light and fragile at thirty degrees, meaning the walk was on despite a restless night for Eli. Ted's understandable charges would surely kill the book before a new contract was signed.

"Leslie," Carly called, as she approached the group on the road ahead. "What brings you out?"

"AB," she groaned. "It sure isn't the coffee." Beth and Bernie were renegotiating the conversational no-fly to include weight, irregular bodily functions, and all dessert items to the existing list of politics, social media, religion, kids, money, and grandkids.

"I'd like to also nominate tabloid stories," Bernie said, warily adding, "and the suspicious demise of anyone who contributes to them."

"Here's another item for the taboo topics list, in case I am suddenly nowhere to be found," Eli groggily announced. "Hadn't heard from the ex until we literally ran into each other at the Shepherd Center yesterday. I assaulted him five minutes in, and then hightailed it back here to await apprehension. Nothing yet," she said, forcing a smile.

"You're extraordinarily reserved for someone who is so often evading arrest," Mela remarked, grabbing her collar from behind.

"That has to be consensual, doesn't it? I mean, a *guy*?" Beth said, with a dubious head jiggle.

"I *slapped* him, Beth," she said. "Not a sexual assault. Stop watching those smarmy dating shows."

"I watch *ID TV* mostly, and I've learned *so* much."

Carly shuddered. "Those shows give me nightmares."

"Now that Pete's working for Ted," Eli said, "and planning a late June wedding—unless I'm incarcerated by then—it could get weird."

"I have to know." AB tiptoed in on the subject. "What did he do to get slapped? Because I've tried counting the many buttons in your firing sequence. I stopped at like a hundred."

"He said something," Eli answered reluctantly. "It's just a phrase, a dumb nothing. My mother used to say it when I would mention anything I wanted to be, to have, or to do. She'd say it to shut me down."

"And that was? Because we sure don't want to accidentally…"

"She would say, 'That'll be the day.' And after I screwed up and told Ted about her using it that way, he did the same."

"Well, now," AB said, smiling at her wounded friend, "I'd say that's an old reaction you can modify, and those silly words could eventually make you laugh."

"Oh my gawd." Leslie's voice carried from the rear. "That was almost touching."

Chapter 11

Who Are You Calling Fubsy?

"Four bags for three days, Carly?" Eli counted, shoving the last behind the seats of her Sport.

"There's no room in Beth's car. The back is packed with 'for sale' signs and boxes. All the deflated tubes are piled behind my seat."

"Even with Leslie backing out this weekend, we're still needing space for six," Mela noted, eyeing Beth's blocked back windows. "Beth, let's take mine, more room," Mela pleaded.

"Oh, I'm one of those people who has to drive. We'll fit."

Eli's phone rang through Bluetooth in the car. "I got it," Carly yelled, hopping in and clicking on the call. "Eli Sledge's phone. May I help you?"

"Carly, no," Eli had shouted, a second too late.

"Yes. This is David Harrison. I wonder if I could speak with Ms. Sledge?"

"That's David Harrison," Bernie stage-whispered to AB, shoving her sideways in disbelief.

"Hello, yes, this is Eli. Go ahead," she answered through the open window as though she were on two-way radio.

"We finally have that new contract, Eli, printing now. I'd rather messenger your copy than transmit electronically, if that's acceptable."

"I'm okay with anything, as long as it gets me back to work on the book. What's next?"

"Are you in Atlanta today by chance? I'm at a law firm in Midtown."

"I could be," she answered, over a jointly mewed "no" in the background.

"Sounds like that would require a change in plans. May I ask where you'll be this afternoon?"

"Well, Chimney Rock was the plan."

"I was on location there once," he commented. "A very beautiful area."

"Holy smokes," Beth shrieked, earning a pop on the arm from Eli. "*Dirty Dancing?*"

"A while before that," he said, laughing.

"Could I meet you there for dinner?" he asked. "I'd like to point out a few clauses."

"He wants to meet us for dinner." Bernie stifled her exclamation, swinging again for AB, who jumped clear in time.

"We're staying at the Lodge on Lake Lure," she said, scanning her phone as suggestions filled the air.

"La Strada," Carly shouted, scrolling websites.

"Ooo, Esmeralda," Bernie added, as Eli cooled their enthusiasm with a steely glare before finishing her sentence, "and I think it has a restaurant. Yes. Treetops."

"Sounds like we may need an event space. Ida will be sorry she missed this."

"You'd be driving all night, Mr. Harrison. And I can be in Atlanta by noon," she said, an upright index finger raised at arm's length shushing her audience—who all responded with a different finger, upright at arm's length. He was already relaying the information to someone who advised him his 407GXP would be waiting.

"If there's a veranda, I'll be on it when you arrive. And if you'll all join me for a late lunch or an early dinner, I'll still be home by evening. Please remember, everyone calls me David. Does that work for you?"

Subdued cheers on Eli's end had the Harrison team chuckling. "Sounds like it does," Eli confirmed. "See you there in three hours."

"He's got a helo," Carly squealed, popping open Eli's lift gate.

"What makes you think that?" Mela asked.

"That bird is a Bell model," she answered, rooting through a stack of luggage. "Probably an executive service. Maybe he owns it."

"Is that a private jet or what?" Beth asked.

"A bird, you know, helicopter. Just as nice and more agile than a jet. I know that like I know this is Range Rover's Sport SVR," Carly opined, tugging on her luggage. "I looked it up after we went to Atlanta. Did y'all notice all this carbon fiber trim? What's your paint color, Eli?"

"Racing red. What are you doing with your bags?"

"We're meeting *David*, and for sure his hot security guys again. I need to repack."

"Uh-uh," AB said, pulling her away from the bags. "We're leaving now, as is."

"I need shotgun on these mountain roads," Carly announced, "or I'll be carsick."

"Me, too," Bernie countered, "and my purse is camped on my spot in the Sport."

"C'mon," Beth called from the old Mercedes, as she inched along the driveway, waiting for Carly to hop in. "One hundred thirty-one miles," Beth reported, whacking the GPS plugged into her console from the dash.

"Wake me up when we can see Chimney Rock," Carly requested, leaning against her purse as a pillow.

"Oh my," Eli sighed, watching Beth turn to Hiawassee instead of heading up through Franklin to Asheville for a mostly four-lane trip. "We're going the scenic route."

"What, where?" Mela wondered aloud.

"Highlands, Cashiers, Sapphire, and Brevard," AB informed her. "Lean back in this luxury craft and have yourself a beauty snooze. I am."

"What I missed sneaking past you people, coming and going," Bernie lamented. "Okay to recline, AB?"

"Go for it. Not you, Eli. Wide awake, child. Unbelievable, this back seat reclines, too."

"So would mine," Mela said from her cockpit-like headrest, "if Carly hadn't stacked her entire wardrobe behind it."

<hr />

In under three hours, they were in front of the Lodge. "I'll sign in and and find out where we go," Eli suggested, as she passed Beth's window on the way in to check-in. "There are six of us in two rooms, so we'll need a couple of rollaways. I'll be right back."

When she returned, her wild expression suggested she was sneaking out with the cash register under her shirt. "We've been upgraded to the lake house for our stay—the entire lake house to ourselves," she raved, perhaps thinking her robotic rigidity looked relaxed and natural from the hotel desk inside.

"How so?" AB inquired, sounding suspicious of a mega bill arriving at check-out. "I see lots of cars out here. First weekend in May and lovely weather. They're not hurting for business."

The answer came from the balcony behind Eli. "I took the liberty of securing the lake house," David explained. "Eli, if you'll join me here in the conference room when it's convenient? And we'll all have that late lunch afterward."

"Oh, this is sweet," Bernie declared, sitting on a queen bed that had a wide view of the lake. "Y'all, I can't believe he didn't recognize me," Bernie added, a little put out. "I should have brought a wig. People need to see I'm enjoying my life." She went to a dresser mirror, lifting her chin and inspecting her profile. "It's my hair," she decided. "I look like an American Girl doll with it pulled back like this. I need my volume."

"Well, I'm ready for that lunch," AB announced, looking for validation.

"I'm hurrying," Eli said, changing into a fresh blouse and smoothing her slacks as she left.

"I am so very glad to begin again on this project," David said, walking her to the conference table, his arm across her shoulder. "Ida and I have grown extremely fond of you, Eli.

"That slowed the contract rewrite as we severed ties with the Wright Agency and substantially revised your compensation. In addition to your fee, we increased your percentage of sales as well, with the rest distributed to benefit the same institutions as were previously named in the contract."

"That's extremely generous, Mr. Harrison, but I wouldn't want to diminish your gifts to the organizations set to benefit from the book. It's back to a skeletal stage, not looking anything like a juggernaut so far."

"That's the other thing we need to discuss, he said, turning his chair to speak more confidentially. Ida insists you tell our whole story, including the sordid aspects about her sister and my father. She thinks someone might remember seeing them, know something that could bring her sister home."

"And Marc? Does he know?"

"Yes, Marc knows. He says it explains everything—everything being his notion that he was always a second-class member of the family. His sense of compensation due, however, has burgeoned with the revelation. Ida says he'll come around in time."

"We should plan to work closely as we weave these elements into your story," Eli advised. "Leaks would be disastrous out of context. And I think Mrs. Harrison, I'm sorry, *Ida*, is right. It could bring answers you wouldn't have gotten otherwise."

"We'll decide as we go. And I have no interest in a launch party in LA, but Molly has superb ideas on these things. Now, if you'll take that contract for review and let me know when it's ready to return, I'll have someone from the firm pick it up."

"You have read it through?" she asked.

"Every line, every word."

"I hope you won't be disappointed in my discernment if I sign it now and return it to you. I wouldn't be taking it to an attorney. I have no doubt that when I read through my copy, it will be more than I ever expected. If I'm indentured for life, that's a perk."

She signed every flagged line and left it on his briefcase as she separated her copy from the stack of documents.

"You certainly feel like family." He laughed, giving her that you-are-loved hug, always with his chin resting atop her head.

David knocked on a door at the back of the room, and as Eli hit "send" on her text to the girls, platters of appetizers were coming in with the menus. When her friends arrived minutes later, David seated them. "This conference room doesn't have the lovely views the dining room has," David told them, "but you won't be all over social media before dessert is served."

"Aw." Carly pretended to pout.

"Huh, the way people have looked at me, I know I'm lighting up the 'Gram right now," Bernie confided in AB.

David cautioned his two-man security team as they took seats at the table. "Bret, Paul—keep an eye on this one, fellas," he said, playfully pointing a finger over Carly's head.

"All right," Carly cooed, sitting erect and shaking her lustrous hair as she batted those fern green eyes in their direction.

After a lovely lunch that included pitcher cocktails, Carly was the last to leave, slowing in front of Bret to ask, "Do you ever get time off for being such a good boy?"

"Sometimes," he responded. "And do your friends really buy this character you're playing?"

"That's no way to talk to Mr. Harrison's guest, Bret."

"We don't usually have to worry about his guests carrying, Ms. Lane. That's no standard issue Sig 229 in your uh," he squinted quickly into her cleavage, "holster, there. I'm guessing a Bodyguard?"

"Ruger LCP II, smart ass. Couldn't leave it in my room. If you know what I was issued, then you know I'm on short notice, so lighten up and keep your mouth shut?"

"I'll just say there's nothing concealed about your carry, ma'am."

"You don't have anything else to say to me?" she whispered, drawing his hands from behind his back before she reached to smooth his collar and let her hand slide.

"Permission to meet you for a drink if I can make it back here tomorrow night?"

"How do I let you know if I have to leave before then?"

"You'll have my number, ma'am. Collected yours when Ms. Parker confiscated phones at the cookout."

"Looking forward to tomorrow night then, Bret."

—◆—

That afternoon, Mela, Bernie, and AB were on the lake house deck, watching Beth glide her drone to capture Carly and Eli paddle boarding.

"That looks fun," AB commented. "We should buy a couple of those when we get home."

"There are two in the storage room at my barn," Mela said. "Girl, I can't wait to see you splashing around."

"They aren't splashing," AB noticed, lifting her sunglasses to be sure.

"There will be splashing." Bernie laughed at the prospect.

Three sharp knocks sat them up in their deck chairs, and sent Mela scrambling to the door.

"Heeey," Leslie said, standing behind her daughter in the doorway. "I'm not lying. Sophie really wanted to be with you this weekend."

"I do, Aunt Mel. Your squad is trill."

"That's a compliment," Leslie said, as she took in the quarters. "Damn, I thought I'd have to get a room. Could we sleep on the couches?"

"I think they make into beds," Mela said, checking out Sophie's crop top. "Want something to eat, Soph? Three trays of delicious stuff in the fridge. Trout cakes?" Mela winked as Sophie gave her an over-the-shoulder eyeroll.

"You're just in time," AB said. "Carly wants to do one of our fire-side questions this evening, and I want to get to bed. What's our question?" she called to Carly, as they came in from paddle boarding.

"What's something weird about you that no one knows?" she answered, walking out to the deck to eat a dessert with Sophie. "I'll start—I have a double uterus."

"Probably runs in your family," AB replied. "I'll go next. Before I got to know y'all, the only place I've been in town since the early eighties is the quick-mart at the corner. Thank you, ladies."

"This is weird," Eli said, self-consciously. "When I'm having an extended phone conversation, I'm horrified to find myself, not mimicking, but reflecting the other person's speech patterns, sometimes their accent."

"Hadn't noticed that," Mela said, "but I may have you beat. I have no memories from before I came to Hiawassee—before the Orrs adopted me. I was six. Crazy or what?"

"I'm calling the last two a wicked tie," AB responded, gagging on her chamomile tea, and shaking her head.

"I guess, mine is that I have no next of kin," Beth said, faraway.

"B," Eli called, clapping her hands to break the spell. "What? Husband, kids?"

"Yeah, I don't know what I was thinking. Leslie, whatcha got?"

"Wouldn't be something nobody knows if I told."

"I'm drawing a blank," Bernie said. "Give me another question."

"Okay, I have one," Beth responded. "But first, I'm wondering if we could try to sort of inoculate our connectedness against political clashes. We have hit on religion plenty of times; money comes up with no problems so far. I never want to have a loss over politics again. It still hurts. So, can I suggest something? Maybe we could relax our rules a little?"

"Maybe we could bring a bobcat and a squirrel to dinner, but should we?" AB countered.

"What do you have in mind?" Mela asked, clearly concerned. "Close families are struggling with political division right now. I do not talk politics with anyone if I can escape it."

"Let's write one line," Beth said, bringing Bernie a note pad, a pen, and a bowl, "about your political viewpoint, fold it, put it in the bowl, and pass it along. Then we read them, guess whose they are, the air is clear."

"Have you taken up drinking?" AB asked, incredulous. "There are eight of us here and only three rides home."

"Then you read them all first and decide what's next."

When Beth handed AB the bowl, she was slow to take it and reluctant to add her own. After she read through them, she removed her glasses. "Nope, this ain't right. Let's just keep going down the double yellow line in our road."

"It will be okay, honey." Bernie nodded.

"Hey, let's write down our guesses, too, about who wrote what," Beth said, passing out sticky squares and pens from the drawer.

Leslie snickered. "This would make a helluva drinking game."

"I hope there's no one intending to stake out any high ground tonight," AB said. "Not one of us has shown an inclination to ridicule or shame others because they hold a different point of view. My wish for us all is the illuminating gift of thinking for ourselves—each investigating without bias what we espouse as true."

"First one," AB said quickly, "says 'I believe in personal freedom,' and it's *signed*, but I'll omit that.

"Number two, 'Nobody tells me how to vote.' There's a mystery.

"Three, 'Without a well-equipped military, we're doomed.' Isn't this fun?

"Four, 'I support candidates, not parties.' Now we're getting somewhere.

"Five, 'Why couldn't he have three terms?' He who? Several possibilities.

"Six, 'It's important that we have a strong economy.' Yep.

"And seven: 'I'm not registered to vote.' That's it."

A rumble of disbelief swept the room after the final response as the who-wrote-it stickies were handed to Beth, who tallied the results.

"We have four votes for Eli as the author of the 'personal freedom' statement," Beth began.

"Nope, not me."

"Number two, 'nobody tells me,' gets five votes for Leslie."

"Ha, no."

"Three, 'our military,' goes to Mela."

"That would be Mac's answer. Try again."

"Four, 'candidates,' is attributed to AB."

"No ma'am, not me."

"Five, everyone wrote in Bernie. But then you quote our former president all the time, so…"

"Seriously, is there anyone here who doesn't agree with that?" Bernie asked.

"Six, the 'strong economy,' y'all thought was me," Beth said, "but I'm the believer in supporting our military."

"And seven is a strong showing for Carly."

"For real? Y'all think I don't vote? I'm so hurt! I said we need a strong economy."

"Enough, this is excruciating," AB groaned. "I'm the one who's not registered. I gave up voting because I wasn't going in that polling place just so those old gossiping biddies at the desk could turn up their noses at me."

"I'm one of those old biddies," Mela said softly. "I take off every election day to work the polls. I would have given you an 'I Voted' sticker. And hey, how come I got the military nod?" Mela said a little louder. "Why wasn't I picked for the 'strong economy' remark? Although it's true, I *always* vote for candidates, not parties."

"I think I'm the only one here with a master's in economics from Columbia," Bernie huffed.

"Can we discuss this?" Beth said, oblivious to rising tensions.

"Ya get two minutes," AB said, glaring at her. "Let's be sure to keep this light and neutral. Don't say anything you don't want to have to wear on a t-shirt to the grocery every Saturday for the next year, and I mean it. Hand printed."

"I don't wear clingy stuff," Beth objected. "And that's shaming."

"One minute, forty-five seconds."

The evening ended peacefully, with agreements made to respectfully see things differently, as everyone was tired and rough weather was closing in.

Having breakfast on the Treetops deck won out over cooking their own after a loud, stormy night. As they waited for their orders to arrive, Carly reviewed the river tubing run from start to finish.

"I did this route all summer as a kid," Carly assured them. "We'll put in a little below where my grandparents lived on the Broad River."

Over breakfast, Carly shared some history of the lake area, along with exploits while spending summers with her grandparents until she finished high school. In the middle of her lost virginity story, Mela sailed a half-eaten piece of toast her way. "Don't spend much time around kids?"

"Aaah, don't worry," Leslie assured her. "Soph knows what goes on."

"Let's get to the river," Carly said, as the plates were removed. "Wear your water shoes if you've got them or sneakers. It should be a wild ride after all that rain last night."

"Wait, what?" AB asked, alarmed. "I brought sandals. I am not here to remake *Deliverance*."

"It's the weekend, so there won't be water releases upriver. It'll be fun."

"We should have brought wet suits," Bernie muttered. "All that cold rainwater coming off those mountains. "Y'all don't mind my rolled-up jeans."

Sophie was behind her mother's car door as Mela carried out a cooler and placed it in the cargo area. "Do I recognize the costume you're wearing?" Mela asked, raising the side of Sophie's long t-shirt.

"I told you, it's a swim tank," the girl grumbled, "and I won't wear it at your house anymore. Hop off!"

"We both know that's the flesh suit you wore those nights you were dancing in my window for boys at the boat ramp. And unless you're determined to attract creeps, you should lose it. Permanently."

Sophie jumped in and slammed the door.

Unloading at the first bridge, Mela was relieved to see Carly connecting a small air compressor to the socket inside Leslie's cargo area.

Sophie was helping, with shorts under her tee and wearing tennis shoes. "Your smarts are showing," Mela whispered to the girl, with a kiss on the forehead.

Tubes were soon fat and ready to go, with Carly demonstrating the preferred launch method of standing in knee deep water and aligning one's tush above the center of the tube before falling backwards into the current. "Use your feet to push away from fallen trees, rocks, or anything you don't want to crash into along the way."

Leslie was nowhere to be seen until Eli noticed her beyond the cars, hiking a swig from a thermos. Beth missed the demonstration, too, preoccupied with filling her tube from a canister at the back of her car.

"What did you put in that tube, flat-tire-fix?" Mela asked, giving it a pat. "You'll sink like a rock."

"That won't be the problem," Beth answered, the giant tube flipping as she steadied it to lower her backside into the high floating ring.

"What's in that thing, hot air? Car exhaust?" Carly said, feeling the surface of the oversized tube.

"Open house balloon filler," Beth admitted, swirling away from the riverbank.

"Ha, won't make a bit of difference." Mela laughed. "Science is not on your side."

"Helium?" Carly fumed. "O-M-G, it's disappearing from the earth and you filled your river tube with it?"

"Is the whole can in that thing?" Sophie scowled, shooting ahead of Beth in the current.

"Two," Beth whispered, a finger against her lips. "And it can still go in the balloons, but I should switch to flag banners, I guess."

The rest of the tubing crew pushed off, Carly sporting a backpack with waterproof compartments carrying phones and keys. "Awful lot of eggs in that basket," AB observed.

"Awful lot of ass in that tube," Leslie scoffed, watching Beth, but from a little too close to Bernie.

"Who are you calling fubsy?" Bernie demanded, kicking Leslie's tube nearly out from under her. "Want to start some personal dialogue? Shall we start with Leslie?"

Mela caught a glimpse of Sophie's t-shirt peeling off and being tucked behind her back. With her shorts invisible inside the tube, flesh-suited Sophie got a few honks from cars on the road along the river before Mela caught up with her. "Put your smarts back on, Sophie, now!"

"Oh, this sun feels so nice. I've dreaded May ever since I can remember, but this one is looking good," Eli commented, as Mela and AB floated closer to her and Bernie in a quiet section of the river.

"I give up," Leslie droned from behind. "Why does Eli dread the merry freakin' month of May? You think you're the only person with troubles, always-whining Eli?"

"I think you're the only one here drunk," Eli remarked, watching Carly and then Sophie pushing off rocks as the river narrowed again up ahead.

"Do you even care what seeing you like this again does to Sophie?" Mela implored, as Leslie shoved between her and AB in the current.

"Divorced a year now, right?" Bernie asked over her shoulder, as she and Eli twirled off the same rock. "I'm just starting that process, and I'm already worn out with it. How long does it take to feel like it was worth it?"

"Gosh, Bernie," Eli answered, doing 360s as she dragged her toes against a steep stone wall. "I'm not the best person to ask about that."

"You came to our school for the last two weeks in May," Mela recalled. "Your mom had died, and you were living with our high school principal."

"Yeah, Aunt Ta."

"That didn't help you make friends."

Wild shrieks ahead had AB paddling for the bank, but the faster moving water carried her through the narrowing channel as each of their tubes gracefully sailed over a low waterfall that splashed into a wider, slower basin. As the last of the floaters came over, Beth was standing with one hand holding her tube tight against her side and the other scooping water to the front of her head.

"Honey, you're bleeding," Bernie noticed.

"Let's take a break on this giant rock while we're all together and see what's going on," AB suggested, leaving Beth a spot beside her.

Beth pushed up to take the seat and yelped in pain, grabbing her right side. AB was concerned about a rib injury, but Beth directed her to a gash above the eye.

"Riding too high, I think," Beth admitted. "Came off that waterfall like a catapult."

"You've got a little tear in your helix but doesn't look like it would need any stitches. Lots of blood supply there."

"Your helix for the helium," Sophie chanted. "Mother Nature got you back."

"Did you hit your head?" AB pressed.

"Yeah, pretty good."

"Why didn't you say anything?" AB asked.

"Why didn't you scream?" Sophie whined. "Why didn't you say... I know things you could say," she trailed off, with a touch of irritable disappointment. Her comment timed to her mother's latest expletive explosion while climbing the blackberry bank to take a whiz in the woods.

"That's how you say it like you mean it," Sophie counseled. "I know better than to cuss in front of teachers. Y'all are like teachers, and you'd get me for it. Legally I can talk that way all the time if I want."

"Yeah, I did, too, when I was little," Eli confided, as the others were hopping back on the tubes. "My mom used words your mom doesn't even know. All the time. So, I did, too, and she thought that was hilarious.

"Then one day when I was visiting Aunt Edie, we were passing an ice cream store. I wanted one but she said that she had to study, and her roommates were waiting. I threw my toy puppy at her feet and let loose with howling obscenities that would impress your fave celebutard."

Sophie sneered, splashing Eli as they drifted. "My dad just leaves the room when I melt down. What did she do to you?"

"She cried, like she was sad for me," Eli recalled. "She swooped me up and drove to the Atlanta Botanical Garden. Dazzling beds of tiny flowers under tall blooms in all colors were everywhere. Even the shrubs and treetops were full of blossoms.

"She said something like, 'Do you love these gardens, Eli? Do you feel the joy from the happy, dancing flowers, and the water singing as it splashes along?'

"She wanted me to see what makes life worth living, saying, 'We think we have to wear cute clothes and have pretty houses, but really, we live in here,' she showed me, with a hand on her heart and one about here, on her solar plexus. 'But mostly inside here,' she said, laughing, kissing my cheeks until we were both giggling.

"Then, touching a finger to each of my temples, she said 'This is where we choose to live in a beautiful garden, or in a pile of smelly garbage. Always see yourself in a glowing garden like this. Thoughts in your mind can become flowers and fountains when we share kind words and ideas. There can be a garden of joy surrounding you anywhere you go.'

"She looked at me, more serious than before. 'Eli, when we say or think ugly things, they pile up like trash in our heart and make us feel *rotten*. And when we damage our garden with sour, mean thoughts, we frighten people away from us. It takes practice to keep a pretty garden surrounding you.'

"I will never forget her. Maybe because I was so little or loved her so much. Sure, there are words I use every day that aren't great. And I mess up and say worse, but I try to clear it away and restore my garden as quickly as I can. Does that sound redic to you?"

"Cringey," Sophie responded, a little side-eye for emphasis.

"Well, that's why I try not to be a total potty mouth. I try to have a place to escape in my mind, a beautiful, peaceful place when I get stressed out."

"I think you should see my dad's therapist," she recommended, boosting off a boulder and waving bye-bye as she sped downstream.

Eli thought she was behind everyone but looked back to see Beth and AB. Beth's oversized tube was making navigating difficult. Just as Eli stood to wait for the stragglers, Beth slipped into what had appeared to be a tributary but was, in fact, moving away from the main current down a new channel.

"Wait, don't leave me," Beth wailed, as she disappeared.

AB stopped alongside Eli, who was fighting a losing battle trying to move upstream. "No phones," AB said, evaluating their situation. "And everyone else has literally gone round the bend ahead. We better catch up."

Eli found the fastest section of the current, watching to be sure AB was close. As they rounded the turn, they saw Carly, hands on her hips, looking back and forth between them and something ahead. *A real waterfall?* Eli worried, heart pounding.

"Beth is missing," Eli tried shouting over the noisy river, as she saw Carly getting on her tube after shooing the others ahead.

"We need the phones," AB bellowed at a surprising volume for such a slight body. Carly stopped, waiting for them to get closer. "We hollered a lot growing up in Tennessee," AB explained.

"Is that Beth up there?" Carly shouted, as they arrived. "Did y'all let her go left at the island?"

"No, Beth took off down a creek or something," Eli called. "We need to call for help."

"Right there," Carly pointed ahead. "She bypassed the island, that's all."

Everyone but Carly was relieved to head home on Sunday after listening to Beth's harrowing tales of wildlife on the shortcut she took. She was almost as excited about dinner that night at the hotel where the cast of *Dirty Dancing* stayed during filming.

Back at the lake house, after Sophie climbed over her passed out mother to go shower, Carly revealed that she might stay out overnight—earning high-fives when her friends heard it was Bret she was meeting.

The next morning, Mela made sure Leslie was sober for the drive back to Atlanta with Sophie; she had Eli search the car for hidden booze. Nothing could guarantee Leslie wouldn't find a source on the way home, but Sunday morning in the South would help. On the way to Hiawassee AB, Mela, Bernie, and Eli worked out the details of an intervention for Leslie. Carly hoped her headphones would ensure a much-needed nap on the drive home with Beth.

Chapter 12

What If May Never Goes Your Way?

A text from Mela as Eli was unpacking from the Lake Lure trip said that Mac was ready to get in an afternoon of sailing, as good sailing days on Chatuge were rare. "Just us," Mela typed, and Eli read it as "Come dispel any rumors." Mela still hadn't finished with Beau's attorney.

Weather was perfect, with a steady breeze, afternoon temps in the seventies, and soft spring leaves crowning almost every tree from the lakeshore to the surrounding mountains. Already a bright pink from spending the day before on the river, Eli opted for an oversized shirt and baggy shorts for her sailing lessons.

She thought she'd been doing especially well for a beginner when Mac leaned starboard, uttering an alarming, "Oh, nooo." He shot a look over Eli's head at Mela, who also saw the problem.

"Eli," she urged, scrambling past the boom, "why don't you go down, uh, just—"

"Hey, E," Mac called, motioning her over. "That's Ted on his 23. He's seen us and is coming this way. Okay?"

"Yeah," she answered, deflated. "I'm good." *A good and rumpled mess,* she thought, considering a fall overboard to mitigate her appearance. *Flowers, gardens,* she recalled, as the usually reasonable voice in her head predicted imminent humiliation.

Eli peered around the sail and caught a glimpse of Ted and the tropically saronged Hannah. Desperate to vanish, she sat on the top step of the boarding ladder and flipped over backward, diver style.

"Idiot!" Eli raged, as she surfaced, realizing her mistake. *Yeah, Ted's boat is more agile. He and Jessica Rabbit will rescue you if another power craft doesn't nail you first.* "Enough, head voice," Eli gurgled in the light chop. "You've been an oracle of hindsight lately. Leave me."

On this steadily warming day, stratified water temps in the sixties soon numbed her fingers, weakening her belief that swimming for the big island would increase her body heat. Eli was fading when a fishing rig with two guys on board roared up and one snatched her out of the water by her voluminous shirt.

"How'd you get out here, kid?" the baffled angler demanded.

"Thanks," Eli chattered. "Not a kid. I slipped off that sailboat," she added, nodding at the approaching boats.

Just then, Mela gently passed alongside, slow enough for Mac to call out, "Thank you, brothers," as he reached from behind and swung Eli upright onto the deck.

"I'm feeling a little like slow thawing cargo," Eli grumbled sheepishly. Mac was too invested in his glare to respond.

Mela pulled a blanket from the cabin and motioned her over. "Next time just say no. Mac doesn't know about your run-in with Ted." They heard the chain feeding as Mac anchored near Ted's 23 at the island.

Mac was astern chatting with Ted, who wore Hannah draped over his shoulder. "That's the guy who can't stand to be touched," Eli said sarcastically. "Guess it depends on who is doing the touching." Just then, Ted peeled her arm off his chest, forcing the rest of Hannah to step away from behind him.

"I don't think he's that into her," Mela observed. "He's glancing at you," she noted, brushing wet strands from Eli's face. "You know, girl, your hair has really grown out. All this copper with bronze tips. You look like shojo anime."

"Do what?"

"That's Sophie-speak. She loves her girly graphic comics."

When they returned to the dock, Mela was surprised that Astro wasn't there to meet them. They found him near the terrace, and though he appeared asleep, his body was cool. Almost ten years old, Mela thought it was probably his heart. Beau's Astro was gone.

Mela was grief-stricken as Eli brought her inside while Mac carried Astro to his truck, then drove to the barn. They buried him beside Zsa Zsa, the Borzoi that Beau's parents loved. Mela stayed the night at Eli's, leaving for work before the morning walk.

As they gathered, Eli broke the news of Astro's passing and suggested they all go in on a plaque like the one marking Zsa Zsa's grave. AB suggested they take Mela to dinner and called Mac to meet them at Brother's in Young Harris.

Midmorning, Eli's phone died as she checked voicemail. She could find no technical issues. It was safe at Mela's while they were on the lake. Nothing left to do but visit the phone store in Hiawassee for answers. The answer was, she needed her own post-marital billing. Her phone had been disconnected by the account holder of record.

Miss Independence forgot to move that line to her own phone service for a whole year, she thought, waiting while the rep added a line for her dead phone to the account she had opened for Aunt Ta's old number.

What else could she have forgotten? Damn, health insurance went with her job. No hurry on that, she decided, and spent the afternoon texting contacts her new number. Dinner was a celebratory wake, recalling adventures with Astro. Mela seemed to lighten a bit.

<hr />

On Tuesday morning's walk, instead of confirming Leslie's family would be at the intervention they were planning, Mela explained that JT, Leslie's husband, had discovered she was in Hiawassee to avoid seeing an oncologist to start treatment for a breast tumor that she'd failed to mention. He was frantically trying to get her in rehab and stable enough to begin the treatments.

"Her ass is outta here to-day," AB said, in a blustering rant. "If we have to hog tie her and shove her in my virtual trunk, she's going to be ready for her oncologist's first opening. Anyone available to help wrangle this heifer? Not you, Carly. You have to be at the airport tonight."

"I can help right now," Carly objected. "You need me to get her in the car. Let's move."

"You heard her," Bernie hollered, herding everyone. "Let's find Leslie."

Weary and frightened, Leslie no longer resisted when confronted about her need for care. Carly cleaned and organized Leslie's things while Beth packed, Mela consoled, and AB counseled. Bernie stealthily saged Mela's house with the pungent herb, bottom to top.

Eli was on the phone, close to Leslie for permissions, as she made arrangements with the facility. Dr. V would cover for Mela, settling the last detail of rescuing Leslie. As usual, AB planned to nap in the car as the three women set off.

Eli went back to work, having already outlined new chapters and identified needed rewrites in the Harrison book. Mela called saying she would stop by after she dropped AB at home.

"Get ahead of those thunderstorms coming in," Eli urged.

"Not due til midnight. We'll be home by nine thirty," Mela assured her.

A few minutes later, Bernie called, asking for news. "Mela and AB are headed home, and I'm expecting her here soon. Should I call and fill you in then?" Eli offered.

"No, that's out of our hands now." Bernie sounded distracted. "This storm, I think it's going to be bad. Eli, take precautions. You hear me?"

"You, too, Bernie. We'll be climbing through limbs and stuff tomorrow morning, huh? See you then."

Pharaoh was unsettled, too, and Eli checked radar, which showed the line was moving in hours faster than forecast. She let the anxious cat out, left the door open to watch for his return, and started cupcakes for Mela's visit.

She put them in the oven, then went to find Pharaoh. As she opened the door, her head slammed against the brick siding. Her knees buckled, and in her blurring vision, she saw Pharaoh leaping from the retaining wall, landing on the neck of her attacker, who angrily slung the bold creature into the bricks over Eli's head. The cat slid to the ground in a heap against her.

A rumble of thunder helped her regain consciousness. Eli was on the ground, on her side, and though it was dark, when lightning flashed, she could see a man at the edge of the lake on a boat. He was pulling the ripcord on a small inflatable raft, throwing it over the side. As the raging storm crested mountains to the west, he was cursing and grumbling—mostly cursing.

Her vision wouldn't clear, but she thought she could see two lengths of anchor chain stretched down the bank. She was wrapped in a tarp with duct tape over her mouth. As she rocked back and forth to loosen the canvas, the movement shifted the covering almost over her eyes. She played dead—not a stretch—when he jumped off the boat and started toward her.

Eli had seen his face for a second or less at the house. *Who is he? Why is he so angry with me?* He gripped the tarp behind her head and dragged her across the bank. She glimpsed the cowhide of new work gloves. He was livid, kicking her legs into place as he worked. "Goddamn storm," she heard him rage.

Rain was thumping on the tarp. She could feel the strands of chain beneath her as he rolled her body nearer the water, the anchor links wrapping around and around until she bumped onto the raft. Then, with a jerk, the line from the boat pulled the raft off the shore.

This is how I'm going to die, Eli realized, her thoughts still hazy. *Did Ted send him? Ah, hello, bright stars, peeking through the clouds. Flowers, fountains, and beatific moons. Thank you, Edie, I remember.*

Chilling water washed into the raft and across her face from the rough chop. The weight of the chains pulled the tarp away from her head enough that Eli could tell the winds were increasing. The boat, struggling to tow, was whirring like AB's sewing machine.

Through the pouring rain, she could see some lights in homes on the shoreline. If only she could scream. No one would notice this boat, near silent in the storm. *Thank you, brave Pharaoh. Please God don't let him hurt Pete, too.* Eli had no idea what time it might be. Mela would come to the door and think she had fallen asleep. *Goodbye, my sweet friends.*

It was hard to calculate progress in the howling winds, but Eli knew they were well out in the lake, and the storm was crashing around them. Suddenly the tow released. Maybe the line broke. An odd, zinging sound was popping around her, interrupted by a powerful lightning bolt striking nearby.

Above the dying thunder, she could hear the boat moving away as the raft was sinking beneath her. *Have I been shot?* She felt nothing but the cold, her aching head, and desperation pounding in her chest.

In her panicked struggle, her hand slipped free. She ripped the tape off her mouth and squelched a scream before it reached her lips. He was the most likely to hear her and might turn back. Two air chambers were collapsing, but he'd missed one. She felt her weighted legs sliding off the crumpling raft.

With her thoughts clearing, she pushed her left arm out, feeling for the carabiners that held the chains—finding one at her chest that she quickly released as her body slid into the water. It was too late to grip the remaining air chamber as it bobbed above her.

Miraculously, or torturously, Eli noticed the tarp had captured pockets of air, slowing her descent as the lower course of chain un-wound from her body. She flipped her legs to loosen the chain and was surprised that the effort could propel her slightly upward.

She needed air to fight. Her forearms broke the surface. She couldn't be more than a foot from a breath; her lungs were burning. She brushed the second carabiner, unlatched it, and kicked again as she fought the blackout coming over her.

The chain was falling away. She was feeling lighter. Or was that just her dying imagination? She tried cupping air to her face but gulped water instead. *Don't cough. Don't cough.* The soft metallic clicking of the chain slipping away stopped. A snag.

Irritation snapped her eyes open, and through those few inches of water she could see the stars, bright among the clouds. Eli managed a last mermaid kick, and the chain cascade resumed. As she sank this time, a buzzing sound filled her ears. Warmth enveloped her body, calm washed through her frantic mind, and her throat involuntarily closed against another gasp.

As Mela pulled in at Eli's, her lights showed Pharaoh, a wet, bloody mess quivering in the rain. Thinking he had encountered a fox or a coyote, she pulled a transport case from the back and called Eli to tell her she was taking the cat to the clinic.

She could hear Eli's phone ringing from behind the house. With Pharaoh secure in the warming passenger seat, she walked around to find the kitchen slider open, phone on the counter, and burning cupcakes—but no Eli. Below the porch light, a patch of bloody hair hung on the wall. She called Mac, and he was on his way across the lake as they spoke.

Dude was already agitated, whining at the door, and leaped up the dock as Mac whistled him onboard. A storm like this was no time to be on the water. His fishing rig would get them across quickly.

Midway, Dude alerted, barking frantically. An overwrought alert, Mac noticed. Looking beyond the dog, he glimpsed an inflated piece of tarp in the storm-churned water.

Mac cut the engine beneath the rumbling sky and shone his mounted spotlight into the water, illuminating chain around a tarp. Bloating would bring a body up after a few days. "Nothing good going on under there," he muttered. "Unless it's connected to Eli—maybe something she saw," he said, trying to calm the agitated dog with his voice.

He called 911 with his coordinates as he dropped anchor. Mac heard the dog hit the water as he tucked his phone away, and dove in seconds behind Dude. Although the dog had a grip on the tarp, it wouldn't budge. Mac sent him back on the boat and dove again with his handheld light. It caught a face peering out of the canvas. As the copper strands of hair lifted in the current, Eli's lifeless eyes stared back at him.

He grabbed her body, but it felt stuck. His light showed one length of chain held her below the water as the rest of the line tangled in an old limb maybe ten feet below. He snatched it away, shoving her to the surface.

As he pushed her body onto the boat deck, Dude gingerly pulled her to the center of the boat. Mac scrambled on, urgently feeling for a pulse he knew would be hard to find in a hypothermic victim.

Rain poured steadily in the fading storm, and the flimsy poncho he'd tented over Eli's head would do little to keep her body temperature from dropping. Watching for a response after two assisted respirations, he saw nothing. Mac directed his dog to stay against her right side while he started chest compressions. He was relieved to see Towns County Fire & Rescue Boat III coming in view in a stunning response time.

"Call in a 9-line, Captain," Mac bellowed, loud enough for the EMS rig pulling into the boat launch across the water to hear. "She needs a bird, now!"

Although her body had not responded to the first rescue breaths, he intended to keep breathing for her until she could. They transferred her to the larger boat and pulled away, leaving Mac's rig anchored for deputies and the dive team to investigate the location.

Dude resumed his warming duties against the blankets, assisting the heat packs under her arms and on her abdomen as Mac shouted between compressions, begging Eli to take just one breath. "Just one, Eli. One breath, for Pete!" At Pete's name she gasped, then her chest sank, still.

"Mac, they're never dead until they're *warm* and dead," the fire captain reminded him, as they continued resuscitation efforts. "Warming, defib, and hi-flow oxygen are 90 seconds out. Let's get her in the air. They're cleared to land in that launch lot."

"Don't leave us now, Little Bit," he whispered, as the air medics approached. "There are things I haven't told you. I love you, kid."

Quickly loaded, assessed, and receiving treatment, Eli would arrive at a Level I trauma center within the golden hour. Mac v-carded the very kind medic who said he would pass it on and watched the helicopter lift back, rotating west under the fast-clearing night sky. It wasn't the first or even the fiftieth time he'd sent someone off in just this way. The last time, he was the one being transported. Yet this was more agonizing than any moment of those tours.

Two deputies were on scene, and one led Mac to the patrol car to provide information while the other was riding out to the rescue site to secure Mac's boat and any evidence until investigators arrived.

With the sheriff listening in on an open line, the deputy directed Mac as a video recording was made of his personal contact information, activities earlier in the day, and when Mela's call came in about Eli being missing.

"I started an eighth of a mile away, around a bend in the shoreline. If this guy was coming from Eli's looking for a deep spot to drop her, his first chance would have been over the Long Bullet section to the Woods Creek current—that's eighty-five feet deep right there. I mean, there was nothing random about this. He was coming for her, right?

"Anyway, that storm had been tearing it up for at least 30 minutes when Mela called to say Eli was gone. She thought Eli had put something in the oven maybe an hour before Mela arrived. There was no sign of any watercraft when I happened on her. So, he was docked very close, or already past the point I came out, which would have him traveling north or northeast."

"Mac, we're going to leave all that up to the investigators," the deputy said, interrupting. "Let's keep going with what you saw, heard, and did."

"Yeah, but there are rental properties along the west side of that shoreline and some nice, seldom-used places on the big water at the stretch on that north shore. Maybe we start canvassing the nearest renters with boat access. Checking for boaters who may have seen somebody hanging around—"

"Let's get back to how you found the body."

"Not a body. She's alive. Listen, I've told you all I know. I have to get to the hospital. Could we finish this by phone?"

"Nope," the deputy answered. "Maybe we can continue on the drive to the victim's place, Sheriff?"

"We can do that," they heard him reply. "GBI is coming this way, too."

"What about the FBI?" Mac added. "She was kidnapped. That storm pushed him all over the state line."

"We'll investigate every possibility," the sheriff answered. "You know how this has to go, Mac. Let's get through everything you can recall while it's fresh."

They finished recording his account on the drive, and then his first call was to Mela. "We found Eli. She's been medevac'd."

"I know, Mac. I heard over their radios. Where are you now?"

"Just gave my statement. Lost my leg again. The deputy is bringing me to Eli's."

"The sheriff was speaking to you from here; two investigators just arrived. I know a little about what's happened. Bernie spoke with her twenty-two minutes before I arrived. You were so close, you might have been hurt, Mac.

"I've been treating ol' Pharaoh for injuries. Dr. V is meeting me at the clinic so that we can drop him on our way. Wait, Deputy Bennett says he'll take him for me. Which trauma center, Mac, Atlanta or Chattanooga?"

"Chattanooga, and we don't have a minute to lose. It's bad, Mela."

She loaded the sedated cat beside Dude in the back seat of the deputy's car as the sheriff came around with Mac's prosthesis in hand. "A rescue boat securing the scene found this in some tape around the tarp. Rushed it over for Mac. If the GBI wants it back in the evidence bin, we know where to find it. That is his name on there?"

"Yes."

"Y'all drive safe, Doc, and let us know about Mrs. Waller?"

"I'll call as soon as we have news on Eli's condition, Sheriff. Thank you so much, for everything you all do." She waved, easing up the drive to wait for Mac. Earlier, she had darted home and raided Beau's closet, getting Mac a shirt, pants, socks, and shoes after listening to their radio reports as the deputies arrived at Eli's. She had to keep moving—no thinking—or she would fall apart.

Mac was out of the patrol car, balancing between the doors as the vehicles passed on the driveway. He spotted his missing leg as he vaulted inside Mela's Expedition. "Aw, I'm glad to see this. Thought I'd lost another Niagara." He sighed, holding it to the window with a thumbs-up to the deputy.

"How are you doing, Mela? Want me to drive?"

"I need to drive, stay focused."

"Mela…" He paused so long she looked over.

"There is something I need to say before I lose my nerve. Just listen a sec, alright? I'm through being too tough to express what I feel, to say that I am thankful for the people I love," he told her, looking from the prosthesis he'd been casually examining to the woman beside him. Interrupted by a voicemail alert, he put it on speaker as it played.

An inflight update to Chattanooga was seemingly butt-dialed to Mac's phone. The reports were hopeful with successful defib, a thready pulse, increasing oxygen levels. The message closed with, "Capnography's brightening our flight, Miller."

As it finished, a call came in from AB at Carly's. Mela was turning onto the four-lane in Murphy heading for the Tennessee line, and the signal was weak. She shared the medic's update and promised to call from the hospital. They rode in silence through the southwest corner of North Carolina while Mac reattached his prosthesis. After a few glances, he leaned over in the dark footwell and could see she was crying.

"Listen, Mela, I don't mean to make you uncomfortable. I was trying to ask if you've ever thought about there being an *us* in the future. I know this isn't a good time, but I can't keep this bottled up. I want to be there for you. I want to be the person you reach for first."

Mela looked ahead, tears glistening in the light from the dash.

"I don't want to lose any more time," he went on. "Tonight, with what's happened to Eli. I'm shook, I guess.

"Did I do enough to try and save her, or too much? Why didn't I trust the dog instead of making a phone call? Did she die while I did that? I'm crashing around like a three-legged bull—no dog, no truck, no clothes, either." He breathed deep, pulling his damp t-shirt away from his chest over shorts and a bare foot.

"I could never be uncomfortable with you, Mac. When I'm around you, I get a sense that things are good, safe," she said, voice quivering. "Yes, I am attracted to you, but I want to know it's more than a physical thing. Maybe we could find out what we are to each other when we have Eli back with us.

"I can't do anything about most of the problems before us tonight," she said, as they passed the Ocoee River Olympic site. "But I did get some things from Beau's closet. Behind my seat."

"I'm twenty pounds heavier and an inch shorter than the towering Beau Johnston," he warned, unfurling the first item. "Shirt's right," he said, buttoning the windowpane check and reaching back for the khakis. "Do you mind?" he asked, holding the slacks out.

"Mind what?"

"If I change here in the truck? No tidies in this stash. It'll be commando."

"Knock yourself out."

"Don't jinx me," he ordered, shimmying out of the shorts and shifting the seat back to step into the slacks. "*Beau*, you lying bastard, you aren't twenty pounds lighter."

"Thanks, Mac."

"For flashing you? Or for calling the man a lying bastard? Honestly, said with love. I'm working on the love thing."

"For not speaking of Beau in the past tense."

"Mela, nobody over there or anywhere could get the drop on Beau. He's somewhere figuring out the best way home," Mac said, over the roar of the rising river echoing against steep stone walls of the gorge. "What will you do when he gets back? And if he's not alone?"

"He's told me about the professor, and Mac, I'm happy for them. You know we were never a romantic thing. I just don't want to let him down. He's made so much happen for me."

"*You* have made so much happen for you, and he'd be the first one to say that. You are invincible, Mela. Beautiful, kind, and unshakable. Will you stay on at Beau's?"

"You know, Mac, I am ready to move on. Feels like I've been frozen in place for years now, and hanging with Eli has brought me back to the living. I want a home of my own, interests outside of my patients, and happy times. Think I've lost my mind?"

"Maybe you've found it. Maybe you're ready for some reckless ir-responsibility. I could sign on as your bodyguard—if I don't have to end Ted first."

"You think he's behind what happened tonight?"

"Who else looks good for the surveillance? The blackmail threat is tied to his servers. Who else has a problem with her now? Well, a big problem anyway.

"This wasn't random," he assured her, putting a sock on his foot. "They came prepared. There was no boat in sight when I crossed *mi-raculously* through that location near the deepest point of the lake. I missed saving her by less than five minutes, Mela. I could swear there was a pulse in her neck when I was pulling her to my boat.

"Even if the guy was running without lights, even in that storm, I would have picked up on any engine. Despite being *blowed up* more than a few times over there, my hearing is good."

"Have you called Pete, or Ted?"

"After I spoke with you. They were coming in from Charlotte, so Pete will probably be there before us-—if Ted shows his face."

Chapter 13

Where *Are* Your Ruby Slippers?

"She should be in Atlanta. I don't want her here," Ted was shouting outside the intensive care unit. He was not getting his way in a heated conversation with Pete and the trauma specialist, who was defending the pulmonologist, cardiologist, and neurologist treating Eli.

"You are doing your wife no good with this, Mr. Waller." The intensivist tried to reason on behalf of his patient. "Our trauma team is second to none, and moving her unnecessarily now would be detrimental to her condition.

"She has experienced a prolonged resuscitation—mechanical ventilation is keeping her alive as we battle hypothermia, hypoxemia, arrhythmias, and the chaos these conditions cause in the body. She is at a precipice. Please do not interfere with her treatment. We are her only hope."

Ted leveled his gaze, roiling exasperation rising off him. "If anything happens to her, if—"

"Don't make any threats that will get you removed from this hospital, Mr. Waller. We will advise you on her condition as often as possible," he said over his shoulder, returning to the bay where Eli was being treated.

Pete knew not to approach Ted, that he was far too anxious to be handled, much less reminded that he was an ex-husband with no standing. "I'll be here if you want to go get coffee, Ted."

"Yeah," Ted grumbled, rubbing his neck. "I'll be right back." He was leaning on the elevator button when the doors opened. Mela stepped out ahead of Mac. "What are you doing here, Mac?" He seemed confused by their arrival.

"Two hours ago, I pulled her out of Lake Chatuge. You remember Mela."

Ted looked her over. "No."

"My parents had the campground on the lake," she gently reminded him.

"Right," he said, stepping into the elevator.

"He hasn't lost that boyish charm," Mela whispered, walking with Mac to the desk.

"Hey, Mac," Pete called from the line of chairs against the wall. "Thank you, man, thank you for saving Eli." He embraced her rescuer. "And you are Mela?" he said, turning to hug her. "Eli thinks you two are, well, she's calling you *Mala*," he laughed.

"Kind of 2010. . ." Her answer faded as she looked up at Mac.

"That works." Mac said, meeting her gaze. "What do we know, Pete?" he asked, taking a seat with Mela between them.

"Thanks to the two of you, she's still with us. We're waiting for—"

"Well, wait no longer, honey. Time to find out what we're dealing with," AB interrupted, bending to hug Mela. "Oh, one minute, there's somebody I know," she said, breezing by and warmly greeting a woman reviewing a digital pad at the nurses' station.

"We see one another regularly at continuing ed seminars," AB said, upon returning to the conversation, which had suspended as they watched her being shown charts, scan screens, and eventually Eli. Pete offered his seat next to Mela. "At this hospital," AB advised, waving a finger at her audience, "I'm her aunt. Everybody got that?

"So, she has not regained consciousness, but her oxygen levels are creeping in the right direction, as are her body temp and ECG rhythms. The ventilator is necessary, at least until this time tomorrow, especially as we watch for any intercranial swelling. Don't be alarmed by all the wires and tubes when you see her. The endo supports her airway, a nasogastric line protects her from aspirating stomach contents, and the rest are the usual manner of support," she explained, holding Mela's hand.

"There is no way to tell how much of her status is due to head trauma, but they will let y'all in to see her after the neurological assessment finishes. Let's hope our girl just pops up and asks for a ride home, which is possible."

Ted had received a call back from the business office as he was getting coffee, advising that the ultra-exclusive medical network he had enrolled himself, Eli, and Pete in years ago at his brother Lew's urging had been recently canceled for Eli. He went to the office to assume responsibility for her expenses before returning to the ICU.

"Pete," Ted called, summoning him. Pete was quickly relating the information AB had received, but Ted angrily cut him off. "Her aunt is dead. That is not her aunt."

"Hello there." AB welcomed Ted as she came past Pete, lowering her voice to add, "As the not-really-her-aunt addressing the not-her-husband-for-a-year-now, I'd suggest we graciously agree to support one another's interest in seeing Eli safely through this. Hmmm? By the way, I'm Annie Blanche Sutton, her kin, her neighbor, and her friend." She angled her head to meet his eyes. "And someone *not* to be trifled with."

AB took her seat next to Mela while Pete filled Ted in on the news about Eli. They were joined by the intensivist, who said two could go in for a few minutes. Pete stood as AB reminded him that Eli could hear him. Ted followed him into the room, shocked by the sight of her battered head, the airway tube, and lines running in and out of her body from under the warming blankets.

Pete pushed her hair back and kissed her brow, saying, "We're here with you, Eli. You are safe, and everything you feel going on is to help. You're fighting, we know, and we're not leaving until you come home with us. I'll be right outside your room. We love you."

He stepped back, easing behind Ted, saying, "I'll give you some space."

Mac was waiting outside, watching through the glass wall. Pete passed without looking up as he dried his cheeks on his sleeve.

Ted stood at the bed, both hands gripping the rail, watching each breath rise and fall with the ventilator against the backdrop of the monitors' multicolored graphs. "Eli, please, wake up. I've only wanted to protect you, to give you the best life I could. I know now you weren't always fighting me."

He dropped his head, sinking against the rail. "You have to get better. I love you, in a way that can't be quantified. It's an energy greater than the sun," he softly confessed. "The things that have happened to us, I couldn't stand it. Maybe I did want you to hurt like I was hurting," he cried out, oblivious to the increasing pulse of her heart rate until an alarm sounding on the monitor overrode his voice. "But not like this."

The chorus of alarms brought him to his feet. "What's happening?" he shouted, as the intensivist pushed past him. A nurse shoved him out and pulled a curtain.

He leaned against the half-wall next to Mac, who was careful to modulate his voice as he asked a question he didn't need answered. "What did you say to her?"

"I told her to get better."

"What was it you did to hurt her, Ted?"

"That's no concern of yours."

"What did you do to her?" he asked again, turning to face him.

"I thought of her as dead, okay? I couldn't get her out of my mind."

"Would it be better if she were dead?"

"No, Mac, of course not. I wanted to stop thinking about her. She couldn't stand me. She left me," he answered, pushing away from the wall and walking off.

Ted went into the stairwell, avoiding the waiting room where Pete was introducing Grace as she arrived from Atlanta. AB could see Mac still outside Eli's bay and heard the exchange with Ted. As she approached, his head was down.

She felt the slightest recoil as she put her arm around him, assuring him this was not a seizure from brain injury; it was a sign that Eli was still in that body and fighting against the ventilator, against the restraints that held her in place.

"She's fighting off Ted," he told her, hands clinched. "I heard Ted tell her he had wanted her to hurt, 'just not like this.' Whatever that means. She seemed to have a clear understanding. It frightened her."

"We try to make sense of what we're seeing, but it could be more benign than that."

⟫•⟪

Saturday morning, an agent from the Georgia Bureau of Investigation arrived to interview Mela, and later, Mac. He brought news. A body had been found, an apparent suicide in a car parked at a rental house on the lake. Both rentals, the house, and the car were in the name of the identification carried by the deceased, Patrick Thompson, a 54-year-old male from Texas.

Under the car seat was a receipt for an inflatable raft that matched the one retrieved from thirty feet of water, snagged on a branch. It was held there by two new anchor chains. A bullet that had passed through an air chamber in the raft was lodged in a seam and submitted for ballistic testing.

"And get this," he said, smacking his knee with his folded notes, "both hands heavily scarred from the base of the palm to his fingertips. Probably done before DNA analysis took a leading role in criminal investigations."

As Eli began to breathe on her own, she had progressed to serious but stable over the weekend. Ted never returned. AB and Mela went back to work Monday, leaving Mac and Pete with Grace. She became their liaison with the medical staff.

Pete continued to update Ted, who immersed himself in facility upgrades in Dallas and Charlotte between weekend races. Mac's curiosity about every level of Ted's communications for the last year had become an obsession. He sat clicking away in a chair next to Eli's bed, tracing every call, text, email, message, and bank draft for a link to the suspect.

Mac was intrigued when Hannah Collins appeared at the hospital thinking she would find Ted there. He plugged her into his suspect board after listening to her excuse for the misstep. Usually gracious Mela detected a stalker vibe.

Mac had also been looking into Patrick Thompson since his body had been found hours after Eli was left to die. Once Mela had fallen asleep on his shoulder in the ICU waiting room, he had been turning up every available detail on this lifelong Texan.

Thompson had brushes with the law as a juvenile, more than a dozen arrests for misdemeanors, and then graduated to felony charges by eighteen. While out on bond, he had been working in a plant when he tumbled from a catwalk and tried to save himself by grabbing a pipe as he fell. But it was a live steam pipe, and he dropped another twenty feet when the flesh burned off his hands.

In those days, a mild brain injury and long recovery had diverted his judicial fate. Then he lived quietly, at least until he came to Lake Chatuge.

On Tuesday, Mela drove over after her last patient. She wanted to catch Eli awake. "Whatcha working on?" she asked, handing Mac a sandwich when his eyes stayed focused on his research a little too long. He flipped the screen down and walked into the hall with her.

"According to a friend in law enforcement," he answered, in a do-not-ask tone, "no one in the area, not even neighbors near his rental house, recognized his photo. He hasn't appeared on any retail or restaurant video so far, and the purchase we know he made—the raft—occurred in Mississippi along the way up weeks ago. He certainly doesn't fit any assassin profile. No known criminal activity since he was a teen. Nearest neighbor in Texas says he lived there over forty years, but alone after his mother died."

"Maybe he wanted a raft to paddle around on his vacation," she said, setting the tray on the chair between them.

"Nah, this was a survivalist model, extremely durable. Then there was a gun, the chains, and that tarp. Oh yeah, no boat. What did he do, chain her and set her adrift on the lake in a monster storm?"

"Maybe he was one of those really lonely guys, and he came to find a companion to take home, willing or not," she suggested, taking a bite of potato salad.

"They usually work a little closer to home," he countered, standing to look into Eli's room.

"How has she been today?" Mela asked. "Can she tell you anything?"

"When she opens her eyes she looks around, gets her bearings, I guess, and she's out again. Doesn't respond to anyone, not even Pete," he said, adding, "He went to meet Grace."

"Have they gotten her up?"

"Said they might in the morning. Her vitals are coming within normal limits. But that was a brutal concussion before she ever hit the water, and the specialists are still conferring on heart and lungs. I think her brain wants to tap outta the game for a stretch."

"Can't say that I blame her. Mac, are you still trying to find a link to Ted?"

"I'm trying to eliminate him. Having you here is a nice diversion. Can you stay, Mela? There are two beds in my room if that sounded—"

"It sounds inviting," she answered, "but I do have to get back. Doesn't look like I'll get to see E tonight. And I *am* going to keep tomorrow's appointment with Beau's attorney."

"I'd like to be there with you, but I know you'd veto that. Listen to what he has to say—everything, Mela. One way or another, Beau Johnston set this meeting in motion. You can believe that."

"I want to peek in before I go," she said, slipping her sandwich wrap in the trash can. Mac was finishing his when he heard Eli's faint voice. "Mel?" He could hear her coughing and gasping. When he looked, Mela had her sitting, leaning against her shoulder as she assured Eli the attacker was dead.

"Dear God. Oh, Eli," she wept, rocking her friend in her arms. "Time to go home and heal."

Chapter 14

When You Decide to Breathe Again

June mornings come softly on Lake Chatuge. Warm evaporation rises through the chill mountain air, the lake exhaling a cloudlike mist that rolls across the water until it meets the sun climbing above the ridges. By mid-morning, the stealthy fishing rigs along the banks have given way to flotillas of jet skis darting among boats until hunger or darkness drives them all ashore.

"What are you doing out here *every* sunny morning, my friend?" Mela asked, carrying coffee cups onto the old stone patio.

"Until the GBI guy came by last week, I was listening to boats. Now I'm watching birds," she answered flatly, nodding her thanks for the fresh brew.

After a week at Mela's following her release from the hospital, Eli insisted on being at home; but her friends weren't granting her much alone time. Mac and Dude arrived by ten each night to camp out on the sofa, replacing Beth or Carly, who visited in the evenings. When he left at sunup, AB or Mela would soon be stopping by. Bernie had brought lunch every day.

And this week, instead of dropping by, Bernie had summoned her with a honk from the driveway. Then Eli would set the GPS for their lunch destination. "If I'm driving the Leaf, we're going incognito," Bernie had clarified, when Eli asked about her extremes in personal vehicles. "If we're in the truck, I'm having a mountain girl kind of day."

"You wanted an F-250 Harley Davidson custom edition for your mountain girl persona?" Eli had to confirm.

"Nope," Bernie said slyly, her shoulder raised as she looked over at Eli. "I bought this for my husband's fiftieth birthday, but I caught the SOB with my producer when I drove it to her place to hide it. Been my truck ever since. Now, let's go back to Fortify for more of those gouda fritters today. It's such a beautiful ride to Clayton."

Eli was smiling, recalling those lunch excursions with Bernie when Mela snapped her fingers. "Hey, I said any interest in a little shopping after your doc appointment in Chattanooga tomorrow? Only two weeks til Pete and Grace are married, and you'll be hosting that rehearsal dinner, remember."

"Switched the appointment to yesterday," she said, studying a hawk at the end of the dock. "They said I'm good, more tests in a month."

"Why were you listening to boats?"

"I would know that weird engine if I heard it again. GBI guy says it's electric."

"Yeah, Mac said the owners were at their lake house and reported damage to one of those super-sporty electric boats—oxymoronic until recently. So, the boat yielded evidence—"

"A couple of Pharaoh's hairs stuck in a smudge of my blood behind the pilot's seat. I've been no help. I mostly remember the malevolence."

"But you picked him out of a photo line-up."

"I *thought*, no, it *was* him. But different."

"I look crazy different in every picture I've ever seen of me."

"Me, too. He just looked softer. There was a gentleness in that photo."

"Only a teen record—no one thinks he was a pro. You know, Mac has all but let go of the idea Ted was involved. What are you thinking, Eli?"

"I think Ted despises me more than I ever imagined. And I'll never believe this guy just happened upon me in his maiden homicidal rage. Never had any contact with his part of Texas. Think I cut him off in Dallas traffic? I need to know the why," she said, exhaling dramatically as she flopped back in her chair.

"Oh yeah," Eli added. "Grace told me last weekend that Hannah has been their *wedding guru*, taking over Pete's rehearsal dinner—really, all of Pete's side of things—for Ted."

"That good opinion won't last long. More like the zombie queen slithering in. When did this happen?"

"Apparently Hannah has been huddling with Grace since Pete joined Waller Analytics. Anyway, not sure I'm on the guest list, but the rehearsal dinner will still be at Enrico's. Pete says their venue, the Creekside Pavilion at Brasstown Valley Resort, went from thirty seats to maxed out, with dinner afterwards in the resort. Ted is best man, you know."

"I should have guessed." Mela groaned, lifting out of her chair and pulling Eli up. "We're going shopping, and trying some spa stuff, and indulging in all sorts of things to get your sparkle on for this wedding. Eli, you're Pete's entire family until those vows are spoken.

"When he looks over at you on his wedding day, Pete will see the only constant he can remember. Ted may be filling the seats with his network, but it's you he needs to see. Your crew will be there. We got you."

⟶•⟵

Warm, breezy days and bright blue skies filled the week before the wedding, beginning with perfect weather Sunday for sailing. Mac was determined to get Eli back on the water, persuading Mela to arrange a get-together at the dock so that he could ease her aboard.

On their walk, Mela invited the girls to come for the gathering. It would be their first since the Chimney Rock trip, and JT was bringing Leslie and Sophie for a visit.

Even though Eli arrived early to help, Carly and Mela already had tables set up on the terrace as well as the dock, where Mac was tying up Beau's sailboat. Bernie's arrangements overflowed with mountain laurel, rhodos mixed with oakleaf hydrangeas and purple coneflowers from the yard, with touches of Queen Anne's lace from the ditch along the road. When Pete and Grace arrived, Beth had woven a sweet circlet of leftover wildflowers for the bride.

AB and Mela were sharing observations on Eli's recovery as they watched her helping Mac arrange a platter of crispy, bite-size appetizers—irresistible for Eli. She sampled a few as she spiraled the pieces inside the dish, her light cotton sundress lifting in the breezes with the ribbons trailing from a coneflower circlet set in her copper curls.

Watching her, Mac saw the little girl who had first come to Lake Chatuge so many summers ago. The one his grandmother had pointed out.

"Well," Eli raised her voice, turning to him with the tray in her hands, "*do* you know what these are called?"

"Sorry. Guess I was on mute. They're pastelitos, and I usually make them with a beef filling. Some are sweet. Mine are always savory. More like little empanadas. These are guava and Gruyere."

"Something you learned in South America?"

"It's Cuban. My father taught me."

"I don't remember you ever mentioning your father before. Was he military, too?"

"Yes, he—"

"*Leslie*, how wonderful," AB thundered from the terrace. "That's a beautiful achievement," she added, returning the thirty-day chip to her beaming friend.

JT kissed his wife's cheek as he pulled her a little closer beside him. She's handling her treatments really well, too," he said, shaking his head in wonder as he looked at her.

At the dock, Will thanked Mac for the name of a contractor who would be handling some major remodeling at AB's house. "He's impressive, and has already given her an estimate and a start schedule," he said.

"Lloyd built my lake pavilion," Bernie said. "He's great, *and* nice, but apparently didn't know I had quite a TV presence," she mumbled, rearranging a vase of flowers. "Guess it's been a while."

"C'mon, Bit," Mac whispered, leaning in behind Eli. "Ready to get back on the lake?"

She wheeled around, almost nose to nose, thanks to his angle. "That again? If I hesitate, do you plan to mention that you have experience rescuing me? Who hatched this idea, you or Mela?"

Just as his arm lifted, leveling his accusation at Mela, he saw her vigorously poking a finger in another direction. He then bobbed, compass-like—to Grace. Eli grabbed Pete and bride by the wrists and led them down the dock, stopping for a napkin full of pastelitos.

With Pete's quick grasp of the basics, he and Mac had the sails billowing and the boat skimming the lake surface as artfully as Beau ever had. Mela watched from the terrace as AB joined her. "Wishing you were on the water today?" her friend asked.

"Oh, I'm half imagining that's Beau at the helm again. But I'm awed by Mac's ability to take on anything and excel. "I've noticed that seeing him doesn't just warm my heart these days—it's racing when he's around. AB, I think I'm in love."

Out on the water, Eli's attention had been captured by the tenderness between Pete and Grace. It was a sight that would have hurt just a year ago. Eli long begrudged PDA between lovers, never having experienced it. That was tenderness she had strived to merit, but something Ted was uninterested in receiving or bestowing—public or private.

As she and Grace spoke over the wind and rushing wake, Eli leaned to hold her fingers in the spray of water alongside the boat, giving thanks for being released to live and learn a little more among people who have so much love to share.

———⊱•◦•⊰———

Days later, the shops of Blue Ridge offered a remarkable selection of outfits during Eli's excursion with Mela and AB. They left with an armload of dresses and detoured south for lunch at the Toccoa Riverside Restaurant. From a table overlooking the scenic, tumbling river dotted with tubers, they order mountain trout pasta, bacon-wrapped filet, a Riverside salad, and fried green tomatoes to share.

"This is fabulous," AB said. "We have to come back with everybody, maybe medicate Beth because I see dogs around tables down by the water. The things I missed in exile."

Their outing gave Eli the boost she needed to get through Pete's wedding. AB's taste and Mela's eye for what would work on Eli left her with abundant selections for the week ahead. "I'll need to adjust one or two of those, but I think you'll get as much notice as Ms. Fatal

Attraction," AB said, yawning on the way to Hiawassee for some pampering at Body Sense.

"You've got a nice shape, girl," Mela added. "Healthy and happy is beautiful. Now no more fretting about going to the rehearsal or the dinner."

With AB's fitting, a little time in the sun, and enough weight loss in recent weeks to pass on slimming understuff, Eli was dumbfounded by her reflection. She looked taller, younger, and felt the confidence that came with. Unpretentious fabric drifted from the Bardot band neckline, skimming her figure and ending mid thigh. Creating the look in a dark forest green absolved the lack of coverage.

She turned away from the mirror and looked back, feeling like a model prepping for fashion week. "Those legs look great in that dress," Mela exclaimed. "Nude heels are genius, AB. From now on, I'm going to find heels to match *me*. It's time, E. Brasstown Valley Resort awaits."

As the valet left in her car, Eli almost bolted for home. Hannah was standing beside Ted inside the BVR lodge entrance, her arm looped through his, head on his chest. As Eli watched, Hannah kissed him. *Ted detests kisses,* she thought, *or* did.

Eli waved off the doorman coming across the entry court, pointing to an annex door that she knew would access the Creekside Pavilion. She entered as Grace, her parents, a brother, and his family were coming through the corridor.

"Eli, you look fabs," Grace squealed, grabbing her face and planting lip prints on both cheeks. She introduced Eli to all her family, apologizing for not getting them together sooner.

"That's on Pete and me, too," Eli said, greeting each of them and freezing as Grace's mom grasped her chin, rubbing a thumb against the lipstick blotches.

From behind the family, she could hear that cackling laugh Ted always uttered to preface ridicule. "Is that a rash?" he howled, feeling particularly witty after downing a few in the bar.

"Ted," she heard Pete say sharply, indignance in his tone.

"Excuse us for a moment, please, Mommy," Grace said, as she pulled Eli around the corner and into what would be her dressing room in the morning. "Sorry," she said, dabbing cream on the lip stain. "I've ruined your makeup."

"Nothing but eye-opener and lip color. Chill," she ordered, taking the tissue to finish as Hannah flew in, bending to Eli's face.

"Still smearing spackle," Hannah broadcast, exiting without a word to either of them.

"That bitch is a lot to unpack," Grace said, totally out of her sunny character. "I'm a wreck, and Mommy, too. She has taken over all our decisions, leaving huge bills behind. This ballooned from a simple wedding party of twenty to eight times that."

Nothing got Eli past insecurity faster than someone in need or a bully. This was both. "Make a list of change-backs."

Armed with Grace's to-fix list, Eli made her way past Ted to where Hannah was calling out positions in the pavilion. Ted chuckled into his drink as Eli confronted her, list in hand.

"This is Grace's wedding, her parents' gift to her and Pete, and these are issues that she wants resolved," she calmly explained.

She called over Grace and her mom, sent for the resort's event manager, then read through the list of the original staging. "With these corrections, any new change will be approved by Grace or her mom. All agreed?"

Hannah stood by in stony silence.

"That would be helpful," Grace admitted, frightened that her husband's career was at risk. Eli took a pic of the list before she gave it to the resort rep, then texted Pete to meet her outside, where she played the audio recording of the event reboot for him.

"I had no idea this was going on," he said, seething. "Grace never lets anyone run over her. It must be the Ted connection. I'll follow up. By the way, Lew is super pumped about coming."

"We talked yesterday. He seems happy to be back at Waller Analytics," she assured Pete, so proud of the man she'd helped shape. "I don't know about this groomsman thing with his walker, though. Good that John will be there, too."

"He parked that weeks ago. Wait til you see him tonight. And you look sensational," he said admiringly, squeezing her hand before he returned to his bride as Eli left for Enrico's.

"There is," Eli remembered Viv Wright asserting, "something about looking the part you're playing that is empowering." The specter of Ted Waller with Hannah his flying monkey didn't scare her anymore.

The rehearsal and the dinner were relaxed and pleasant, with two exceptions: Ted got wasted, and Hannah was sullen throughout. Lew and John's happy arrival lightened the festivities and brightened the Waller family image with Pete's future in-laws.

Grace and Pete enjoyed a beautiful day for their afternoon wedding with an indulgent morning for the girls at the resort's Equani Spa, while the groom and companions hiked Miller Trek Trail, meandering above the golf course and below Rocky Knob.

The bride's gown was ethereal in antique Belgian lace flowing from the Queen Anne neckline of her great-grandmother's wedding dress. Eli wore a demure sleeveless sheath in a richer coral than the bridesmaids, with an inverted pleat of fabric flowing behind each shoulder.

Grace's sister sang as originally planned, accompanied by the small orchestral ensemble hired by Hannah. In an otherwise traditional service, the couple spoke vows that touched guests deeply, revealing an inspiring bond.

Dinner offered a variety of food stations among the tables that were arranged to encircle the dance floor. Hannah's band proved its worth, the cake cutting was genteel, and just two mercifully classy speeches concluded the program.

Carly was still dancing her way through the groomsmen when AB, Mela, and Eli were ready to leave. Beth was MIA, responding only with a "see you tomorrow" text.

As the three of them approached Pete and Grace at the edge of the dance floor, a tipsy Hannah could be heard over the microphone. She was requesting the band behind her play "Without You," coyly mentioning that it was in honor of her engagement to Ted. "A New Year's Eve wedding," she announced, arms around the neck of a fiancé barely able to stand, much less respond. Deep groans swept the room.

Pete ushered the four women back to the bride's table. "Maybe a round of caffeine?" he suggested to the server, nodding at the pair by the microphone.

"Are you sure that's the guy you were married to for eighteen years?" AB asked, squinting past Pete to Eli. "He just doesn't fit the description."

"He hasn't been the same person for months," Pete answered first. "And I've never seen the guy here this weekend before in my life. He's been a disgusting drunk. And what an ass tonight."

"Yeah." AB nodded "*That* one fits, if it means he's the drunk and she's the ass."

<hr />

On her way to Eli's for an after-wedding ash-it-out—but on the patio due to formalwear—AB drove off the road reading the fresh church sign message: "Eternity is a long time to suffer for where you went wrong."

"Okay, Buster, truce over," AB grumbled, making a U-turn and cutting her lights as she coasted along the drive behind the first row of gravestones. After her dust mop surfaced in the lake so conspicuously, she'd bought a back-up, a telescoping travel model, and kept it in the car for just such emergencies. She had used it only twice—more due to recent events than an improvement in the weekly messages.

Teetering on the stone wall, AB swept off each letter, pulling it out of the mop and stacking them at her feet. "Long winded this week, you old goat," she muttered, leaning down to place another letter and coming face-to-face with a man who had been standing right behind her.

She braced against the sign support. "Get away from me," she rumbled. "You're messing with the wrong woman!" And with that, she gave a menacing wave of the dust mop, which he promptly grabbed, pulling her off the wall and catching her under his free arm.

"What is your problem with this church?" he demanded, trying to release her.

"Get your meaty paws off me this minute. My problem is with the miserable jackass that posts these messages. He's an angry, heartless poser who regularly insults the loving, compassionate, patient God that hasn't got a vengeful *whatever*. Anyway, he's a jerk, and if you ever read his crap, you'd know it. Now let me go."

"I'm trying, but your lace is tangled on my buttons. Let me put this mop down," he said, striding to her car.

"Don't you go carrying me off in the dark, dammit, stop! I'll hold the mop, and you untangle me. Who the hell do you think you are?"

"I was about to ask you a similar question. I'm the interim pastor here, Will Shafer, and that's my message you're pulling down. And yeah, I thought that one might get my vandal's attention."

"You baited me," she fumed, squirming against his arm and noticing he was surprisingly muscular for an older guy. And that handsome smile showed he was more amused by her than annoyed.

"If you'd hold still, I'd have a better chance," he shot back, thinking she was as pretty as she was feisty. "You were welcome any time to come in and express your opinion," he advised, freeing the first of several lace-bound buttons.

"You could put me down for this," she responded, trying to reach over her shoulder to feel for the problem. He lowered her to the ground, which resulted in an awkward moment, bent over her with his face on her neck.

"Nope," he said, lifting her again, then asking if she'd been to one of their services as he walked to a gravestone.

"Haven't had the time," she said breezily, appreciating his body heat in the cool night air. He sat on the upright stone, snugging her against him to have both hands free.

At that, she tried to stand, her lace yoke ripping away from her dress as she tore three buttons from his shirt, a fourth still holding. She arched back to see her lace gaping as he tugged it free of the last button. She exhaled slowly through puckered lips, not so much at the damaged clothing as at the extraordinarily toned chest now catching light from the church sign.

"I'm very sorry about the trouble," she said, moving from his lap onto the stone beside him. "This spot used to be a special place for me a while back. I'd sometimes wander through, reading the older head-stones. I made a friend doing the same thing. Her name was Suze. And—"

"Sewz," he repeated, turning his face away.

"Yes, you should know she thinks a lot of you. Several times that summer we talked for hours sitting here. When I complained about the signs, she said you were going through a rough patch. Then I took a new position that kept me busy, and even though I've come here a few times, I haven't seen her again. Did she move away?"

"Sixteen months ago, Sewz died. We were married almost four years. She was in remission, but it came back," he said, without emotion. "And I'll tell you this, dustmop vigilante, it took my faith away. Maybe you're seeing that in the messages."

"You don't sound like a preacher, or is that pastor?"

He laughed and said, "Ex military. USMC colonel with two tours in Nam as a very young pilot. I killed anonymously. That never leaves you. Can't pray it away, can't drink it away, can't talk it away, can't atone for it at all, apparently. I can't anyway."

"There's a lot of that going around up here," she said, not just for herself, but for the vets she'd met through her hospice work, and through Mac. "You think God's shut you out of the program? That He's told Sewz you won't be joining her, ever?"

"I don't know what I think anymore," he said quietly, one eye tilted to the heavens. "I visit the sick, pray with the dying, advise those who seek my counsel, and just keep on waking up every day. I'm nearly seventy. This can't go on forever," he shouted, quickly laughing at how startled she appeared.

"Almost seventy? Really?" she blurted, sending him into long, loud laughter.

"I can't put into words how much I've enjoyed meeting you to-night," he said, standing to offer his hand. "Ms.?"

"Sutton," she answered with a hint of apology. "Annie Blanche, but everyone calls me AB."

"Does anyone call you Annie Blanche?"

"Only in Tennessee," she advised, trying not to stare into his open shirt. "And there aren't many of them left."

Crunching gravel alerted them to an approaching truck, which eased forward until the headlights lit their location and the driver stepped out. "Colonel Shafer, sir," the shadow spoke.

"Lieutenant Miller? Can I help you?"

"Looking for AB, sir. Thought she might have had car trouble. We were expecting her over an hour ago. I'll be on my way now."

"Wait, Mac," AB called, as he returned to his truck. How did you know I was here?"

She noticed he was looking at the torn lace flopping over her shoulder and back at Will's open shirt.

"He caught me taking down his sign, okay? A little tangle as I was removed from the structure is all, no hanky-panky here, got it? Now how did you know where I was?"

"GPS, ma'am."

"My GPS?"

"Yes, ma'am," he hollered, backing quickly and disappearing down the road.

"How do you two know each other?" Will asked.

"Friend of a friend," she replied. "And you?"

""His father and I were lifelong friends. And I know Mac well enough to say that of anyone who could have seen us in this misleading situation, he's the one who would never bring it up anywhere, no matter what he thought."

"You do, huh? I think I'll never live it down. He will gig me with it for eternity."

"But only you. So, we're back to eternity, are we?"

"I'm putting the mop under house arrest. Your messages will go unmolested. By me, anyway."

"I'll replace the dress. You are lovely in it."

"A dress damaged in the commission of my crime? I can fix it. Let me put buttons back on that shirt, and it'll be good as new, too."

"Well, the laundry could—"

"Hand it over, Reverend Colonel. I'll drop it off when it's done."

"Call the number on that sign up there," he said, not noticing her awed expression as he pulled the shirt over his head to preserve the last buttons. "I'll pick it up, along with you, if you're open to having dinner."

"Dinner would be nice," she called, waving as she pulled onto the highway. "Annie Blanche Sutton," she said, looking into her rearview mirror. "How could you look at a *preacher* like that? *HA, ha ha hahahah...*"

Chapter 15

Why You Seek to Hide

"Hello?" AB called out, walking around to the patio at Eli's.

"What happened to you?" Bernie demanded, twisting in her seat.

"First things first," Eli said, as AB came under the porch light. "Where's the rest of your dress?"

"Oh, I stopped to talk with somebody. Didn't Mac tell you? My lace got snagged. I can stitch it."

"Bernie told us everything," Carly taunted. "Let's hear your story."

"Huh, I don't know anything to tell," Bernie laughed. "But now that you're sitting next to me, I get a whiff of my ex's aftershave. So, either you have really, really bad judgment, or you're swapping scents with a man whose grooming tastes run to the '80s."

"Oh, my friend, you got me on the judgment thing," AB confessed. "Nothing but flashbacks the last ten minutes. My first *intimate* experience was the hospital chief of staff, and it happened twenty feet from where his brave wife lay dying. I was his pregnant bride two months later.

"My second husband was my psych professor—lasted all of ten months and put me back years in my recovery. Now I'm tearing the shirt off a stranger in a cemetery, and he happens to be a colonel subbing as a pastor. Think I got a type? Have I mentioned my daddy ran off with Momma's best friend?"

"Well, Mac said you were catching up with someone and that you'd be on your way soon," Mela said, rattled by the outburst.

"That boy is such a gentleman." AB hooted. "Where's Beth, I know she can tell me all about this fella."

"She was sidetracked, too," Mela advised. "Text said, 'See you tomorrow,' so you'll have to wait for that resource. Anyone I might know?"

"Only the writer of the worst church signs in plastic letter history."

"C'mon, not the grumpy preacher," Carly said, leaning in. "Spill!"

"I had just extended my new dust mop and was popping letters off that damned church sign—"

"Hold up, AB," Bernie interrupted. "I cannot appear in any tabloids being perp walked into the Towns County jail with you. Any charges pending?"

"Nah. We're going out."

"Wait, *who* is he?" Mela asked.

"Will Shafer. Turns out he was married to Sewz, the sweet gal I met walking in the cemetery summer before last."

"Now was that meeting before or after she died?" Bernie inquired.

"Oooh, Colonel Shafer is that pastor?" Mela said, connecting some dots.

"Out with it, Mela. What do you know?"

"Dude has issues," Carly interjected.

"More like a quirk," Mela said. "He was already a little OCD before Sewz died."

"That's a broad brush you're swinging there," AB noted. "And now?"

"He may be struggling," Mela advised. "But from what our reception girls said, that doesn't slow the stream of ladies hoping to get his attention with casseroles. He's a super nice guy, and nice looking, too."

"Yes, yes he is," AB agreed. "Now, what about this struggle? How do you know?"

"The girls at our front desk would say that, when he brought in his old Jack Russell, he kept getting up to stack brochures or magazines, or to adjust the ceiling fans so they were all going the same direction. I noticed him rearranging supplies in my exam room."

"He's a great guy, with some anxiety issues. What's not to love?" Eli defended from the depths of her subconscious.

"Probably not doing well after losing Sewz," AB suggested, "and this likely isn't his first bout. Compulsive behavior is sometimes associated with PTSD, and he's a prime candidate for that. He surely knows there are meds and therapies available. A little distraction might lower his stress levels," she added suggestively.

"You go, AB," Carly cheered on her way to the kitchen.

Does all this harassment mean y'all have covered the wedding announcement without me?" AB asked Eli quietly. "That was some world class bad form."

"I think it shocked everyone there," Eli said. "Grace's family was stunned by the intrusion, Pete and I were mortified, and most people didn't seem to believe her, with Ted staggering off to the side."

"He didn't deny it," Mela scoffed.

"None of that will happen," Bernie commented, sliding her shoes off and resting her feet on the cool stone floor.

"Your opinion, or straight from Spirit?" AB wanted to know.

"The last thing I heard from Spirit was to keep Eli out of the storm, and you saw how that worked out. Last time I fully connected was the night we all met. I was on fire again. I truly miss being able to bring healing messages."

"What derailed you, anyway?" Eli asked, darting through the opening.

"Forgot what I was about. Stopped focusing on helping people and decided I was something of a rock star." She laughed weakly.

"You are a rock star, Bernie," Carly insisted. "I've been watching your shows online, and you were *amaz*. I got all the feels."

"A lot of editing that made it look faster and more pinpoint than it really is," she conceded. "But it did feel good—easing sorrow and lighting up memories.

"The more I got caught up in expecting to be treated special—not honoring the gift—the more it faded. We found ways to cover in production that weren't going to fly with Spirit at all. I had to quit."

"Did your family abandon you when things fell apart? Is that why you're alone here?" Carly asked, with supercharged compassion.

"Oh, honey, I kicked those money-grubbing users to the curb. Cheatin' husband; back-stabbing producer; tweet-happy personal assistant; my son, whom I treated like royalty; and his princess wife—all off the payroll. Wait, now, I don't think like that anymore—"

"Explains why you didn't know I've been standing here," a male voice said from the corner of the house.

Instantly, Carly was in a shooter's stance. "Hands behind your head," she shouted, pulling a flashlight alongside her weapon to illuminate the intruder.

"Whoa, whoa, whoa!" he responded, hands clasped over his head.

"Carly, that's Seth Taylor, from the GBI," Eli shouted.

"Wish that would happen *every* time somebody tries a psychic joke," Bernie muttered.

"What has you skulking around in the dark?" Eli asked, as he walked over to take a seat on the wall with her.

"Been fly fishing on Fires Creek and thought I'd check out the security system you planned to install," he said, amid glances over at Carly.

"Since when do you carry a gun, Carly?" Mela whispered.

"Since I was eighteen, I think."

"A little dark for fly fishing, idn't it?" AB questioned, adjusting her flopping lace.

"Didn't you come by earlier?" Eli asked, as she showed him an infrared option through her phone app for the security system. "Because I thought that was your fancy Gladiator gliding by."

"Busted," Carly jeered from over his shoulder. "Bet you could get anywhere in that truck. Oh, and sorry about the, well, you know."

"Hey, I very much appreciate your restraint. That was careless, walking up in the dark, especially after what happened here.

"So, Eli, I was thinking you might enjoy some fly fishing with me tomorrow. I have a cabin in Hayesville. You could come by for breakfast, and we'll get an early start?"

"That sounds exciting, and I would love to learn, but I have tons of work to catch up on tomorrow before I meet with a client Monday. Invite me next time you come?"

"Isn't that fraternizing with the assault victim, or some other ethical breach?" AB asked, still ruffled by his entrance.

"Is David Harrison coming here Monday?" Carly asked, squeezing in between Seth and Eli. "I have to be here if he is, you know—"

"We're meeting in Atlanta, sorry."

"Not the Hollywood David Harrison, right?" Seth asked.

"One and only," Carly answered.

"Are you sure you're a GBI man?" Bernie said, with a touch of side-eye. "Because that Harrison has set off a whole string of fireworks here recently."

"How's that, ma'am?"

"Don't go all 5-0 on me. You know that dead man didn't fall off the short bus, happen upon the fastest electric boat on this lake in a helluva storm, and find his way to *this* cove and *this* house and *this* girl all serendipity-like."

"Let's not forget the uberwealthy ex-asshole," AB noted, "who hasn't missed an opportunity to spit in her eye since she left him."

"You had your chance to leave as you were listening from the corner over there," Eli teased. "Not many thoughts go unspoken when we're all together. I'm sure y'all will get to the bottom of this soon."

"Well, we are clo—"

"Duuude," Mac bellowed, as the big blond dog dashed through the patio after Pharaoh, who playfully struck a fierce pose on his way to Eli. "He's only been out since we came home," she apologized, scooping him up as Mela's eyes widened.

"No showing off," Mela scolded the cat, as he rubbed his chin against Eli's cradling arms.

"There's the boy who helped Mela save me," Eli tutted, kissing his ears.

"Oh no, over *here*—we're the boys who saved you," Mac announced, catching up with Dude and absently bumping fists as he passed Seth. "Ain't that right, Dude?"

"Guess I'll be going, early start tomorrow," Seth said, dusting off his jacket as he stood. "Cat allergy. We'll try another time," he suggested to Eli before disappearing.

Mac walked back into the driveway after he heard the Gladiator start, waiting for it to leave. Meanwhile, Mela caught everyone up on Pharaoh's amazing recovery despite losing an eye.

"I thought that cop would *never* leave," Beth said, following Mac to the patio.

"You are not going anywhere with that blue falcon," Mac ordered, pointing at Eli as he flopped in a lounge chair and snapped for Dude. "Sorry, Pharaoh, but I had to get that character out of here. You were a great help, buddy."

"You sicced Dude on Pharaoh?" Mela screeched.

"Nooo, just signaled him to trail. Figured that would bring him to one or the other of you. Close enough to run off Nancy Drew."

"Oh, I've been waiting to toss this one." AB chuckled from her seat next to Bernie. "So Beth, where the hell have you been, and what the hell happened to your dress? We look like a demolition derby for formal attire tonight."

"I went for a walk and got lost in the woods and my phone didn't work so Mac came and got me."

"Well, well," AB said, exchanging gotcha glances with Bernie. "Which superpower did you use for that one, Mac?"

"As much as I love sparring with every one of you, I've had enough playtime on this side of the lake for today. Mela, can we go—uh, I mean would you like to get something to eat with me?"

"Oh, where are y'all going? Because I am so hungry after those prissy dabs of wedding food," Bernie said, slipping her shoes back on.

"I'm in. Ride with me, Bernie," Carly said. "I'll get you back safely."

"I don't doubt you, girl."

"Beth," AB whispered, as the others gathered their things, "should I stay or go?"

"Stay. Please. I just got upset when a big ol' pickup had me blocked in. Clowns shouldn't be driving things they don't know how to get in the parking space."

"Now before you pounce on pickup truck drivers like you do on spam callers, or social media, or people using fake vests to misrepresent their pet as trained service angels because they can't go anywhere without the dog—"

"Or laundry detergents you can smell from a block away," Eli chimed in.

"That was a righteous one," AB agreed, "but let's get to what's fueling all this upset. Tell us what really happened this evening?"

"Guys, I'm in trouble. Could I stay tonight, Eli?"

"Yes, of course. Shouldn't we call your husband?"

"There's no husband, no kids. Nobody."

"Did something happen at the wedding? I didn't somehow drag you into any of my stuff, I hope," Eli said, trying to remind her she wouldn't be alone in whatever it was.

AB was mid-breath when that comment surfaced, bringing her squarely around to Eli. "Do you *ever* stop beating yourself up?" she earnestly wanted to know. Flustered, Eli looked blankly at AB, who took her hand as she reached across for Beth's.

"Now, let's have it, Beth."

"It's all because I'm not really Beth. Well, I am Beth. My name is Elizabeth, like Beth's was, but my gram called me Bibi, and that's the name I went by til I was fifteen."

"And how did that get you stranded at Brasstown Valley Resort tonight?"

"I have a real estate ad running on BVR's internal TV channel. Mountain scenes, info, and me talking over it. Today I got a voicemail, a call from the resort. The name unnerved me. I agreed to meet her in the lobby after the wedding, and when I got there, I panicked. I know it's Beth's older sister. She's tracked me down."

"Maybe," Eli suggested, "she's one of those people who just wants to see the area while wasting the real estate agent's day."

"Let's back up to the higher order problem for a minute," AB said. "How did you happen to take on her sister's identity?"

"Short version? Because it's a lot."

"Bib-bee—that's going to take some getting used to, girl—it would do you good to air the whole story. And the more time I spend here, the less time I'll have to lay awake thinking about snuggling up to that fine preacher."

"Beg pardon?" Bibi asked, startled.

"You don't need that in your head right now," Eli assured her.

"K. Gram raised me, and by the time I was nine, we had to go live with her sister-in-law, Margaret, on the coast in St. Mary's, Georgia. Gram found a job cleaning and stocking at a nice gift shop just a few minutes away on the river, a branch of a fancier place in Fernandina. When she got sick, I was twelve, mature for my age. Claimed I was fifteen and took over for her after school and weekends to maintain that little bit of income.

"Three years later, new owners for both shops were introduced one October afternoon saying they would close for remodeling to reopen in the spring. They kept me on, a fifteen-year-old they believed to be eighteen, to clean out files and organize records as they relocated their lives to the area.

"The offer to buy couldn't have come at a better time for my employers, Joe and Emma Parker. Their property in Missouri had been purchased by Branson developers, allowing them to retire and move—with the two girls they adopted late in life—to St. Mary's and open the gift shops.

"That luck started to reverse soon after, beginning with the presumed riptide drowning of their younger daughter, Beth. She was at a Florida beach with her sixteen-year-old sister Sarah and friends as a Labor Day hurricane was moving off the coast. Her body was never recovered, and they never accepted she was dead.

"By the time the buyers came in, Emma's diabetes had worsened dramatically, and Joe's mind was failing as fast as his eyesight. Their daughter Sarah had left them behind, having met and married a corporate attorney based in Japan.

"As the new owners took over, I was still grieving my gram, doing my best to keep up with school, and tend to Margaret as well as my failing employers. The Parkers were moving to a senior care community in Florida and creating a multi-million-dollar trust in their older daughter's name, in hopes she would return to find Beth.

"This left me trying to figure out a way to repay money I had stolen from the business over the last two years to pay overages for Gram's heart-failure treatment. My earnings were always handed over to Margaret, who had relied on Gram's pitiful income to make ends meet.

"About that time, a relative had figured out the value of Margaret's coastal property and invited her to live with them. I would be homeless at fifteen, probably turned over to the state. Still with?"

"You're quite the little soap opera, Ms., well damn, what's your last name?" AB wondered aloud.

"Spillett. No kidding. Just sounds odd under these circumstances."

"Not so odd," Eli argued, reaching over to put a throw around Bibi's shoulders as she shivered from the racking exposure and the cooling air.

"As I sifted through boxes and file drawers that week, whittling down the heaps of paper to essential documents, I found a box labeled 'Beth.' Inside were all the girl's records, from pediatrician notes to a baby book and assorted report cards, school art—even her birth certificate and a social security card.

"I read through all the Missouri documents and found the Parkers had adopted Beth at the age of four and probably from relatives not unlike my own messed up parents. After that sad start, she had a fairytale life ahead, then lost it so young. But legally, Beth was still alive.

"I saw this as an answer—become Beth, and as an eighteen-year-old, I wouldn't be at risk of getting turned over to the state. There was no one to say I wasn't her. I loaded my backpack with most of the contents of the box and put the rest through the shredder.

"I needed driving lessons and a ride to Kingsland for the test. I told Margaret I would be living with the Parkers, and then I stayed in a Fernandina shelter while saving for a room of my own. I worked days at our main shop, nights serving burgers, and I got a GED. Eventually, a lady who was often donating at the thrift store where I shopped gave me a job answering phones at her real estate office and later helped me get licensed. I was only going to be Beth until I was old enough to get a life of my own."

"So, you worked with Sarah in the shops?" AB asked.

"No. No, I don't remember her ever coming in when I was there."

"How did you know her tonight then?" Eli pressed, confused.

"Well, I didn't. Wow, Sarah Parker can't know who I am. Now I can focus on getting Ca—"

"Her name is Sarah Parker? Any guess how many Sarah Parkers live right here in Georgia?"

"Baby, your stressed-out conscience pulled a fast one on you tonight." AB giggled, delighted to see a faint smile, even if Bibi wasn't sure what she was smiling about.

"It's getting chilly and we're tired," she added, standing to leave. "But we will get you through this, Bibi Spillett."

Before Eli could get back from the kitchen with fresh decaf, Bibi was asleep on the sofa. No sense waking her to move to the guest room. Eli opened her laptop and asked Mac for help in quietly researching an Elizabeth Parker, who went missing below Fernandina Beach.

As she typed, thunder was rumbling in the distance. Pharaoh left his bed and slid into the chair against her, tail swishing over the keyboard. "Nice to have Beth, *nope,* Bibi here with us, isn't it, fella?"

When Bibi finally stirred, her open eye focused on a dozing Eli, still cross-legged, in the chair. "Aw, that's going to hurt," she mumbled, stretching herself upright. Pharaoh raced her to the door and out as she watched the darkened sky shedding steady rain.

"Ow, ow, don't tell me it's time to walk," Eli moaned, trying to straighten a leg. Her phone showed it was after seven.

"Let's see who wants to skip the walk since we'll be having Mela's birthday party by the lake this evening if the rain stops," Bibi suggested. "What were you working on so late? The Harrison book?" she asked, on her way down the hall.

"A little," Eli responded, limping to the kitchen. "Bathrobe on the back of the guestroom door. I'll start some breakfast."

"Holy smokes, I don't have any clothes," Bibi called through the door. "Could you drive me to BVR for my car?"

"It's parked out front," she answered, pans rattling. "Mac brought it last night."

"You don't find it a little freaky that he makes things that cannot happen, well, happen?" she asked, gliding out the front door barefoot in the fatigued A-line guipé that even pouring rain couldn't make worse.

"You have no idea how deep his freak streak runs," she muttered to the empty doorway.

A tap on the glass door behind her coincided with AB hollering, "Do I smell bacon and coffee?"

"Coffee, yes," Eli said, sliding the door aside. "And you can start the bacon once you're out of that rain gear."

"Bacon sounds good," Lew said from the front door, ushering Bibi and Kit inside.

"I've heard of farms where injured or lost animals are mysteriously compelled to show up, but you've got something even stranger going on here lately, and I may have an idea about it," AB whispered over Eli's shoulder.

"I met these guys coming down the driveway," Bibi said. "Anybody need this bathroom? It could be a long shower."

"Kit, what a wonderful surprise." Eli rushed to hug and introduce her to AB before she bear-hugged Lew. "Where did you find Kit?" she marveled, tucked under his arm.

Lew waited to see whether Kit would respond first, and when she looked away, he answered. "I was north of Atlanta, heading home when I got a call from the security desk at corporate saying there was an anxious young woman there attempting to contact Eli Sledge, so I swung by and met Kit—who is just as lovely as you described her in your paddle boarding story. I offered her a ride to Hiawassee," he said, taking coffee from AB.

"I was stuck and scared—then so happy to meet you, Lew," Kit said, both hands tight around her coffee. "Eli, I'm sorry for barging in this way. My phone broke during a situation with someone I've been involved with for a while and couldn't break things off with last night. Strange way to take you up on that offer to see your lake place."

"When they come up with that communication chip to implant behind our ear," AB predicted, delivering a plate of bacon to the crowd gathering at the kitchen bar, "the phone insurance racket will be *over*."

"I think I'll stick with losing my phone," Bibi declared, freshly robed from the shower, a towel turban on her head. "Maybe we should call Bernie, Carly, and Mela for a birthday breakfast instead of the bonfire tonight."

"I think we could use a juju-clearing fire," AB said. "And we're already late planning our entries into the July Fourth boat parade. Don't forget Leslie and Sophie are driving up for the party."

Eli was distracted by a "Where are you?" text from Mela and was going to the front door as Lew responded to AB. "I could use some ideas and a few hands with my entry," he said, helping himself to another biscuit.

"What is all this?" Mela asked from the door, as Carly breezed by to the kitchen.

"Ummm," Carly crooned, filling a plate with biscuits and scrambled eggs, "if I'd known we were doing this I'd have been on time."

"Save me something," Bernie warned her, taking off a raincoat on the porch.

"Our *walk?*" Mela said, still shaking her umbrella and parking it outside the door.

"I can explain," Eli said, guiding Mela to the bedroom hall. "First, happy birthday," she whisper-shouted, handing Mela a small box that contained a sterling relief pendant with a fat labradorite moon hanging over mountain ridges. On the back was a Ram Dass quote, which read, "We're all just walking each other home."

"Oh," Mela exclaimed. "It's a Melanie Miller piece." Then she read the inscription. "You get me, E," she said, giving her friend a rocking hug.

"Right back at ya," Eli said, as they returned to the kitchen. "I'll introduce you, but that's Lew, the brother-in-law I declined to relinquish in the divorce; and Kit, the sensational marine biologist from Beaufort."

"Where did all these people sleep?" she said, as Eli guided her to meet them.

Chapter 16

Where Your Secrets Go on Parade

L ater that afternoon, Kit returned with Carly, wearing cuffed shorts and a pullover they found while scouting Carly's closet. Their snickering suggested the two had bonded over Gen-X humor. "Okay if Kit bunks with me? Carly hollered, as they trooped to the lakeside patio.

"Yes, girls," Eli called out, in her best Carol Brady impression. "Remember, no TV after nine, and lights out by ten. Seriously, come peel some oak branches for these hot dogs."

"Let me help with that," Lew offered, turning away from the fire he and Bibi were building. Mela had opened a tote filled with identical gifts that attracted attention, while Leslie and Sophie delivered a festive floral cake spiked with candles.

"You're looking a bit thinner, my already slim friend," Eli chided, as Lew seared branches over flames. "Is this a racing tactic or due more to Ted's inability to make a sandwich?"

"There's no shortage of food in that building. I'm working over-time at the office trying to earn my keep since the company insurance had covered my near-death experience as though I'd been showing up for more than the occasional board meeting. By the way, Ted was livid when he discovered your health coverage had been dropped. His attorneys buried that in the settlement?"

"Gosh, no. My oversight after the break with the Wright Agency. I just found out that Ted had signed for all my expenses at the hospital that night. And no one at Waller will talk to me about getting copies of billing to pay him back. Could you help me get that?"

"I can tell you none of it has come through Waller Analytics be-cause I've looked at every fiscal file that's been opened for months. I suspect they imprinted his personal card, and that is between him and his CPA.

"I can also tell you that I'm suspicious of his self-proclaimed fian-cé's activities, both at corporate and as regards my brother. *She* may be what happened to your insurance. I'm drilling down on transactions she's initiated. And I'm convinced she is medicating Ted—with some-thing that would explain his newfound openness to a social life and to her ambitions."

"Can't imagine Ted taking anything other than those few supple-ments and an occasional aspirin, Lew."

"I agree. Initially he had little interest in her, but *this* Ted can be persuaded. Alcohol seems to hit him much harder these days, too. The shift is too dramatic not to be enhanced. But how to catch her at it? She's very, very good at covering her tracks."

"Then maybe he's not so much a happier man as an anesthetized man in her company?"

"Something like that."

"No way, Sophie," they heard Leslie shouting. "Your dad did one, and I'll do one."

Lew kissed Eli on the cheek after he wrapped his second hotdog to travel. "Time to go. Take care of Kit, and I'll see you next week at the parade."

"It's no big deal, Leslie," Mela said, trying to settle the blow up. "I mentioned at the clinic that DNA testing was interesting, then came all these tests as birthday gifts."

"My mother said my gift for *seeing* came from her side," Bernie muttered, as she read the test insert. "But that isn't going to show up here."

"Shouldn't you *know* the answer, though?" Bibi wondered.

"With all your secrets spilling, you hit me with a shot like that, *Bibi Spillett?*"

Mela handed out tests, suggesting the results could be revealed together to share their discoveries. "Eli, take the last one for Pete," Mela offered.

"E, this way," Mac said, wagging the box to get her attention and heading to the dock.

"I've done a test," he admitted. "Scots on Mom's side, as expected, then a half-Cuban line on my father's combined with a solid streak of early American settlers—adventurers some call patriots," he said, stopping to face her. "Yet I've had the impression you're none too fond of military people. Am I right?"

"No, Mac, I admire and respect the people, it's the concept of being battle-minded and warring and all that. It sickens me. Look what it did to you! I know it's unavoidable sometimes, I—"

"What if *your* bloodline was full of warriors? What if they were fighters only when they needed to protect the people and places they love?

"What if they are just as sickened by war, but step up and put their lives on the line to secure what matters most? Their families, countries, and the freedoms they protect for all people, even those they can't agree with? Would you disown them," he asked slowly, a break in his voice, "as fathers, mothers, sons, daughters, sisters, or *a brother*?"

"Mac, what are you getting at?"

"My father, the jet jockey who sortied over Nam," he stammered. "I'm thinking he could be your father, too."

"Why would you think a crazy thing like that?" she blasted. "Based on what, Mac?" She turned away in a storm of confused irritation. "Tell me what you think you know that I don't."

"Why are you yelling, angry with me?" he finally responded, his voice low. "I wanted to give you a heads-up. I've registered on a few websites in case he had other *offspring*. If there are two of us right here, well…

"When you came to live with your aunt and were at our place a few times over that first summer, my gran told me she thought you looked more like me than my older half-sister, Kathy. She brought you to my dad's attention."

You're saying this to me because of some comment your grandmother made?" she raged.

"Because my dad saw you the summer he died and said you looked just like his mother, Rosa. He had me sorting through his things for a picture of her. He was too sick, it was too late to pursue it, but he remembered a Julia coming to a party at the old Fieldstone Resort when he was here visiting Will Shafer one Thanksgiving. Let's just say they got bored with football."

"No one ever told me any of that," she said, finally listening.

"He and my mother had been a thing when he was visiting Will a few years before that, not long after her divorce from Kathy's dad. After I was born, Gran said Mom was afraid of sharing custody and never contacted him. She didn't see him again until I was eight.

"We literally bumped into him shopping at Alexander's, looking through jeans. She told him she had tried to find him. She was remarried by then, but he immediately bought a lake house, retired, and was here until he died of prostate cancer at fifty-two."

"*That* Julia couldn't have been my mother," Eli said dryly. "She claimed the sperm donor was an unnamed encounter at a Grateful Dead concert in Atlanta. Although I heard a relative tell the story of her dinging her boss for two years of support until he got a paternity test."

"Then I'm not disparaging your mother by suggesting another candidate?"

"Momma set a very low bar for reasonable disparagement," she assured him, rolling her eyes toward the party up the hill.

Mela moved away from everyone seated around the fire and tried to catch some of the intense conversation Mac had started, as AB joined her to watch.

"Think those two are figuring out they're related?" she chuckled.

Mela grabbed her arm. "Mac told you?" she yelped.

"Well, no, but geez *Doctor* Mela. Those unusual eyes they both have, the hair, the smiles, and—"

"Who's the referee," Bernie asked from behind them.

"Oh, we're not arguing," Mela said.

"No, between Eli and Mac there on the dock, the man in the fine blue uniform. Who is he? Ray, Raf. No, Raphael," she shouted, answering her own question. "He's laughing, throwing his hands in the air, and saying, 'These are my children.'

"Can't you see—oh, Lord in Heaven, y'all *can't* see. You can't see, but I can see!" she sang, clapping her hands and dancing in place, the silk threads of her embroidered tunic glinting in the afternoon sun. "Thank you, Heaven, for letting his spirit speak to me."

※

Monday morning's walk moved along slowly, with lots of topics to cover and a crowded field, despite Eli being in Atlanta. Sophie made a shopping list for boat parade supplies; Carly was pressing Bernie for details about her show at the lakeside Concert Hall, benefiting the area first responders; Leslie and Bibi were comparing paint colors for the redecorating underway at AB's; Kit was coaching Mela on paddle boarding; and AB was considering ways to help Eli process the "heads-up" from Mac.

Afterwards, Leslie, Bibi, and Sophie went shopping, while AB and Bernie headed home. Once Carly and Kit had met the barn menagerie, they saddled up for a trail ride through the woods surrounding the neighborhood. After the horses were cooled and turned out, the girls went with Mela to find the paddle boards stored at the barn. Eli was waiting at the terrace when they returned with the boards.

"Were you doing stuff like paddle boarding in your twenties?" Eli asked, as she and Mela watched the boarders gliding out in the lake. "Because my twenties were spent buffering a grade-schooler from a bigger, brattier kid who resented sharing his home and wife."

"Nope, I was working my way through school, marrying out of my sexual orientation, and caring for venerable folk. Did I mention I've been there, vicariously done that, and will not be a participant in feeble old age?"

"Isn't it supposed to beat the alternative?"

"Naaah, they say you forget there is one."

Eli was astonished by how young and sweet Kit had seemed since Sunday. Her reality TV bravado disappeared with the lavish designer wardrobe. Laughter rippled across the water in the voices of little girls at play.

"Why don't we ever get out there like that?" Mela stewed. "They're what, maybe fifteen years younger?"

"Not quite. And do you remember how slowly we moved the day after we followed Carly up Wyah Bald to reach the stretch of Appalachian Trail she helps maintain? I'll need some pre-play conditioning."

"So," Mela wondered, "are you and Mac good after your smack-down at the dock yesterday?"

"What did he say about it?"

Mela hesitated, collecting her thoughts. "Mac has come a long way from the angry recluse who came home in pieces a few years ago—his military career abruptly ended, his life mission canceled. He has fought his way back, E, opening up little by little, but that accelerated when you came home.

"He told me once you were here that he has believed you are his little sister since he was a boy. That he watched out for you as well as he could until you left with Ted and were out of his reach. He's been a different person with you around again. Even told me that he's had feelings for me since we were kids. He's a very private guy with deep, deep feelings."

"Then you believe Bernie *seeing* his dad saying he was my father, too?"

"I can't say right now because Mac's coming our way. But he was concerned that he'd messed up. Talk to him? I'm going back to work."

Mac caught Mela as she was standing to leave, giving her a gentle kiss on the lips, which surprised and delighted Eli.

"Something else I should know? Can I call you two Mala now?" Eli asked, as Mac sat next to her, a warning glance included with his smile.

"How about your fugitive friend's records? Prints as Elizabeth Parker—same birthdate and birthplace—are already on file for everything from a carry permit to a purveyor of real estate, but otherwise clean."

"Thanks, Mac," she said, kicking a pinecone from under their bench. "How did you get her prints?"

"Swiped the birthday card she gave Mela at the party, printed it, then gave it to Mela last night."

"You were at Mela's last night?"

"Mela was at *my* place. She owns my heart Eli, always has."

"What about the girl you brought to Road Atlanta, and the Ohio one, and—"

"Plenty of not-the-one girls have come along, and not one compared to Mel."

"So, Ms. Parker, or Spillett, she's wanting to reverse her identity? If she goes for a legal opinion, I think they would explain the likely sentencing in that conversation. Anywhere she talks about it, that's one more layer of potential exposure should she decide to pass. It's chilling, the ID theft that goes unnoticed unless someone gets turned in or overplays it.

"Assuming a complete identity like she did, having established it so well, maybe live with it? That's a very common name, and if the only person liable to figure it out is the adopted sister? She never accessed any of the dead girl's accounts. What would send the sister looking? Prison and a ruined life are powerful disincentives.

"Thanks. I'll let her know what you've told me and, listen, I uh—"

"Hey," Mac said, pulling her into a side hug, "I hit you with huge news. Remember giving me your one-and-done password a while back? I realized then this was something you needed to hear. I'm really sorry he wasn't around long enough to know you, but I think you'll be relieved once *you're* convinced."

"You've run my damned DNA, haven't you?"

"C'mon, who leaves a hairbrush in their kitchen? It was meant to be."

"You neat-freak ass."

"Stubborn brat." He laughed, pulling her up from the bench and turning her to the lake. "I've waited a long time to tell you that the house in the cove to your left across the lake there, pale blue house with the wraparound porch? That was our dad's house. I lived in it after I separated from the Eighty-Second, while I worked on Gran's house to make it livable again. Been renting it out since. Want to take a look at it this afternoon? I'll show you some of the old man's pictures."

Eli was too zoned to answer, leaning against her brother, listening to his heartbeat and the resonance of his voice through his chest. "I won't be a brat again," she whispered.

He tugged her closer, lifted her chin, and said, "Nobody calls my little sister a brat. *Nobody.*"

"Mac, what if you hadn't made it home? What if we never connected? Why didn't you tell me years ago?"

"Until I had confirmation it was too speculative, but you've been on the deed to the house since I left Auburn for my first tour. It's a big relief to know you're good with this."

"I am over the moon that I know, finally *know* who my father was, but mostly that I get you in the surprise package. Only thing better would be you and Mela tying the knot," she said, without filtering. "I mean, you know, someday if that's how things work out, maybe."

"She couldn't stand it." He howled with laughter. "She showed you the ring, didn't she?" he said, once his laughter subsided.

"Seriously, is there a ring? I'm going to choke that—"

"Almost sister-in-law? I said she's the one, Bit. I'll let her tell you when. This is new. You haven't missed much. Let's get those boardettes off the lake and hit Carlotta's for a late lunch, huh?"

——————◆————————

Thursday morning's walk was skipped in favor of an early start decorating Lew's prized wooden boat, an antique Chris Craft. AB was smitten. "Get a pin-up shot of me back here," she directed Carly, her photographer, as she struck a pose in her capris and conservatively tied sleeveless camp shirt. Next, she perched on the gleaming varnish beside the fluttering flag.

"I really should have an Instagram account," she decided. "What's the hold up?" she asked, as Carly angled the phone from the Waller dock.

"Waiting for you to tell me what a pin-up filter is," Carly answered blankly.

"This boat looks expensive, and fragile," Mela said to Eli, who was handing off streamers to Bernie from the dock.

"It is both," Eli replied, watching AB climbing over the seats. "It's the 1941 Deluxe Runabout Barrel Back, the 19-foot model. Of course, Ted had to find the more rare 23-foot version."

"Enough," Bernie shouted. "Photo shoot's over. Let's get some festoons on my pontoon."

Mela was shaking out the folds of bunting to drape around Bernie's railing as Kit approached Eli with her phone held out. "Please, tell Molly that I am here with you. She's freaking because my phone goes straight to voicemail."

"Hi, Molly," Eli said. "Yes, she's been here since—" she paused to read Kit's lips, "Saturday. Yes, we are getting ready for the boat parade and the fireworks show tonight. Sure wish you were here with us. It's Carly's number, the friend she's staying with. I will do that, Molly. Great, talk to you then."

"Kit, you disappeared and didn't let your mom know where you went? Now I'm in trouble for not letting her know. How did she find you?"

"Carly made me call. Thanks, E. I'll keep in touch," she said, tucking the phone in Carly's back pocket as they joined Mac and Lew discussing the fishing rig.

"Naaah, I'd never pay that much for a boat," Mac assured him. "This Skeeter's three years old. Bought it off a fella whose wife was having them move back to Virginia to be close to grandkids. Never seen a man cry like that over a boat."

Lew was helping him set the fishing rods upright, outfitted in wired mylar ribbons to look like exploding fireworks overhead. As Kit came on board, he pointed to the young man approaching the dock with a cooler of iced drinks. "Kit, that's John, my son."

"Dad," John shouted. "Uncle Ted is here. With *her*."

"Thanks, JB. Put those drinks on the pontoon boat, will ya?"

"Yeah, Dad. Mac, mind if I go with you? Looks like Dad's boat is booked."

"Sure thing. I'll move down the dock and give Ted some room for the 23," he said.

"Food and drinks on the shaded boat, everybody," Bernie announced. "I'm just saying."

"Where's the chill deck?" Eli asked, stepping onto Bernie's floating resort. "I'm ready to relax. *Or barf*," she amended, at the sight of Hannah sashaying along the dock. "Are we ready for take-off or whatever, Bernie?" she urged, grabbing at dock lines.

"All aboard," Bernie announced, revving the engines from the pilot's seat. As they cast off, Mela, Leslie, Sophie, Bibi, and Eli were sprawled on the benches, pelting Mac and Lew with Cheetos before Hannah completed her runway strut. Mac met Ted on the walk down, and they talked as Hannah approached Lew's boat.

"Aw, Lewie, you have a new friend." She smiled condescendingly at AB. "Is it true the old ones are grateful, no matter *how* long it takes?"

"I guess you would know, sweetie," Carly gushed, popping up from behind the seat where she was slipping off her shorts and t-shirt. Her Supergirl pose couldn't boost the wattage any higher on her paint-tight, brimming bikini. "That's my mom, AB. I'm Carly, and here is the best lay I have *ever* had, but you'd know that already, huh?" she said, grabbing Lew and planting a face-sucking kiss that left him weak in the knees.

"She's gone. You can let him up for air now," AB drawled. Lew staggered to a seat and watched Carly stroll over to Mac's rig, where Hannah was posed. Carly yelped, hopping as she feigned injury until she neatly bumped Hannah into the dock's fashionably deep water.

Raucous cheers went up from the pontoon boat—inaudible to Ted, who was just as far underwater as his fiancé, trying to shove her to the ladder. Kit and Carly high-fived as they returned to their respective rides, with Kit again in possession of Carly's phone to get pics of the surfacing for Eli.

"I am in love," Lew told AB, as he watched Carly breeze to his boat.

"You and every other male, straight or not, in this parade today. And I should include some women in that count."

As they joined the boat lineup behind the floating Tiki-Bar, AB put another towel on the seat beside her for Carly. Her giggles bubbled into laughter as they watched Ted trying to push Hannah on the dock while Mac and John pulled.

Then she turned to Carly. "Ditch the ditzy, Lambchops. I never bought it for a minute. Now tell me who you really are in there," she said, with her usual look over the top of her shades.

"Ditzy is my cover for work. Do not share this please. My marksmanship got me into the Federal Air Marshals. My appearance almost kept me out. Our training officers emphasized invisibility—blending into the background on every flight we take. I created an airhead vibe and always wear simple, baggy clothes when I work, so that I don't stand out."

"You really blew your cover over there." AB laughed again, stretching her legs over the seat in front of her. "It's nice to finally meet you, Carly Lane."

"Will you keep my secret?"

"Are you available for adoption?"

"Yeah, I would have been a few years ago. My sweet mom is such a conformist, even before social media began driving everyone in that stampede. Her son and younger girl fit her mold, but I couldn't get there.

"My body rebelled first. Even though we had tons of veggies, no sugar, plenty of fresh air, and sunshine, I was a little big and already busty at twelve. She took me for a breast reduction consultation when I was thirteen, and the surgeon said there was no medical necessity for it.

"There's the 9-11 factor," she said, with forced detachment. "Kids my age either became fixed on making the world a safer, healthier place, or living under an ever-falling sky. Sure, I'm a recycling freak—especially electronics, I preserve non-renewable resources in every way I can, but I will never panic, and I try not to blame."

"Yep," AB agreed. "Those are two lethal pollutants in this super turbulent world."

"I think most of my life choices embarrass our mom, but please our dad. There's not much about me she would want to post, which is a plus with what I do for a living."

"In a demographic with a pathological need to over-share, I think you're a very healthy young woman, Carly."

"Did you know," Lew shouted over the engines between their seats and his, "that a man's hearing is most keen in a noisy situation? That he can pick up conversations across a crowded conference room, or an open watercraft? AB's right, Carly, you are a gem, and if I were ten years younger—"

"Try twenty, there buddy," AB shouted back. "And never follow a compliment with a cheeseball line like that. We really need to tune-up your openers."

As the parade rounded the Georgia Mountain Fairgrounds and then passed under the Anderson Bridge, hoots and whistles greeted Lew's vintage Chris Craft. "I don't know whether it's your boat or the beautiful young thing waving to everyone, but I think you'll take an award for crowd favorite," AB said, climbing over to the seat next to Lew.

"This ol' Runabout has the two hottest women in the whole damned parade on board," he said, beaming—with a chin jut to acknowledge another vintage boater anchored off the Hiawassee Beach.

"Aw, that's much better, Lew," she said, popping the top of his antique admiralty cap.

⟱•0•⟰

Within the hour, three parade entries had arrived at Bernie's spacious boathouse dock. "That was some reaction your fancy cruiser got along the route," Mac said, walking over to assist with tying it off securely while Lew helped Carly and then AB disembark.

"Don't bother," AB said to Lew's pursed lips and raised eyebrows. "Just agree it was the boat."

"Oh my gosh, send me all of these." Eli squealed, holding Carly's phone as she swiped through Kit's photos of Hannah's melted face breaking the surface. "Would a giant canvas in the laundry room be tacky?"

"Title it 'Basic Aqueuse.' No need for photo credit," Kit suggested, waving toward the hill above. Bibi was at the wheel of a bright red Retriever grinding down to the shore from the enormous house.

"Bernie sent these paddle boards," she called out to Kit, as she struggled to keep the paddles stacked in the seat beside her.

"Zowie," Eli exclaimed, shading her eyes as she looked up at the multi-wing home. "That place has more rambling decks than the great lodge at BVR."

"What did you do with our hostess?" Mela asked, unloading the first of four brand new boards.

"She had company waiting when we walked in. She was super happy to see them. I slipped away because it seemed kind of special. I think it was her son and his wife."

As Eli iced drinks and Beth ferried trays of chopped pork barbecue and all the sides to the pavilion, everyone's frequent peeks at the house were rewarded with the rumble of her last load: Bernie and guests easing down the path in the four-seater. "Everybody," Bernie crowed, "this is my handsome, amazing boy, Alex, and his beautiful, precious wife, *Teeena*. She's from Hawaii—and they are expecting."

With Kit and Carly, the young arrivals went straight to the boats as Bernie bubbled with the news that they had relocated to Atlanta and her son was a principal in an established film production company.

"Before they come back," Leslie asked, "pronounce that Hawaiian name again. Did I hear Tea-ni-ah?"

"Not even. That was *Tina*, with enthusiasm."

"Yeah, Les, so exotic." Mela chuckled, clinking lemonades with Leslie as she left to check on Sophie's paddle board lesson.

"Bernie is a happy girl today." Mela sighed. "She needed this—her son back in her life, and now a baby."

"For sure," Eli agreed. "It was really so nice of her to share that news with us, *wasn't it?*" she taunted, twisting to look squarely at Mela.

"Between you and your brother," she responded, mildly exasperated, "I will never have a moment's peace. And I'm loving it." She laughed, extending her hand to give Eli a look at the ring from Mac.

"Wow, beautiful. What is this stone?" Eli asked, confused.

It's a polished, uncut sapphire. Mac told me to say he found the ring while fly fishing."

"No, what? He gave you someone's lost ring?"

"Since he was a kid, Mac has taken a teensy cloth sack when he's wandering these mountain creeks, to carry the bits of gold he finds. In high school, he showed me a box holding a collection of rubies and sapphires he's found, too. I remember saying he could make an extraordinary ring someday.

"When he gave this to me a few weeks ago, he said he had a jewelry designer craft it from his gold and his best sapphire *before he went to Auburn*—for me."

"That is crazy romantic. Mela, I'm thrilled for you both," Eli whispered, eyes welling.

"I will cherish my Mac, my Eli, and this ring he found in the mountains always. Now what do you think about Thanksgiving weekend? Will you be around, or in LA with that new client, or what?"

"Oh, I'm here," Eli assured her. "Don't you think you two are going down any aisle without me there."

As Mela scampered out the pavilion's screen door in answer to Mac's call, Eli joined Bernie, watching the paddle boarding beyond the boat house. "Can you believe how quickly life can change, Eli?" she crooned.

"It's scary business, alright."

"You're always waiting for that other shoe—the one with the dog mess on it—to drop, aren't you, girl? Isn't finding a brother right here something of a miracle?"

"Well at this rate, I have to wonder if there's a brood of us out there," she speculated. "Bernie, if I have this total busybody voice in my head, one I yell at out loud sometimes, am I nuts?"

"The one insisting you apologize to your brother?" she laughed.

"How'd you—"

"You'd been broadcasting that battle to the universe."

"But what am I hearing?"

"Heaven inspires gently. The prods God offers, they do not interfere or badger or mislead. That was all you, baby. Your *ego*.

"Ego's the thing that's always slapping a blindfold on you, spinning you around, playing hide and seek with your peace of mind. We silly humans are all about righteousness and vengeance and punishment; but the way home to Heaven is filled with understanding—learning how to heal, be kinder, love more.

"Now who's that AB's talking to in the almost dark, Eli? You see him, too, right? Some fella in a bass boat, but it isn't Mac."

"It looks like that preacher, Will Shafer. Busy lake tonight. It's a local tradition to watch the July Fourth fireworks from your boat," Eli explained, as they approached.

"I've heard about this beauty for a while," said the commanding voice. "Saw it for the first time this morning. Hope you don't mind me tying so close," he said, as Lew invited him out for a spin in the twilight.

The open docks flanking the boathouse held the guests watching Bibi climb in next to Lew while AB and Will took the back bench. The water was glowing as the perfectly restored craft eased toward the disappearing sun.

"AB's son is so proud of her," Bernie said softly, watching them go. "Brave, strong, and beautiful as ever, he says. Guess I'm supposed to tell her that."

As the boaters returned, the skies teemed with exploding fireworks, vividly fulfilling the hopes expressed by a future president. Eli remembered reading that John Adams wrote, after celebrating our nation's independence, that it should forever be celebrated under the glare of such rockets. She also remembered his letter was written July second. *Maybe it arrived on the fourth,* the voice in her head suggested.

As the show ended, Bernie was deluged with grateful thanks for a spectacular day at her home. Mac dropped Kit and Carly at Mela's dock as she, Bibi, and Eli were thanking Lew for the ride home. John reluctantly boarded his dad's boat, preferring to trail Kit and Carly around forever. AB, they noticed, hadn't taken Mela up on the offer to come in at her dock with Will.

"They have more sense than to test that rickety relic at her place, surely," Eli said, as they walked to the terrace.

"Maybe there's a better one at his," Mela said with a wink. "Now what was the somber conversation with Lew before we left Bernie's?"

"Brace yourself. He assured me it was nothing he couldn't resolve, but that I am the subject of another investigation. That during the divorce, my name was used to get an enormous mortgage on Ted's penthouse, and they can't trace the money. I'm still shaking."

"No way!"

"Oh, way. Lew believes Hannah is behind it. AB said Hannah was goading Lew—nasty stuff. Lew is also trying to prove she's drugging Ted."

"Drugging Ted with what? Could she have wanted you dead to cover up the mortgage? Mac should be looking at her again. She's bold enough to be causing all of this."

Chapter 17

When There's Frost on Your Campfire

C old fronts penetrating the deep south are rare summer events, even in the Georgia Mountains. Still, an adventurous mass of Canadian air had refreshed mornings with starts in the fifties and afternoons with low humidity. The walks were lightly attended, as everyone tackled outdoor projects in the fine weather.

Eli spoke timidly to Mela and Bernie as they entered a downhill section. "You know, I'm completely new to having people in my life who are real friends. People I look forward to being around. I think we're especially protective of our connection; but in light of our many revelations, could we become less restrained, more genuine? Does that sound needy?"

"Not at all," Mela answered. "And except for the two of us," she noted, "I agree that we've stayed on the surface. Considering your celebrity background, Bernie, weren't you always surrounded by people? But I don't recall you mentioning a close friend either."

"I didn't make time for the friends in my life as Bernie Carter, once Bernadette Montgomery landed a network show. Or family. I blew it with everybody, deciding people who stayed close to me were there for the perks, not me. I've discovered so much hiding out here—reading, praying—but I wasn't doing the work to rebuild."

"I've blamed coming from such a big family for my seclusion," Mela said. "I enjoy time alone. I told myself I would *get a life* when I was no longer taking care of Beau's parents, then my mom. But after they were gone, the blame shifted to Beau—waiting for him to get home."

"Don't laugh," Eli said, "but having a career while taking care of things for Ted and Pete, well, I was *too busy* to have time for anyone else in my life. The truth was I couldn't let anyone close enough to see what a lost cause I was—apologizing for *breathing*, so ashamed of everything about me that I couldn't even face a doctor's appointment for most of those years."

"What do you mean, 'Don't laugh' and 'so ashamed' when you talk about your talented, caring self, Eli Sledge?" Bernie demanded. "You would defend any one of us if someone spoke about us that way. You stood up for Leslie in the middle of her snarknado. Why is it okay to demean yourself, Eli?"

"Slow to change, but thanks, Bernie."

"No, you've come so far, E. What if," Mela ventured, "at Sunday night's campfire we can each ask a question if there's something we're curious about, and answer one? Not truth or dare, but a trust thing?"

"I dunno," Eli said, squinting at the prospect. "Sounds dangerously like our political *outing* at Lake Lure."

"But that worked. We're able to discuss the subject with mutual respect—so far, without bloodshed," Mela reminded them.

During a lull at the campfire Sunday night, Mela was eager to reassure Eli, and pitched the idea of getting to know more about one another by suggesting the round of questions. Uneasy shifting on the stone seats as everyone stared in different directions sparked Carly to speak up.

"Here goes. I've been wondering, Mela, are you a virgin? Because—"

"Okay, noooo," she responded, frosted.

"Wow, so was it Beau? Because—"

"It was *not*. No follow up questions," she ordered, with a regretful look at Eli.

Kit called out her question rapid-fire. "Eli, can you see the person who attacked you when you close your eyes, or did you block the memory?"

"Oh God." Eli rocked forward, hands on the edge of the stone bench. "I…It's something I try not to think about," she answered, clearly reliving the moment.

Bibi jumped in with her inquiry. "Carly, do you own rental properties in Towns *and* Union counties?"

Carly divided a glare between Mela and AB, utterly chagrined. "Yes. I do. Would you like to rent one?"

"No, just wondered if there could be two Carly Lanes with all those houses showing up."

Giggles erupted from AB as she opened the cooler for a water. "Anyone?" she offered before closing the lid.

"Me," Bernie said. "You're a fine, stylish woman, AB. Why do you have gray hair?"

"Ha, ha hahaha." She laughed loudly in reply. "Why does anyone have gray hair? Melanin failure? I like it so much better than the original mouse brown.

"I started a thing in my forties," she said, nodding to Mela to suggest she was sticking to the program. "I wanted to be authentic, to stop disguising myself to fit in. There are exemptions: Spanx and eyeliner."

"Is that a dig at my *inauthentic* life?" Bibi snapped.

"No, honey. That's just me trying to share. Let me try again. Okay, everybody," she added, obviously uncomfortable, "I disappeared down the rabbit hole when my widely scandalized husband of two years and my eighteen-month-old son died within days of each other after an accident. I was twenty-two. I survived several deeply dark years, got sober, and was a student for another ten until I married a professor, divorced on my way back to rehab, and recently ended a stint as a professional repenter—"

"I'm stuck. Stuck being a fake," Bibi shouted, "because I'm trapped in an identity that I stole when I was fifteen. I can't do anything legally in Florida—no matter how much I need to," she raged. "I'm a *criminal* in Florida."

"Aw, sweetie, that made you a criminal anywhere in the U.S. and most reciprocal countries," AB said playfully.

"Not everything is a joke, AB," Carly said flatly. "And please stop calling everybody sweetie, sugar, baby, and stuff. Not even flight attendants do that anymore. Just stop."

"Got it," AB said. In an aside to Mela, she added, "This kind of went over like calling the football team into the locker room for a group prostate exam, huh? Now you see why I never wanted a practice? Handing out the cartoon Band-Aids is more my speed."

"I know I don't fit in with y'all," Bibi said, tugging synthetic extensions out of her hair and throwing them in the bonfire. "Yes, I'm a criminal. Yes, I stole from people who relied on my honesty. Yes, I disappeared, and I've been paying for it every damned day since. For like thirty years I didn't dare trust anyone," she said haltingly. "I confided nothing to coworkers. I pretended to be some happy wife and mother. But I worked hard and tried to be a good person.

"Then my kidney blew New Year's morning after hemorrhaging for weeks, being alone in ERs, waiting on gurneys in different hospitals where they kept badgering me about giving *someone's* name. I had no one."

"Oh my God, you had us, B," Carly exclaimed.

"Not then. There had been someone, but I couldn't say so without revealing my crimes. I discovered a younger sister of my gram's six years ago on a genealogy website. She had also lived in Florida and then moved to Hiawassee. I came here and found her. We had so much fun.

"I didn't want to frighten her with whatever I was going through. Weeks later, after my kidney was removed, she had been abducted by her former Florida neighbors. I saw it on her camera system recordings.

"This was a couple who had taken over her Florida home right after her husband died, slowly taking over her life until one day she slipped away from them—her sweater stuffed with documents. Left them in her house and started over here," she explained, voice breaking. "And I suppose they had been looking for her since. I have to find her because I worry they're mistreating her again," Bibi sobbed.

"As soon as I was able, I drove down to get her, and the people who answered the door said she had moved to a senior living place but wouldn't tell me where. I can't hire someone to search for her because I've liquidated everything I had—my savings, my car—and gave up my apartment to pay hospital bills and expenses at her house. I'm about to lose the shop. She must think I abandoned her."

AB and Bernie settled beside her, promising to help find Carol.

"We'll get her back. I'll start planning tonight," Carly added, scooting in front of her.

"Surely to goodness, any statute has run out on the stolen money," AB said, looking across the fire to Eli and Mela. "But if you would feel better, we can help you make restitution payments. Are we talking six figures, or—"

"Twenty-two hundred sixty-eight dollars. I have it all written in a notebook," Bibi confessed. "I could have paid it off, but the risk of exposure…"

"Good Lord, we got this." Bernie laughed. "And if she was fifteen when she took this identity, isn't that a juvenile crime?"

"We need an attorney's advice," Eli suggested. "The identity thing is an ongoing situation. But Bibi, I don't understand. You were having a medical crisis when you did all that redecorating at my house?"

"I had helpers with the furniture. You met the boys," she reminded Eli.

"But I could have been there for *you* then. Stayed at the hospital with you!"

"It's stupid to admit, but I couldn't risk anyone finding out. You seem really obsessed with right and wrong. I couldn't understand why you were complaining so much about a guy who gave you everything just because he didn't say things you wanted to hear—"

"Oh, but Bibi, you were so alone! I do get fixated on things I can't make sense of," Eli acknowledged. "I'm sorry, everybody. I'm working on it, I promise."

"We all have things we're working on," AB said, her heart breaking for her friends.

"Why did you rip your hair out?" Carly asked, still sitting at Bibi's feet.

"Everything about me has been fake for so long," she said. "And using the weaves helped me feel normal after most of my hair fell out from all the hemorrhaging or stress."

"This is a strong start to ending your pain," AB assured her. "We got this. No more sleeping on—what'd you just say—a sheet of plywood on top of paint cans in the garage beneath your shop? No more hiding. We have each other's love and protection.

"I read recently that this *finding joy* thing happens, not through improving circumstances, but through the attitude we choose. I've watched that happen—successful people come from luxurious homes to our spartan hospice, and there, find more peace and joy in those last weeks than in a lifetime. They often mend relationships, shed trappings, settle their minds, and finally understand the only things that were ever important were not things.

"While I'm preaching, I'd like to recommend a filter I'm *trying* to keep in place on my big mouth that you will appreciate. The idea is: before we speak, let that filter determine if what we're about to say adds to the world's hurt or to healing. We are so in need of healing. I'm counting on the millennial/centennial hearts among us tonight to keep brightening this world. Or are y'all social-app obsessed, too?"

"My mom posts all day," Carly answered, adding, "and I had a fake page for my ex to see. Mostly I slay him with my Insta."

"Yeah, no, Molly won't," Kit said. "But my grandma and her sisters stay busy on it. Too much arguing."

"Seth Taylor has his whole life in photos on social media," Eli said. "I feel like I know everything about him."

"You know everything he wants you to," Bibi answered warily. "I believe it's mostly a charade. And full of political enmity, but that's just my opinion."

"So you and Seth are becoming a thing?" Mela teased Eli. "Having dinner at Lake's End, kayaking the Ocoee, and what else?"

"Well, he's nice," she responded defensively. "And I did go fly fishing. That was a mystical experience."

"Let's have a mystical experience tomorrow evening, watching the Perseids meteor shower," Bernie suggested.

"I have to work tomorrow night," AB said. "What time is the peak expected?"

"Before midnight," Carly answered. "But bring jackets if we're going to the Bald because even in August it could be way cooler up there."

"Can't we see it from my dock?" Bernie asked.

"That sounds much better," Mela said. "I wish Sophie could be here to see it, but she's back in school. And did I tell y'all, Leslie has her last chemo this Friday? They're coming up next weekend."

"Another excuse for dinner out," AB said.

"Oh yes, let's try that Toccoa Riverside place," Bernie suggested, pleased to hear unanimous approval as drinks were emptied on the waning fire.

AB and Mela went home to bed as the rest settled in at Eli's to plan Bibi's rescue operation. They established the last time she had seen her Aunt Carol, what was missing from the house in the way of personal documents, that she was of fiercely sound mind before she disappeared, and that Bibi was terrified of involving law enforcement.

Eli mentioned her trip to Beaufort, suggesting Bibi and Carly come along and use her car for a preliminary assessment.

"Oh, I'm in," Carly said. "I've never been to Beaufort."

"That's pronounced *Bewfert*," Kit chided. "If you ask for directions to *Bofart* they'll point you up the coast to North Carolina. Plan on staying at my place whether I'm there or not," Kit offered, reminding them her classes resumed Monday.

"The first night I might be at Bret's place," Carly said, with a deep sigh. "But I hope you'll be around for that excursion boat thing you mentioned."

"Can't wait," Kit assured her friend.

Skies were clear, loaded with stars, when everyone reassembled twenty-four hours later. An unexpected spread of finger sandwiches and cookies covered the catering counter inside the pavilion as Eli parked a box of soft drinks on the island. "This looks delicious," she exclaimed to Nancy, Bernie's longtime housekeeper, who was opening a bag of chips for a star-gazing snack.

"Didn't want to crash the party empty-handed," she laughed, folding a hand towel by the sink. "I've never watched a live meteor shower."

"Me neither," Eli admitted. "Let's check it out."

Will and AB were on a wide chaise lounge next to one shared by Mela and Mac. Carly and Kit were sitting on the end of the dock as Nancy and Eli walked to the benches outside the boathouse, where Bibi and Bernie were already noticing activity in the sky.

"Take a seat before you look up," Bernie advised. "We don't need anyone falling in, as cool as it already is this evening. Where's your boyfriend, Eli?" she asked.

"Haven't heard from my friend in weeks. Maybe a big case came up."

"Or maybe he's ghosting you. Is there something worrying you right now? Besides him?"

"Nah, he's entertaining, but not special."

"I'm getting a worried vibe from you lately," Bernie said.

"There's something unresolved that happened during the divorce and involved my name, not me," Eli admitted. "It's a big deal, but I've been told not to worry."

"He knows about it," she answered. "He's bothered that you didn't tell him."

"Where do you get that?" Eli asked, bewildered. "How does that come on your *screen* or whatever?"

"Your mama tells me most of the things I get about you. She wishes she could have been a better mother, you know. She just wasn't equipped. Lately your mama Julia and her sister have been helping to set things in motion for you and Mac. Her sister just laughed and said, 'It took long enough.' Little sis is a brilliant light."

As the meteor flights increased, AB found Bernie in the pavilion with Nancy while Will and Mac reviewed a starter switch problem on Bernie's pontoon. "You're so generous, sharing this beautiful place with us, Bernie," she said, hugging her friend. "And Nancy, the snacks were scrumptious. I have two of those delicious little sandwiches in my purse to enjoy tonight at work."

"I have some sacks here for take-homes," Nancy waved in answer. "Will Shafer is a lucky man to have found you," she added, slipping sandwiches in bags for Will and for Mac.

"Oh, you wouldn't say that if you knew about me," AB said, studying the sandwich packing.

"You know what a small place this is," Nancy replied, not looking up from her work. "I've lived here all my life. And yes, there are folks who love to make ancient tales new again, but everyone I know is happy for you both—very happy."

"You have made my week, girl, and it's Monday," AB said with a hug, hurrying off to get Will and make it to the hospice.

The week flew as they celebrated Leslie's last chemo treatment and finalized plans for Bernie's already sold-out fundraiser. The following Monday morning, Eli, Carly, and Bibi stopped for breakfast at the Sawmill before heading south over Blood Mountain. Eli was on the porch taking a call when the platters were served.

Carly was hot saucing her Nottely omelet as Bibi added blackberry jelly to the toast that came with her brisket, hash browns, and egg. "Umm, ummm," she swooned as the blackberry smeared over the melted butter. "There's something so decadent about getting toast already buttered. Makes me a little giddy," she giggled.

"Really? *That* thrills you?" Carly laughed. "How long has it been since you had sex, B?"

"I was fifteen," she answered, separating her running egg from the crispy hash browns.

"Oh. When was the first time?"

"About three weeks before that."

Bibi saw Carly's troubled expression and set her fork on the plate. "When I stole Beth's identity, I needed to get away, get established somewhere. First, I needed ID, preferably a driver's license, but before that, I needed lessons.

"This guy, a *friend*, said he would give me two driving lessons and take me to Kingsland to get my license if…" She picked up her fork and stuffed in a bite before adding quietly, "if I had sex with him each time. It was pathetic. Nothing like the movies."

"Right. You want my toast?"

When they arrived in Beaufort, Eli dropped Carly and Bibi at Kit's townhouse before registering at the hotel. "Why the change in plans?" she asked Carly, as they unloaded bags and entered the code on Kit's door lock. "I thought we would share my hotel room, do some sightseeing. Y'all could take my car Wednesday while I meet David to get the book off."

"Well," Carly responded, "Bret has some free time until he meets the Harrison's flight Tuesday evening. So, we're strategizing tonight and will reconnoiter tomorrow."

"Holy Smokes," Bibi muttered, as she entered first. "This place is fantastic. It looks like an *Architectural Digest* spread."

"Here's a note from Kit," Carly said from the kitchen. "It says, 'Make yourselves at home. I'll be back tomorrow afternoon to show you around.' Y'all, her place is stupid sweet."

Eli awoke Tuesday morning to a text from Carly saying they were en route to Florida with Bret. What she didn't say was that they were in a rental car, shadowed by Bret in a black Explorer. Once they saw the aunt's house for sale online, Bibi called to schedule a showing so that she and Carly could check out the premises. With the Harrisons in Milan, Bret could be nearby for official-looking back-up if Carly had to flash a badge.

As they cruised down I-95 south, Bibi was thinking aloud as she drove. "If she's not here, or if we find her and she's not able to communicate, what do we do?" she said, quickly looking over at Carly.

"They need her to complete the sale of the house," Carly assured her. "That and accessing investments gets a little trickier than draining bank accounts. Her physical condition may not be good, but they have to keep her available."

"Bret seems really good for you," Bibi observed, raising an eyebrow as she glanced over. "He has a way of raising your IQ, if you know what I mean."

"Yes, I do bring my work persona home," Carly droned. "Like I said last night, I'm sorry I didn't trust you guys to still like me if you discovered I was an air marshal, a fed. Think about it. You hate law enforcement. Mela forbids guns anywhere around her. Eli's politics are very different from mine, and I—"

"I don't hate law enforcement," Bibi squirmed. "I'm afraid of the consequences of being found out. I avoid po-po at all costs. Mela is afraid of guns, and I can't blame her after her younger brother used one to take his own life. And Eli isn't politically hostile like some whacka-doos. People seem to let what they fear color their relationships. Like AB says, we can all do better."

"You're awesome, Carly. You and Bret are taking an awful chance, helping me." Bibi choked, as tears slipped down her cheeks. "If things go wrong, promise me you'll take off and not look back. Promise me!"

"Stop with the negative thoughts, Bibz. I'll bet we find Carol before lunch. And with every restaurant billboard we pass, I am thinking about a fried seafood basket from somewhere along here.

"Let's make sure we have eyes on the house well before the ten o'clock appointment. Maybe we can watch them leave and see if they take her with them. Now tell me what you know about the house that I didn't see in the listing or the virtual tour."

"Umm, she said that when they built the house, it was right after Hurricane Andrew hit south Florida. You saw the pool house. She never mentioned attic access or a storage room. Oh, but they created a small safe room accessible through the back of a closet. Her husband used it for gun storage mostly. That feature wasn't in the listing, which is not unusual."

"Good to know," Carly said. "If the agent doesn't tell us about it, and Carol doesn't leave with them, we'll find that first."

South of Jacksonville, Bibi eased to the side of the road and reached into a bag on the back seat, pulling out a long black wig. She leaned forward and tucked her hair beneath it. "Whatdaya think?" she asked, batting her eyes as she smoothed the hair down her shoulders.

"You look hideous," Carly said, snatching it off and tossing it over the seat. "Was that a disguise, or a *GOT* costume?"

"Something more subtle?" Bibi offered, reaching into the bag and pulling out a blonde Wintour cut.

"If you must," Carly said, whipping her own lush mane into a loose French braid and straightening the starched collar on her white blouse under the navy jacket that matched her skirt. "I call this faux federal styling—it's what people expect to see," she said, playfully grinning to ease Bibi's nerves.

"Remember," Carly said, reviewing their strategy, "we take a quick look around, tell the agent it isn't what we're looking for, I'll set up an entry point, and we leave. Then wait for her to lock up and go so we can come back and search before the freeloaders return. Bret will park behind us to hide the tag while we're inside. Be calm, confident."

Minutes later, they had exited the interstate, driving through the lauded golf community as Bret surveyed the area for anything that might interfere with a fast retreat. A circular drive widened at the garage bays where a minivan was parked outside.

"Carol mentioned a Caddy here," Bibi said. "Maybe it's in the garage." As she spoke, a door in the breezeway connecting the garage to the house opened, and a couple entered the van. "No Carol," Bibi sighed.

"Think positive," Carly admonished. "She's in there, waiting for us." She used the phone Bret had given her to contact him as they traveled, having placed both their phones in a dead box in his headliner. She gave a detailed description of the van, discreetly raising her binoculars to read the tag to him and give specifics on the physical aspects of the couple driving it.

"Good news," Carly said brightly. "They're carrying Publix totes. Going grocery shopping. Someday we'll have a Publix." The light rain they had been driving in all morning began pouring as they watched the sales agent arrive.

"Heavy rain is good," Carly was quick to explain. "Obscures security camera range and we get to wear hooded gear. Remember, I'm Lizzie, you're Jane."

"Oooh, this is very dated," Bibi declared, as they came through the front door and looked across the living room to a family room that joined the kitchen at the back of the house.

"But sis, it has a beautiful pool," Carly said, walking to the wall of windows. Bibi was already fidgeting with the fireplace, asking the agent to ignite the gas flame. As she fumbled around on the mantel for a remote, Carly was slowly opening the back door, but darting right to unlock the last window and return to Bibi. "Never mind," she said, from the doorway. "All grout and tile out there. We'd have to gut this place, Janie."

"Do you have anything similar in this community that we could see?" Bibi asked. "But more updated? We're only here today. We could meet you after lunch."

The agent quickly locked the back door and joined them as they walked to the driveway. "Please let us know right away what else we can see today," Carly urged, hoping to delay any feedback to the couple. Carly directed Bibi to the left lane when she saw the agent behind them indicating a right turn.

As her taillights disappeared in the downpour, they traveled a short distance before doubling back to the house, where they blocked both ends of the drive with their vehicles after Bret joined them. Carly was counting on this very senior community having equally aged, low resolution camera systems as she slipped around the garage and in the unlocked window, then let Bibi in the front door as Bret kept watch.

As soon as the door closed, Bibi was shouting Carol's name, adding, "It's me, Bibi. I'm here to take you home." Meanwhile, Carly checked the garage, laundry room, and was in the office when she heard Bibi call from the back of a bedroom closet. She was pushing boxes aside as she banged on a padlocked, metal door.

"Carol," Bibi was crying, as Carly reached her.

"We're in too far to quit now," Carly advised, pulling short bolt cutters from her shoulder bag.

"I will never comment on your geardo ways again," Bibi swore gratefully.

"When someone is being held," Carly grunted, as she forced the cutters to close, "restraints are usually involved. Get your video running," she said. "We need to document our version of what happened here." *No matter what we find,* she said under her breath.

When the padlock fell away, Carly signaled Bibi to stay back as she stepped inside and found a light switch. A pile of clothes moved slightly, and Carly pulled away a coat, then saw defiant brown eyes flicker with hope as Bibi bumped her aside getting to the frail figure on the floor.

"Grab some cream off the counter," Bibi ordered. "This damned tape will rip her skin," she shouted, furious over the duct tape across Carol's mouth, around her wrists, and binding her legs.

"We should call the police," Carly suggested, handing Bibi a jar of cream as she recorded.

"Yes, the police," Carol whispered weakly, as Bibi eased the adhesive off. "I want to tell the police what those fools have done. Water, please, Bibi," she said, a tear trickling as she looked up.

"You and Bret get out of here," Bibi ordered. "Awesome thanks to you both. I got it from here. Carol can tell her story," Bibi said, smiling through her own tears. "Go get that seafood basket."

Bret and Carly watched from a distance as an ambulance, fire truck, and several police cars responded to the 911 call Carol insisted on making. Bibi was shaking as she heard the sirens approach.

"I *am* your aunt, Bibi. We *are* family," the emaciated woman declared, tape hanging from her legs and wrists. "Even if you had been the child adopted by the Parkers, tests would still prove I'm your biological aunt," she said, sounding reassuringly rational to Bibi until she added, "I do so hope we can get home to Hiawassee today. I must have my hair done."

"Maybe tomorrow. First, we get you checked out, and see these people are arrested," Bibi said, gently releasing her hand to greet the first responders. "But I'm not going anywhere without you."

Carly changed out of her suit, then rummaged in a bag behind the seat before selecting shorts and a crop top while Bret struggled to hold his lane on the coastal highway. She stayed in touch with Bibi by text as she and Bret ate at the Reef on A1A north of St. Augustine and then took a long stroll on the beach with Bret, relieved that the rescue was a success, and their careers were intact.

Chapter 18

What Possible Good, You Say

While investigators were still combing Carol's home for evidence, they received a report that the couple who had been presenting themselves as Carol's guardians had turned themselves in.

Soon after, Bibi got a call at the hospital while awaiting the results of Carol's evaluation. It was the detective assigned to the case, saying they had found a scribbled timetable among statements from various investments that indicated the imposter guardians were trying to close on property in Ecuador as soon as they could access her accounts. The D.A. anticipated they would face kidnapping in Georgia and accumulating charges in Florida—deeming them flight risks with no bond.

On Wednesday morning, Bibi brought Carol to her home to search for any surviving personal items. She had been confined to the pool house, which had a kitchenette, but any trace of her personal effects in her home, other than documents in her husband's desk, was gone. She gathered a few books and some paintings she had underway.

Her personal attorney met them there, agreeing to support the necessary steps to ensure prosecution, and work with her investment advisor to assess the damage inflicted, as well as prepare and sell the property. Carol advised him she would make a new will in Georgia and establish Bibi as her guardian and heir. "Even though I've barely made it to ninety-two, don't get too excited," she cautioned Bibi. "I may be financially ruined after this."

"I can take care of both of us," Bibi assured her.

———◆———

The news Tuesday afternoon that David and Ida Harrison would be delayed a day returning from Italy was a break for Bret, who kept trying and failing to get out of bed at the ocean front hotel he and Carly had discovered the day before.

For Eli it was a disappointment, as she wanted to be off the highways and back in Hiawassee ahead of the Labor Day weekend. Postponing was out, with the publisher awaiting final signatures; and she had reservations for her trip to Watkins Glen for the following week.

It wouldn't be the intended celebration, but Victor had suggested a signing lunch so that the publisher could get the book in production. He mentioned that his wife Liz would like to join them to propose another client who was seeking a biographer. Eli couldn't say no to Victor, as protective and trusting as he had been when things were in chaos, but Liz would be displeased to hear that within the marketing rollout on the Harrison book, Eli had found a strong solo career and was already contracted for over three years.

As Eli was searching for directions to the restaurant, Kit called. "Liz asked me to bring you to lunch in Savannah. 'K?"

"Good news to me," Eli answered. "You all right? Sound rushed or stressed or. . ."

"I'm fine. Pick you up in ten?"

"Sure."

Eli was waiting out front in the sundress Mela helped her select before Pete's wedding—a daffodil float that suddenly felt childish as Kit arrived in a shimmering cowl neck blouse; short navy skirt, with antiqued buttons down the side; and exquisite Romy pumps in navy and silver degradé leather. The future billionaire's OOTD.

"Went by my place to change and didn't see Carly or B," Kit said, as Eli approached.

"They're scouting Carol's neighborhood today. How far is Savannah?" Eli asked, sliding into the seat of a meticulously upholstered, '70s-era TR6. "Love this car."

"Thanks, saw it at a Hilton Head Concours show and had to have it. We're about forty minutes out from the restaurant, but if we had jetpacks, maybe fifteen or less. These coastal roads go forever."

"Coastal jetpacks, huh? A side development while you build your mariculture empire? Are you the bio client Liz is proposing?"

"That's another prehistoric Hollywood associate of hers. She's always trying to stroke that creep; does anything to make him happy. I hate the sight of him."

"Is Liz sort of a mentor to you, like Viv Wright was to me?"

"In the sense that your publicist boss Viv *misdiagnosed* your husband's neurologic status, derailed your marriage, and got you mixed up in this mess, yeah."

Eli was feeling queasy as they hurtled along the winding roads, not up for an in-depth discussion. "Did you do the restoration on this Triumph, or—"

"Already done, and it wasn't for sale." She snickered. "But when my friend made the offer, he took it."

"Nice. Is this friend still a friend?"

"We see each other."

They rode quietly through the traffic coming into Savannah and found a suitable parking spot for the Six along the riverfront. As they approached the restaurant, Victor stood to greet them from a table under the streetside trees. "Liz made our reservation," he mentioned, seating them. "She should be here anytime. Let's have refreshments, submit these signatures, and enjoy this pleasant summer breeze."

With a few sweeps of the stylus, they dispatched documents that could have been done digitally from anywhere, while Victor endeavored to make it an event with luscious shrimp skewer appetizers, crawfish beignets, and signature drinks.

Eli amused her companions with tales of rehabbing the old Sutton place on the lake, and Kit reviewed the festive boat parade for Victor, including the care taken with Lew's magnificent Runabout.

"My dream is to have a vintage boat," he said. "Maybe one day, if David will ever slow down."

"Ah, but I have pictures," Eli offered, getting her phone and bringing up the gallery folder of the parade. "Here's Lew's pride and joy," she said, lifting the phone as Victor leaned across the table.

"Yes!" he exclaimed. "That would be a boat—"

His upper body jerked and fell, sprawling across the table, scattering plates and drinks. Eli jumped back, wondering whether this was an awful comic move. *No, a stroke?* One look at Kit told her it was neither. Eli yanked the arm of Kit's chair, slamming the blood-spattered girl to the ground and dropping beside her.

"Victor's been shot. Are you hit?"

"I don't think so," she whispered slowly, teeth chattering.

"Don't move, Kit. Call 911," she shouted. "He's been shot!"

Voices were anxious and muffled as tables quickly emptied around them. She heard a man crisply detailing the situation and turned her head enough to glimpse him waving people through a doorway.

"I didn't hear shots," Kit whispered in gasps, hands over her face as she lay shaking on the ground.

"Stay flat. That weird thump must have been a bullet. There's blood all over you. They can't hit us down here," she fervently hoped.

Eli moved to evaluate their exposure and looked straight into Victor's face—framed in a bloody field, flat against the frosted glass tabletop. Her phone was teetering on the table edge as she snatched it off, waiting for the shooter to react.

He's been gone, she decided, avoiding the direction of Victor's body as she called Mac over howling sirens. Then she called Carly to alert Bret.

Liz had arrived as patrons were rushing into the building and was not informed of Victor's death until after the police had secured the scene. Kit—unable to speak to investigators—was taken by ambulance to be treated for shock.

<hr />

By early afternoon, an officer returned Eli's phone while she was still answering questions about the meeting and how it had been scheduled. As she thanked him, she observed Liz in a similar interview across the room. *Is that Bret being escorted over with Carly in tow?* she wondered, weak with relief at the sight of the couple.

"Could I clean her up a little?" Carly asked, with a look to Eli as she searched her purse for a hand-wipe packet.

Bret stepped away with the supervising detective to provide background on Victor's relationship with David Harrison.

"Do we have photos?" the remaining officer asked.

"Plenty," Eli said wearily, taking a shaky handful of wipes from Carly as she studied the performance Liz was giving. They could hear her wailing complaints punctuated with loud exclamations of "to me," or "about me" throughout.

"Wish I could hear that line of questioning." Mac's voice came over Eli's shoulder as he pulled a chair beside her. "They tell me that's the grieving widow."

"You're here? And in two hours? That's a six-hour drive," she whispered, dumbfounded. "How did you get in? Tell them you were one of those hundred or so witnesses back there?"

"Nuh-uh," Carly answered. "I heard Bret say, 'my brotha squirrel' when he saw Mac talking to an officer posted outside. There's a connection somewhere."

"My 313th tat works in mysterious ways," he intoned, gripping Eli's hand between his. "That, and one of my excellent friends-with-birds got me to you. Brother Bret's over getting grease with the locals. Now I know you've been through this many times already, but can I ask you similar questions until they get back to you?"

Before each question, Mac seemed to review video on his phone. "What's that?" Carly finally asked, leaning in for a look.

"Collected plenty of security videos from buildings for a couple of blocks on the way in," he answered, watching the screen. "Not many systems hardwired these days—too expensive. The cameras out front gave us two angles on their table," he told her, looking up. "Where is Kit now?"

"Paul took her mother to the hospital to get Kit," Carly said. "He told Bret she had nothing to say to the detective there with her, just wanted to go home with Molly. Bret called the Harrisons on our way here. Had to, before the news picked it up. That was heartbreaking to overhear."

"How horrific for David and Ida to come home to this. What's happened to Bibi?" Eli asked, suddenly aware of her absence.

"She and her aunt Carol are probably halfway to Hiawassee by now," Carly whispered, bending down for a low-five with Eli. "She's one tough little lady. And furious about Bibi *not* staying at her house or using any money from the accounts she had added Bibz on. Although she's glad B is using that Mercedes."

Bret dropped Eli at her hotel while Carly and Mac took the TR6 to Molly's house. She invited them in, but with Kit resting, Carly gave Molly a hug to pass along, and she rejoined Mac for the walk to Eli's hotel.

Soon they were both admiring a classic Thunderbird as it passed. "That is sick," Carly said, whistling as it eased to a stop before turning onto the main road.

"Oh, yeah," Mac agreed. "It's a '57, Starmist blue, with a V-8. Pretty sure it was sitting at the security hub on the Harrison's driveway back there. I saw that color through the trees."

Eli heard a knock on the door as she was drying her hair after a shower. Carly was coming to share her hotel room and it was a mess, the second bed loaded with her open suitcase and all its scattered contents. She released the doorknob and swept up the last armload of clothes off the bed. "Hop right in," she called, then glanced at JC Harrison.

"Oh!" Eli gasped, dropping the load onto her bed and swooping it back into her arms as she realized her towel had dropped with the clothes.

"I'll come back," he offered, moving behind the door. "I had asked the desk to let me know when you came in."

"One sec," she said, as she pulled a blouse, shorts, and undies from the heap, then scampered to the bathroom. "Come in. I'll be right out."

He pushed the door almost closed, and when he heard the hair-dryer running, decided to lean back on the extra bed, pulling a pillow loose for support. He was there, looking through his phone, when Carly came through the door ahead of Mac.

"Oh, wrong room," she squeaked, pushing back against Mac and looking at the door number, then turning slowly to the man on the bed. "Hey, you are—"

"I know," he said, apologetically. "But this *is* Eli's room, if that's who—"

"Yeah? I don't know who *you* are," Mac said, stepping around Carly and suddenly slowing his advance. "Unless you are James Harrison, which you could be, now that I think about it. We should go, Carly, before Eli—"

"Too late." Carly dismissed him as the hairdryer stopped, keeping her focus on the man occupying her bed. "Now how do you know Eli?" she asked, lifting her chest and smoothing her hair as she sat on the bed across from him.

"I met her last Thanksgiving at my parents' house. And you are?"

"Yeah, I'm Carly Lane, Eli's bestie, and this is her brother, Mac Miller," she said, pointing to a chair by the window for Mac to take.

"Hey, Mac," JC called, sitting up. "Mind if I ask you how that happened?" he said, gesturing to Mac's left leg.

"Afghanistan, 2012," he replied, phubbing JC as he texted.

"It isn't curiosity," JC explained. "I have a role starting the first of the year. I'm playing a disabled vet with a similar injury, and I want to be authentic in my representation."

"Not likely you'd want to do this authentically," Mac answered dryly, putting his phone away.

"Well, hello," Eli said, peering around the bathroom door. "I thought I heard voices."

"I was thinking you and I could get a bite," JC said, looking first at Eli, then at Mac. "The hotel has a private dining room. We could all have dinner, or at least drinks."

"I could use a drink," Mac agreed. "Girls?"

"C'mon," Carly urged Eli. "You need to eat."

At dinner, JC shared moments from a lifetime watching his father and Victor bond as brothers.

"I found brothers and sisters in the Eighty-Second," a loosened Mac commented.

"Yeah? I thought I had a brother, until recently," JC responded, raising an eyebrow at Eli.

Bright light crossed the room as a door opened. Mac and JC called out, "Brother Bret" in unison, resulting in a hard stare between the two.

"I don't have much time," he said, scanning the plates and over-looking the sudden discord.

"You can have my stuffed flounder," Eli suggested. "I ate the salad, though."

"And what have you been up to?" he asked, pulling Carly's chair away from JC's and sitting between them with Eli's flounder platter. Carly described their afternoon, ending with the walk from Molly's to the hotel and the classic Thunderbird that passed them.

"That's JC's car," Eli interjected, delighted. "Isn't it the most *beautiful* little thing ever?" Even she was surprised by the gushiness of her remark.

"Yes, you should take Eli for a ride," Bret suggested. He whispered to Carly, "Think what could happen in twenty minutes alone upstairs."

"If Eli's up to it, we will," JC agreed. "I'd also like to spend some time with you, Mac, before you leave, if that works?"

"I want to turn in early," Eli announced, fading fast.

"Really dark tint on my windows," Bret whispered again to Carly, as she slid her hand along his thigh.

"How much time do you need?" Mac asked, stretching against the back of his chair.

"As much as you can spare. Bret and I are meeting my parents' flight in two hours. Until then I'm open."

As she left, Eli assured Mac she could manage to find her room. They watched Bret and Carly hurry out the door, then Mac was alone with JC.

"Before we start this authenticity session," Mac said, drink in hand as they walked over to club chairs at the balcony window, "how in-volved are you with Eli? Let me make it simple. Have you gotten my sister naked?"

"Aw wait, now," JC stammered. "I did not *get* her naked, and it happened just before you came in."

"Yeah, she texted me from the bathroom," he laughed. "I was messing with you. So, what do you need to know about my tours in the sandbox?"

———◦———

Eli's reunion with the Harrisons the next morning was bittersweet. "The book is on hold for now," David advised her, as their visit ended. "We'll discuss it after I've had a chance to… Well, soon, Eli," he said, kissing the top of her head as they hugged. She knew thoughts of getting Victor's perspective would crackle throughout every conversation David Harrison would have for months.

Eli, Mac, and Carly were invited for brunch Thursday, where David told everyone there was no progress on identifying a shooter and that Liz had arranged her own admission to a private Atlanta hospital for a stay. "Victor's body was transported to the GBI," he said gruffly, trying to maintain his voice, "with no date for release. I can't guess what Liz may do at that point."

JC was standing with the travelers in the parking court behind the house as they gathered at Eli's car to leave. Mac was arranging luggage in the back as Bret pulled up, offering to show Carly the target range under the west end of the house. "I know a blind spot," he mentioned, leading her away.

"It was good seeing you again, Eli," JC said, "despite the circumstances. You've been on my mind. Before the meltdown over Marc's story and more since. Lately, I can't get you out of my mind at all," he said, taking both her hands in his.

"Please don't tell me that's since yesterday afternoon, because I'd like to edit that particular mental picture for you," she said, responding to him tugging her closer.

"A PG first kiss, to better remember you by?"

"'I'd like that," she said, as he leaned to her for a tender goodbye. While the kiss didn't offer the thrill she'd expected, the heat of the long embrace relaxed every taut nerve in her body. A piercing whistle from Mac snapped her rigid again and brought Bret out ahead of Carly.

"We have promising video," he said, putting a hand on Bret's shoulder as they watched a possible suspect walk out of a building south of the restaurant, time-stamped just after the shooting. "Check out that jacket over his left arm. See that grip under there? Has to be off an SA Saint pistol."

"You're convinced he used Blackout 300 ordnance," Bret said. "So, a soft shooter, subsonic, suppressed."

Mac agreed. "Yeah. Small, but distance accurate. A guy like this, he was in a hurry. Grabbed one of the pieces he built in his garage. Parts now scattered along the road from here to wherever. Had to get the gun out with him. This meet came together too fast for planning."

"Fedora, glasses, collar up, shirttail in the breeze, tell me we've got him getting into his vehicle," Bret said, scrolling back through the frames.

"Nope," Mac said, shaking his head. "He's too exposed for this to be his way."

"Thanks, man," Bret said, clasping hands with Mac as they walked to where Eli and Carly were waiting. "If you get anything else, I'd like to know."

"You got it."

———◆———

On Sunday evening, Lake Chatuge was still swarming with watercraft when the first log went on in the firepit Mac had built into a corner of Mela's terrace. AB was loading a table beneath the kitchen window with a ribs-centric buffet from Bitter Creek Market.

"I'm over *frankfurters* until summer rolls around again," she confided in Bernie, who was laying out plates. "Getting anything on Bibi's aunt?" she prodded. "Just keeping you on your game for the show at the fairgrounds."

"I don't need reminding, thank you," Bernie answered, casting a look at AB. "I'm feeling a very spunky lady—kind, and fun. I'm told she'll bring our Bibi to a happy outlook."

Bibi was the last to arrive, introducing Carol to the weekly crew expanded by Will Shafer, Leslie, and Sophie, who were up for the long weekend, and Lew, who did his best to cheer a lonely Carly.

"I'm elated to be here in Hiawassee with you all," Carol announced. "I wish I could race around this house doing cartwheels; but I learned, when I survived an ultralight crash landing at eighty-three, not to promise a better trick than I can deliver. So," she called out, while distributing hugs, "thank you for welcoming me home."

Everyone had stopped to listen, then broke into applause and whistles, disturbing Dude's nap, while Sophie cartwheeled around the terrace for Carol. "Heard anything from Kit?" Mela asked, as she handed Sophie a buffet plate between Eli and Carly.

"No." "Not a thing," came their replies.

"I'm calling Molly Tuesday if we haven't heard by then," Eli said. "I've hardly slept. This has shaken me to my core, and Kit grew up with Victor around, so I can't imagine," she continued.

"I've heard once from Bret," Carly added. "He's been arranging extra layers of security for the Harrisons and scouring Victor's communications."

"It's what Liz has communicated that we need better access to," Mac said, wrapping his arms around Mela from behind. "She's plenty cagey for a talent broker."

"Kit showed me some photos from her modeling jobs that Liz arranged," Carly told them. "She is so photogenic, just gorgeous."

"Yeah, I saw those on her phone," he said quietly to Carly. "Thought it was strange that she was using end-to-end encryption as a student who models part time. I need to get back on cracking that data."

"Remember, y'all," Eli said, scooping slaw into her pork sandwich, "I'll be at Watkins Glen next weekend."

"And has refused my offer to fly private," Lew added.

"Cannot believe you got medical clearance to race," Mac said, shaking his head.

"Oh, I didn't think I could love being home any more than I already do," Carol told Bibi, as they sat by the fire. "But this get-together is food for my soul."

"This bunch has restored my sanity," she answered softly, scanning the many friends who had come into her life recently.

As Eli was packing for New York after their walk Wednesday morning, she noticed a missed call from JC. The message said a memorial service was scheduled in LA for the following Tuesday, and in Atlanta that Thursday. "Dad and Mom are attending both," the recording continued, "and I'll be there if you decide to go to one. I'd like to see you again. Soon, Eli."

For several minutes she stood over her repacked bag, wondering whether she was completely dead to having another relationship. AB was falling in love again after decades alone, *but what if I never find real love?*

Who wouldn't think they were dreaming, to have James Harrison showing interest? Who would keep blowing off a thoughtful GBI agent until he gave up? Who could be divorced over a year and not remember noticing one hot guy? She decided to be open to any reawakening experience the testosterone storm at Watkins Glen might offer. *Single* testosterone.

Chapter 19

When a Gentleman
Starts Your Engine

After a connecting flight to Elmira, New York, Eli put her name on a list for the next shuttle—the final leg of her travel to Watkins Glen—and went in search of her luggage. She had arrived a day early to avoid interfering with Lew's track activities and to allow time for sightseeing ahead of the vintage-themed Grand Prix Festival.

Her hologrammed butterfly tag led Eli to her bag. It wouldn't budge off the rack. She pushed her purse onto her shoulder to tug with both hands, but it was packed to roll, not lift.

"I'll get that for you," she heard, as the bag lifted clear of the rack and swung to the side of a nice looking guy who was already handling his own large duffle with similar ease. "Where to?" he asked, with a gallant smile and flirty gray eyes.

"I'm here for the SVRA Vintage Grand Prix at the Glen. I can manage now. Thank you so much."

"No problem. I'm Eric Hobbs, by the way. I'll be taking the Dix shuttle, too," he said, striding toward an outside door.

"Eli Sledge. Truly a pleasure to meet you, Eric."

They discussed track interests as she followed him out, noticing the sculpted taper of his shoulders to the toned glutes under the khakis. Maybe she wasn't so dead after all. *Maybe you're spending too much time with Carly,* the voice in her head harangued.

They were seated in the shuttle, making small talk about Lew's car and Eric's own racing team, when he leaned back, groaning. "Oh, no. That jerk ahead of me at the rental car counter is heading this way. Did you hear that guy? 'This is unacceptable. Get the airport manager.' They gave away his car. Mine, too, and probably to a tip that was worth losing the job. It's survivable."

Eli heard the door behind her open, and the vehicle rocked as the irate rider dropped in his seat.

"Andy, unload the Big Healey for me," he said, placing the phone on the seat beside him as he browsed his tablet. "I'll need it to get around while I'm here. Thanks."

He might as well have poured ice water over her. Eli, hidden by the headrest, was fighting the urge to crawl under the seat. Eric must have noticed her visibly shrinking.

"You okay?" he asked, curious as to what had shut down his previously vivacious seatmate.

"Mm-hmm." She feigned sleepiness with a confined stretch. "Might catch a nap," she whispered, as her phone brightened, blaring a ring tone consisting of three dramatic chords usually heard in cartoons or silent movies when the villain enters.

"I thought that was your goofy luggage tag in the back," the unhappy man in the seat behind her surmised.

"Eric," she responded with reluctance. "You said you know Lew Waller? How about his brother, Ted?" She sighed, flipping two fingers over her shoulder.

"Well, Lew's brother Ted," he said, extending his arm between the seats. "Eric Hobbs. I think I have heard the name. Good to put a face to it."

"And how do you know my wi—my *ex*, Eli?"

"Got it now," Eric chuckled. "Met Eli at the luggage carousel," he said, winking at her and asking the driver to drop him at the track's east tunnel.

"That's my stop, too," Ted said loudly over his screen.

"Oh goody. Make it three," Eli said, flatly.

When they found Lew's garage space, Ted's 1959 Austin-Healey 3000 Mark I BN7 was show-ready. John was replacing the transponder in his dad's white 1958 MGA with Andy supervising. "Couldn't find any rooms on short notice so we rented an RV in Corning to drop off Monday," Andy explained to Ted. "Room for a third if you want to bunk with Doug and me."

"It's loud at the track. Where are you and John staying?" Ted asked, as Lew came in.

"A room with two beds, across the road at the Apex. I can check on a cot," he offered. "You have to make reservations for the SVRA Grand Prix well ahead."

"Lew, you and John can take the A-frame cottage I reserved at the Seneca Lodge, and I'll take the Apex room," Eli suggested. "It has two bedrooms, a couch, a bath, and kitchen."

"They're racing," Ted said, shaking his head. "Closer to the track is better. If you have an extra room… Did you say Seneca Lodge? Why in the world would you—"

"Because I want the Watkins Glen experience," she said indignantly. "I could see online that it's *rustic*. I want to have a drink in the tavern and walk where the legends gathered. Anyway, where's your betrothed, Ted? Isn't that where you should be sleeping tonight?"

Way to sling a hatchet, the voice in her head cheered, as Ted stormed out of the garage with Lew on his heels. Eli knew something was going on when Ted appeared the week of his fabulous Alaska cruise, arranged by his bride-to-be. She felt entitled to twist the knife after months of investigation into the mortgage fraud had hung over her while Hannah slowed the process.

"I get you're upset, but don't ruin this trip for Eli after what she's been through," Lew said, pitching his room key to Ted. "You go ahead and unpack. John and I will go with Eli."

"Wait." Ted called his brother back. "Been through? What? I've been buried with work. Explain."

After Lew had detailed what little the news was reporting, Ted slapped the keys back in his hand. "Leave Eli to me. But you take that win," he said, clapping his brother's shoulder.

Ted took the paperwork for the Concours d'Elegance and keys to his rare Austin Healey from Andy, promising to get it back safely. He cranked the engine, calling Eli outside. "You drive," he said, leaving the door open as he switched to the passenger seat. "You can have it if you'll let me stay in your extra room tonight. I'll find someplace else tomorrow."

She balked, thrown by his affable demeanor. "I don't remember this one in your collection. It's exquisite, but I certainly don't want your car," she assured him. He came back around, stopping inches away from her, causing a wild release of emotions or hormones, maybe inhibitions, that brought heat rising to her face.

With his hand on the small of her back, Ted coaxed her into sliding behind the wheel of the primrose yellow-over-black restoration. "I would love to drive it," she conceded, tingling from his touch as she watched him drop in beside her. "You never offered—"

"I *never* a lot of things," he said, pointing the way out.

They came back with six pizzas, feeding Lew's team and passersby. The evening was pleasant, and the overnight arrangements, cordial. Still, Eli kept her distance, but she noticed Ted didn't make or receive a call all evening and was almost uncomfortably attentive to her.

———————

Quick taps on the thin paneling wall against her bed at 5:30 AM snapped Eli awake as a voice said, "Want to meet the team for breakfast?" Ted sounded so close she expected to see his face as her eyes flew open.

"Where are you?" she shouted, jumping out of bed and wrapping a sheet around her.

"I'm at your door, now," he said, with another quick tap.

He twisted the handle, and she stepped aside as the door opened a few feet. He spanned the frame, resting on a forearm, boxers hanging low. *Calvin would love to have you on a billboard,* she thought, as he leaned close before they both recalled their diminished relationship status. "Ready in five," she promised, scurrying around in the sheet to find clothes.

"You dress faster than any woman I know," Ted said from the passenger seat of the warming car. Eli stepped back from the headlights, pleasantly surprised by a sensation she couldn't define. Ted had spontaneously spoken of her approvingly for the first time—ever. *And how many women* has *he waited for as they dressed?*

Lew, John, and the guys hurried through breakfast and hustled to the garage to have everything a go for the early afternoon practice. "See you two at the Research Center at six?" Lew asked.

"Beer, wine, and hors d'oeuvres," his nephew reminded them.

"We'll be there. Little John," Ted said, tugging the cap on John's six-four head, "text me the numbers after your dad's run."

Who are you? Eli wondered, watching him engage and even play with people he'd seldom conversed with in the past. *Is it Hannah, or Hannah's potion? What is she giving you, and how is she doing it?* Eli was worried, unwilling to consider it merely his sultry fiancé's positive influence.

Ted drove as they followed the Old Course, riding the original race route used from 1948 to 1952. Sailing along past roadside homes and open pastures, Ted recited the history of Watkins Glen racing and of the legendary Collier brothers, Lew's heroes. He explained each of the eight historical signs marking the old track as they flew by, taking the right turn so close at the old stone bridge that she jerked her arm in to avoid losing it.

Eli missed some of his details as she studied the old homes, including one with a dustpan dormer like hers in Hiawassee. Almost every time she looked his way, Ted was already looking at her. Did he want to tell her the ponytail looked silly? That the make-up was clownish? *Was that almost a smile?*

Back in town, they decided to walk through the State Park and wandered in among bird calls Eli didn't recognize. Bulging walls of stone strata overlooked whirlpools that narrowed into waterfalls of varying speeds and widths. The espadrilles Mela had her pack for this tailored-skirt, loose-tank look had not been made for hiking old stone stairways through a gorge long enough for nineteen waterfalls.

During a break on a ledge beside a basin fed by triple waterfalls, they both were turned in to the view. Eli reached out to feel the water rushing past, leaning so far that Ted swept her back from it. He kissed her carefully, as though executing a long-planned intention.

"Don't tell me I shouldn't have done that," said the most disciplined man she believed ever existed. He pulled her against him, kissing her again, this time solidly connecting with her sacral response. "This is right, Eli. Don't argue about it now. Decide Sunday. But being with you, it's right."

Feeling very much like an engine component just evaluated by a voltage meter, Eli faltered as he steadied her descent to the parking lot. They passed a sign about Friday's gymkhana on the site, and Eli stopped to find out more.

"That'll be an easy traffic cone course on this parking lot. Fun in the Big Healey," Ted suggested, dangling the keys.

To prepare, Eli drove the flawlessly restored sports car the rest of the day until they left the gathering at the track's research center, where everyone toasted Lew's return to racing. Conversation over dinner with Lew and his team centered on mechanical issues, competitors, and strategy. That carried over to their after-dinner stop, the tavern at Seneca Lodge, where the crew left Ted and Eli still early in the evening.

To her continuing amazement, Ted mingled, greeting and chatting with SVRA members paying homage to the venue. All the while he held on to her—his arm around her waist, across her shoulders, or on her backside. During all the years they were married, the events they attended invariably passed without him acknowledging her presence.

Despite reminding herself throughout the day of all the reasons they weren't a good fit, she was infatuated with *this* Ted. He seemed to find her attractive for the first time in a decade, and would certainly do for that racetrack fling, the increasingly impaired Eli reasoned in response to the handsy attention of her soon-to-be married ex.

Eli remembered making out in the car but not the short drive across the property to the A-frame, or anything afterward. She was aware, however, that the bed in which she had awakened was Ted's, that the clothes strewn around his room were hers, and that if he came out from his shower naked, she didn't have to wonder anymore about what happened last night.

She was entirely too hung over to detect whether the stress-relieving boosts of oxytocin and dopamine usually awarded by an orgasm or two were registering in her neurosphere.

Ted was shaved, dressed, and ready when he exited the bath, whistling cheerily into the kitchen as she pretended to sleep until the room was clear. In the bath, she turned on the shower and texted Mela to update her on Project Testosterone Storm.

"OMGWTFBBQ!!!" came the reply. Then her phone rang.

"Ted is there, and you slept with him," Mela shrieked. "Have you lost your mind? And Mac is on his way there. If he thinks Ted has picked you up as a side piece…"

"Wait, what? Mac is coming?"

"He's determined to be there for Lew's race. Wants a video of John crewing at the Glen with his dad," Mela explained.

"And OMGWTFBBQ? *Barbecue?*"

"That's our receptionist's meltdown response, like when I let her know a big emergency surgery is coming in at closing. Never thought I'd have the occasion to use it, but Ted as your Project Testosterone target?"

"You are not hearing me, Mela." Eli backtracked. "I don't remember anything after getting good to go while we were sitting in his car. Maybe…"

"Maybe you better ask him," Mela said cautiously, "and then call me. If I'm with a patient, tell them it's urgent."

Ted was knocking on the door. "All right in there?"

"Yes," she answered, whispering a promise to let Mela know what she discovered.

When Eli emerged from her bedroom, she was wearing a multi-color floral on pale blue dress with a fitted bodice, box neckline, and cap sleeves above a flounce skirt. Her hair was swept in a high French twist, and she was wearing gloves and dark glasses as she entered the kitchen.

"Close as I could come to a fifties look for the festival today," she announced, revolving for effect.

"Yeah?" he answered, glancing at her and turning back to the fridge. "I have a smoothie every morning. Nothing in here. We'll stop somewhere."

After breakfast, Eli bought some groceries, leaving them in the A-frame fridge before returning to the track. As Eli walked to the garage, she was flattered by the smiles and appreciative stares, but the wolf whistle from Lew was a bit much for Ted. "The hell?" he grumbled, shaking his head.

Lew had completed the tech inspection and first round of qualifying, saying he would come by the Concours d'Elegance to scope out the cars during the lunch break.

"Might not be there," Ted said, "but I'll see you at the Old Course Reenactment later."

"Could you drop me off at the festival?" Eli asked, unsure of where she fit into Ted's schedule but intent on exploring the event.

Ted drove to the registration table at the Concours, picked up his bottle of wine and picnic basket, then returned to Eli in the car. "We don't have to find lunch," he said, dropping the basket behind the seat.

"You're not staying for the show?" Eli asked, surprised that Ted would blow off a major commitment.

"Nope."

"Then you've participated in your last Concours?"

"Probably."

As they left the field, he pointed out the 1979 Datsun 280ZX raced by Paul Newman, circling again to get a better look at a few other cars. As they wandered through town visiting festival vendors, Eli noticed he wasn't studying her today and had much less to say. Was he put off by her outfit? Did he remember he was never that into her in the first place?

He watched while she drove the festival's Glenkhana, an adventurous automotive obstacle course. Afterward, she presented him with a purchase she'd made, an SVRA logo, long-sleeve t-shirt emblazoned with their motto: *Some People Collect Art, We Race It.*

"You've forgotten," he said indifferently, stuffing it behind the seat with the empty lunch basket. "I never wear t-shirts."

Mac found them along the street in front of the courthouse as Lew and John readied for the Old Course reenactment. "Girl, you look fine," Mac said, taking her hand and spinning her around.

"A little worse for wear," she admitted. "Should have seen me before the Glenkhana."

Back at the lodge, Eli cut holes in a black trash bag to wear as an apron while she made beef chili over rice with coleslaw and crostinis for all the guys. Ted ignored her through dinner, talking track while John and Mac helped clean up. Lew and the crew left early, but not before Ted fell asleep in front of the TV. Mac bunked in the loft.

Ted and Mac went to the track early Saturday before the last round of qualifying, but Ted came back for her to get lunch and return in time for Lew's early afternoon race. Because they were attending the SVRA party after the race, she wore the dress AB had fitted for her.

On the rack it looked like a collarless, sleeveless, cream trench coat; but after AB's touch—loosely belted, and the hint of black satin added at the neckline and 1960s hem—it was perfection. With the morning to herself, she had piled her hair in loose curls, subdued her make-up routine for Ted, and promised her toes a massage after the hours ahead in stilettos.

Although Ted didn't seem to notice her effort to look polished for Lew's return to the Glen, he did pull her along with him through the crowds at the track. She thought Lew raced brilliantly, but Ted claimed he had backed off his more aggressive pre-wreck style, and that cost him the lead.

Lew rolled into his garage to plenty of cheers and whistles, with Mac and John lifting him out of his car onto their shoulders as Eli got the videos Mac wanted.

———◆———

The Waller team didn't stay long at the party but lingered in the dining room of a local marina, celebrating the day. Ted was standing in the corridor as Eli made a call to Pete, sharing details of Lew's triumph. Ted intercepted her as she started to the dining room.

"Eli," he said, putting his hands on her waist and sliding them over her hips, evidence that he was already over his drink limit. "I want to be with you tonight. I forget how much you mean to me, and then when I'm with you..."

She was flush with surprise but couldn't let him know how steadily he had been on her mind the last two days—not just as a candidate for her weekend project, but for the glimpse of the man he had been that first twenty-four hours. She wasn't sure which Ted was propositioning her, *But either one would do,* she thought. "What about Hannah?" she said, defensively.

"I don't have sex with Hannah," he broadcast, incredulous, to any number of people within earshot. "I could, but I haven't. Just you, Eli," he announced, almost groping her as he spoke.

"How stupid do you think I am, Ted Waller." She shoved his hands off her and rushed around him.

"Hold on," he said, sweeping her back in front of him. "You don't believe me? Then who do you believe carried you in and put you in your bed the other night, only to have you come to my room, strip, then climb on top of me and pass out in *my* bed? It took me hours to fall asleep after that. In *your* bed."

"You're telling me we didn't…"

"You were wazzed, and there are rules about that."

She laced her fingers behind his neck—stiff with affront—and kissed him. "Thank you, fine man. Wait, we can't be together tonight. Mac will be in the loft."

"I'll find a place. I'll text you. Go back to the table and say I left."

"Where do I say you went?"

"You don't know."

The Waller crew dropped Mac and Eli at the A-frame on the way. "What do you and Ted have going on?" Mac said, after they were inside.

"Just being civil," she answered, thinking better of their intentions as her alcohol level receded.

"I could have sworn you were over him, kid. You were so unhappy when you were with him. He's no different now, Eli. He's just familiar," he warned, giving her a hug and starting up the stairs as he heard the Healey pull in. "Don't worry, I won't wait up."

Mac heard the door lock behind her as she went out to Ted.

"When did you get the new breasts?" Ted asked casually, as he turned toward an Inn with a vacancy northeast of Watkins Glen.

"More than a year before we split. I was beginning to think you'd never notice," she answered, wondering whether his grasp of sarcasm had improved. "Viv said my clothes would fit better."

"Do those have the same density? Is the supported mass rigid?" he asked, gearing down for an intersection.

"I suppose we'll find out," she said, feeling more like a science project than the object of his passion. Eli found enough wine left in the bottle from the picnic basket to constitute a drink or two, and she swigged it as they approached their destination. "How did you find this place?"

"Called every lodging listing until I got to this. Like I said in the text, it's a honeymoon suite."

"I didn't get a text. I've never been in a honeymoon suite."

When they parked, Ted took out his phone to prove his text. "Oh shit." He exhaled. "I texted that to Hannah."

"Sorry, all the wine is gone," she said, giggling.

"This will show you how much I want us to be together," he said, waving her out of the car.

"Is it a demo then," she answered sardonically, "in the honeymoon suite?"

Ted delivered on his promise. It wouldn't be easy to put this evening out of her mind, she realized, pulling a sheet over his back. He was sleeping soundly in the bizarre round bed, adjacent to the heart-shaped hot tub he was certain constituted a respiratory biohazard throughout the suite.

Eli kept dozing off, her brain awash in oxytocin and all its illusion-inducing brethren, blaming herself for the reckless breakdown of their marriage. *If only I had tried harder, been more patient...*

———◆———

A ping from Ted's phone woke her. She heard the shower running, and his phone was on the bed. Unlocked, she discovered. A slew of texts from Hannah were stacked on the screen, all unread. Hannah sounded charmed by his reference to a honeymoon suite, taking it as an olive branch opening after ghosting her since his decision to pass on the cruise.

Then came Hannah's litany of all that he was missing—illustrated in attached excursion pics in case he wasn't reading her posts. The texts became terse as he failed to respond. Finally, in early morning on Alaskan waters, she changed her tack to being overjoyed that the wedding was back on. Eli reset them as new messages.

"I'll drop you off and find Lew," Ted said, as they pulled in at the Lodge. "He wasn't sure last night if he would race again today."

It was the first thing he'd said since they'd left the Inn before daylight. "You can fly back with us this afternoon if you want. Takeoff is at 3."

"I'm good. My flight is 1:20, and I have to catch the shuttle first," she said, appearing to check her phone for this information. She was feeling the old familiar disconnect. The same superficially pleasant, emotionally absent aura of their entire relationship—until last Wednesday night—settling dense over them again.

"Ted," she began cautiously, as she closed the car door, knowing this sort of conversation always set him off. "If you've reconsidered and decided to work things out with Hannah—"

"So you're mad at me again? What this time? I never said I changed my mind. Is this you letting me down easy? Fine!"

Eli watched him tear through the property to the highway, gears taching out as he disappeared.

Ted arrived as John was helping Andy and Doug load the trailer. "Better let her cool down before we load the Big Healey," Andy advised.

"He's through then?" Ted asked, watching his brother pack his gear into a duffle.

"He's worn out," Doug said, pausing to speak quietly with Ted. "Reasonable with all the work he put into getting here, but he made it."

"I invited Mac to fly home with us this afternoon," Lew said, as Ted sat by him on a bench in the garage. "Did you get Eli to join us and skip that miserable commercial trip home?"

"No," he snapped, walking back to the car to get his phone.

"Where's Eli?" Mac asked, carrying the communications case to the trailer as he passed Ted.

"Packing probably."

"She spent the night with you, then?" Mac pressed, dropping the case in the trailer.

"That's none of your business. Can you not understand that?"

"I understand you don't have any idea how to treat women," he said in a low growl, coming back to Ted at the car. "After my discharge, I saw how alone Eli was with you. That wasn't a marriage. She was your domestic manager.

"I told you eighteen years ago to leave her alone, that you weren't right for her. You've always been the center of your own universe. You want an assistant-to, not a partner. She's got more to give than that, Ted. So *do not* run off with her again. I'm telling you the same way I told JC Harrison last week and that GBI guy before him. She's a concours, not your in-town SUV. Let her be."

"*Really?* She's been dating two guys?" Ted noted with a tinge of disgust.

"Don't look down now, Turbo, but you're closing on the drop zone for your next wedding," he said, brushing close to Ted's face as he walked out of the building. "So fuck off."

"Waller Racing never needed you, and you're not welcome back." Ted responded, dropping over the door into the driver's seat and squealing out of the garage.

"Wait up, Mac," Lew called from the door of the garage.

Lew gripped Mac's shoulder as they walked back inside. "He'll cool off. He knows these guys are waiting on him to get their truck on the road. And *you* know Ted sees only his own perspective on everything. Looks to me like Eli is perfectly capable of fighting her own battles these days."

"I might have agreed with you before I found her drowned under a tarp in Lake Chatuge."

"You need to see this," Andy said, approaching Lew with his phone.

"He'll be late to the office tomorrow," Lew said, showing the screen to Mac. "Says he's driving that car to Atlanta. Nothing we can do now. Let's go, fellas."

After takeoff, a noisy video game battle ensued between John and Mac in the lounge of the Waller jet as Lew settled in a cabin seat across from Eli. "Glad Mac persuaded you to come," he said, handing her a cocktail from his shaker.

"No thanks," she said, waving it off. "I've had enough of that for a while. And yes, Mac has a way of syncing people's decisions with his." She laughed. "I've been wanting to tell you that I'm so proud of you, Lew, the way you fought to get to Watkins Glen, and how beautifully you raced yesterday. I wouldn't have missed it."

"You sure about that? I mean with Ted showing up."

"I'll never get over him, but I'm going to get past being *messed up* over him," she claimed, pressing the footrest up on her seat. "He's such a wonderful, maddening man."

"You saw what I've been telling you, right?" Lew insisted. "That he was fundamentally more perceptive, at ease with people. Then it fades once he's out of her reach. I'm telling you, Eli, she is drugging him. He refuses to believe me, says nothing is different about him."

"No doubt, Lew. Being with him that first day was like he had awakened from a coma, able to communicate and be with me like *never* before. By this morning, he was totally gone again. How is this lost on him? He turns into a brick wall."

"Dealing with Ted is easier for me. He's my brother, and that allows a magnanimous viewpoint. Ted's the one who lives with it. Like Mac's leg, his disconnect makes life harder for him. But you don't love *Mac* any differently, maybe more, for his strength and determination. It's a difficulty he manages from day to day. By a different measure, it's the same for Ted.

"Ted loves you deeply, Eli. I know this. Can't imagine how frustrating it must be to have devoted yourself to someone who didn't return that passion or even appreciate it. My ex had plenty of grievances about me, and I have learned from that loss. Maybe Ted has, too.

"I don't see him intentionally hurting you, ever. Because of the basic attention that you needed from Ted but couldn't get, I wonder if that makes you see his issues as something of an offense? He doesn't get how abrupt and uncaring he comes across.

"And the greatest obstacle to your love life right now may be your big brother. I heard him tell Ted that he'd booted two admirers in the last few weeks and one of them, I understood him to say, was James Harrison?"

"Oh, no, he did not," she screeched, bolting upright.

He laughed, finishing his drink. "Don't jump him now, but the certified brother role has gone to his head. Perhaps Mela can help. By the way, text me the campfire schedule? I feel like family when I'm there with your bunch."

Chapter 20

Where You Find What Sets You Free

Lew didn't get back to Hiawassee until the weekend of Bernadette Montgomery's first responders' benefit. She hadn't been on stage in four years. Local restaurants were jammed, hotels were full, and the event had sold out online in minutes. Bernie Carter's lifelong battle with anxiety would be won or lost here, she had decided, listening to the rumble of voices in the Anderson Music Hall at the Georgia Mountains Fairgrounds on that October day.

"You got this," AB promised, combing every wig hair into place after Bernie changed her outfit again. "Your breathing is crucial, so let's focus there," she added, taking her hand. "Your pulse is good; that quiet time you took to pray helped."

"That always brings me peace," she said, breathing deeply. "I won't let my insecurities get to me."

As the curtains parted, Bernie caught sight of her son and his wife sitting alongside his father. From her first big event, Henry Carter's enthusiastic whistle brought her eyes to him before she could react to the massive crowd—a gift at the start of every show. She was touched to see him there. AB's frequent advice echoed in her mind. *Forgiveness sets our joy free.* As his whistle echoed, Bernie blew them kisses through her tears.

"We're here tonight to honor those whose lives are dedicated to helping others," Bernie said, arms extended to the uniformed guests in front rows. "Your ticket proceeds will go to first responder support organizations throughout these mountain communities. Our thoughts and prayers remain with these beautiful souls, and with all the brave hearts in medical fields, outreach programs, care facilities, and everywhere love flows in service. Now, let's get some of your messages flowing, shall we?"

⟫━●━⟪

"I had never seen so many people at the Fairgrounds," Bibi marveled, as she followed Carly down the hill to the bonfire Sunday night. "Even the campgrounds were full. Probably a fraction of the audiences in all those big capacity venues she's done."

"Bernie was *dope*," Carly said, waving to the group gathered below at Eli's, all waiting to share the results of their DNA testing. "I'm surprised to see her here. She was exhausted after three hours of going out through that crowd. If her ex hadn't shown up like he did, hadn't been there to catch her when she almost passed out..."

"I don't think she has ex'd him yet," Bibi said.

They slowed their descent as Leslie stood in the path, arms folded. "Get this, Bibz. I went by AB's to drop off your fabric from Marietta, but no one answered the door—even though her car and a pickup were there. I stepped in to leave it on the table and heard splashing. The hall to the pool area was open, so I peeked to see if she was swimming because I would wait. But it was Will, getting out of the pool and drying off. Stark naked, I swear. Very naked. All over."

"Full pickle, huh?" Carly chuckled. "Sounds like you got more than a peek."

"Pickle? No. It's a heated pool. Have you ever overlooked a zucchini in the garden?" Leslie hooted, as they walked ahead together.

"Thanks for bringing the fabric," Bibi said evenly. "Now grow up, you two, before they hear you."

"Enough, my kind friends," Bernie said, raising her hands. "Being with all of you recharges my batteries, and it's your love and support that brought off last night's show. I'm very grateful," she said, taking a seat next to AB. "Especially to you," she declared, clinking soda cans.

"As we all agreed," Eli announced, "Mac and I handled submitting everyone's DNA sample, setting up the accounts with email support, and researching the results, so we can provide a full spectrum reveal for those of us who benefited from Mela's trove of tests. Still time to go private," she reminded the gathering.

"Make it happen," Lew cheered, then chomped his loaded hotdog, sneaking a piece to Dude at his feet. "Umm, fire roasted. This place is heaven," he said.

"Then we'll start with you," Mac said, taking the Waller folder out of the stack. "There is a Viking among us tonight," he declared, reading off the Wallers' descendancy as cited by a related researcher, who traced the line to the Duchy of Normandy established by Vikings in the year 911.

"That explains so much." Eli laughed, reaching over to him for their *feed the birds* gesture she and Lew adopted while watching *Castle* reruns at the Shepherd Center.

"No need to bore everyone with all the generations of pillagers since." Lew grinned, taking the folder from Mac.

"Next up is Bibi," Eli said, lifting the first page. "Ancestors from Wales, Belgium... Wait, Mac, this says she has two brothers in Newnan, Georgia? Bibi?"

"Oh, yeah, I didn't test because Carol and I already have, so I let Sophie spit in it."

Leslie sprang from her seat and snatched the papers. "How dare you," she shouted, and then fell silent. "Two brothers in Newnan," she repeated, struck by the words. "Oh, my God. *Oh my God.*"

Leslie turned to her daughter, who was bracing for whatever was headed her way. "My precious baby girl. Oh, Sophie," she cried, sobbing into the frightened girl's hair.

"That was close," AB whispered to Bernie. "Could have been another Sunday night dumpster fire. Didn't you get any warning? You know..."

"Warning? About a healing?" she answered. "Actually, I've been hearing beautiful voices murmuring all day, and I less-than-humbly thought it might have something to do with last night. Now it's stronger and even lovelier. There are so many here with us today, telling me that this," she said, circling her index fingers around at the group, "is family. That we are *all*," she said, shifting her circling to the sky, "one family."

Mela went to Leslie and sat with Sophie huddled between them. Leslie was beaming at Mela, lips tightly pressed, as if that would contain her emotions.

"We did find your mom," Eli continued quietly, bringing two folders to Leslie, "and she has a website dedicated to you. Your father is an injury attorney in Birmingham. Big family. Your mom's a teacher in Macon. Married, two other children, and grandkids. I spoke with her last night, and she's on her way here."

"Thank you." Leslie said faintly, hugging her sister and then Eli. "I was so afraid of this day, and it's nothing like I imagined. Come on, Sophie, let's find your *grandmother*."

"Mela?" Eli asked cautiously. "You want to go ahead with this?"

"Been waiting all my life. Hit me," she said, pulling Mac to join her and Dude by the fire.

"Surprise, you are not half-Italian, as your adoption records suggested," Eli said, glancing at the page. "And you guessed close—you are 41.3 percent sub-Saharan African; but the 40.7 percent Northern European—over half of that is French with English and Irish. Plus 12.5 percent Ashkenazi Jew; 3.9 percent east Asian and Native American, with remaining percentages undetermined."

"What? I figured DNA would be a final, crushing disappointment. Did you..." She exhaled hard. "Do I have any family?"

"Do you ever. Your mother was easy to find. Lauren Post. An only child, parents deceased, but she has cousins. She is single, living in Louisville, Kentucky, where she's an orthopedic surgeon, *Doc*. It appears your parents' connection was Vanderbilt, where they were both students the year before you were born."

"Vandy, really?" Mela said.

"Yep. Your father, Luke Bailey, is one of four kids. He is a musician and songwriter living in Nashville, also unmarried. You have scads of cousins in New York, Kentucky, and beyond."

"Let me see that," she said, releasing Mac's hand to take the report. "So, I guess... Busy people, obviously."

"Babe," Mac said, turning her to face him. "Dr. Post called me back yesterday after I got a lead from her uncle, who was surprised to learn his late sister had a grandchild.

"Lauren's out of her mind excited. Didn't want to look for you in case you didn't know you were adopted. Didn't want to complicate your life, she said. Her number is on the bottom of that page, and she will meet you anywhere, any time. I haven't reached your dad. This contact info is new, and he's damned reclusive."

Mela kissed him solidly, then returned to scouring the papers while Eli delivered Bernie's folder.

"It's entirely possible Mela's dad has no idea," Will said, joining AB and Bernie. "DNA is how I learned I had a son, Ewan. As I told you, I became a father at sixty-two."

"You… Your hair is wet," AB said absently, when Will noticed she was staring at him.

"Went for a swim, then came to find you," he responded, smiling warmly.

"My boy, his name was Ewan, too," she told him, distractedly stroking his damp hair.

"Annie! Was it!" he said, tucking her under his shoulder, kissing her forehead. "Are you ready yet, to tell me all about him?" he whispered.

"Yep, nothing new here," Bernie declared, rummaging through the files. "A little different emphasis from my sister's website, but she's been working on our history for years. Rosie has viewed documents in court-houses and libraries across the south. Traveled the country to gather our story. Thank you, sweet Mela, for sharing your birthday gifts with us."

"Sorry," Carly said as she squeezed by Eli. "I never turned mine in, but Mom is totally into genealogy, and she updates it all the time."

"Annie Blanche Sutton," Eli announced. "Cousin AB. It seems our Sutton line goes back through Virginia's Tidewater. Then your ma-ternal line descends from the Boone family in Kentucky. *That* Boone family. None of your roots show an immigrant after the 1600s."

"That's a snooty sounding bloodline to have devolved into a bunch of feuding hillbillies. Thank you. I'll give this to Louise," AB said soft-ly. "Her kids will get a kick out of it."

"That leaves Mac, Kit, and me," Eli announced. "Kit's busy this weekend. Mac already had testing, for *both* of us it turns out, resulting in his dad also being my dad, as you all know now.

"And AB and I have great-greats in common. Thus, I can no longer poke fun at the mountain gene pool from which I emerged. This test showed that like Mela and AB, I have a small native American percentage to go along with my momma's Mayflower folks who somehow made it to these mountains. Going to be an interesting Thanksgiving this year."

"That it is," AB added, cuddled against Will. "Let's tell them now," she suggested, patting his knee.

"Annie Blanche has agreed to marry me," he joyously declared, rotating to everyone as he spoke. "And what more appropriate day could there be than Thanksgiving? We want to share that special day with all of you."

"Eggplant. Butternut squash." Carly giggled in Bibi's ear. "Give me a minute. I can think—"

"Would you hush," she grumbled, elbowing Carly as the happy congratulations continued.

<hr />

"So, Cousin AB," Eli said, when the chatter had slowed. "This test still doesn't have enough indigenous tribal DNA to determine locations of our trace amount, but it does support your suggestion that we have a Cherokee grandmother many generations back. Crazy, huh?"

"Yeah. Bernie says she often sees a native American woman around me. I do like thinking that great-granny is dropping in on us—that the old story is true."

"What's the story?" Carly asked, as she handed out cupcakes.

"My grandma often told us kids that her great-grandmother—a descendant of the Bird Clan—stayed behind with her brother when what officials thought was the last of the Cherokee were forced on the Trail of Tears that had begun in May of 1838. They weren't among those exempt from the removal, but took shelter with the son of our ancestor, the settler William Joseph Sutton."

"The two young men, Billy Joe and Wohali—who also went by Edward—were close friends," AB said, adding that the tragedy was felt by many families in the area. "As the danger of discovery passed, and winter was coming, they built a cabin deep in the Sutton property for Wohali and his sister, Walela, who had taken the Christian name Sarah. But by the time it was finished, Billy Joe and Walela were in love and wanted to marry. Her brother and the Sutton family celebrated the union.

"Billy Joe and Wohali established a mill on the river below the Sutton homeplace, and as Wohali had been learning the healing ways since he was a boy, he also continued that practice throughout his life from the cabin he shared with his wife and their children.

"When William Sutton moved away to live near a son who was well established beyond the Ocoee River in Tennessee, there were two Sutton homes standing on a rise overlooking the river and the mill— one left by William to a younger son, and one built by Billy Joe and Wohali, not far from the cabin. Wohali was said to have had a massive mantel stone set above the hearth in his friend's new home with a carved inscription invoking a blessing of love and healing to transfuse the place forever.

"Now it may be my imagination working overtime," AB cautioned as she brought her story to an end, "but I get a sense of healing every time we're here together. I feel it powerfully. Maybe these bonds of friendship bring us blessings, but I like to think it is helped along by Uncle Wohali's prayer."

"I've never heard that," Eli said, spellbound. "Your house and mine, then?"

"That's what I'm thinking," AB said. "A while after my husband died, I confirmed that his house was probably one of the Sutton houses, and that the Clarks were in the other. It appears both have been remodeled enough to have obscured their history."

"But the mill on the river?" Carly asked. "There's no river here."

"About 1942, the Tennessee Valley Authority plopped this big lake on it," AB said, pointing behind her. "As the dam was built, that mill was among the places burned. Trees were felled. Farms are still under that water, but there are a few people who can remember how it looked."

"AB, could we talk to you and Will for a sec?" Mela asked, walking them past the bustling food table. "Mac and I want your absolute honest answer," she said, looking at Mac for support.

"Why so serious?" AB responded.

"A few weeks ago, Mac and I had decided to have a justice of the peace wedding on the Wednesday before, then celebrate with dinner on Thanksgiving, so, would y'all consider a double celebration? No hurt feelings if it's a 'no' to that."

Will and AB erupted in relieved laughter and threw their arms wide to embrace Mela and Mac. "We would be thrilled to have a double *wedding*. This is wonderful," AB answered, her chin on Mela's shoulder. "I'm looking forward to meeting your mother, and we'll find your dad."

"We have another big question that I hope you'll consider," Mac said nervously before whistling Dude back from the lake.

"You know that Beau's estate has been settled," Mela said softly. "He left everything to my discretion, but he had intended, after his parents were gone, to dedicate their home as a retreat for military veterans.

"Mac has attended reunions that we would like to model these retreats on. A nonprofit supported by Beau's family trust will encompass all of this. With your backgrounds, we're asking you to think about being the on-site administrators."

"Mel and I are moving to my place across the lake after the wedding," Mac added. "It would be full time for both of you and a live-in situation. It's a lot to ask, but we can't imagine anyone else who could pull it together as well as y'all would."

"Do we need to think it over, Colonel Pastor?" AB asked, looking up at Will.

"I've found the church members have a forgiving, healthy resistance to my clumsy efforts to whip them into stalwart Christian soldiers. And although it has been an extended temporary gig until they find a genuine man of the cloth, I'm sure I'll be available to start by the end of the year. Sounds like Annie will be available sooner. How does that fit into your timetable?"

"Perfectly, sir," Mac answered, as their friends swarmed the couples with congratulations and ideas for the festivities.

<hr />

Morning walks buzzed with plans and revelations. One day it was just Carly and Eli listening to news of Mela's joyous reunion with her birth mother, Dr. Lauren Post, and finally, with her dumbfounded father, Luke Bailey, who had called her every day since with questions—mostly about Lauren.

"His grandfather was Jewish," Mela said, relating her newfound roots. "And Luke is originally from New York. His mother was French Canadian, from Quebec, and his songwriting led him to Nashville. Lauren is coming for the wedding and will stay with me. She is sensational. Impressive, accomplished. I'm waiting for someone to call and correct my DNA results. This can't be real."

"But it is real, Mel, and we're thrilled for you," Eli said with a hug. "Only wish it had happened sooner. By the way, I've been trying to get in touch with Kit, but she's ghosting me. It has to be more than her workload."

"Yeah, about that," Carly said, wincing as she stared ahead. "I don't want to put her on blast, but she's at my place. Arrived Sunday night. Y'all, she's really frightened. Could we get Mac to talk with her?"

Kit cowered in the seat of Carly's Miata as they made the drive around the lake to Mac's. Mela and Eli were there when they arrived.

Initially, Kit again claimed she was still trying to end a long, troubled relationship with someone who wasn't ready to end things. "Basically, they told me they would accept it was over if I'd take one last fantastic trip to be sure that's what I wanted. Then they said, 'Bring as much as you can, most of your clothes for the differing climates.'

"Always before, shopping for everything was a perk on these excursions. I got scared, that I might never come back—disappear," she said, bending to hug Dude, convulsing as she cried.

"You're saying 'they.' Is that the friend you mentioned?" Eli asked. "The one who bought you the TR6 you were driving?"

"No, he's just one of... That's another person." She wept, unable to speak and barely able to catch a breath. She moved to the floor by Dude as the big dog gently nudged her. "I'm in with dangerous people. I think I was supposed to die, not Victor.

"Since he was killed, Liz has been pushing me to tell the cops that Victor was behind what she and Johnny have been doing at that bogus talent acquisition firm. But it's *her*, and she's going to end me because I won't lie anymore!

"Eli, the day after I refused that trip, she insisted Victor needed me to drive you to an important meeting. That gun was aiming at me before Victor leaned across the table."

"Kit, I thought that, too," Eli said, rocking in her seat. "I thought it was another attempt on my life. We've been through an awful shock, and it's reasonable to—"

"No, Eli. These people are total degenerates," she cried. "I am, too. I'm one of them now."

As Mela comforted her, Mac noticed Carly's phone position and texted her. She indicated she had recorded it all from the beginning. "You're safe with us," Mac promised Kit. "Feel like explaining how you got involved with Liz?"

"She was always saying that I was *so pretty*, that I should be modeling. She asked me to stay with her dog at their Beaufort condo while she was away. Then she came busting in and caught me with a boyfriend. I was fourteen but looked his age, twenty. She threatened him, said she had video and would give it to the police.

"Liz threw him out, then acted all sympathetic. She said I could be something special. Took me shopping everywhere, then had me modeling a couple of times. I was amazed by the photos. I was spending every other weekend at her place in Atlanta. Molly objected, but Liz said it was jealousy over how close we were.

"She took me to celebrity parties, traveling, telling Molly I was her apprentice, that this was educational exposure for me. Within a few months, I wasn't just spending time with men who came to her place. She started sending me out to men she claimed were David's friends. They were obsessed with me, but I didn't know what pervs were. I kind of got into it. Felt like I had some crazy power over men.

"My modeling jobs explained the wardrobe and travel. Every attempt to quit brought bigger incentives, especially from her nasty pig partner. They told me Victor and David set me up for this, that Mom would be fired, and they'd take her house if I didn't go along. I didn't understand then that *everything* was a lie.

"I was always at Liz's place. Mostly for entertaining her people, but sometimes she was just lonely and called me over. Those nights after so many more drinks, she would ramble on, crying and telling me all this crazy shit about a guy who worked for them, how much he liked watching things die.

"A few times, she told me terrifying things that had happened to other girls, but I thought she was trying to intimidate me. I didn't believe her until Victor died." She wailed, burying her face in Dude's fur. "That was real," she said. "What if Liz had lied all along about Victor and David? What if, when she drank til she was blasted, she was telling me real secrets? That she is a murderer?

"I just want to go home, but I can't. They've been using me. I'm disgusting, and I was never anyone's lame goddess," Kit lamented as Mela reached to hold her.

"I want to wade through estuaries and tend to nature. I want a simple, useful life," she said, sobbing. "People think I was just this spoiled brat, but I've been in hell forever now. I haven't looked Molly in the eye for years. I miss my mom."

"This isn't on you, Kit! You were only fourteen," Eli assured her. "Did this all start about the same time you began calling your mom Molly?"

"Yeah, I don't know."

"Eli," Mac said softly. "Would you call Seth Taylor? Maybe he could come by?"

Weeks later, as charges loomed for Liz and her partner, LA producer Johnny Grant, she changed her story. Liz was no longer trying to implicate her late husband, Victor Hernandez, but was now preparing to claim Grant extorted her into the decades-long sex trade hidden within their agency. Only Johnny Grant had taken a plea deal first, flipping on Liz, painting her as the mastermind.

That turned out to be a fatal misstep, as an interested third party experienced in silencing potential witnesses left Johnny dead in his flagstone driveway. It appeared to be a taxpayer-friendly suicide until labs came back. Johnny Grant did not jump from his third-floor study after all.

A usual dose of opioids and a surprise injection of veterinary suxamethonium had preceded his fall to the roof of his Lamborghini. Medicinally paralyzed, he would have been initially aware but powerless to interfere as he was pitched out the window. The tactic was obsolete as a forensic ruse, but may have afforded other satisfying benefits to that third party.

When informed of her codefendant's peculiar manner of death, Liz Hernandez was said to have visibly withered. All too familiar with that staging, she changed her plea to guilty and negotiated for protection in exchange for information on the killer—information she was slow to provide.

A loud discussion preceding her new plea hearing carried into the corridor on the second floor of the courthouse. Prosecutors were making a final demand for Liz Hernandez to reveal specifics about Johnny Grant's unnamed associate.

As she hurried by to the courtroom, Eli felt a chill pass through her. It was the first time she had heard the partner's last name. She recalled having spoken with producer Jack Grant's son, Johnny, while researching Ida Harrison's missing sister, Alma Garcia.

"I had nothing to do with him. He was Johnny's man. All I know is that he takes care of things, of people, for Johnny. I don't know his name," she swore. "You *must* announce that to the media."

Kit was determined to attend the plea hearing where Liz would admit her guilt. Eli was joining the Harrisons there to comfort her and Molly. As they gathered, the small group overheard the intense exchange regarding the death of Liz's partner being reclassified as a murder, and the prosecution's subsequent reluctance to allow her plea to go forward.

As they followed Kit to their seats, the volume in the adjacent conference room increased. Eager to get before the judge, Liz again loudly claimed she had no knowledge of her partner's killer. "I've never seen him. I don't know who he is."

"Yes, you do!" Kit shouted from her seat, emboldened by the judicial setting. "He was there when you shot that woman."

Scanning the room in terror, half-expecting an attack to silence her, Kit brushed away her mother's grasp and turned to the Harrisons, breathlessly apologizing to David and Ida as the judge peered out from his chambers, dispatching a bailiff to subdue the disruption. A prosecutor left the meeting with Liz and her attorneys after hearing Kit's accusations, and signaled the bailiff to bring her forward, to where he and his investigator waited.

"Please don't blame my mom," she begged the Harrisons, as he led Kit from her seat. "She didn't know any of this. Only me. Liz told me."

Eli watched the couple, both reaching over to Molly, sharing looks of frightened concern. She scooted to Kit's empty spot by Molly, then turned to the front row where Kit met with the prosecution team. She was shaking violently, but answered every question the investigator asked as he slowly moved her through her accusation.

"I was always at her house—Liz's house," she said, her soft voice echoing through the cavernous courtroom. "Liz drank a lot, and she would talk about things that scared her." She looked back around the near empty room.

"Several times she told me the same story—being young, dating the guy who became her business partner, Johnny Grant." She glanced, broken, at the Harrisons and then continued. "Johnny wanted the Harrison man dead because he was taking away the girl Johnny wanted, Alma."

Ida gasped, and David held her tighter. Eli saw Molly was trembling at this point, tears spilling freely, and took her hand. The prosecutor sat beside Kit, urging her to continue as Liz and her attorney remained out of view. She repeated the story of how the murders came about, in offices at the back of a movie lot. The foursome was planning to go out drinking together, when Johnny changed the plan.

"Liz said it started when Ray Harrison made a comment Johnny didn't like, and Johnny just shot him in the back. She said Alma ran, screaming, and this kid who was always hanging around Johnny chased Alma down.

"Liz said he offered to 'take care of her,' and Johnny put his gun in Liz's hand, saying something like, 'You say that you don't want her around, make her go away.' He shoved her toward Alma, who was on the ground, begging them not to kill her, that she had a baby. Each time Liz told me this story, it ended with her saying, 'If I hadn't shot her, they would have killed me.' Then she would cry for a while and pass out."

Kit slumped forward, her face in her hands as she listened to Ida's muffled sobs against David's chest.

"That was all I could do—promise her I would take care of her baby," Liz shouted from an adjacent room. "And I did. I did! I helped him, gave him jobs, made Victor get financing for his projects. I was always there for her boy!"

"Go ahead, Kit," the investigator said gently.

"Liz said the young guy dumped their bodies in a pit behind the studio that was used to bury horses. She said he had been a 'fixer' for Johnny all along, getting rid of girls and 'meddlers' who caused trouble, and that he would like to take care of me if he ever got the chance. She was always saying things like that.

"I know he meant to kill me and shot Victor instead. I wish it had been me."

This revelation persuaded the prosecution to go to the judge and ask for a continuance, postponing the plea hearing.

DNA confirmed that some of the half dozen or more human skeletal remains uncovered among those of the horses buried on the long vacant property were those of Ray Harrison and Alma Garcia. A pistol that had belonged to Jack Grant was also found there and was being tested for evidence. At trial, Kit's testimony would be critical.

Chapter 21

When You Just Can't Get Over Yourself

With charges pending against Liz, and a loose killer bent on dispatching witnesses, Molly and Kit agreed to temporarily move in with the Harrisons, where security was tighter than ever.

"Kit says they will visit before the autumn leaves are gone," Carly reported on the morning walk, as they discussed the recent developments in the saga.

"How did we miss Kit's situation?" Eli asked, zipping her jacket in the brisk, mid-October air. "She always seemed focused and on course, but there were clues."

"We can't change what's happened, but we can support Kit's recovery," AB suggested. "When she and Molly come, these mountains will lift their energy. The Folk School festival is awesome. The Fair is coming. Hiking in cool air is easier, and there's always this magnificent lake. From what you've said," she continued, glancing at Eli, "Molly is having a harder time with this than her daughter."

"She's crushed, but sees this as a turning point for them," Eli answered. "She talks about having been so controlled as a girl that she wanted Kit to be a free spirit and felt that within their close circle of acquaintances—having known Victor and his wife so long—that Kit was safe. She understands now why Kit became so distant, and they are in counseling."

"By design, we learn and grow," Bernie said, pausing to inspect a small tree along the road. "Now, what is this pretty little shrub?" she asked, examining the vivid oranges, yellows, and swaths of green in the leaves.

"Break a twig and sniff," Mela suggested. "See these lower leaves with three lobes, then the mitten-shaped leaves above them, and higher up, these deep orange ovals?"

"All on one tree?" Eli marveled.

"Root beer?" Bibi guessed, sniffing the twig Bernie snapped.

"Sassafras," Carol hollered.

"How many of these twigs to make a batch of root beer?" Bernie asked.

"Honey, why do you think they call it *root* beer," AB said, waving them to move on. "I've seen these on your property, Bernie. They spread easily and stay relatively small. Most people clear them out as scrub, not knowing how pretty they turn."

"I've been trying to find some fabric the color of those hickory leaves," Mela said, pointing to a stand of golden trees beyond quarter horses grazing in a pasture. "Should I be looking for any particular fabric, AB?"

"I may have that color in something that might work for the sketch Bibi made of the dress you described to her. I cannot pass up fine fabric on sale. I'm using a remnant of silk for my suit."

"But that's brown silk," Bibi reminded her. "Why brown?"

"It's slimming, it's autumnal, and I already have brown silk," she said, pinging an acorn off the back of Bibi's head.

"I hope I can say this right," Bibi ventured, rummaging through a pocket inside her vest. "AB, you dress like the first female executive on *Mad Men*. You're more fun than that. If you're set on brown silk, how about this," she said, presenting a folded sketch.

"Oh, my," AB said, seeing a dramatic wrap neckline—high across the back and dropping as it rounded the shoulders to cross in front. The bronzed brown silk fit closely at the bodice, with an elegant flare beginning below the waist. AB's bright smile and bright eyes were captured in the sketch, as were upswept soft curls, with light bangs escaping. "Bibz, you are a wizard. I think I can make this. The hair will take some doing."

"Alrighty then," she said, pulling out a swatch with the second sketch. "Leslie found this fabric for Mela's dress, and she's waiting for approval to make the purchase," she added, handing Mela the fabric and a revised sketch.

"This color is made for you," Eli raved, holding it across Mela's cheek as they walked.

"It's exquisite," Mela said. "And this design is so detailed. Can I help somehow?"

"Lots of fittings," AB warned, "but it will be stunning with the portrait neckline and sleeves in lace. Have that, B?"

"Yep, lace, too. Say 'yes' and my text goes," she said. "Leslie is super psyched about this."

"Send." Mela laughed, laying the fabric over her arm. "What is this color?"

"Persimmon," Carly answered, running through crunching leaves to a luminous tree and returning with a handful of crimson leaves that almost disappeared on the fabric.

"A scarlet wedding dress," Mela squeaked. "Lauren brought her mother's gown, insisting I try it on even as I was explaining how much I wanted a dress that's *me*. I couldn't say I didn't want to see it or touch it or think of the woman who sabotaged several lives to preserve her pride."

"Your wedding, your decisions," AB advised. "I've only met him once, but I can see you're Luke's daughter—easy going, quiet, with support and patience to spare. Lauren sounds like her mother, expecting to have her way. Start this relationship off right, Mela. You decide."

"I have," Mela declared, raising the sketch and swatch in defiance. "And the color is persimmon."

"Then I'll call mine autumn white oak," AB decided, pulling coppery brown leaves from a branch as she passed.

"I wouldn't miss one of our walks this time of year," Carly said, collecting maple leaves mottled in bright red and yellow. "Can we use these on tables for the weddings?" she asked, passing one to AB.

Mela held it to the sun. "Think if we press some, they'll keep a few weeks? I have some fat acorns that I can gather to weight them on the tables. Terrace might get windy in late November."

"No terrace weddings," Bernie forbade them, wedging between the brides. "The pavilion is the only place for this. We have a kitchen, the water views, plenty of room, glass weather panels, and heat, which I expect we'll need. Plus, you girls will have the house to get dressed.

"In fact," she added, "let's have a sleepover the night before. With the specialties that April will bring from Epic on Wednesday, plus dishes Nancy and I will put together at the house, there's no shortage of good eats. How about it?"

"You are hopelessly generous, Bern. It would be a dream location," AB said. "You don't need weddings and construction going on at your place, Mela."

"Not worrying about rain would be great," Mela said, as they linked arms behind Bernie for a hug. "A sleepover will be fun," she added. "I've never been to one."

"Who here has?" Eli asked, anticipating a low response.

"Me," Carly said cautiously, surveying her friends. "Those things get uggz."

"Aw, you were with a bunch of brats. I'll bring the booze," Carol said, from twenty feet ahead. "Come on! Y'all walk like a bunch of old ladies."

"Oh, I can't," Mela said. "Lauren is coming for the weddings. Mac's sister Kathy, too."

"Six bedrooms and sleeper sofas in the big room downstairs," Bernie countered. "Bring your new sister and Momma."

"Margarite Orr was my momma," Mela said, emotional at the thought of a wedding without the woman who had nurtured her. "And, like Bernie keeps telling us, we are family. The best kind because we found each other—amazingly—at such tough times in our lives. Not that you were having any problems, Carly. You keep everything under control."

"You don't know what finding legit friends has meant to me," Carly replied, stacking the leaves in her hand, stammering, "I love you guys so much."

"Hey, you're our shining light," Bibi said, handing over her leaf collection. "Stop fretting. Bret is nuts about you, just busy."

"Thanks, B," she murmured. "You're the best. You're not just a different name, you're a different person the last few weeks. You're, I dunno, *content*."

⋟•◉•⋞

Morning walks were sparsely attended as November arrived. AB was especially busy with dresses for Mela, herself, and Sophie. One afternoon, after dropping off a box of ribbon at Bernie's, Eli noticed Will's truck wasn't at AB's and stopped by.

"Back here," AB hollered from her sewing room when Eli knocked. "Your timing couldn't be better," AB groaned, with fabric heaped across her shoulder. "Help me get this hem in, would you?"

"AB, you've done so much since I was here. The low ceilings are gone and those are some hunky rafters up there. Oh, the old wood floors are restored. It's transformed," she exclaimed, helping AB on the footstool. "What's in these shadowboxes in the foyer?"

"Shards of pottery, pieces of pipes and stone tools—really old items that turned up when the pool was excavated. Will framed them," she answered, rotating as Eli pinned.

Will is doing all this construction, too?"

"Will and Mac, working with Lloyd's crew. Then Will retiled both bathrooms," she answered, beaming. "Go look at my kitchen. Totally redone. Now they're working with Lloyd on Beau's house, getting it ready for hosting retreats."

Halfway around the skirt, Eli was relieved the hem looked level. She and AB discussed asking Bernie about renewing her vows with Henry on Thanksgiving instead of Christmas, and whether the custom furniture maker who frequented Bibi's shop was looking for inspiration or a date. "He's popping in on her the way that GBI fella keeps showing up around you," AB teased.

"Seth is fascinating, with or without his career," Eli said. "And he volunteered to do the photography for the weddings, which is so kind. I'm just not feeling it," Eli said, tugging the hem as she worked.

"My feelings for Ted overwhelm me when we're together, but we don't fit. He simply doesn't like anything about me, but he has said he still wants to be with me. Well, not lately.

"Once, last fall, I was able to ask about his dissatisfaction, briefly, where before he would have exploded on me. I didn't get an explanation, just a fresh litany of what he doesn't like. Why do I keep trying?"

"Doesn't appear to be a self-destructive obsession," AB said, peering over her glasses. My personal take is that there must be some special pheromone emitted by a good man—a decent, capable man who has quiet strength and a generous heart. Maybe some of those assets are obscured by emotional scars and things that life builds in, but you feel that energy. It's not about looks, or money, or success. Although Will is one fine looking man, and I don't know if I'll last another ten days without jumping his bones."

"Wait, what?" Eli gasped, almost swallowing her pins. "You two..."

"Not my idea," she said, stepping down and removing the dress. "Although I am a little apprehensive. It's been a while. He believes it would be a bad example. Like anyone would care. So he swims and works out frequently—very frequently.

"Back to you. Here's the thing about why we keep trying with people we love," she said, sewing again. "When our efforts or relationships get derailed—I believe it's because we're being given a hint to change our approach, to refocus our perspective.

"I came to love my life and my old house—even before the renovations, not because circumstances changed, just me. I chose to change how I relate to others around me, to see the soul beyond the body we each wear.

"Back when I started hospice work, I figured there was less potential for me to damage anyone for long. But I found myself mostly listening. What people have to say as they prepare to leave this world...

"It's an accelerated course I'm privileged to audit. Most of these people grow radiant, those lovely souls shining through failing bodies. For those who are suffering terribly, or are fearful, I can usually make a difference. But every one of them teaches me.

"And this year has taught me that when we choose to climb out of the hole we've dug so deep—give up wallowing in our sadness and grievances—we can find a beautiful world full of lovely people waiting for us.

"It sounds like you know Ted Waller loves you, whether or not he reveals it. If the nerves in his hand couldn't tell his fingers to grasp, you would understand that, and adapt. Isn't it just as possible that the synapses firing in his brain can't spark the words to reassure you of his love and appreciation? You must change your expectations of him because you *cannot* change who he is.

"As I see it, you have a couple of ways out of your misery: decide to embrace that boy's wiring glitches and love him as God made him, or put some real distance between you and Ted. In this life, we are always, *always* free to choose again, to choose that loving perspective."

—◦—

Lauren arrived the Saturday morning before Thanksgiving. A colorful Hermes scarf tied thick, shoulder-length hair back from an utterly flawless face. Her red flats, jeans, and half-tucked denim shirt over a red-flecked navy cami were impeccably casual.

As she and Mela unloaded her car, the guys were making their way to the terrace after kayaking on the lake since daybreak. When Mela returned for a second load, she saw Lauren at the tailgate clutching a garment bag and watching the men, studying one. He was walking toward her.

"Lauren," he said warmly, as he hung back next to Mela. "I'd know you anywhere."

She was uncharacteristically silent, alarmed by the physical response to hearing his voice after so long. He looked taller, his face, more defined. His body, too. Then he flashed that killer smile.

"Yes, it's good to see you," she managed to say.

"Let me take that bag," Mela offered, leaving them to reacquaint. "I'll see y'all inside."

Behind the front door, AB and Bernie were totem-stacked at the side glass. "Aw, he's holding her. Look at that, Bernie Carter."

"You two get out of that window," Mela hollered, descending the stairs. "Let's have an early lunch so these guys can get to work on the barn ramps."

"This remodel is going beautifully," AB said, as they built sandwiches smeared with red pepper jelly on one half and creamy brie on the other, mounded with her delicious chicken salad full of toasted pecans, strawberries, and minced green onion. "Adding baths between new bedrooms has doubled the space for folks who'll be coming to retreats."

"Yep," Bernie said, peeking at the front door. "I was thinking we should nickname this *the love shack*, but that's tacky, and not somewhere you'd let your spouse go on a retreat. How about, *the place for mending hearts?*"

"Much better," Mela said, putting another plate on the bar as the crew came in.

"Henry, having an engineer on site is a Godsend," Will said, clapping Bernie's husband on the back.

"If every project had a team as much fun as this one, went kayaking before work, and gave me time to see my girl, I wouldn't have retired early," Henry said.

"Sounds like somebody has been living it up in retirement," Bernie mumbled, sprinkling a tower of chips on the last plate.

"You think I don't notice his truck driving in at your place every evening and not coming out?" AB whispered, elbowing her friend.

"There's plenty of consulting work around here," Mac noted, dropping Dude a bite after stealing a look at the kitchen. He was mildly alarmed to notice a low volume squabble underway, with Bernie poised to fire a spoonful of chicken salad at AB.

"I'm thinking about it," Henry admitted. "But this isn't a big market."

"These mountain towns create a lot of enterprise zones within driving range," Mac assured him.

As Mac was moving to join everyone on the terrace, he noticed Mela at the front door, arms crossed, watching through the sidelight. She jumped when he kissed her neck.

"What are you thinking, babe?"

"How sad it is that they never had a chance," she said, watching her birthparents sitting on the tailgate. "That Lauren gave him up, gave me up, to meet her mother's expectations—and her father's, of their only child being the next surgeon in the family. She's had a very successful, very lonely life, Mac. Lonely like me, until you."

"My life didn't start til I finally kissed you," he said, as she continued watching.

Sunday morning, Lauren joined the walkers, but not for long. "C'mon, ladies," she rallied, stretching. "This is a perfect route for a run. Strolling doesn't have the cardio benefits we need."

Leslie ducked behind Mela, agitated and swearing. "I've only been around her a few hours but this woman cannot be your natural mother. Is she always like this? Maybe she'll be too busy to visit much."

"Walking cardio-izes me just fine," AB said.

"I'll run with you," Carly called, her face reflecting the involuntary conscription. Bibi performed a papal gesture of blessing as Carly took off.

"Dr. Lauren is extra-extra," Sophie observed, as the runner slowed with a look of disappointment, expecting her daughter to catch up.

"You've got her pegged, puddin'. This is going to be an interesting week," AB prophesied.

———⟶•⟵———

On her way to meet Mela the next morning at the Aquani Spa for a massage, Lauren turned in AB's driveway and passed Will, who stopped splitting wood to greet her. As he directed Lauren through the open front door to AB's workroom, he was suspicious of the white lace bundle she carried. Seemed like a good time to take a load of logs around back.

Humming from AB's old Singer led Lauren to the right door, and she knocked softly as she peered in. "Hi, Ann," she chirped, dramatically tiptoeing in. "I need your help with a surprise for my daughter's wedding."

"Oh? How's that?"

"My mother's gown. It was custom from Hubert de Givenchy, and with your skills and the measurements you have for Melanie, it will give my mother a presence, a bond with her granddaughter."

"You're planning to spring this on her the morning of?"

"That's what makes it a surprise," she said, absently looking at AB's many sewing projects.

"Lauren. Around here, we call that an ambush."

"Do you? If you'd rather not help, don't spoil it for her."

"Coffee?" AB said.

"No, thank you, I haven't time for—"

"Me neither, but since you've involved me... Mela made plain what she wants to wear and why. I get that you are a woman who knows what she wants, and I can admire that when it doesn't involve steamrolling anyone. You can push good people like Mela and Luke, but not as far as you might intend. I'm guessing that relationship tactic hasn't served you well."

"Are you quite finished with your unsolicited analysis?" Lauren said, seething. "I came here on a mission for my daughter, not for your intrusive opinion of my more than successful lifetime of relationships," she snapped, quickly gathering the dress as she stormed out.

⟫•◦•⟪

During lunch with Mela at Brasstown Valley Resort after their massages, Lauren presented her daughter with earrings from their earlier visit to the John C. Campbell Folk School's gift shop. "Beautiful. Ah, from the Alchemist's Garden. Eli and I love her work. Thank you, Lauren. I will treasure them," Mela exclaimed.

"I saw you looking in that display case," Lauren said. "They were titled Warrior Goddess, and I thought that was fitting for my daughter."

"I strike you as a warrior goddess type, really, Lauren?" Mela asked, looking up from her grilled trout.

"Melanie, since we met, there's been a concern I have given a great deal of consideration," she said, eyes bright and eager to share her ideas. "I have researched a fast track for you to an M.D., with a surgical residency, living with me in Louisville. Let me make up for the education you should have had, the future you can still have."

"I appreciate your—"

"This disabled man you want to marry, he'll step aside for the career you were meant to pursue. You can join my practice, take over soon after, and live beautifully. Picture yourself there, doing what you should be. We can make up for lost time together. Sleep on it, darling."

"Lauren, I don't need to think about it. I'm twelve years in on a career I love. My practice—"

"Sweetheart, I know you love the little animals, but I'm talking about being a real surgeon, a—"

"I *am* a real surgeon, Lauren, a good surgeon. My colleagues and patients fill my days with challenges and contentment. And as exquisite as these earrings are, you chose them to promote a different mindset in me. You know by now that I don't have anything like a warrior mentality, or a goddess, for that matter. I value healing and comfort.

"Mac Miller gives me that. My friends keep me grounded in just that. As of this week, I am on top of the world with joy. I want you and Luke in my life more than I can express. But you must stop thinking about running my life, now, *please*, Lauren. Can you accept me *and* Mac for who we are?" she asked, her jaw tense and eyes filling.

"Well, yes, darling. I only wanted to help, but if this is what you want..."

"This is all that I want."

"I see," Lauren responded, forcing a smile as she stabbed at her salad. "Great." They ate in silence, briefly.

"Truthfully, I don't understand you at all, Melanie. Why not live your best life? I imagine you're relying on the fortune behind this estate you've inherited to sustain you, but dear, your clothes, those shoes. Even your hair could be transformed with very little effort."

"I'm not the rapacious American female, molding herself into what the leading influencers are pushing," Mela retorted, maintaining her composure. "Yes, my hair could use more conditioner. My shoes are usually selected online for function, not to impress anyone. My clothes are local purchases I love. I'm happy with my life. Overjoyed with it lately. And as for the Johnston estate—"

"I see. Just a sanctimonious bohemian then. How quaint."

"You don't get me at all, Lauren, and I'm not sure you want to. Maybe we should go now."

⟫━◉━⟪

Not long after they returned home, Lauren was coming down with her bags. "This construction is too much for me. I'll be at the resort."

"You're moving to BVR? You're that upset about our conversation?" Mela asked.

"We need some space," she said, pecking Mela's cheek as she left without speaking to Eli and Lew as they came in.

"Hi, guys," Mela said, embracing them both as Lauren drove away.

"Why does she have her things?" Eli asked, holding Mela's arm.

"Too much construction," she answered flatly.

"That's a laugh," Mac commented, as he carried a sheetrock panel through the room. "She's been keeping Luke up all night every night since she got here. This morning he said he'd be staying at the resort for the rest of his visit. Bro's a goner."

"I'm here to take up the slack for a fallen brother then," Lew assured him. "No chance of me spending any evenings in the foreseeable future bedding anyone. And I don't require lodging, just good weather to come across the lake."

Lew steadied the sheetrock as Mac reached for Mela. "If you're there with me on Thanksgiving, no one else matters," he whispered.

"None taken!" Eli groused, pushing him back to work. "Show Lew the ropes, would you?"

"So, Mel," Eli said, with a crooked smile. "Pete just called, and they may not make it for the weddings. Grace is indisposed," she giggled.

"They were at dinner two nights ago, and Grace was cataloging the disorders she detected in the attending physician she reports to, when someone in the booth on the other side of the partition answered his phone, saying, 'Yes, this is Josh Williams,' and Grace nearly fainted. Practically crawled away to the ladies' room. Dr. Williams is her attending, oversees her psych rotation. You know how that little voice carries. Pete says she's hardly spoken a word since."

"He is a psychiatrist. Maybe Dr. Williams will see the good in this," Mela said, stifling a smirk. "If not, she could claim trainee identity crisis. I've heard that's a thing."

Lauren didn't reappear until the Wednesday luncheon that welcomed everyone arriving for the wedding. Leslie and her tribe; Bernie's Alex and his expectant wife, Tina; Kathy, Mac's older sister; Will's Ewan, with his wife Becca, and their Liam, all gathered in the private dining room at Enrico's. AB's sister Louise would be delayed until morning.

"I'm thrilled that she's coming at all," she assured Will. "Louise is the only one of my siblings who has communicated with me in forty plus years. I always hoped to earn Mama's forgiveness for doing to someone what was done to her, but..."

"Before Christmas," Will promised her, "you and I are going to drive to Tennessee and visit your momma. We'll find your reconciliation."

As guests arrived, Bibi handed out color coded name tags by wedding. Seth Taylor was already in photographer mode. "Taylor," Mac said, "thank you for doing this. Much appreciated."

"It's a pleasure to be here," he responded. "I've never photographed a wedding. A triple wedding will be a challenge."

"Two weddings, one vow renewal," Mac noted.

"Yeah. Hey, who's the guy with Eli?"

"Brother-in-law. Not a *thing*."

"So, Miller," Seth said quietly, "I hope you know I didn't set out to get your friend at the GBI. He did himself in. It's just that networks like yours, they can be dangerous—"

"I think you know better in this case. But suggesting he was covert? Some kind of militia?" Mac interrupted, staring defiantly.

"If he was FBI, I'd have done the same."

"You did the world a favor. He's doing important work. 'Sall good."

Carly devoted her time to shepherding Carol through the crowd, all of whom were delighted to meet the 92-year-old who would be officiating. When guests commented on her sweetness, Carly was quick to advise. "Don't let that marshmallow coating fool you. Carol's a total badass—blackbelt in karate at seventy, crashed in a hang glider at 83, and had to be rescued from a tree."

That afternoon, with everyone settled in somewhere, the sleepover attendees gathered at Bernie's. Mela and Kathy relaxed on the dock swing, talking with Mac while watching Will and AB cruising the lake until almost sunset. Henry and Bernie finished setting up the nursery for their grandbaby as the parents-to-be sampled Nancy's stuffed mushrooms.

Mac took Kathy to see what he had done with their grandmother's place, and to spend the evening catching up. Once all the men had left for home or retired to bedrooms, the gigantic TV downstairs screened *Bridesmaids*, followed by *Father of the Bride*. AB had unilaterally vetoed *Steel Magnolias*.

Bernie tried on a rackful of glitzy gowns until the assemblage agreed on the right one for her vows—all in the midst of their group facials and manicures. Carly was snapping and editing pics, including one after-facial for Carol, shot with a filter that smoothed fifty years from her face, leaving her ecstatic until she encountered a mirror.

AB, Bernie, and Carol caucused upon discovering they were all reading their way through—and struggling with—the same spiritual work from the 1970s. Despite their busy Thanksgiving ahead, no one was ready for the evening to end. With the exception of mom-to-be Tina, they agreed to make a group trip to Times Square for New Year's Eve, and to plan regular travel destinations for the year to come.

⫸•⫷

Still in pajamas, and bundled against the cold front that arrived over-night, Eli and Mela slipped out early to walk Thanksgiving morning. Nancy passed them with her teen nieces in the car on the way to pre-pare a few more recipes and finish setting up. The weddings were set for two in the afternoon, preceding the holiday buffet in the pavilion.

"Have you and Lauren talked?" Eli asked, changing the subject from Luke's long career of celebrity collaborations.

"Finally, yes. She says she feels twenty again since reconnecting with Luke. Maybe it will work if they both haven't been too single too long. That's what Mac and I are compromising our way through."

"I'm impressed that he doesn't give in to her on everything. Your bio-mom is inclined to get her way."

"True, but Lauren isn't ice cold like demanding people can be. She has a heart. Has to, right?"

Headlights accompanied the low rumble of a Montreal metallic blue roadster coming off the highway. It was the Z3 M presented to Ted by his dad after he enhanced his physics and analytical chemistry degrees with a PhD from the University of North Carolina, a doctorate source close enough for weekends in Hiawassee.

"Did you invite Ted to your wedding?" Eli asked, leery of another encounter.

"That's Ted? I remember that pretty little car."

"He must be looking for Lew, but…"

"Good morning," came his greeting over the purring engine. "Mela, I hope you and Mac will be very happy," he said, exiting the car with anxious squints at Eli's feet.

"Thank you, Ted. Would you stay? It will be small and simple."

"I would like to talk to Mac before I leave.

"Eli," he said, trying not to stare at her bunny-slippered feet. "Take a short ride with me? Back in an hour."

"Like this?" she said, to Mela.

"See you soon," Mela answered. "And Ted, please come."

The Déjà vu theater opened wide before them as Ted pushed the M through each gear. He suggested a ride across Rainbow Springs Road—the same holiday, car, and route he had chosen nineteen years before to propose Eli leave, after three months at Young Harris College, to live with him while he finished at UNC. It was an offer she had no trouble refusing—initially.

"I brought a couple of blankets," he said, looking behind her seat. "You're wearing pajamas? Anything under them," he asked, reaching across, frisking beneath her coat.

She yelped, smacking his arm. "Oh, no, Ted Waller. You are not getting me naked in these woods ever again. That was a satellite TV truck we just passed on this sliver of a road. Houses are all along here. Look! A bear hunter's truck. It's below freezing. No!"

He couldn't hide his laughter as she railed against his idea of a romantic outing. Once she quieted, he advanced again.

His blunt suggestion this time was to come back for a trial run. He was willing to make changes—talk to her, do things together, remember to initiate sex, whatever the hell it would take.

"It feels pathetic to say it out loud, Ted—and don't get angry, this is not intended as an insult, it's offered as an insight—but I have never felt loved with you. I want to feel cherished, to be precious to someone. You are a phenomenal man—all sorts of interests, magnificent career, busy enjoying life, and your mind dazzles me.

"Yet, I've never had any indication," she continued, after a peek to see whether he was listening, "that the admiration is in the smallest way mutual."

"I take you as you are, Eli. That's all."

"Confirmation that you tolerate me. Maybe we're just people flirting across the way in glass buildings, who will never figure out how to find one another."

"I don't have any problem finding you, Eli. I just can't make you happy."

"I know my frustration bores you. Compare it to when you're talking about metabolomics, or peptidomics approaches, or things that sort molecules by viscosity. I hear a few words I recognize, I *hmm* appreciatively but not enthusiastically, because I understand nothing and just hope it's over soon. Is that how you feel when I talk about *us*?"

"It is," he answered, as they rumbled along.

"Why can't you be happy like me?" he said forcefully, as the roadster slid to a stop on wet leaves above the Nantahala River. "I want us to be happy together," he demanded, staring at the gauge panel.

She studied the few grays highlighting his sable hair, backlit by morning sun. "But after today," he finished, with quiet determination, "I will not ask you again."

"Ted, we've come to this impasse a half dozen times, tried again, and always reverted to the same patterns. There is so much about being a couple that does not suit you. I don't want to be that lonely again, ever.

"I've asked you before—am I your fallback plan because things aren't working out with your fiancé? It feels like this visit is a side bet."

One expressed thought too far.

The M roared the way they came along the single lane gravel road above the river. Their ride was ending as badly as the one that morning nineteen years before—his proposition falling flat, as experience and distrust chased her back into the wood line.

In half the time it took to reach their turning point, they were back. Eli spoke to Ted quickly, knowing he would be gone as soon as she exited. "I'm sorry I've upset you again, Ted. I want you to have a good life, and I want that for myself, too. I do love you and always will."

He left without responding. Eli listened to the M fade away.

With a heavy heart, she texted Mela, reporting for bride support duty. Mela called immediately, dissecting every detail, and was astonished by the effort Ted had made—even if it was a doomed sequel of an awkward episode in their history. "That was big for him, E. It took guts to open up that way."

"Or a dose of Hannah's magic potions. I don't think he could have done that otherwise. I'm going to find a professional, not a future professional, to help sort me out." She sighed. "One of us is hopelessly intractable, and I'm beginning to think that it's me."

Chapter 22

What Is Not Your Dream Come True

B y noon, the pavilion had become a wedding venue, with dressed tables beneath the expansive windowed walls. At the lake end, Nancy was arranging rustic wood trays of acorn squash and pomegranates riding waves of kale, sprinkled with Brussels sprouts and mushrooms, all set among a backdrop of peace lilies. Fiddleleaf fig trees flanked Carol's unwanted chair, creating a screen for the ramp down to the boathouse.

Lew came by early looking for Eli. Ted had come in at the Waller place to leave the M and pick up his car, but Lew couldn't engage him. He and Eli sat on the dock talking until Mela texted. Lauren had brought over a make-up artist she'd met at the resort, and Mela was uneasy with her photo-adapted face.

"How can I assist?" Lew asked AB, as she scurried through her checklist before changing. "What's the music plan? A digital sound system? An ensemble?"

"Lew, with the three-ring circus this has become, music was overlooked. Anything you can Bluetooth from your phone?"

"I play an acoustic guitar. Back in 30 minutes. How about 'There is Love,' as you come in? Too cliché?"

"Paul Stookey's inspired piece? Perfect. You are a gift, Lew Waller," she said, kissing his cheek as he rushed out.

"This is more radiance than I'm prepared to emit," Mela said, hiding behind the door as Eli came in. Her brows, undereye, and jawline were gleaming with highlighter, while her eye shadow, cheek hollows, and upper neck were visually recessed. "I think Halloween may be too fresh in this artist's mind for me," Mela said, dabbing with a tissue. "I look disembodied."

"Wowser, that's intense. I saw AB downstairs, and she had passed on this make-up offer. Bernie looks great, though."

"Bernie does her own. She said she picked it up from the pro who did her stage make-up."

"Then Lauren had an artist come just for you. That's thoughtful."

"For Lauren and me. She does look spectacular."

Lew was strumming outside on the dock, and Bibi was drawn into the chilled air to listen. She was soon harmonizing as he sang. "Lew, what a nice voice," she exclaimed, as he played the last chord.

"Sounded better with yours," he said with admiration, seeing a very different Bibi than he remembered. "Just guitar as they enter, and we do the lyrics as they finish?"

"Love it. Let's rehearse in the garage. It's freezing out here."

On their second run-through Luke appeared, apologizing for interrupting. "I thought I heard a Hummingbird," he explained, walking around Lew to view his guitar. "That is a Gibson Montana Hummingbird."

"Yeah," Lew answered, grinning. "You have quite an ear."

"Got one at home. The vintage Cherry Sunburst. Like this, but worn," he laughed.

"We met at the luncheon, right?" Lew said, standing to extend his hand.

"This is Mela's father," Bibi reminded him. "Luke Bailey."

"Lew Waller. It's an honor to have you look in," he said, prolonging the handshake. "We're working on something for this afternoon," he added. "Not interfering with any of your plans, I hope."

"No, no, grateful for your gift. Let's talk after," he said, as he left the garage.

A commotion in the hall preceded Carly bursting through the door. "Bibz, come quick. Bret is here. Oh, and he's with Kit. And Molly. And the Harrisons, and a case of champagne."

"Luke Bailey was bad enough." Lew coughed. "Now we're performing for David Harrison?"

AB, Bernie, and Mela abandoned their grand entrances to welcome the influx from Beaufort. The house reverberated with joyous noise as Kit introduced Molly, Ida, and David to her friends' families. Carly had already absconded with Bret.

As the atmosphere settled, Will found AB in the pavilion working to precisely space the floral displays and chairs. He watched quietly, muffling his laughter as she aligned chairs in the wide semi-circle so that they symmetrically crossed the lines of the hardwood floors.

"How did I get along before you, sainted Annie Blanche?" he teased, taking her in his arms and waltzing her down the aisle to the tables loaded with lilies and cornucopious dough bowls. There, he began shifting and pushing the planters and trays into loose, organic groupings, and then pulled chairs apart—groups of three here, two there, some forward, some back—until any suggestion of a line was gone.

"It should be good therapy. Nothing could distract me today," he promised, taking her in his arms again as she looked warily over her shoulder at the changes. "Maybe the chairs could be better," he said, following her gaze. "I'll fix the chairs."

As they finished the reset, a shivering crowd surged down the walk from the house. It was 1:45. "We two are almost one," he said, nuzzling her neck. "Almost."

"Promises, promises," AB murmured.

Seth Taylor was already on site with his camera, and Eli worked as his assistant, directing subjects for his photographs, including Dude in his black bow tie. Seth suggested a pose with Liam kissing Sophie on the cheek, which was met with a firm, "Swerve, bro! I'm not kissing any babies," from the preteen, before she marched away, belted bow swishing.

As everyone filtered in to their seats, the crush slowly parted. AB's sister Louise appeared at the back. "Oh, honey," AB shouted, her voice breaking. "I didn't think you'd make it."

As she rushed forward, Louise stepped aside. AB faltered, fearing she might collapse as a mirage, her grandmother, came into focus. Both hands flew to her face as AB realized it was her own mother. She rushed to the frail woman on Louise's arm, embracing her tenderly and pulling Louise in for the same. "Momma," she cried, awestruck.

"Let me see you, Annie Blanche," the tiny woman fussed. "You're much taller, girl," the flustered octogenarian observed through cataracts.

"Well, you shrunk, Momma," a man behind her pointed out.

"Good Lord, *Tim?*" AB called, astounded.

"And Sarah, Kay-Kay, Billy Joe, and me," another brother said from the back. "Sissy, you look like a million bucks."

The ceremony started late, after the Sutton clan was introduced and AB heard highlights from the last forty years. In the new millennium, the farm's primary crop became pumpkins and corn, essential for the Maze-Maze every autumn. Camping sites, zip lines, and glamping yurts covered the rest of the riverfront property.

"We've missed you awfully," Sarah said, hugging her sister as Will took AB's hand to gently signal it was time. "Louise was the only one of us who ever dared defy Momma. Sissy, this is a wonderful, happy day."

Carly was still tending to Carol, grabbing her water bottle for a quick refill. "Uh-uh," Carol shouted, catching Carly's skirt. "Put that back."

"Just topping it off," Carly said, giving it a shake.

"Maybe water, maybe not," Carol answered. "Whatever, doesn't need diluting."

"Are we sure Carol's authorized to do this?" Mac asked uneasily, as he waited nearby with Henry and Will.

"Oh yeah," Henry assured him. "Bernie says she was real big at it in that golfers' retirement community before she moved to the mountains. Busy at funerals, doing marriage counseling, then marrying the recently widowed. Steady work in Florida."

While Lew strummed his Hummingbird, Liam and Sophie entered carrying baskets of ribbon-paired wedding bands, turning to stand in front of the grooms. Then came Mela in her persimmon gown, Bernie in a crystal-encrusted eggplant caftan, and finally AB in her brown silk by Bibi.

Their Internet-certified officiant warmly welcomed those gathered. Her address to the couples was interrupted by a gust of freezing air that drew attention to the pavilion entrance.

Guests looked back to see Luke standing aside, taking Lauren's hand as she postured regally in a strapless, mercilessly-snug, lace gown that appeared to rise from a deeply layered flounce at mid-calf. The sixties-era, custom Givenchy gown so limited her gait that the toddle to the bridal zone was comically slow. Luke followed, casting a subtle, apologetic touch from his lips to Mela.

Lauren broke the long silence with a meandering announcement—to a crowd of mostly strangers—as she navigated the narrow aisle with her five-foot-wide flounce.

"Yesterday, after looking at houses all morning, Luke and I decided on a whim that we were wasting time. Why not have the wedding we wanted years ago right here at the Towns County courthouse. You can get a license and marry, same day. But then we thought, with three weddings on the schedule, well, what's one more? Surprise," she sang, toned arms outstretched as she inched toward the bridal jam ahead.

"One vow renewal, two weddings," Mac testily corrected.

"With a side of ambush," AB muttered. "Grandmother Post crashed the wedding after all."

"Four weddings, and I'm feeling a funeral—not mine," Carol grumbled.

Each couple shared tender, touching vows until it came to Lauren and Luke. He gave an emotional declaration of his lifelong devotion and unfailing love, to which Lauren responded, "Ditto, darling."

Soon Carol was able to say, "You may kiss your brides," and was startled by a collective "Ahhh" from the guests, until Carly pointed to the snow beginning to fall. Bibi's harmony with Lew thrilled the newlyweds and reweds as they slow danced to "There is Love."

<hr>

Nancy and her nieces were loading the buffet tables with fruit-wood-smoked mountain trout; sliced rows of en croûte turkey with dressing; gravy boats; Epic's cranberry and orange relish; crispy potatoes galette; cauliflower steaks with mushroom gravy; pumpkin risotto; sweet potato casserole; ambrosia salad; bud-shaped figs stuffed with bleu cheese; swirling lines of pecan tarts; baskets of popovers alongside bowls of honey-chive whipped butter; and three tiers of petit fours decorated with microscopic pears, grapes, and mums.

"Mac, any idea how this sweet potato casserole made it on the buffet?" Mela asked, as she and Kathy watched a third marshmallowy, pecan-coated spoonful land on his plate.

"Babe, it may not have been on the brides' menu, but I believe a woman like Nancy could see this as long-single men's last tango with an old flame, which they will encounter hereafter only as a stark superfood. Look, I've got Brussels sprouts, too."

"No safety concerns," Bret said to David and Ida Harrison, as he joined their table, looking across the lake to the mountains of North Carolina. "Foreflight radar shows this is an isolated snow shower, and temps are holding. Dolly-Bird's on standby. You'll be there before six, in time for more dinner with Doc Kiley's family."

"Bret," David said, taking Molly's hand, "don't let these two out of your sight until you bring them home next week."

After the crowd had cleared from the scrumptious buffet, AB led a toast to Nancy and her nieces, leaving for their own family gathering. Then the Harrisons left early, reluctantly parting with Molly and Kit, who were staying for a visit. Leslie, JT, and their children hurried out to get through Atlanta.

The Miller contingent joined those chatting with Luke and Lauren— who was wrapped in Luke's jacket, ostensibly against the chill, but also to hide the failed zipper that left the back of her dress gaping. Bernie found scissors, which she used to snip away layers of ruffled lace encasing Lauren's legs, then stuffed the couturier's remnant in the garbage.

Will and AB sat with Ewan and Angie on one side and AB's gabbing family on the other. Young Liam slept in AB's lap, as her mother napped against her shoulder. "You are a vision of joy this evening," Will whispered to his wife.

"Don't you fade on me tonight," she whispered back, eyes twinkling. "You ain't seen nothing yet."

Bernie's table was the liveliest—despite her daughter-in-law Tina snoring in a wing chair—with everyone engaged by Alex's stories of movie production in Georgia. Carly and Carol were getting advice, eager to work as extras, while Eli walked Seth to his car, thanking him effusively for his time and his patience.

"It was an interesting night," he said, eyebrows arched in amazement. "I don't expect to see anything like that ever again."

"Oh, this is Cray-Cray Lane, Seth. Not long until the next show."

———➤•◀———

Honeymoon travel held no interest for any of the four couples wed on Thanksgiving in the Enchanted Valley of the North Georgia Mountains. Henry persuaded Bernie to try fishing. In addition to starting a civil engineering consultancy, Henry was angling to join Mac's venture as a guide on nearby mountain lakes, and was planning some Black Friday boat buying.

A "Do Not Disturb" sign hung on Will and AB Shafer's gate. Lauren and Luke were shopping for a weekend place for their *weekends only* marriage, while Mela enjoyed a few days vacay as she and Mac hosted Kit and Molly that first week of December. Carly revamped her work schedule for Bret's stay. Despite the construction throughout, the Johnston estate's available bedrooms were fully occupied.

An early morning huddle at the kitchen table focused on Bret's news of Liz negotiating a guilty plea on the two major counts, with sentences running consecutively—for her foreseeable lifetime despite the possibility of parole. Liz professed to truly believe she had enhanced Kit's chances in life with "exposure to only the best people and places." She had decided that telling all was her surest protection against the man she swore to know only as Poke.

"In her statement, she claims the guy was twelve when his father died in a bizarre accident while working as a prop man at the studio, and that Johnny Grant put him up on the lot, let the kid do odd jobs," Bret said. "Problem was, they figured out the boy was killing things— birds, stray dogs, even a horse set to be put down. They said he made it slow and painful. Word got around, and people were angry.

"Only to Johnny, it was funny," Bret continued. "Liz admitted she didn't think Ray Harrison and Alma were the first murders involving the kid. I've been told that investigators in LA haven't found one person who will say anything about him. No employment records or paper trail of any kind through the studio or the Grant family."

"No way she doesn't have more current info," Mac said. "I've been analyzing tower dumps for months trying to isolate this guy's phones. Could be in stashes, probably with his weapon reserves and IDs. Having no sort of identification is stalling the hunt, but that gun is demolished by now anyway. We need to draw his attention somehow."

"Don't let David Harrison hear you say that. And there's the small matter of interfering with a federal investigation. So, what do we know for sure? Not much. Our guy would be pushing sixty at least, which could fit with that low-res image you scrounged in Savannah suggesting he is approximately six feet, slender build, and possibly right-handed."

"Couldn't be a more general description," Mac said, checking stills in his file. "Head down, hiding his face under that hat, a jacket likely concealing a weapon. But with so many cameras in that area, to get only that one video tells me that even if he were working on the fly, he knew what he was doing. His set up anticipated any form of Shotspotter, and included an exit plan to elude response vehicles."

"Tipped his hand with a few old school moves," Bret noted. "Keep mining those dumps, and he'll show up somewhere. Some investigators think he's in Central America by now. I think he's a guy who holds grudges. They're slow to run."

"No doubt. If he is savvy enough to use the kind of phone surveillance I found in Kit's devices, and he's a totally depraved old bastard, we might get a lead on some of the dark sites online that cater to his combination of sadistic preferences. Beyond that, I have scanning set for all the matching location calls that we haven't cleared. If he brings any of those lines here, we should know. Meanwhile, I'm playing a hunch on an old connection."

"Enjoying all the sunshine this morning?" Carly sang, as she danced down the stairs with Kit. "Bret, don't forget we're picking up Bernie and Eli, then meeting Molly, Mela, and Lauren for lunch at noon—or whenever they're finished shopping."

"Yeah, Bret," Mac chided. "We'll be thinking about you while we're out fishing this morning."

When Mela pulled in at Fancy This Mercantile, Bibi was out front wrapping fronds of fir and cedar with wire to make fluffy garlands for her store. "Love your antique shop." Lauren swooned as she admired the arched brick surround at the wood framed glass doors.

"The store is early 1900s, but this isn't an antiques shop. There's a little bit of everything," Bibi explained as they entered.

"How long will this last outside?" Molly asked, delighting in the rich fragrance of the woody mix Bibi held.

"My entrance faces north, so no direct sun. This garland will be green into the new year, but I won't dress the big windows for another week or so. Would you like some to take home? This one's almost done."

"Oh, I would love that," Molly said, picking up a loose stem of Fraser fir. "But in Beaufort it would be toast. This piece will be my little Christmas inhaler."

"Kit, put that out of your mind," Eli begged, after Kit whispered another apology about that night at the campfire when she'd asked whether Eli remembered her attacker's face.

"Liz was demanding to know, and I was terrified," Kit recalled, as Eli hugged her reassuringly, aware that Kit might never feel safe again.

⟹•◈•⟸

Mid December, Eli and Bibi sent boxes of garland to Molly and to the Harrisons, sharing a touch of the mountains. Pete and Grace would be staying with Eli the weekend before Christmas on their way to Virginia, and Lew had been invited to spend Christmas Day with his ex, Carolyn, and their son John.

Regrets from Mac's family, Luke, and Lauren, dashed Mela's hope of getting them together for her last Christmas in the house that held so many memories. Newly christened Beau's Place, it was scheduled to open in early March as a retreat for military vets to reunite and reconcile their pasts with the present.

"Tell me again why you get this kind of tree?" Eli asked, stringing jewel-tone bulbs in the lower branches of the ten-foot fir.

"I love this fragrance, the soft needles, and strong branches with these elegant little fingers at the end," Mela said, plugging in the last strand of tiny, soft-white lights illuminating the trunk and interior of the tree.

"Mac likes Fraser fir for that beautiful blue green color, and because they don't shed as much. He says they are native only to the Appalachians at elevations of over 3,000 feet, discovered by a Scottish, of course, botanist, John Fraser, in the 1700s. Just don't get Mac started on the woolly adelgids."

"Yeah, no. I have never seen a prettier tree than this. I wish Kit could have stayed to see it. Oh, I heard from her father's sister, the one we found through the DNA testing, and she said he went missing after his last tour. Died ten years ago, homeless in Baltimore. Never knew about our girl. Unless Kit asks, I'm not mentioning it until she's in a better place."

"Right," Mela agreed. "We can do much more for our vets. Mac said the first reunion he attended a few years ago refocused priorities for him, seeing the people he served with also struggling to return to civilian life. The meet they had at Brasstown last spring was a big boost for all of them.

"There is such a bond there—men and women who have served. Beau's Place will be his tribute to that bond. After 911, when so many of his friends joined the military, he felt he wasn't welcome to serve without misrepresenting his orientation. As always, he found his own way."

"He would be so proud," Eli said. "I know Mac is, too."

"There's something else," she said, descending the ladder. "Before we tell everyone on Christmas. Well, not Lauren and Luke—she's already suspicious because we're not coming to his family gathering in Nashville."

"You're radiating joy. Am I going to be an aunt?"

"We think, about the Fourth of July," Mela said, as Eli jumped up for a hug.

"She'll be a little firecracker."

"Mac's hoping for a he, to name him Raphael, his dad's name. Easy enough to add an 'A' on the end. If this is a dream, Eli, I don't ever want to wake up. I'm so content it's embarrassing."

Garlands swagged every window and door around Eli's house. Light snow completed the look an hour before Pete and Grace arrived. A crackling fire and hot cocoa thawed the travelers as they caught up since their visit Thanksgiving weekend, when Pete mentioned the surprising results of the DNA sample he'd submitted.

"Remember the concentration of distant relatives the report showed in Louisiana and Mississippi? Out of that cluster I have an uncle—not a Cooper—living somewhere in Costa Rica these days, although his extended family is still in Mississippi," he said.

"From what I can tell, this is a half-brother of my father, who grew up in foster care. Very tight-lipped folks, his kin. It's on my figure-this-out list for next year."

Eli decided to save the baby news for Mela to keep or share at dinner later. Something was going on with Pete. His casual air was tinged with apprehension.

"What's on your mind there, Pete?" she asked, forcing a smile.

"Yeah, that. Things aren't going well for Ted. He left yesterday for some ancient fishing cabin of his grandfather's on Lake Guntersville. Said he would be back in the offices January second. Things have gotten tense, hostile really, between him and Hannah. I think Lew has finally convinced him that she will be facing charges soon. He's messed up."

"Oh no," Grace gasped. "I wish you had told me before we left. I might have—"

"That miserable bitch," Eli spat. "I am beyond ready to be cleared of what she has been doing in my name. I feel like the recurring villain on *Law & Order* that no one can pin anything on. My life has been overrun with creeps and criminals. This year cannot end soon enough." Grace and Pete silently stared at the floor during Eli's outburst.

So much for easing Pete's anxiety, the voice in her head snarked at their reaction. *No gardens, no fountains?*

"And," she added, in a calmer tone, returning to Pete's point, "I really am concerned about how she might retaliate against Ted. He's backed out of his engagement, then?"

"Yesterday. Kicked her out of the guest condo, too."

"Lew has been weirdly quiet," she noted, wondering why he'd kept this from her. "Said he 'had a fine time at the most delightful Thanksgiving ever,' but just one call since then."

"Lew has been preoccupied," Pete explained. "Maneuvering her to make a mistake the feds will act on—anything to conclusively implicate herself in those transfers from Waller Analytics accounts. He told Ted he doesn't care if she avoids prosecution; bottom line is he wants the funds restored."

"The spyware Mac tracked to Waller Industries," Eli said. "That was her. And that guy who came after me? Maybe she could bunk with Liz Hernandez in prison." Eli brightened, swizzling her cocoa with a candy cane.

At dinner with Mac and Mela, topics were far ranging, starting with Mac mentioning that Carly had dumped Bret by text without explanation. After Grace's take on the personality type most likely to do that, the talk came around to Ted's situation and Lew's determination to corner Hannah.

"I wish Lew had discussed this when he was here," Mac responded to Pete's update.

"The wild and crazy wedding day might have had something to do with that," Eli said, sampling his bread pudding.

"Wouldn't take much for this to go sideways on him," Mac muttered, thinking aloud. "I'll get back to you," he told Pete.

⟫•◦•⟪

On Christmas Eve, Bibi helped Carol reestablish her lasagna dinner tradition. Her long dining table would seat all their new friends and special guests. The house glistened with greenery and elegant decoration—another benefit of persuading Bibi to live with her. Carol had extended an invitation to Jeff, whose custom wood furniture often brought him to Fancy This on days she kept the shop open for Bibi.

"Yes, Carol, for the hundredth time, he's a nice guy," Bibi answered. "But he says that's his sister living with him. *Sure, buddy.*" She laughed, hoping to close the subject.

"That makes him an even nicer guy," Eli said, as she opened the pastry box with a Buche de Noel from Melissa's, surrounded by cocoa mushrooms and glistening with fondant sprigs of holly leaves and berries.

"Lew will regret missing this dessert," Carol raved. "Carly, is Bret coming?"

"Nah," she said, shaking her hair. "His six months are over. That's how long my relationships last, so I'm going to stamp an expiration date on them at the start."

Jeff and his sister Marilyn were warmly welcomed, with many fans of his work around the dinner table. After Marilyn shared her frustration over being delayed at the grocery earlier, almost calling a manager while waiting for a woman to finish swapping out eggs in cartons, Bibi was won over. "I know, right? People are at their worst in a grocery store."

"I thought you said, 'while driving,' Bibz," Carly teased.

"Pretty sure *the worst* was opening a restaurant without a website, just a social media page," Mela recalled.

With everyone seated, Carol lifted her glass, offering a toast. "Bibi's adoption was final two days ago," she said, over cheers. "We have always been family, and now it's official," she declared, hugging Bibi.

"You're good with this, right?" Eli asked, surprised by Bibi's subdued behavior.

"It's wonderful, really. I'm still snagged on the identity thing. I've legally changed my last name to Spillett. But the social security number, the birthdate, all that is Beth's. I can't fix that."

"Don't let it get to you, B, baby," AB said, forking an abandoned carrot from her plate. "Do not let a frightened young girl's decision define your life. You can make peace with this."

"Bibz," Eli whispered. "Do you still have the video from Ted's penthouse?"

"Maybe," she replied cautiously.

"Shoot me a copy? I want to take another look at that bathroom."

Before dinner was over, Marilyn had accepted a part-time job at Fancy This to supplement her days as a substitute teacher. Finally, Mela and Mac shared their happy news, as well as her plans to lighten her workload for the new year. "I'm feeling homebodyish these days," she admitted, as Mac took her hand.

"I'm on board with that," Bernie said, winking at Henry. "The new year does not feel adventurous. Maybe it's just the chill of winter setting in."

"How about having a lit NYE right here at BVR's bash; and saving the New York City ball drop for next year?" Carly proposed. "The new virus that's reported overseas will make it onto a flight here soon. It has me thinking about a job change, because duh."

"I thought you had decided," Seth objected, pausing the basket of rolls midflight.

"Not publicly," she answered frostily.

"Don't mind us, you two," AB said, nudging Will.

"I might be starting a sixteen-week GBI training program," Carly broadcast, chin in the air. "*That's all.*"

"We are one hundred percent professional," Seth added, gesturing between himself and Carly.

"Have you thought about working with a private outfit?" Mac asked, avoiding Seth's stare.

"I don't know any," Carly said, puzzled.

"I do," he assured her. "You'd be a good candidate. Pay is way better."

"Now girls, if we're going to the resort for New Year's," Carol warned the single women present, "I've got dibs on Lewis, and I want a picture of us arriving in his *beautiful* car," she added, striking a red-carpet pose. "Because: *Pics or it didn't happen.*"

"Why are you still calling her Carol, when you're her daughter now?" Carly whispered.

"What do you want me to call her, Auntie Mom?" Bibi protested. "I did this for her protection."

"And she did this for yours."

As dessert was served, Bibi began handing out knit pullovers embroidered with "Baes of the Blue Ridge," to everyone's delight. "All these love stories inspired a new line of sweats for Fancy This," she explained. "Just don't pack it if you're heading for Denmark. Bae doesn't translate well."

"That reminds me! Before we leave the table," Eli said, waving two cards, "I'd like to read this note from Kit, and I'll pass around a New Year's card to her for anyone who wants to sign. It says:

Hello, Hiawassee and Merry Christmas to everyone in Bibi-land, what she calls the Far North of the Deep South. I love that. I'm wearing the sweats with that swirly logo now.

I feel sweet peace these days. I brought that gift home with me from my Georgia Mountains friends. I have a mom again. I am a daughter again. And someday I may be a mariculture entrepreneur, but for now I want to be a person who rescues people from dangerous situations. I'm adding criminal justice and social work courses to start. Sksksksk. Swear, this isn't a professional student gig.

Lots of love,

Kit

⸺◆⸺

A few days later, Mac reached Lew, and didn't like anything he learned of Lew's plan to snare Hannah. Lew intended to promise a substantial personal payoff for her to go quietly and avoid publicity that would undermine the reputation of Waller Analytics, in exchange for the recovered funds.

His expectation was that the authorities would want to be present to apprehend her as she discussed the deal at the penthouse. Mac planned to reason with Lew after the party, on New Year's Day. First, he wanted to check into why Eli's old phone number was showing up in tower dump data. Probably been reissued.

On Lake Chatuge, the last day of the year broke to flurries drifting through the first light of morning. Eli was watching Pharaoh on the patio as he tried to ignore the swirling flakes, when an email from Bibi pinged.

It was the video from the penthouse. The last few seconds showed Hannah at the undercounter fridge. Eli zoomed in and saw blueberries, bananas, coconut milk, and medication bottles next to the blender on the counter. *Ted's morning smoothies?* Months of snide speculation chilled into horror.

She wondered whether Ted had been in touch with anyone the last ten days, certain he would never answer her call. What she couldn't know was how many calls her old number was placing this quiet, frosty morning as Hannah Collins prepared to shed the bullseye weighing on her.

Eli's old phone number was still on Ted Waller's personal account, where Hannah had transferred it to a new phone, leaving Eli believing Ted had it disconnected. Hannah had used it only occasionally to authenticate most of her fraudulent activity, due to extensive financial records documenting it as Eli's—an impression reinforced by preserving Eli's voicemail greeting.

※─◦─◆

New Year's Eve morning, Lew saw Eli's text and ignored what he expected was another reminder about the BVR party. He had given up on hearing from the agent considering the case against Hannah. She was ready to run, he could feel it.

The meeting took an extra day to arrange, and now he would be late to that party at the resort. He'd promised Eli, when she insisted on meeting for Sunday brunch, that he would come. She ensured his promise by swapping his Levante Trofeo for her Sport as they parted, claiming she needed it to shuttle Carol to BVR on New Year's Eve if he ran late. He would call her on the way up.

Lew had assembled the audits, all his evidence, and left a message for the agent in charge saying that he expected Hannah to be collecting the missing funds on another continent by morning. In his suite at Ted's penthouse, Lew neatly laid out folders and notes on his bed, set a Bluetooth data skimmer, then locked the door. The information in his room would help find her and the funds.

Hannah arrived thirty minutes early. She refused to go beyond the foyer, or set down the locked briefcase in her grip.

"Bring up the transfer file so I can look it over," she demanded, keeping the center table in the foyer between them.

"You do the same," Lew said calmly, carrying his laptop nearer to her.

"Set it up and back away," she repeated.

"Not on your life, Hannah," he scoffed. "This has to be done precisely. We dispatch the transaction orders simultaneously. I'm giving you these personal funds; you're agreeing to return the total amount shown that you illegally acquired by accessing accounts at Waller Analytics and through fraudulent loans. Is this screen correct?" he said, slowly approaching with the open laptop facing her.

Hannah became alarmed by what sounded like a script. "You miserable little shit. Give me that!" She lunged for his laptop and caught her briefcase against the table, sending it skidding across the floor.

"They're waiting for you downstairs," he bluffed. "Just hand that back. Let's settle this now, and you can go anywhere you want," he added encouragingly, realizing she could indeed be capable of murder.

Hannah kept two fingers between the screen and keyboard as she backed away, scooping a key fob off the table and kicking it against Lew, knocking him to the floor. "Screw you," she hissed, racing to the penthouse elevator and banging the button to private parking.

Lew pushed off the heavy antique and arrived in time to see the elevator light dropping. He ran down the stairwell to the parking section Hannah knew would have a car matching the fob she took.

She repeatedly clicked the fob and was surprised to see the lights were flashing on Eli's Sport. Glancing around for security or worse, she sprinted to the car and slid in as Lew charged across the exit lane before her.

"You lose, Waller," she screamed, gunning the engine, racing toward him, exploding into a fireball as Lew dove from her path.

Chapter 23

When You Choose Again

An explosion shook the ramp as Ted approached his parking garage in the late afternoon of New Year's Eve. He ran to the open deck and found Lew, bleeding and crumpled against the curb. Security quickly rushed in, directing 911 to the site and reporting at least one fatality as the smoke receded.

Ted crouched to shield his lifeless brother from the heat, glancing back at the smoldering vehicle. He recognized it as Eli's Sport—with a blackened head leaning on the blown-out window frame. He lurched to the gutter, vomiting.

"I've got breath sounds," a voice behind him said over clattering equipment. Ted was braced against the curb, wiping his face with his handkerchief. His eyes moved slowly to Lew, flecked in bloody wounds. "Let's get him out of here," the paramedic treating Lew said, as they loaded him.

Two officers spoke with Ted at the curb. He identified the victims as his brother and his ex-wife, then called Lew's son, leaving a barely controlled message about his dad. "I'll meet you there, John."

Ted could offer little information, explaining that he had just arrived and pointing out his E63S Mercedes parked by the ramp. Cameras confirmed his arrival. He sent the building supervisor along to give the investigators access to his properties, then he went to Lew. Soon, he would find Pete and Mac.

Eli's calls and texts to Lew had grown frantic. There was no response when she attempted to track her Sport. Was he acting alone on the smoothie evidence? Confronting Hannah?

Pete and Grace were staying at the resort. Bernie and Henry joined them there with AB and Will. Mac offered to ferry the rest of the partygoers if Lew hadn't arrived by eight.

At the hospital, Ted learned that Lew's shrapnel injuries from the explosion were not life threatening. His relief overridden by anguish, Ted left to find Pete before the news reached him. His days-overdue shower and shave would wait.

Leaden with grief, Ted was on the road to Hiawassee where Pete and Grace would be wondering why Eli wasn't ready for some party. He would have to face Mac with the news, too. He fought his emotions as darkness fell. Memories of Eli filled his mind, breaking his heart.

Several calls had come in from the same 404 number, and Ted had ignored them. Exasperated, he listened to the last message, an APD investigator.

"Mr. Waller, I have a photo of our victim's left hand we received after the medical examiner removed her glove. This may allow you to confirm your preliminary identification of your wife. Get back to us immediately."

Ted had pulled over to hear the message. "Identify a hand?" he shouted angrily. "Are there no prints?" He groaned, chilled by the thought. Ted couldn't clear his head as he paced behind his car, steeling for the image. Finally, he tapped the link—the cropped photo captured a huge diamond solitaire. *Eli doesn't wear diamonds*, his mind screamed.

"Hannah Collins," he bellowed, remembering the extortionate ring, wanting to run the last miles to the house that surely held Eli. Uncertainty flooded his thoughts. Had he been wrong before, or was he wrong now? *What if...* Sailing off the highway and skittering through the turns, he came sliding in next to Lew's car at the old lake house.

Eli swung the door wide, set to chasten Lew Waller over losing his phone, but saw his disheveled brother instead. Ted reeled at the sight of her, hardly noticing the shimmering attire.

"Ted?" She blurted, perplexed by the switch. "What are you—"

He plucked her from the doorway, hoisting her in the air, then folded her in his arms, weeping quietly, repeating her name.

"What's going on? Where's Lew," she asked, squirming to see his face—trying not to reveal the sweetness of his embrace again.

"Lew will recover," he answered. "Hannah," he said, with a shuddering breath, "is dead. I saw... I thought it was you. She was in your Sport," he choked, pulling her tight again.

"I don't understand," she cried.

"An explosion," he said, still in disbelief.

"Where? Ted, are you hurt?"

"Could not be better," he mumbled, grasping the back of her neck as he nuzzled her face until he reached her lips.

Eli flinched as she felt Pharaoh slip past into the darkness. "One sec, Ted. He can't be out. Coffee's in the kitchen." She pointed, scurrying down the steps.

He watched her disappear, then noticed a package against the porch post. He picked it up and, as he walked to the kitchen, saw it was from the Harrisons. Tempted to throw it in the trash, he sailed it onto the kitchen table, where it slid across as he turned to the living room to mix a drink.

Eli was peering under the porch when the blast slammed her against Ted's car, setting off the alarm as debris settled around her. She was disoriented, huddled against the warm tire, minutes later when Mac came running, almost falling over her.

"Bit, don't move!"

"Ted is in there," she wailed, unable to look at the house.

Mac gently placed her on the seat of Ted's car, then called Mela asking her to advise 911 of injuries. "She needs you," he whispered, ending the call. "Dude, stay!" he commanded, leaving to find Ted.

The heavy front door was intact but jammed, forcing Mac to climb through a blown-out window. Dust obscured his way as he searched by the weak light of his phone, yet he could see the moonlit lake through the opening where the kitchen had been. Approaching headlights drew his attention. It was Seth Taylor. "Leave your lights on," Mac shouted, as Seth bailed out, stopping at Ted's car.

"I'm here for Ted. They want to talk to him in Atlanta, tonight," he answered, stooping to check on Eli. "Help is coming. Try to remember every detail you can for me, Eli," he said, crossing the drive and going in the window where Mac had been.

"Eli said Ted was in here. The back of the house is *gone*," Mac stated grimly. "He may be under the wreckage."

"No, no, Ted, please," Eli shouted from behind them. "Answer me, Ted!"

Twisted frames from the glass sliders and a section of roof covered the walkway to the buried patio. The old root cellar—later expanded into a basement—was now a gaping pit open to the night sky.

"Get her, Seth," Mac shouted, landing his prosthesis in the rubble as he climbed across the remains of the demolished kitchen, then dropped into the void as sirens neared.

Mela arrived and led Eli to her car as first responders were assessing the situation. "Get out of there now," the fire chief ordered Mac, as they set up work lights.

The cellar side of the basement narrowed along granite outcropping walls. Mac pushed a section of hanging floor and staggered back when his faint light crossed a headless body. As the dust drifted, he could see it was Ted wedged under a granite layer— his head only hidden by an outstretched arm.

"I've located Ted Waller, Captain," he called over the sound of floor joists shifting, his voice, shaky. "Drop a Stokes and a backboard, A-SAP."

"What?" Ted groaned. "MacLellan?"

"Really good to hear you, brother. Time to un-ass," Mac said calmly, releasing a fierce whistle to the rescuers up top. "We got a live one," he hollered, hearing jubilant whistles returned from above.

"Eli?" Ted shouted in a panic as his awareness cleared.

"With Mela, man. She's okay. We're getting you out," Mac assured him, contradicted by a sharp crack from a beam overhead.

"Fell through the floor," Ted mumbled, wiping blood from his eyes, steadying against the granite. "Hit my head," he added vaguely, looking skyward. "You need a boost, Footlooze?" he asked Mac, as a ladder extended.

"Been a while since you called me that, *T-dub*. How about I boot your ass?" Mac warned his old friend, holding the ladder. "Patient one coming up. Refusing assistance."

Ted also refused medical transport after the paramedics looked him over, which wasn't easy as he shifted to keep Eli in sight. Pete and Grace arrived with trays of coffee as onlookers appeared.

The young publisher who'd bought the newspaper from Eli's uncle was on scene before Mac and Ted emerged. Hank was not wearing his usual jeans and Columbia vent shirt but was shooting photos in an aubergine velvet blazer over a gray dress shirt and charcoal slacks. He and his partner had detoured on their way to the party, Mac noticed, seizing the opportunity to razz his friends.

"Hank, Jed," He greeted them, over handshakes as they waited for Ted to be checked out. "You guys stringing for GQ, now?" he said, admiring Jed's black suit over a burgundy turtleneck. "And me in this beat-up rag." He laughed, brushing away plaster dust.

"Not enough urban, too much decay," Hank critiqued, photographing Mac in front of the many response vehicles.

"No, not me, guys, your story's in the back of that bus," Mac said, thumbing at the rescue truck. "Compared to him, I look fine."

⋙─●─⋘

Mela suggested going to the house for some warmth and hot coffee until Seth could join them to explain his mission. Mac stayed on site after he learned of the earlier explosion.

"Entirely too familiar to me," he informed Seth, as they watched the firefighters review the destruction. "I'm betting acetone peroxide. Same scent as IEDs used ten years ago. Mother of Satan, the bomb makers called it, because it killed plenty of them in the process. The recipe is simple but very unstable—an insidious bomb.

"But no fire," Seth noted, looking at the wreckage.

"Any fire is secondary. Its energy is an entropy burst. Extremely powerful, very contained. Triggered by lots of ordinary influences—from heat, to static, a bump, even UV light. From what you've told me, all it took was a baggie staged on Eli's engine. Ignition did the rest."

The Carters and Shafers had noticed as Pete and Grace rushed from the dance floor. Will reached Mac, who informed them of the blast. They all gathered at Mela's, rejoicing in the close calls survived that day.

Bibi stayed home with Carol, who wanted quiet to pray. Carly phoned from work after a text from Bibi. A call inexplicably came through Ted's mangled phone. It was from John's number, but Lew's were the words he gratefully heard.

As fireworks were going off at an unnerving rate, welcoming the new year, Mac and Seth arrived ready for coffee. "I don't think you'll need to come back to Atlanta tonight after all," Seth said, taking a chair next to Ted.

"I know your brother was frustrated with the slow pace of the investigation your attorneys initiated," Seth began. "What he didn't know was that Ms. Collins was making similar charges against your brother, claiming he was framing her for his crimes. She swore her life was in danger. This complicated an already difficult case.

"When you initially identified Ms. Collins as your wife, our attention shifted from your brother. The possibility arose that Eli *could* have been behind the mortgage fraud; and perhaps you, behind the Waller Analytics transactions.

"Tonight, we had to consider that you and Eli might have been looting assets, planning to claim insurance benefits from Eli's supposed death, and lead everyone to think Ms. Collins had disappeared with the stolen funds. But the explosion didn't destroy all the evidence."

"That is insane," Ted snarled.

"When you didn't bite on IDing the photograph as Eli—or respond at all—we had to decide whether you were gone already, or not our guy. Finding you in the root cellar had us leaning toward the latter.

"Finding the trove of data laid out for us by your brother, *that* will make the case. We're still evaluating the contents of the briefcase she dropped in the penthouse. With Ms. Collins dead, your chances of recovering those funds may be, too."

"You can be sure Lew Waller already has that traced," Pete advised.

"But you're not addressing the bombs, Taylor," Ted insisted. "Whose bombs? Why?"

"We found a second phone in the bombed car, along with Lew's obliterated computer," Seth responded. "That phone has layers of surveillance apps embedded. The voicemail greeting on that number is Eli's, as was the line at one time, but still on Ted's personal account."

"What?" Eli said, from her blanketed cocoon with Pharaoh, suddenly mystified.

"When your line went dead last spring," Mac reminded her. "Hannah had access to all Ted's accounts. She stole your line to shield the mortgage fraud after attempting to discredit you with the blackmail hoax," he continued, as Ted's head dropped, realizing that his gullibility had almost cost Eli her life.

"You're saying Hannah was trying to kill Eli with both bombs?" Ted demanded.

"This is conjecture, for now," Seth said.

"Seth's not ready to say Hannah's schemes landed her in the way of someone intent on killing Eli," Mac interjected. "And she's not the first. Victor Hernandez may have taken a bullet."

At that, Eli shattered. "These people are dead instead of me?"

Mac came over to put his arm around her, but she pushed him off. "I don't need coddling. I need answers," she raged. "Who is doing this? Why?"

"I think they're going to find a tracker on your car," Mac said quietly, sitting on the arm of the couch. "I think this is tied to the suspect in Victor's death. I think he tried to kill you that night on the lake when—"

"No!" she screamed, fighting confusion. "He's *dead*, Mac," she said slowly.

"Maybe not. I think this guy killed his brother that night, someone who worshipped him, former neighbors say. One believed his early criminal record came from the older brother using Patrick's name for those arrests when he was visiting from California. A lady I reached this week in a nursing home blamed him for the accident causing the younger brother's brain injury, and those burns that damaged his hands.

"Said he was a mean, sick boy. Today she called me back to mention that although his name was Arthur," Mac revealed, cutting his eyes to Seth, "everybody called him Poke.

"I think, Eli, that he brought his brother here to set him up for your murder if his plan didn't go right. It just went wrong sooner than he anticipated. He shot his brother in the head, left the gun in his hand, and waited for another opportunity."

"His face was older than the picture they showed me of Patrick Thompson." Eli was shivering uncontrollably.

"I also think that he believes you can identify him," Mac added. "He got involved because he was given your number when Johnny Grant panicked over you asking about Alma Garcia. He cross-tracked Hannah when she took over your phone.

"According to the tower dumps on a number we linked to him this morning, he's come close several times. Likely tagged your car with a tracker in Beaufort last September. Once Hannah kept that phone on steadily the last ten days, he closed in, waiting for his chance. The phone and the car tracking to the same location gave him his window."

"Then why a bomb here?" Eli insisted.

"He was in view of the parking deck, we're sure," Seth answered. "Just haven't determined which vehicle was him. He knew it wasn't you when she came out to the car. Left for Hiawassee with a backup explosive, apparently."

"So, he was watching here, too?" she asked quietly, tugging the blanket around her.

"That's what we think," Mac said carefully, "but—"

"Get the video on my dashcam," Ted shouted, launching out of his seat, tossing his key fob to Seth. "I was in a hurry last night, but there was a guy wearing a ball cap, sitting in a '16 or '17 GMC Canyon across the road when I pulled in. Gray with a black toolbox behind the cab. Might have been four-wheel drive—"

"What, no tag number?" Mac shouted, racing Seth to the door. "Stay, Dude," he ordered, as they left.

"We're going," AB said as Will took her hand. There won't be much sleep tonight, but I am grateful. We've each come through firestorms this last year," she said, leaning to hug Eli.

"I believe that," Bernie added, as she and Henry stood to leave. "I know that I was self-isolating, hiding from my mistakes, until I found you all. My sweet AB was living in exile, evading judgment that no longer existed.

"Our self-sufficient Bibi was suffocating in the wrong identity. Our Carly, determined to conceal her savvy and skills from the world. Carol was rescued from an unimaginable situation. Then Leslie, who long believing she had a secret that would destroy her family. Beautiful Mela existed in suspended animation, waiting for circumstances to change. Kit lived trapped in an invisible stranglehold almost half her young life.

"And our perpetual fugitive, Eli—who ignited this spiritual controlled burn—experienced a powerful push from the universe to these sacred mountains, where she escaped a murderer. I'd say this confluence of waylaid women had a very good year," she concluded, amid hugs as the gathering ended.

⟞•⟝

Eli persuaded Mela to get some rest, promising to do the same. Ted wasn't letting Eli go to bed without him, and she didn't object twice.

Grace sat in bed with her phone light dimmed as Pete slept, texting AB about Eli's bedmate. She was regretting the disclosure, and the pre-dawn timing of it, when a reply appeared—a string of hearts interspersed with naughty emojis.

Sleeping with windows open in winter was one of Eli's least favorite things about Ted, but a third-floor bedroom made it feel safer on this senseless night. As they spooned under a pile of blankets, she could tell by his breathing that Ted was out.

Oh, no, you don't need anyone's protection, the ol' voice weighed in. *But there's nowhere you'd rather be than close to this man.* Quick tears of shame spilled freely as Eli recognized how her egotistical perception of others—of who's right, who's wrong, and who's mistreated, were arbitrary and baseless.

Ted awoke to her trembling and tears. "What's this?" he said, still groggy as he rolled her to face him, gently rubbing her back as he pulled her closer.

"I've been so foolish, so determined to be right no matter what it cost me or how it hurt people I love," she wept. "You are precious to me, every little thing about you. I love you so much, Ted. I'm sorry I've hurt you. I thought I was protecting myself, but—"

"Eli," he whispered. "Nothing is coming between us again. Whatever it takes, I can meet your expectations," he said, finding her lips, sliding his hand way down her back.

"Whoa," she said, eyes wide. "Do you have, uh, *protection* with you?"

"What, a gun? Oh. *No.* C'mon, Eli. If nothing happened when you were young and fertile, what makes you think—"

"Oh my God, you did not just say that to me!"

"What?" he asked, propping up on his elbow.

"You're an idiot, that's what. Mela is barely older than I am, and she's, well, they're expecting in July."

"A kid? You're joking. Miller and Mela?" he yelled, loud enough to carry beyond their room.

"Yes," she answered softly. "I'm sorry I called you an idiot. Sometimes the things you say are miserably blunt."

"We've never done that," he responded, pulling the comforter around her bare shoulders. "We didn't do it—"

"Much at all, remember? I do believe you, that things could be different. But for how long?"

"Yesterday, when I thought… It changed everything," he said, kissing her neck in that rumbling, immobilizing voice as he pulled the blanket away.

⟶▶◦◀⟵

Pete and Grace were whipping up breakfast in formalwear until Pete could bring their bags from BVR. Mela and Eli met on the stairs, following the bacon aroma to the kitchen and lauding their visiting chefs. "Up all night?" Grace deadpanned, handing Eli orange juice.

"Not quite," Eli responded, exchanging sheepish looks with Ted as he came in ahead of Mac.

"Hope you don't mind," Pete said, setting a plate of pancakes and bacon with scrambled eggs in front of Mela.

"If this is how you two *guest*, drop in anytime, Coopers," she said, as they clinked juice glasses.

"Any news since I saw you last?" Ted asked Mac, who struggled to focus after a long night shadowing Seth.

"That truck was spotted six miles north of the bridge over Lake Lanier, still tagged and registered to a private seller in Mississippi. Driver took off. After a chase, a pit maneuver skids him, he counters, goes airborne ahead of the bridge approach. Sails off the highway, hits the water, and lights up like a depth charge. No body so far. Might not be anything left."

After a minute or two, the silence was torture for Grace. Pete could see her suppressing the urge to counsel. "What time is the walk?" she asked, squirming next to Eli. "Can I join?"

Mela and Eli were exchanging eyebrow waggles as she continued.

"First day of the new year, we should start it off right, no matter how the last one ended," Grace said earnestly.

"I don't know." Eli sighed. "This has been a lot…"

"Grace is right. Not much can be done on New Year's Day," Mela said, picking up her phone. "I'll text everybody."

"Up for a walk, Ted?" Mac inquired, unenthused.

"I'll get back to you," he mumbled from the terrace, as he called Lew with Eli's less-fractured phone.

"How are you adjusting to so much togetherness?" Mela said, when AB walked out to the road.

"Bliss," AB breathed. "I know that can't last, but since we're so old, maybe…"

"You're a baby," Carol hooted. "Charlie and I were going strong until he passed—stirring oatmeal one morning at eighty-nine."

"Oh, don't think we aren't. Let me just say, if you have access to a heated pool—"

"Uh-oh, 5-1-1," Carly said, covering her ears.

"Not X-rated," AB declared. "But the water reverses sagging. It lifts your—"

Mac interrupted AB with a spurt of coffee bubbling from his nose, then veered across the road and out of earshot.

"Mela," Bibi called out, as she approached the group waiting at AB's driveway. "I just got a call about a house next to Carol going on the market next week. Can you get Lauren here for a look?"

"Absolutely not," Mac shouted, startling the paint horse he was befriending across the fence. "Hide that listing, and I'll make it worth your trouble," he added, fanning imaginary cash her way.

"What are you doing here this bright and beautiful morning?" Bernie asked, as she arrived, giving him a hug.

"Are you suggesting I'm a contradiction to bright and beautiful?" Mac asked, still blotting coffee.

"Mac is our escort," Mela explained. "The person behind all the horror this year hasn't been apprehended."

"I'm carrying," Carly assured her, looking over at Mac, who nodded approvingly. "Sounds like I was away at the worst possible time," she added.

"Carly," Mac said, beckoning her. "You volunteered to work yesterday to avoid that party, right? Bret doesn't get what happened. Could you just talk to him?"

"No," she said, walking back to her friends, then wheeling around. "I was just a good time for him, right? We'd been arguing over which of us could change jobs to be together, and he said it was obvious, me.

"A little later, I heard him talking to someone as he was waiting for us outside Bibi's shop after Thanksgiving. He said, 'Because Carly is a crazy *dolly bird.*' I looked it up. It's British hipster, describing an attractive, *un*intelligent girl. Why would I waste another minute on him?"

"Hold it there, Carly," Mac said, palms up. "He was on the phone with me about arranging flying lessons for you up here. What he said was, 'Because Carly is crazy about Dolly Bird.' The Harrisons call their helicopter Dolly Bird."

"Oh?" she said, wide-eyed. "Gotta bounce," Carly called, sprinting away.

"This is what they do every morning? Take turns jogging?" Ted asked Mac as he arrived, watching Carly round the bend ahead.

"Who is this rocket scientist?" Carol whispered to AB.

"The real deal, baby. You're looking at a certified wunderkind. That's Eli's former ex."

"And that pretty little girl?"

"An aspiring psychiatrist with wobbly training wheels. Do *not* get her started."

Lew was released this morning," Ted told Eli, as he pocketed the phone. "Went home with John and his mother, who has separated from her latest husband. Lew told her he's through racing. Ha! Says security told him my building's Residency Board is calling a meeting to discuss the Waller brothers. That should be interesting," he said, pausing to make another call.

"You know he's got *your* phone," Mac told Eli, staring at Ted. "And he's damned chatty. What's up?"

"Replacement phones arriving tomorrow," she answered. "And he says he's been seeing a specialist Lew found for him. AB has set me up, too, with a therapist. Interested?

"Anyway, Lew said that after Ted analyzed one of those morning smoothies and threw the rest out, their exec team noticed his stress, or anxiety, intensify within days. Said Ted had literally been consuming a witch's brew.

"He's trying a med for anxiety and practicing behavior modifications this professional recommends. I think I see a difference already, in both of us. Mac, I believe now that I can love him for who he is, and let go of who I expected him to be."

A truck rumbled out of Bernie's driveway towing a fishing rig.

"Love that Harley truck," Eli called out to Henry, who couldn't see Bernie's Cheshire Cat smile.

"Not a bad pick on the trailer. Looks like you found your way to Boundary Waters without me," Mac commented, admiring the glossy boat.

Henry rummaged through papers on the seat beside him. "Eli, I made some rough drawings this morning of a re-grade on your property that would give you a walkout basement on the lakeside. The minute you're ready to talk rebuilding, you call me."

"Henry, thanks so much," she said, taking the sketches and putting her hand over his on the window frame.

"I mean it. Anytime, Eli. Now Mac Miller, why do I always find you hanging with the ladies?" Henry complained. "A man's gotta fish."

"I hear ya. Just don't go casting around those honey holes behind my back."

"And when does this walking happen?" Grace asked, hands on her hips.

"Let's go," Eli hollered, taking Ted's arm, which he unconsciously pulled away, then quickly took her hand.

"How long?" he asked, as they walked ahead.

"You can let go now," she answered, loosening her fingers.

"How long is this walk," he enunciated.

"Two point six miles, up to the highway and back," she answered, squeezing his hand.

Mac and Mela were answering baby questions as they all rounded the curve. Then the chatter fell silent. Behind strands of yellow tape, a partially bared skeleton of hand-hewn timbers stood stark against the backdrop of the lake and mountains. Siding that had dangled after the blast was still falling away, revealing more of the dogtrot-conjoined cabins—their chinking and plaster reduced to dust.

"Ted, how did you survive this with only bruises and a banged head?" Mela asked, appreciating the force required to do so much damage. "And Eli, not a scratch."

"Most of the blast was in the direction of the lake," he noted. "That's why the back of the house is gone. I was almost in the living room, and the floor dropped under me *ahead* of the blast. Perhaps energy was baffled by the granite under the house."

Mac went in, making his way to Seth, who was climbing through the wreckage with the fire marshal. Ted followed, signaling Eli to stay back. Mela gripped Eli's shoulder and guided her to the road, saying, "Mac promised he would look for anything salvageable."

"E, honey," AB ventured, moving alongside them. "Mel and Mac are full time at his house after today. Will and I will be moving to Beau's Place later this week to prepare for retreats. Will you stay in my place until you rebuild, for as long as you need?"

"That's very kind. I don't ever want to go back to Atlanta," she admitted. "I've no idea what's ahead, but I can work from anywhere. The house was insured. Not for a lot. Pete and I will decide. He may want to build himself something there."

"Eli, Pete says that's your home," Grace insisted. "Last night we talked about chipping in because he said rebuilding will take five sponge baskets."

"Oh, Pete. Oh, my holy freakin' cow!" Eli shouted, running back to the house. The walkers shared clueless looks and turned to catch a glimpse of Eli bounding through a window opening and disappearing as Ted and Will failed to intercept her.

"It's here," she whooped, snatching loofas from a basket wedged under the cast iron tub. Eli caught her breath as she squinted between the rows of logs into the living room.

Heads popped up like so many prairie dogs around the structure to see what she had recovered. Pete and Jeff were standing at his truck, discussing a piece of furniture he was taking to Carol when Eli shouted. Seth and the fire marshal came peering out of the root cellar. The girls were crowding at the front of the house as Eli pointed to the fireplace.

"Annie Blanche Sutton, look at that. It's real," Eli shouted, stepping carefully around the gaping hole, ignoring warnings from the fire marshal as she pulled AB up.

"Dear God in Heaven," Ab breathed, inching around the missing floorboards and collapsed fireplace mantelpiece. She reached over, tracing the carving on one of a pair of mammoth oak tree trunks holding the broad stone spanning them both. Seth joined the women, crouching to see beneath.

"The entire mantel wall is resting on granite. This is the original house we're seeing now," Seth said, wiping centuries of dust from the inscription. "I know this. It's Cherokee."

"So, what does it say?" AB challenged him.

"Didn't say I'm fluent, but I know someone who is," he answered, clicking off a series of shots to send with a text.

"Magnificent," Jeff said, evaluating the ancient structure. "Get a new roof right away, start rebuilding. These log walls are solid," he added, looking around. "You must restore this."

Eli smiled at Pete, tossing him the loofas one by one. It's a joint decision," she advised, looking into the rafters. "Our shared weekend house?"

Ted was baffled. "I already have a house here you can live in. But why would you want to stay here after everything that has happened?"

"Why would I not? This is home. This has been the best year of my life, so far."

"Go for it," Pete said, tossing each loofa back, then his wallet. "I mean it. We can restore this house—your home."

"Well then," Eli murmured, stuffing the loofas under her sweatshirt and thumbing through his wallet.

"I was making a point. Gimme that," he said, jumping onto the window opening and lowering Eli to the ground after retrieving his wallet.

"Get those things out of your shirt. That looks stupid," Ted barked, jumping down beside her.

"What, these?" she laughed, patting her expanded belly. "They do itch," she commented, peeking in each one to fish out the stashed cash.

"Come on out, Danny," Mac shouted to the fire marshal, steadying the ladder.

"I'm waiting to see how many of you fall through what's left of that floor," he said, testing the ladder before he ascended. As he surfaced, Seth's phone was blaring a J. S. Bach concerto. "Very funny, Taylor," he grouched.

"That's a ringtone," Seth explained, scrambling to answer.

"Hilary Hahn's violin concerto?" Jeff asked in amazement. "My sister loves her music."

"It is. Hello?" Seth answered. "Yes, uh-huh. Let me write this," he said, taking a tablet and pen from his jacket. "Got it, thanks. You've been a tremendous help, Mr. Long.

"That was a linguist at the Cherokee-speaking academy. Great guy. He could make out these words from the inscription photos," Seth said, passing Eli the sheet from his notepad. The English alphabet list was "didanvdo, ayiawa, kanvwodi."

"So, Didanvdo is a plural form of *spirit*. Ayiawa is one of the words for *rest*. And kanvwodi is translated to *heal*. He also says those are the three sisters—corn, squash, and beans—carved into the oak trees that are this original mantel's legs, and those plants carved at the base are ramps—symbols of plenty and sharing. That's all I've got."

"That's fantastic." Eli gasped. "Thank you, Seth, and especially Mr. Long. This is thrilling. Don't you think so, Ted?" she asked, trying to involve him as AB and Bernie took a seat on Mac's tailgate.

"That's one of the guys you dated? This GBI agent?"

"Nothing serious. It isn't like I was *engaged*, or anything. Sorry, unnecessary."

"And the Harrison guy," he continued, slapping the dust off his slacks. "Was he fantastic, too?"

"Haven't spoken with him since I was in Beaufort. I don't know anyone as fantastic as you." She faux frowned, slipping her arms around his neck as he stiffened slightly. "But then, I have no actual basis for comparison, Dr. Waller."

"No one calls me Dr. Waller. Don't do that," he complained, taking her arms down as her friends noticed the interaction, making him even more uncomfortable.

"Got it, Dr. Waller," she said, turning away as a faint look of disappointment crossed her face.

"Wait, Eli," he said urgently. "The thought of you ...I—"

"Never have been *with* anyone else," she said, cautiously embracing him again. "Convince me you've been my right choice?" she said, raising her face to his stubbly chin.

"I will," he swore, becoming oblivious to their audience, whispering before his lips reached hers. "I will."

AB and Bernie could not hear the exchange but enjoyed the show. "I don't need your gift to see that their battle will continue." AB laughed, swinging her feet from the tailgate. "Will they make it?"

"It won't be easy, or soon. A lifetime of breakthroughs and defeats. Remember, our future is fluid, altered by each choice we make. But I believe they will get to where they always choose love.

"Your great-great tells me to say to you and your husband that she 'rejoices that you are finally one.' Isn't that nice?" Bernie messengered, bumping AB's shoulder.

"Bernadette! You have no idea how cheeky that was." AB blushed. "*That's* where I get my mouth. And while you've got the line open, please tell Heaven that we're forever grateful for all the mighty angels sent our way," AB requested of her friend.

"You just did, honey. No *line* necessary. And Spirit says we became one another's angels, walking each other home, as Heaven intends."

CPSIA information can be obtained
at www.ICGtesting.com
Printed in the USA
LVHW092257230721
693520LV00002B/5